EVERYTHING TO LOSE

DANIELLE GIRARD

ITP
Everything to Lose

Third Edition: June 2019

Cover and Formatting: Damonza

ISBN-10: 0996308989
ISBN-13: 978-0996308984

Please Note
This is a work of fiction. Names, characters, places, and incidents either are the product of the author's imagination or are used fictitiously, and any resemblance to actual persons, living or dead, business establishments, events or locales is entirely coincidental.

Your Free Rookie Club Short Story is Waiting

San Francisco Crime Scene Analyst and aspiring Rookie Club member Naomi Muir is passionate about her work, especially the cases where she works alongside seasoned inspectors, like Jamie Vail. But this latest case has her unnerved. A serial sex offender is growing more aggressive. He attacks in the dirty underbelly of the San Francisco streets… and eerily close to Naomi's inexpensive apartment. Each crime is more violent than the last and also nearer to where Naomi herself lives.

To solve the case, Naomi will have to rely on her own wit and an unexpected new partner as the attacker gets too close to home...

Go to
www.daniellegirard.com/newsletter to claim your copy now!

THE ROOKIE CLUB CAST, IN ORDER OF APPEARANCE:

Jamie Vail, Sex Crimes Inspector (Featured in *Dead Center*; also in *One Clean Shot, Dark Passage,* and *Grave Danger*)

Alexander Kovalevich, Sex Crimes Inspector

Sydney Blanchard, Senior Criminalist, Crime Scene Unit (Also in *Dead Center, One Clean Shot, and Grave Danger*)

Roger Sampers, Head Criminalist, Crime Scene Unit (Also in *Dead Center*, *One Clean Shot*, and *Grave Danger*)

Annabelle Schwartzman, Medical Examiner (Featured in the *Dr. Schwartzman Series: Exhume, Excise, Expose, and Expire)*

Hailey Wyatt, Homicide Inspector (Featured in *One Clean Shot*; also in *Dead Center, Dark Passage*, and *Grave Danger*)

Hal Harris, Homicide Inspector, partner to Hailey Wyatt (Also in *Dead Center, One Clean Shot, Dark Passage*, *Grave Danger*, and the Dr. Schwartzman Series)

CHAPTER 1

IT WAS THE way he held her hand. His long fingers wrapped around her hand and held firm like he was saving her. His skin was warm and dry. Boys her age never had dry hands. He thought about what she'd said before answering, considered exactly what she was asking. He was calm, sometimes so serious. A grown-up. She studied him standing in the doorway.

It was the way he laughed. Not some hysterical cackle like guys at school, and not the I'm-too-cool-to-laugh that others put on. Though serious, he laughed softly, more with his eyes than his mouth.

Such a silly schoolgirl crush thing to say, but she swore his eyes changed colors. They might be the exact color of toffee, or they could deepen to the shade of black coffee. They could change in an instant. "On a dime," as her father liked to say when he was lecturing her about how lucky she was and how much she had been given, and how easily it might all go away if she made one wrong decision.

It was also that she knew he was the wrong decision, at least to everyone but her. He was not the one she was supposed to choose. Not one of the boys she'd always known, whose parents knew her parents, whose mothers were on the opera board with hers and only worked outside the home to raise money for the "underprivileged." Not one of the boys in designer jeans and shirts that were washed by someone who worked for them. In fact, not like most of the boys at City Academy.

He had lived on the street. He had been given nothing. His father had been in jail. Yet he was the one who asked the tough questions. What would she do? How would she be someone who counted? Challenging her to move beyond her comfort zone. And he talked about the chances of survival for someone like him, the slimmer chances of not repeating the patterns set by his father.

It was the way he stood at the door, giving her plenty of time to speak up, to say she didn't want to, that it was too much. They could go back to the way they'd been. To talking and holding hands if she wanted. But she didn't. As he closed the door, she scanned the mattress that lay on the floor. Covered in faded green sheets, a gray comforter. A single pillow lay at the top, propped against the bare white wall. One pillow, while her bed was a mountain of them. Why did anyone need all those pillows?

They had never come here before. This had been her request, but he'd tidied up for her. Although she didn't know if he'd moved things elsewhere, or if this was everything he had. The room was almost bare—no dresser and no closet. His clothes were stacked in three piles along one wall, two pairs of shoes lined neatly alongside. Books were stacked on the small table he used as a desk. Candles provided soft light, giving the room the smallest bit of ambience. The air smelled of ocean and coconut.

"We don't have to do this," he said again when they reached the mattress.

It was that he didn't apologize for the room or try to play off the way he lived. He was the first person she'd ever known who was truly real.

She took his hand, felt the tremor of energy as they touched. "I want to."

He waited a beat, watching her, scanning her face.

"Really."

Only then did he reach up to unzip her jacket, moving slowly, reassuring her that he would stop any time, for any reason. But she didn't. She wanted this. They both did. She was awkward. He was kind and careful.

It was that he didn't tell her he loved her just because they'd had sex. Afterward, he lay beside her, running his finger along the profile of her hip. She'd thought his naked form would make her uncomfortable; instead, she felt calm.

She wasn't a stupid high school girl at City Academy. She wasn't Gavin and Sondra Borden's daughter. She was just Charlotte. Charlotte naked in bed with a man.

It was how he was afterward. As he convinced her that she had to go home before her parents started worrying. She'd texted to say she was staying late to work on a school project. He wasn't into rebellion. He didn't need to make a point. Better to play by her parents' rules, he said, than to risk not being able to see her again. It was that he wanted to see her again.

He blew out the candles and reached for the door.

He grabbed his baseball mitt off the floor and tucked the ball deep into its pocket.

"You going to play some ball?"

"Thought I might toss it around a little. It'll distract me when you're gone." He took her hand and, together, they crossed through the darkened main room. The smell of burnt food lingered along with something like sour milk. He didn't live alone. Where were the others? The candles had been meant to mask the smell and the mixture was like something rotting on a beach. Anywhere else, she might have felt slightly sick.

Anywhere else, she might have walked out to the car by herself. As they crossed into the hallway, she was reminded of how different his world was. Along one wall were doors; on the other, a single dingy window that faced a patch of dirt in front of the building where, maybe once, there had been grass. The air was cold and the hallway dark but for a single bulb behind glass that was blackened with dust but miraculously unbroken. He led her down the corridor and into another hallway where the light hadn't been so lucky. Slowly, the light behind them faded away until the light pollution from the city's surrounding buildings and a few early stars cast shadows in the darkness. She stayed close to him as her eyes adjusted to the darkness. A door opened behind her and she turned back. Nothing there. She stumbled to catch up as they came around the corner. He gasped and shoved her forward.

She squinted in the darkness. His expression startled her. "What is it?"

Glass crashed. A grunt. Then he was no longer beside her.

She screamed and reached out, but he wasn't there. She called his name. She huddled against the wall and fumbled in her purse for her phone. His hands were tight on her shoulders. No, not his hands. These hands gripped too tight. He twisted and she fought to break free. He launched her forward as she caught sight of dark brown, angry eyes. Familiar eyes. "What—"

The brown of his eyes flashed to black as he threw her from his grip. She reached out, hand caught in her purse strap. The stairs rushed toward her. Cement closed in. An explosion of blackness.

CHAPTER 2

IT WAS ALMOST 9:00 p.m. when Sex Crimes Inspector Jamie Vail snatched the phone off her desk. She caught it before the Dr. Dre ringtone could play all the way through. Every time it rang, she reminded herself to ask her son to change it to "Brave" or maybe "Roar." Something empowering, and by a woman. Something that might make a victim feel a little stronger. Something more acceptable for a thirty-nine-year-old sex crimes inspector. "Vail," she said.

"It's Maxi."

Maxi Thomas was the trauma nurse Jamie worked with most often at San Francisco General Hospital. For almost fifteen years, the two of them had worked side by side on some of Jamie's worst rape cases. When Maxi called, it only meant one thing. "We've got another one." Jamie grabbed her blazer off the back of her chair. She glanced at the paperwork scattered across her desk that she'd promised herself she'd clear today. "Where?"

"Sixteen years old. Came into General about 7:40. Her parents just arrived. I've talked to them, but they haven't let me near her yet. Doctors are doing everything to protect the evidence. It should be intact."

Intact meant that no one had washed the girl's body yet. Probably because her condition wasn't stable enough. "Who brought her to the hospital?" Jamie asked.

"Don't know. Maybe a Good Samaritan who didn't want to stick around. Or maybe the perp dropped her off."

That would be a first. "I'm on my way."

"I should warn you," Maxi said, and Jamie recognized the tone.

Jamie forced herself to keep moving. "It's bad?"

"She's unconscious. Coma. They're not sure she'll make it."

"Drugged?" Jamie asked.

"Head injury."

"We looking for a beater?"

"Don't think so," Maxi said. "It might have been a fall. A little bruising on the wrists, so maybe a struggle."

"Are we sure it's a sex crime?" Jamie asked.

"The admitting doctor noted fluids. Tests came back positive for lycopodium."

Lycopodium was one of the powder-like substances used by condom manufacturers to keep the rolled up latex from sticking to itself. "Which indicates she had sex," Jamie said.

"Safe sex, no less," Maxi added.

There was obviously more to the story. "But—"

Maxi sighed. "But according to her parents, she's a virgin."

"And, of course, every sixteen-year-old tells her parents about her sex life. What did the doctor find?"

"There are signs of trauma," Maxi added. "Some tearing, bruises."

"Could indicate assault but could mean it was her first time," Jamie said.

"Right."

It was Jamie's turn to sigh. "But the parents want us to treat it as a possible assault."

"They do," Maxi confirmed. "And these are some particularly opinionated parents. With some serious pull."

Jamie pushed through the department's door and headed for the stairwell. Since she'd stopped smoking, the stairs were her best ally in the never-ending war with her size six pants. If she could afford a new wardrobe of size eights, it would be enough to surrender. "What kind of pull?" Jamie asked.

"The attending got a call from the mayor, requesting tightened security."

"The mayor's office called?"

"Not the office, Jamie. The mayor. No press, no outsiders. He also spoke to the head of security. All the video surveillance has been sent to you guys. They think they caught the guy on film."

"Well, that's good news." Jamie jogged down the stairs. "Who are the parents?"

"Gavin and Sondra Borden."

"I should know them?"

"If you read the society papers you would. Her grandfather was the first black attorney in San Francisco. Gavin Borden joined the family practice. They have two daughters. Charlotte, our victim, is a junior at City Academy."

Jamie's heart skipped a beat.

"That's where Zephenaya goes, right?" Maxi asked.

"Yeah." Her son was at City Academy on a scholarship. "I've never heard the name though. Z's a freshman, so junior girls are out of his league."

Maxi chuckled.

"I'm on my way."

Jamie reached the station's main floor, out of breath. Panting from the trip down the stairs. That was pathetic. She emerged into the hallway. Nodded to one of the crime scene techs she knew and a patrol officer who had helped her make an arrest a few weeks back. She caught the eye of an assistant district attorney she didn't want to talk to and ducked her head.

She was about to cross through the department's rear doors when her phone buzzed on her hip. She pulled it from the holster. "Vich," she said. "You get a call from the lab? SF General sent over some surveillance footage."

Vich was the nickname given to Alexander Kovalevich when he'd been in the police academy thirty years ago. A Boston transfer, Vich had joined SFPD sex crimes about four months ago. After the fallout from her divorce, Jamie had largely worked alone. Mostly because she was too surly for anyone to stand. At least until Vich.

"I got it all right," he confirmed.

"I'm heading over to the hospital to try to get the parents to agree to a rape kit."

"You need to see this first," he told her.

Jamie groaned, thinking about climbing the stairs again. Swearing off the elevator was plain stupid.

"We got the perp dropping her off," Vich said. "I'm

in the lab with Blanchard." With his Boston accent, he pronounced Sydney's last name "Blanchud."

At least the lab was only one flight away instead of three. She tried to do it without panting. Only partially successful, she found Vich leaning against a table. Behind him, the lab's fuming chamber was humming. It looked like they were trying to pull fingerprints off a broken wine glass. At the other end of the table sat the evidence drying cabinet, not currently in use.

Sydney Blanchard stood over the shoulder of a lab tech who was frantically typing on a keyboard. "There," she said, and the tech froze the image on the computer screen.

It was a grainy shot of a man holding a woman in his arms. The victim's feet were closest to the camera, making it hard to tell much about her. Jamie studied his face, the way his head was turned. Something about his stance was familiar. She scanned her memory for the suspects she'd interviewed over the years. Hundreds of them. Maybe a thousand by now. "We can't ID him from that," Jamie said.

"Can you enhance it?" Sydney asked the tech.

The tech was already running commands. Slowly, the image crystallized. The screen went black. "It will reload and hopefully be something we can use."

The image built one tiny layer of pixels every few seconds. Jamie resisted the urge to sit down. The ping of a text message.

DA wld b grt for Z. Not nearly as homogenous as CA. +C's a grt town. A frsh start.

Leave it to Tony to send a text in all sorts of outdated shorthand and type out the word "homogenous." No way he was taking Zephenaya when he moved to Cincinnati for his new teaching job. She didn't care if the school in Ohio, Davidson Academy, was a better school or more diverse. Staying with her was best for her son. And best for her. She tried not to think too hard on whether she was confusing the two things.

On the computer screen, the top of the photo had appeared. In it was the dark sky in the background and the shape of cars in the parking lot. "We don't get a shot of his car?"

Sydney shook her head. "The camera only picks him up a few steps before this. Right here is the only time he looks in the direction of the camera."

Her phone buzzed again. *U know this = wht he needs.*

Tony wasn't wrong about that. Something was going on with Z. He'd been caught smoking, was suspended for cheating on a biology test. Not to mention that City Academy was determining whether he would receive a scholarship for his sophomore year.

Sending him off to Ohio was too extreme.

On the screen, the suspect was revealed in thin lines, top to bottom. First, the very top of his head formed. His hair was cut short. Next was a prominent forehead then the furrow in his brow. The screen froze, the clock icon spinning. "It's thinking," the tech said.

"Wish it would think a little faster," Vich said.

The phone buzzed again, reminding Jamie that she hadn't answered Tony's texts. Certainly, she couldn't afford to send Z to City Academy without the scholarship. But he was her child. She couldn't send him away. She hated the idea that Tony was moving to Ohio and breaking up their family, as untraditional as it was. Tony was like her brother. She hated the idea that he wouldn't be close. Losing her son was unthinkable.

The layers began building again. Slowly, the suspect's hooded eyes were unveiled followed by his wide nose. It was his full lips and the angular jaw line that gave it away. Jamie grabbed hold of the table.

Vich touched her arm, but she couldn't pull her gaze from the image.

"I'll put it through face recognition software to see if I can find a match against the database," the tech said.

Jamie cleared her throat to get the words to come out. "You don't need to do that."

The tech spun in his chair. "You know him?"

"His name is Michael Delman," she said.

"Delman," Vich repeated, putting it together.

"Right. The man who dropped off our victim is my son's biological father."

CHAPTER 3

WHENEVER JAMIE DROVE to see a victim at San Francisco General Hospital, she needed quiet. It was a time of meditation for her. No fifties radio that she blared when no one else was in the car because it reminded her of climbing on the fire trucks and sliding down the poles at the station when her father was working. No ESPN radio that she and Z compromised on when they rode together because she'd much rather hear sports than his music.

On the way to meet a victim, Jamie wanted silence for the chance to clear the fray from her intentions. For the victims, she was often their first conversation, their first eye contact, their first touch after an attack. She believed how she handled that had an impact on how they recovered. Whether they recovered.

After a particularly harrowing case a couple of years back, a nurse tried to convince Jamie that she ought to take ten or fifteen minutes to meditate. She taught Jamie to imagine using a huge broom to sweep out any thoughts that entered her mind. This drive was as close to meditation as she got.

Today, though she tried to keep them at bay, sounds

of the world rose and batted against the car as she drove. Electric buses emitted high-pitched hums as they pulled away from the curb. Music blasted from another car—Robert Plant singing "Since I've Been Loving You." The rev of a motorcycle, a distant siren.

She prayed the phone didn't ring. Not even Vich, who would manage dispatching the crime scene team to the hospital parking lot and contact their captain to try to get a warrant to search Michael Delman's home. She drove with purpose, breathed with purpose, and she did not think. Not on any one thing and certainly not on whether Captain Jules would rule this case a conflict of interest because the suspect had fathered her adopted son.

More than five years had passed since Zephenaya last saw his biological father. Michael Delman had been in prison twice. Jamie pulled Delman's rap sheet every few months. She kept track of where he lived, how close he was to their son. Her son. She had no way to find out where Delman worked, to really know where he was, so she settled for knowing if he was in or out of jail.

Her thoughts stirred like a dust storm. Using the big brush that nurse had described—one that always looked like a broom that a witch might ride—she brushed them out. She needed to come to this with a clear head.

Even if Charlotte Borden was in a coma, Jamie wanted to be in the right frame of mind.

Maxi had said that Charlotte Borden was in the ICU. Most of their cases were seen in a room Maxi and Jamie called "2R." It had been called the "Rape Room" before Jamie joined the department, although no one seemed to know exactly where the nasty and inappropriate nickname had come from.

A patrol officer accidentally dropped the words "Rape Room" in front of a victim, causing a bout of screaming hysterics that lasted until a doctor pumped her full of Valium. The officer was suspended without pay; the name of the room permanently changed.

2R was a small, pale yellow exam room with a single bed and bright, glaring lights—both overhead lights as well as several that could be moved around the room. Other than that, the room had gloves, tissue, and almost nothing else. If a victim required an x-ray or scans, she (or, rarely, he) had to be moved. Unless a victim was physically unstable, she stopped at 2R. Charlotte Borden had bypassed 2R, which meant samples and photographs would have to be collected in the ICU.

Jamie showed her badge to the security officer seated behind the desk. "I'm here for Charlotte Borden."

"I don't have a Charlotte Borden," he said. "You sure she's at General?"

Jamie dialed Maxi. "I'm at the front. She's not listed."

There were voices in the background. "413."

"Why isn't she listed?"

"Uh huh," Maxi said, letting Jamie know she was with the parents.

"They requested her name be kept out of the hospital registry?" Jamie asked, as she started for the elevators.

"Oh, yes. Definitely."

"There's more?" Jamie guessed.

"Much."

Jamie hung up and felt the vibration of her phone. A

text from Vich. *Warrant's a no go. Delman could be a good samaritan. We need more.*

That the warrant had been denied to give Delman the benefit of the doubt was comical, although not at all humorous, but Jamie understood the argument. Arresting people for bringing an injured woman to the hospital would create a disincentive to help people out. They didn't want to do that. They had no reason to bring in Michael Delman. Until they could tie him to Charlotte's injuries.

Coming down the hospital corridor, Jamie didn't need a room number to locate Charlotte Borden. The hallway outside her door was congested with people—mostly men, and a token woman—dressed in expensive suits. Jamie held up her badge as she made her way through the mass. The suits watched her, but no one said anything as she knocked on the door and it opened to reveal Maxi's face.

As Jamie entered the room, she went straight to Charlotte. Without touching her, Jamie stared. Beyond the breathing tubes, she had a beautiful face. With small, delicate features and high, round cheekbones, she looked older than sixteen. Charlotte's mother stood on the far side of the bed and two others sat in chairs across the room. They watched her, but Jamie wanted to focus on Charlotte first. There would be plenty of time for everyone else.

Careful not to touch anything, Jamie took note of the left side of her face. Her eye was swollen shut; blood pooled thick under her skin where the bone in her cheek may have been broken. There were no apparent injuries on the right side of her face. Her hands lay at her sides, tucked under the blankets. It was something parents did. Nursing staff usually kept the hands out so as not to tangle the IV and to make it easier to check vitals. Parents tended to cover their children as though they were tucking them into bed for sleep. Jamie pulled two gloves from a box beside the bed.

"Excuse me—"

The man behind her had to be Charlotte's father. The lines in his face were pressed deep into his skin as though he'd slept on a wrinkled sheet. His tie was pulled loose, and he smelled faintly of sweat and expensive cologne. "Mr. Borden, if you could give me one minute."

Charlotte's mother backed away from the bed and began crying.

Her hands gloved, Jamie turned Charlotte's right hand over in her own. She noticed the bright orange nail polish, a ridiculous color that managed to be gorgeous against the young woman's brown skin. She repeated the process on her other hand, then pulled out her notebook. She would do an entire exam, but not with her parents in the room.

"What are you writing?" Charlotte's mother asked.

In the room were Charlotte's parents and a gentleman seated in a chair in the corner. He rose and crossed to Mrs. Borden, placing his hand on her shoulder. "What are you writing down?" Mrs. Borden repeated.

"I appreciate you giving me a moment to see your daughter before we spoke," Jamie said without answering the question. "I'm Jamie Vail. I'm an investigator with the San Francisco Police Department."

Neither Mrs. nor Mr. Borden reached to shake

Jamie's hand. "Has the doctor been in to talk to you about her condition?"

The man behind Sondra Borden stepped forward. In pressed slacks and a dark denim button-down, he was probably from the mayor's office. Or an attorney. Jamie tried not to dislike him immediately. It wasn't easy. "I'm Dr. Travis Steckler." He reached out his hand and, maintaining her game face, Jamie pulled off the glove on her right hand and shook. While her skin was rough and callused and probably clammy, his felt like it had been recently dusted with baby powder, warm and dry. "I've explained to Sondra and Gavin that Charlotte has suffered a contrecoup contusion. A contrecoup contusion means—"

"That her head hit something hard, and her brain struck the inside of her skull," Jamie interrupted the medical lesson. "Most commonly associated with a fall."

Dr. Travis Steckler smiled, and Jamie was frustrated at his condescension. Except, he wasn't actually being condescending. She looked at his casual attire. "Are you the attending?"

"I'm an emergency department physician, but I practice out of UCSF," Steckler said. "I'm here for Gavin and Sondra as a friend."

Jamie turned her attention to the parents. "If it's okay, I'd like to ask you both a few questions."

Sondra began crying again. Gavin went to a chair and sat, rubbing his head and staring at the ground. He was a tall man and in the small chair his knees rose almost to his chest. "Go ahead, Inspector," he said, ignoring his wife's crying.

"When was the last time you saw Charlotte?"

"This morning. Before school." Gavin glanced at his watch and rubbed his face. "Fourteen hours ago."

"Was there anything unusual about this morning?"

"I left around 7:00," Gavin said. "Lotti was having breakfast with her sister. They were still in their pajamas." Gavin Borden winced as though the words came with a painful image. His daughter in her pajamas and now in this hospital bed.

"Her car was found in the hospital parking lot," Jamie continued. "Does your daughter drive to school?"

"Yes," Sondra said.

Jamie flipped a page in her notebook although she remembered the car exactly. "She drives a red Mercedes 510?"

"It's a 520," Gavin said, his voice fading over the last number.

The "2" Jamie had written looked like a "1."

"But that isn't her car," Gavin said. He started to turn to his wife but didn't make it that far. Instead, he crossed his arms and sat stiffly in his chair.

"Whose car is it?" Jamie asked.

Sondra Borden seemed to shrink. "It's mine," she said, then quickly added, "I was picking up a silent auction item—a curio bookcase—and I needed the Jeep."

"Is it unusual for your daughter to take your car?"

"Yesterday was the first time," Sondra said. "But I've only had the car a couple months."

Gavin stood. "I need a cup of coffee."

"Mr. Borden, I know this is hard, but I'd like to get as much information as I can to help our investigation."

"I don't know anything," Gavin said. "I left and she

was in a pair of polka dot pajamas." His eyes were red and swollen. "Purple and yellow polka dots," he continued. "Next thing I know, I find out she was driving her mother's car, wearing her mother's clothes, that she was—" He choked on the next word, clamped his mouth shut, and strode from the room.

"He blames me," Sondra said, sinking into a chair.

"I'm sure that's not true," Steckler told her.

Jamie made no such promises. "What did he mean about her wearing your clothes?"

"She borrowed a sweater of mine. And a scarf. Shoes."

"Did she do that often?"

"More and more. We're almost the same size and you know how teenage girls are."

Jamie said nothing. She couldn't remember being a teenage girl herself—certainly not the kind who shared clothes with her mother—and she had no frame of reference with Z, either.

"Gavin didn't approve," Sondra went on. "He thought she was growing up too fast, but it was just a scarf or a pair of earrings. My boots. It wasn't like she was wearing high heels to school."

"Is it possible she was dressing up for someone?" Jamie asked.

"She wasn't dating," Sondra said without hesitation. "She didn't have a boyfriend. I'd know if she did."

Travis Steckler's gaze held a silent plea not to tell Sondra Borden that she was crazy to think she'd know everything about her daughter's love life. "I know this is difficult to hear."

Sondra went still.

"I'd like to do a rape kit on your daughter. It will allow us to collect evidence of what happened to her."

Sondra looked to Steckler.

"Let the police do their job," he told her.

"Okay." She went to Charlotte's side and smoothed the covers over her daughter's motionless form.

"I'm going to ask you to wait outside."

Sondra nodded without taking her eyes off of her daughter.

"While you're waiting, I'd like you to make me a list of Charlotte's closest friends. Names and phone numbers. It's important that I talk to as many people who know Charlotte as possible."

Steckler led Sondra from the room. A beat after the door closed, Jamie turned to Maxi. "What do you think?"

Maxi waved at the door. "I think that's the whitest black couple I've ever seen. You hear how they talk to each other? My mother's white family is blacker than those people."

Maxi's mother was white, her father black. Married forty years, Maxi described her parents as the perfect couple. Like Jamie, Maxi had been married too. Hers only lasted a couple of years. Jamie's had ended with finding her husband in bed with a woman she'd thought was a friend. It was understandable why the two of them almost never talked about men in any positive way. It was also probably a natural side effect of the job.

"They obviously love their girl," Maxi added in a quieter voice. "They both look torn up."

Jamie imagined the expressions on Sondra's and

Gavin's faces, then forced them away again. "What do we have so far?"

Maxi handed Jamie the initial exam results. "I've started her file. The on-call nurse got initial images of the surface injuries. The hospital's CMO ordered a full set of scans, so she's already had those, too. I should be able to get those e-mailed to you this afternoon. All that's left is to do a rape kit and get it to the lab."

"Wow, you're on it today, Maxi."

"Well, it's easy when you've got everyone paying attention," Maxi said. "Didn't have to ask twice for anything. Not like most times."

"Okay. Nail scrapings first?"

"There's some sort of gray chalk under a couple of the nails on her right hand," Maxi said.

Jamie placed a collection sheet on the bed and lifted Charlotte's right hand. Carefully, she scraped the substance onto the sheet.

"What do you think it is?"

"It's too rough to be chalk."

"Sand?"

"I don't think so. Not uniform enough. We'll get the lab to work it up."

Maxi and Jamie fell into a comfortable silence as they worked Charlotte's rape kit. The victims usually required constant reassurances, confirmation that they were safe, that it would be over soon. Maxi uttered these to their comatose patient. "We're going to comb your hair, see if we find anything. I'll try not to pull," she told Charlotte. Charlotte didn't respond in any way. Maxi would have said the same thing to a victim who never made it to the hospital, to the ones they did rape kits on in the morgue. She had before.

When they were done, Jamie checked that each sample was labeled and collected it all into a single bag.

"There is one more thing I think you'll want to take." Maxi started across the room to a small veneer locker above the sink. From it, she pulled out the white bag that held Charlotte's personal items. Still wearing her gloves, Maxi removed a lace bra. It was bright orange.

"Not the kind of bra I was wearing at sixteen." *Or thirty-nine*, Jamie thought.

Maxi showed Jamie the tag. "And check this out."

"Agent Provocateur," Jamie said. "Never heard of it."

"Me neither, but Carly down in Labor and Delivery says she sees it all the time at Pacific Medical, on the mothers who come down from Sea Cliff and Pacific Heights."

"So, it's expensive," Jamie said.

Maxi snorted. "I Googled this Provo-ca-whatever. This shit's not expensive; it's like a car payment. We're talking a hundred and eighty bucks for the underwear, which is only about four inches of lace. The bra?" Maxi paused for dramatic effect. "The bra costs another two hundred."

Jamie looked over at Charlotte. "And she had a matching pair?"

Maxi lifted a paper evidence collection bag off the table and handed it to Jamie. Jamie unrolled the top and looked in at the matching lace underwear, no larger than a cocktail napkin. "Four hundred dollar underwear. Makes it seem like she had plans for someone to see them."

"Damn straight," Maxi agreed.

CHAPTER 4

WITH THE EVIDENCE collected and bagged, Jamie emerged from Charlotte's hospital room about an hour later, somewhat surprised that—despite the late hour—the crowd had not dispersed. If anything, it may have grown. Or maybe the attorneys or assistants or whatever they were had simply grown restless and were beginning to pace rather than sit quietly. Tucking the paper bag of evidence under her arm, Jamie waded through the bodies, scanning for Sondra or Gavin.

The nearest suit turned toward her. "May I help you?" he asked, peering down a long, hooked nose with an expression that suggested she'd walked into his office without an appointment.

"I'm looking for Sondra Borden. She was supposed to be out here, waiting. She was making a list of Charlotte's friends for me."

The man's sour expression tightened around his lips as he shook his head. "No. No, I'm afraid Mrs. Borden has been called into a meeting."

"A meeting?" Jamie repeated.

"With Miss Borden's medical team."

"And Mr. Borden?"

"Obviously, he would want to be there, too," the man responded.

Jamie replayed his words in her head. He hadn't answered her question. "That's not—"

The attorney's puckered lips stretched out into a thin line that might have been a cool smile as he drew a phone from his pocket. "Shambliss." A beat passed. "Yes, Mrs. Borden has requested I handle that in light of the current situation." With that, Mr. Shambliss walked away.

The current situation was that Mrs. Borden had a child in a coma. Jamie watched him for several seconds. She considered going after him. A few years ago, she would have done it without a second thought, the prick. But she checked her emotion. The mayor had personally requested that the police give the Bordens the highest level of latitude. Not to mention that the suspect had fathered her adopted son. She would be smart not to create a big scene. She had a feeling she would throw one eventually with this crew.

Instead, she headed for the elevator. She would track down Sondra and Gavin after Michael Delman.

"Detective?"

A woman in her early twenties, dressed in a navy pantsuit, clutched her iPad to her chest. She wore simple silver hoop earrings and a necklace with a small pendant in the shape of a circle with a flower at its center. "I'm Tiffany Greene. I work for the Bordens."

"Inspector Jamie Vail," Jamie said without offering her hand. Tiffany seemed slightly terrified.

"I overheard you speaking with Mr. Shambliss, and

I wanted to let you know that Mrs. Borden is making a list of Charlotte's friends—or she was until the doctors came out."

"Do you have that list?"

Tiffany hesitated. "It only has one name on it."

"What name is that?"

"Amanda Steckler."

"Steckler."

Tiffany nodded.

"Is she Dr. Steckler's daughter?"

Another nod.

Jamie made mental note of the name. "You work with Mrs. Borden?"

"I'm one of her assistants."

"One of—"

"Well, between the opera and the foundation and, of course, running the house and the girls—Charlotte and her sister, Kitsy—it's a lot."

Jamie remembered Charlotte's father calling her Lotti. "Kitsy?"

"It's a nickname. Short for Katherine."

"So, you know the girls well?"

"I pick Kitsy up from school. We're together most afternoons."

"Do the Bordens have a nanny as well?"

"No," Tiffany said. "The girls convinced their mother last year that they were too old for a nanny. Kitsy's thirteen."

"How about Lotti? Do you see her at home?"

"Charlotte? No. She's not around that much."

Jamie waited.

"I mean, with her activities and everything."

"What sort of activities?" Jamie asked. She refrained from pulling out her notebook for fear Tiffany would stop talking.

"She plays lacrosse—well, played. She quit the team this year." Tiffany licked her lips. "And she took art lessons for a long time as well as viola and piano."

"She still takes lessons?"

Tiffany said nothing. Her tongue made another swipe across her lips.

"Tiffany, the more I know about Charlotte, the better I can understand what happened to her. I want to find out who did this to her, so he doesn't do it to someone else."

"I thought you knew who did it. You have him on tape."

It was Jamie's turn to fall silent. She always worked every angle to make sure they hadn't missed anything, but in the attack of Charlotte Borden, she was working extra hard to find another viable suspect. Why was that? Did she really have any loyalty to the sperm that created Zephenaya? "We have one man on film, but he may not be the attacker," Jamie said carefully. "We need to pursue every angle. Can you think of anyone who might have wanted to hurt Charlotte?"

Tiffany took her lower lip into her teeth.

"This is important, Tiffany."

Tiffany glanced over her shoulder at Brandon Shambliss. "There was some sort of disagreement about her art teacher."

"Do you know his or her name?"

"His," Tiffany said. "Heath something. That's all I know."

"Were they arguing?"

"I'm not sure."

"How did you hear about it?"

Tiffany licked her lips. Shambliss was still talking on the phone. "One of the cleaning people heard the argument. I don't know who Charlotte was arguing with."

"She wasn't fighting with the teacher himself?"

"No," Tiffany said. "He never came to the house."

"What is the name of the person who heard the argument?"

Tiffany said nothing.

"I need to talk to the person who heard them."

"I don't know her name," Tiffany said. "It wasn't the normal cleaning person."

"But she told you about this argument?" Jamie pressed.

"I overheard it."

"You overheard it," Jamie repeated.

"I wasn't eavesdropping. I was in the kitchen making Kitsy dinner and the two women were speaking Spanish. I don't think they knew I understood them."

"Can you describe the woman you saw?"

"It wouldn't help," Tiffany said. "She's not there anymore."

"I really need to know who Charlotte argued with."

"She had a small tattoo on her neck—of a turtle." Tiffany touched the area behind her left ear. "Right about here."

Behind Tiffany, Shambliss looked their way, his nose tilted into the air as though he were sniffing out people not worthy of his company. Or perhaps he smelled the ones who were asking the wrong questions.

Shambliss walked over to them, put a hand on Tiffany's shoulder. She jumped slightly at his touch.

Before Shambliss spoke, Jamie handed Tiffany a business card. "If you don't mind having Mrs. Borden call me to schedule a time to meet, I would appreciate it."

Tiffany took the card. "Of course, Detective. I wish I had something I could tell you. Mr. Shambliss would know more."

Jamie watched Tiffany's face.

"He's your best point of contact." Tiffany handed Jamie's card to Shambliss.

"Great," Jamie said to Shambliss. "Please contact me if you learn anything that might be useful."

"You can count on it, Detective," Shambliss said.

Inspector, Jamie thought, but said nothing. When she walked away, Shambliss's hand remained pressed on Tiffany's shoulder.

Jamie passed the elevator and opted for the stairs. What kind of relationship did the two of them have? And what relationship would Shambliss have had with the Bordens' sixteen-year-old daughter? She'd have to find a way to talk to Tiffany again.

Jamie walked down the stairs, feeling off and out of sorts. There was nothing unusual about this case, she told herself. She'd dealt with rich victims, powerful victims. She'd dealt with people who didn't want her asking any questions, and she'd seen situations where the obvious suspect had done it and cases where he hadn't.

All the variables of this case were common enough. What she couldn't remember was a case where she'd let the control slip through her fingers so quickly. Letting the

Bordens leave without having a chance to fully interview them or get a list of Charlotte's friends—even Tiffany's comment about them having caught their rapist—felt like a step away from finding their attacker, not toward it. Her phone buzzed. A text from Tony confirming that he would pick up Z after baseball.

Jamie unlocked her car and sat in the front seat. It was cold, the skies dark, cloudy, and threatening rain. She started the engine and let it run, waiting for the cold air from the vents to warm. She texted Tony back. What would he say if he knew Zephenaya's father might have raped and beaten a girl at City Academy?

A girl Z went to school with.

Her phone rang. Vich. "Vail."

"Hey. Wanted to catch you before you left the hospital."

"I'm still here."

"You see the victim? How'd it go?"

Jamie ignored that question for the one burning in her own mind. "How did Zephenaya's biological father meet Charlotte Borden?"

Vich blew out his breath. "Yeah. I thought about that, too. Sounds like the Bordens are pretty wealthy. Wealthy folks tend to keep their kids insulated. Means the most likely place is where she spends most of her time."

"City Academy High School," Jamie said.

"And that's the same school where Zephenaya goes, right?"

Jamie didn't answer him. Was it possible that Delman had gone there to see Z and Charlotte had caught his attention? But who was the expensive underwear for?

Not Michael Delman. God, she prayed not him. Plus, if Zephenaya had seen Delman, he would have told her. Wouldn't he? She stretched for some logical explanation to the coincidence. God, she hated coincidence. "Do we know what Delman does for work?"

"Odd jobs as of late," Vich said. "Part-time at a hardware store. Part-time with a construction crew. There any work being done at City Academy?" Vich asked.

"Not that I know of. I can ask Z."

"Don't bother. I'll call over there," Vich said.

Jamie was relieved.

"I'm over here at the car," Vich told her.

Jamie scanned the hospital lot. "Which lot?"

"Around back. Looks like he drove her in the Mercedes."

"That took balls," Jamie said.

"Indeed," Vich agreed. "Left a real mess, too."

"A mess?" she asked.

"Blood."

"Charlotte had a head wound," Jamie told him. "She was probably bleeding a lot."

"A lot of it's hers," he said. "She's O-positive, most common blood type. Just confirmed it with the hospital."

Jamie cracked the door to the car. "Anything interesting?"

"As a matter of fact, yes."

Jamie held the door handle. "You gonna make me beg?"

"I'm old, Vail. We move slower." Paper rustled in the background. "Here it is. We got two types of blood. Hers and another one, B-negative. And that one is the rarest type. Only one percent of African Americans have type B-negative. Two percent of Caucasians."

B-negative. Damn it. "You get a warrant on Delman?" Jamie asked.

"Yep. Judge issued a warrant to collect DNA."

The image of sitting across the interview table from her son's father made her ill. There was no way he would recognize Jamie, and he wasn't Z's parent anymore. She was. "We pick him up?"

"Not yet. Trying to get the landlord to let us into his apartment. I've got to watch the video again, but it didn't look like he was bleeding. Blanchard is trying to figure out how much of the blood is that second type. We can't confirm the blood is his until we find him."

Jamie pressed her eyelids shut until the blood rushed across her ears. "Maybe not, but Zephenaya has blood type B-negative and, like you said, it's pretty rare."

"Less than one percent," Vich repeated.

Jamie sighed. "Like you said…"

CHAPTER 5

HE PACED THE small space. How long had he been at it? Didn't matter. He was alone and it helped, the pacing. His mother used to complain about it to no end. Scream at him to stop, but he couldn't. Not when it got bad like this. What he needed was sleep. A shower, a meal. He reeked. Fear. God, he hated that smell. When had he last eaten? Not since it happened. It had been an accident. He'd never intended for her to go down the stairs. Some part of his brain knew that wasn't exactly true. It had been intentional. Sort of.

He had been angry. There was no denying that. So angry. The anger had gotten so much worse recently. It used to be that he could keep it bottled up, run it off. He had become a professional at pretending that nothing bothered him. He beat the angry man down. He became easygoing.

That's how everyone knew him—happy-go-lucky. Easy to laugh. He never yelled. He couldn't remember the last time someone had seen him angry.

The truth was he couldn't be angry because someone was always watching. They had expected him to fuck it all up. Just a matter of time. For so long, he'd held himself in a fortress that protected him from that reality. He convinced himself that they needed him, that he couldn't be replaced.

Over the years, the doubt had trickled in. The signs were all there. Hints that he wasn't as important. Decisions made without him, in spite of him, for him.

The doubt had grown and built until he collapsed under the pressure of it. Her cry. The crack of her head striking the metal railing. The echoing hum of the metal vibrations and the scratchy thrashing as her body was thrown against the cement. The sounds of it played over and over in his brain. It made him sick.

He shouldn't have left. He should have stayed with her. He pictured her face. Her beautiful face. These were not people to fuck with. They would ruin him. He would never see the light of day again.

He forced himself to sit. He was terrified she wouldn't wake up. What if he'd killed her? They would never let that rest. They would never give up figuring out what had happened. Dwight Stewart couldn't talk but someone else would. Maybe that little girl who ran into the street. She could wake up.

Should he have gone back for her, too?

And what if Charlotte woke up? What then? He pressed the heels of his palms against his eyeballs. She had seen his face. She would know it was him. She would tell them. Then what? It was too late to say it was an accident, that he hadn't meant it. They had to know he wouldn't hurt her. No, she couldn't wake up. That would be worse.

He had to bide his time. The longer Charlotte was in

a coma, the lower the chance that she would come out of it. And if she did? He thought about killing her. Again.

He cupped his hand over his mouth and tried to silence the rattling of his sobs.

CHAPTER 6

AFTER ENDING THE call with Vich, Jamie crossed to the rear parking lot, carrying with her the evidence from Charlotte's exam. She yawned, fighting off fatigue. She'd been up at 6:00 that morning. Tony and Z would be home, getting in bed. That was where she wanted to be. The wind had started up, whipping her hair across her face and stinging the skin on her cheeks and ears. Her heavy coat was at home. April in San Francisco had a way of fooling her every year. It could be beautiful and clear, the wind low, and she'd be sweating in a blouse and slacks at night. A day later, the temperatures would drop into the 30s and the thin windbreaker she kept in her car would offer no protection. Walking outside was like wearing a bathing suit in the Arctic. Today was one of those days and, as darkness set in, it only got worse.

She zipped her wind shell up to her chin and walked around the side of the hospital. The lights created a halo over the scene. Halfway there, she wished she'd driven over.

Now she'd have to walk back, too. She saw Vich first. His back to her, he stood up on the curb in front of the parked Mercedes. Between them was a thick hedge, about chest high, which divided the lot she parked in from the back one. It was beech or Ligustrum or one of those green, small-leafed plants that grew everywhere in the Bay Area. Near her house, someone had carved two of them into bunnies. Maybe for Easter, though it had been there since February.

Crime scene tape blocked off ten or fifteen feet on either side of the Bordens' Mercedes. Industrial spotlights shined down on the scene, providing light for the techs to work. Outside the tape, three news vans and a small crowd of reporters were being held at bay by a half dozen officers. Standing behind the crime scene tape with his shirtsleeves rolled up and his arms crossed, Vich watched Sydney's team at work. This was one of the things Jamie liked most about Vich—he didn't try to get in everybody's business. He could stand by without commenting while people did their jobs and gave him what he needed to do his. Something Jamie could work on.

Sydney Blanchard was one of two senior criminalists at SFPD. The other senior criminalist was Roger Sampers. Along with a staff of ten or twelve techs, Sydney and Roger managed the collection and processing of evidence from every crime scene in the city. Though Jamie liked them both, Sydney's high energy was occasionally too much for Jamie. Especially in the morning. And at night, like this. Or pretty much always. Watching Sydney with her slim, athletic build also made Jamie feel like she should go running. Or swimming or biking or anything other than what she did do, which was go home and eat dinner and watch the latest season of *Lost* with Z and

Tony. The fact that Sydney was never anything other than kind to Jamie made it worse.

You're kind of a monster, she told herself. *Yup, no argument here.*

The car doors were closed. Most of the work of collecting evidence would happen in the department's garage bay where the team had all the right tools. Not to mention no audience and better light. Right now, they were searching for things that they might lose in transport—anything on the outside or around the car and anything that might deteriorate before they got the car downtown.

Jamie passed by several reporters with her head down and her hand up. What she called her "no comment" walk. She went to the crime scene truck and checked the rape kit in with one of the techs, Naomi Muir, an attractive woman who looked barely older than Zephenaya. "Thanks, Inspector."

When Jamie reached Vich, he was on the phone, calling for an all-points bulletin. "Get an APB out and let's find out where he might have gone. Family, friends, his job? Call me when you've got something." He ended the call and pocketed his phone.

"Delman?" she asked.

"Took off," Vich said. "Apartment's empty. Looks like he left in a hurry."

Sydney came around the front of the car. She nodded hello to them and motioned to the Mercedes. "We're about ready to haul it back to the bay. Do the rest there."

"What did you get?" Jamie asked. "Vich told me about the two blood types."

"We've got some paint transfer on the driver's side mirror," Sydney said. "No way of telling how recently."

Jamie pulled out her notebook. "It's a new car, but might not have happened last night. I'll check with Sondra Borden."

"We have some hairs and at least four sets of fingerprints."

Vich crossed his arms. Jamie had never seen him take notes. "Assuming all three Bordens have driven the car, that last set might belong to Delman. Easier than waiting for his DNA."

"Right. We'll run those first," Sydney agreed. "Blood in the backseat suggests that the victim was put back there for transport."

"Where was the second blood type found?" Jamie asked.

"So far, only on the outside of the car—" Sydney pointed to where a tech was covering an area of the rear window on the passenger's side with a sheet of cardboard and tape. "Thankfully, no rain last night or we'd have lost it. There may be more in the back. I won't know until we have a chance to work on the area." Sydney called to one of her techs. "Raj, can you bring the camera over?"

A tall man with small square glasses and a thick, dark goatee loped over carrying a brick of a camera.

"Can you show them the blood print on the window?" Sydney asked.

"Sure thing." Raj quickly thumbed through a number of photos before finding what he wanted. He turned the camera so they could see the display.

"Can you zoom in?" she asked.

He focused in on the image. Against the bluish-green glass was an area of blood that was maybe two inches by four and slightly oblong in shape. Along the lower edge, the blood was coagulated in a dark smudge, its center marked by several cross marks. Above that, the oblong shape had a void at its center. Lines of blood crossed the void, but not in any sort of pattern. Jamie pictured someone pressed against the window. "A hand?"

Sydney shook her head. "Too uniform to be skin but could be material with some absorbency. A jacket maybe." She pointed to the dark X-like smudge. "This might be some sort of button on a sleeve."

Jamie stared at the form, unable to make anything of it.

"I'll call you guys as soon as we finish processing the car." With that, Sydney returned to her evidence, her ponytail bobbing. Nice as could be. Jamie felt like an ass.

Vich stared down at his phone. "Delman's got a sister. You know that?"

Jamie remembered Delman's sister from her adoption of Z. "I've met her once. Tanya."

"Right. She lives in the same building he does. With her kids. Patrol made it sound like she's got a bunch of little ankle biters."

"Should we go pay her a visit?"

Vich pocketed the phone. "Sure. You feel like a burger?"

Jamie stared at him. "It's 11:00 at night."

"Tanya Delman works at the Jack in the Box on Geary. What, you're not hungry?"

Sad thing, she was.

CHAPTER 7

ANNABELLE SCHWARTZMAN WAS awake when the phone on her bedside table began to quack. Her heart had stopped racing; her gaze no longer darted across the familiar corners of the room to remind her that this was her own place.

She was safe.

"Schwartzman," she answered.

Twisting the knob on the bedside lamp, she swung her legs over the side of the bed, 1:00. She'd only been asleep an hour or so. That always made it easier to get herself up. She wasn't one who fell into a deep sleep quickly. Or ever.

Oversized, gray cotton pajamas pooled around her wrists as she wrote down the address. "I'll be there in thirty."

She hung up and rose from her bed, crossed to the closet, and turned the knob. The door swung open like it had a mind of its own. It took a while to figure out that the room was at some sort of slant so that gravity pulled the door open. Used to bother her.

For months, she blocked it with a shoebox or one of

her medical textbooks before growing stubborn enough to get a screwdriver and move the door strike over so that the latch caught properly. That kind of obsessive perfectionism was a legacy from her time with Spencer and the one legacy—perhaps the only one—that she'd finally stopped fighting to undo.

She pulled the white cord and a single bulb illuminated the square closet, easily large enough for two people or for the kind of woman who loved clothes. Schwartzman was not that person. Much to her mother's disappointment. She slid hangers to the left, one at a time. Three, four, five, until she found the gray slacks she wanted on the last hanger.

Her slacks and skirts hung on the left, shirts straight ahead, and the three or four dresses she owned hung to the right above her shoes. Within their ranks, clothes were arranged by color, shades of neutrals mostly.

Once upon a time, her closet was a mismatched patchwork of yellows, blues, greens. Poppy was popular in the old closet, a color her mother swore brought out the blue in her eyes and the color in her cheeks. The poppy was gone. As were the green, the blue, the orange.

And especially the yellow.

She owned not a speck of yellow.

She had come to dislike bananas and corn, though she was fully aware that this dislike was only in her brain. It did not matter. She gave herself permission to disown yellow a long time ago.

Only a few months ago, she tried on a beautiful pair of black boots. Tall and narrow enough for her slim calves, they had a slight heel but nothing too high. Perfect with the skirts she wore to work. She'd been ready to buy them when she turned them over to check the price. The stitching on the bottom of the sole was yellow. There hadn't been the slightest bit of remorse as she slipped her feet back into her own shoes and left the store.

Schwartzman arrived at the scene a few minutes ahead of the promised thirty minutes. The street was blocked off in either direction. People who lived in the adjacent apartment building were milling about, outside the crime scene tape, straining for a look at the body. Dispatch had informed her that two people had been hit, but one, a young girl, was alive and had been taken to the hospital.

Her victim hadn't been as lucky.

Officers were crowded around the body. Overhead, the streetlights flickered, casting all kinds of strange shadows. A team was unloading large spotlights. Standing along the crime scene tape was a patrol officer she knew. Ken Macy. "Evening, Doctor," Macy said, lifting the crime scene tape so she could cross beneath.

"Officer Macy," she said, trying for a polite smile. Her medical bag in hand, she passed several crime scene techs, unloading equipment from a van, as well as two other patrol officers. "Officer Munoz, Officer Kidd," she said.

"Evening, Doc," Munoz answered. Kidd nodded. The two were silent as she passed, then the talk started up again. There was something absolutely soothing about the cop banter that filled a crime scene.

As long as she didn't have to be a part of it.

Another officer directed her to the body, wedged up against the tire of an old Chevy truck. Her view of the head was partially obscured by the shiny, dented front fender. The tech, whose name was Alan Wigby, though his colleagues called him Wiggy, was on his knees taking photographs.

"Evening, Alan," Schwartzman said, unable to bring herself to say the nickname out loud.

"Just finished up documenting the body."

"Perfect." She motioned to the assistants from her office. The victim's body was in an awkward place for an autopsy and rigor had set in, making it impossible to lay him out flat. "We need to crack it."

Alan, along with two other officers, took hold of the body—one at the shoulders, two at the legs—and laid him out on the pavement, then proceeded to straighten his legs and arms where the rigor had set in and locked the joints.

The slang for the process—"cracking the body"—came from the sounds that came from the corpse as it was straightened out. Once the body was laid out flat, Wigby and another crime scene tech worked to collect the blood and matter under the truck, Schwartzman focused on the body.

From her bag, she removed a white disposable Tyvek pantsuit and stepped into it, sliding her arms down the sleeves and zipping it up to her neck. Not all examiners wore the suit.

For Schwartzman, it was a no-brainer. Once she was done with her on-scene examination, the suit, along with other evidence from the body, would go to the lab on the off chance that there had been some transfer from the body to her. Any evidence that had transferred could be collected there.

The first time she wore the suit as a new ME with

the department, she'd gotten a few odd looks. Shelby Tate, whom she had replaced, had been known to come to scenes in the scrubs she would wear to the morgue to perform the autopsy, sometimes overlaying them with a protective coat if there were a lot of biologicals.

Schwartzman preferred the suit. She left the hood down in the back—the hood was more than a little goofy-looking—and pulled her wavy dark hair into a ponytail. She donned booties and gloves and knelt beside the body.

"Ready?" Schwartzman asked.

"Ready," Jason answered, clipboard in hand.

"Victim is male. African American. Approximately six feet one inch. Appears to be mid to late sixties."

Jason made notes as she voiced her observations.

She put the victim's weight at two hundred pounds. Relatively fit, he reeked of malt liquor. His shirt was open in front, exposing his chest and abdomen. Likely the paramedics cut the shirt open.

"Were you able to obtain vitals when you arrived on the scene?" Schwartzman asked him.

"No vitals," he said. "My partner thought he heard a thready pulse, so we opened the shirt to be sure."

It was what she had figured.

"Better safe than sorry," he added.

"Absolutely," she agreed, and the paramedic seemed to relax. She didn't need to look far to know the victim had been dead for hours. The body was cool to the touch, but that could have been hypothermia. Because of the color of his skin, the lividity was harder to see, but it was present. The areas where the blood had pooled after death were darker than his skin and with a purple hue, like the color of eggplant.

Most obviously, the victim's face muscles showed obvious signs of rigor, which began around the mouth and in the jaw within a couple hours of death. Full rigor had yet to set in. Time of death was less than eight hours ago. She'd have to cut him to measure liver temp. Before she did that, she wanted to be sure they had photographs.

She glanced at Sampers's group. Chase was closest; he shifted toward her, but, before their eyes met, Schwartzman turned back to the victim. It was instinct. She took a breath. Most of the crime scene techs were male. Especially on the night shift. There were a few she liked, but Chase was too flirty, too playboy.

She needed to get the tread marks on the victim documented before she could cut. *Schwartzman, do this.* She clenched her hands into fists. "Chase," she called over.

When he glanced up, she raised a finger to motion him over.

He jogged over, and she stepped back from the body and from him. "I'm ready to check the body temp, but I don't want to cut until we have documentation of these tire marks."

Chase squatted beside the body. "No problem, Doctor."

She stood with her hands at her sides. It had taken time to train herself not to cross her arms and touch her hair. Her therapist had pointed out that those were safety stances. She didn't need those now.

Chase took a series of pictures. "Think I got it. Anything else?"

She shook her head, and Chase walked away without a word. She scolded herself for assuming the worst of every man she met. Then, gave herself permission to feel what she felt. Hokey stuff her therapist said. No. Not hokey. Touchy-feely. Being kind to herself was not hokey. Or only a little hokey, another part of her brain protested.

Schwartzman squatted beside the body and pulled a #10 scalpel from a hard plastic case. Pressing her fingers along the ridge of the ribcage, she made a clean cut about one centimeter long and slid the thermometer's probe up under the ribs and into the right lobe of the victim's liver. She switched on the digital thermometer and set the timer for two minutes. Most examiners used an analog thermometer, but Schwartzman liked the digital. The temp reading was more exact, and the timer function helped ensure she gave it enough time for an accurate reading.

When the timer beeped, the temperature read 89.6. According to her car, the ambient temperature was 41. Humans ran at 98.6. Subtracting the 89.6 gave her 9. That, divided by 1.5, put the time of death approximately six hours earlier.

Almost 2:00 a.m., which meant the victim was hit somewhere between 7:00 and 8:00 p.m. How was it possible that no one had seen it happen? She studied the buildings in the area. The apartment building had the best views, but the building was set back from the street. But it was unlikely that the street was empty at that time of night. Finding the witness was on someone else. Maybe the girl who had survived could describe the car and driver.

She reached for her notebook and remembered Jason

beside her. She recited the numbers and told him she'd make notes on the rest on her own and get him a copy. She preferred to work alone, but she was new to the San Francisco job and she wasn't going to make any requests until they knew her.

With her notebook open, she moved down the length of the body, noting debris and marks on the victim's clothing. Once the body was removed, the crime techs would make sure nothing else had been left behind. Her domain was anything attached to the victim. She'd made her first pass on the victim when she heard a woman's voice, "Evening, Doctor."

Hal Harris and Hailey Wyatt were in front of her. They were her favorite homicide team. "Evening. Just starting the examination. Looks like the victim died between 7:00 and 8:00 p.m."

"That's not that late," Hailey said. "No one saw anything?"

"Haven't heard a word about a witness," Schwartzman told them.

"No surprise," Hailey commented.

"How about the other victim?" Schwartzman asked. "The young girl?"

"She's in the ICU at General," Hailey said.

Hal pointed to the victim's chest. "So, someone ran him over? That what killed him?"

"Yes, to your first question." Schwartzman got down beside the body. "These marks are definitely made by a tire's tread." She touched his neck. "There is evidence of early stages of bruising and the formation of some abrasions, so my inclination would be that the tread marks occurred perimortem."

Hal and Hailey squatted beside the body in a motion that looked coordinated. They appeared oblivious to their synchronization. Hailey and Hal were sometimes referred to as H20 or H&H, nicknames that suggested they'd been together a long time. The first time Schwartzman met Hal, Hailey wasn't there.

At that first meeting, Hal's size had made her distinctly uncomfortable. Worse, the case was a woman who had been strangled in her apartment. Hal had come in and gotten down on his haunches right beside Schwartzman and the body in a cramped corner of the woman's apartment.

It was all she could do not to shrink right into the wall.

Seeing him with Hailey made him much less intimidating. It was hard to imagine that she'd ever relate to a man the way Hailey did to Hal. She preferred physical space, and a lot of it.

"What do you think, Doc?" Hal asked.

One of the things Schwartzman most appreciated about this particular homicide team was that they never told her how they thought a victim had died. Most homicide inspectors had their own theories, often well-developed, before Schwartzman made any determinations of her own.

She appreciated that Hal and Hailey deferred to her.

"I suspect internal bleeding, but I won't know for sure until the autopsy. What's interesting is that there are three distinct tread lines. There's one here, across his collar." She pointed to the impression torn into the skin of his neck. The clavicle bone was obviously fractured there, creating a dent in the area between his shoulder and his mandible. "The weight of the car crushed his trachea."

"But that didn't kill him?" Hal asked.

"No. Eventually, he would have died from oxygen deprivation, but it's more likely that the car tire shredded his carotid and he bled out first. If something else didn't go wrong before that. There are no signs that he lasted long enough to asphyxiate. Plus, I don't see cyanosis—" Schwartzman scanned the victim's face for the bluish tint that would show that he'd suffered from inadequate oxygenation.

Schwartzman opened the victim's left eyelid and shined her penlight into his eye. "We do have some signs of petechiae, but that's not unusual, considering the pressure caused by the vehicle." She pressed the eye closed again and repeated it on the other side. "I'm betting on internal damage. There is tread on his neck and tread here." Schwartzman walked her fingers across his sternum. Broken ribs poked up against the skin and she was careful not to exert any pressure that might cause them to break through the skin as she pulled his shirt aside to expose his left side.

"That's not surprising," Hailey said. "The car drove off at an angle. The front tires went over one area and the back wheels over the other."

"I apologize, Doctor, for my partner's interruption," Hal said, smiling at Hailey.

"That's fine," Schwartzman said. "I thought the same thing at first, but look at this." She moved down to the victim's right foot where his shoe was missing and shined her flashlight across his ankle to show where the white sock was blackened with tread. Schwartzman had tried to imagine how his body might have been curled to achieve all three sets of marks simultaneously. Unless his back had been broken and turned at one hundred and eighty degrees, it was impossible. The spine was completely intact.

"Two cars?" Hailey asked.

"To the naked eye, the tread is consistent across all three locations," Schwartzman said.

"It's possible two cars have the same tires," Hal said.

"But unlikely," Hailey said.

Schwartzman didn't comment. Tire tread was outside her area of expertise.

Hal frowned. "How did the same car run over him in three places?"

Again, Schwartzman said nothing.

Hailey and Hal rose slowly. "Thanks, Doc."

"We'll know more tomorrow." She glanced at her watch. "Well, I guess that's today already, isn't it? I'll do the autopsy first thing in the morning."

Two assistants arrived with a gurney.

"You can take him," Schwartzman said.

She watched as the assistants rolled the victim into a black body bag and zipped him up. They counted to three and lifted him onto the gurney. The rigidity of rigor would make him feel heavier already.

Once they had taken the body away, Schwartzman scanned the area for anything else that might be relevant to the victim. As she left, she told Chase that she was taking the body and the area was open for the techs to search for evidence.

With her job done, she spent the next few minutes scanning the dark crowd for Frank. She found him holding a light for the techs who were sweeping the gutters at the far end of the street, probably for pieces that broke off the car after it hit the victim.

Frank Taylor was a patrol officer who'd been on this particular beat for twenty-plus years. He was married, talked about his wife and their three little girls as often as anyone would let him. He was huge, intimidating, jovial, and totally safe. She'd made it a habit to check for Frank first when she needed an escort to her car.

Clutching her bag and holding her coat tight to her chest against the wind that had picked up, Schwartzman made her way down the street.

"Officer Taylor," she said from a few feet away.

"Dr. Schwartzman," he said, smiling.

"How are those girls?" she asked.

"They're doing great, thanks." He handed the light to another officer. "I'll be right back, DeSoto," he said. "I'm going to walk Dr. Schwartzman to her car."

"Thank you," she said, slightly embarrassed. "Jaden's birthday was coming up last time I saw you," Schwartzman said to deflect attention from herself.

"Turned thirteen. Man, it happened overnight," he said, laughing softly. "Suddenly, she's practically her mother's size."

Schwartzman stopped at her car. She opened the trunk and set her bag in the back. "You have any new pictures for me?"

"You know, I don't. I keep saying I'll get some, don't I? Next time, I promise, Doctor." He gave her a little wave. "You go on and drive safe, Doctor."

"Thank you." She got into the car and locked the doors, put on her seatbelt and started the engine. She moved quickly, her heart rate always racing a little when she got into her car alone.

Taylor waited on the curb. He would wait until her car was out of sight, and she didn't want to keep him waiting. It was kind of him to escort her to her car. He seemed to sense her fear but never addressed it. And he never made it seem silly that she asked for an escort.

Walking to a crime scene, there were always cops milling around on the street, crime scene folks loading and unloading. She liked the scenes. Didn't mind coming at night.

When the lights were up and the scene was busy with people, it was like a bright world all its own. By the time she left, though, the streets were quieter, eerie.

She hated to ask for someone to walk with her, but her fear of whatever else was out there was a thousand times worse.

CHAPTER 8

ROGER SAMPERS STEPPED off the curb, careful to walk around the plastic orange numbers that marked evidence found beside Dwight Stewart's body. The body had been taken to the morgue about ten minutes prior. The victim's blood had darkened to a shade that might be mistaken for oil if not for the distinct spray pattern and the bits of skin and clothing. The smell of blood and burnt flesh, though, was unmistakable and, although subtle, Roger could have found it without any light at all.

He had been there for more than an hour, first walking the entire scene and beyond to ensure the boundaries had been established correctly. Next, identifying evidence outliers while his team placed small orange markers to note debris that might be related to the crime. He was in charge of making certain that every potential piece of evidence was mapped, photographed, collected, and labeled, then transported to the lab for processing. As always, he would be the last to leave. The Sweeper. There was a certain natural frenzy to a crime scene, but getting it right meant lasting beyond the frenzy. Finding the calm. Roger could do that.

He sometimes thought of a crime scene as a woman's body. Every man naturally took interest in a few specific locations and largely ignored the rest. It was those other places—the skin at the base of her neck, the dimple on her lower back, the pad of her palm—where he could make a difference. A crime scene was no different. It was a woman who deserved to be explored completely. This was not an analogy Roger had ever shared with his wife.

With the evidence collected and his team heading back to the lab to begin processing, Roger's last task was to talk to the homicide team. Most of the teams would have been badgering him for the past hour for his theories on the case, but Hailey and Hal were patiently waiting for him to process the scene completely first. He found them in the street, staring at fresh tread marks.

Hal turned as he approached. "Hey, Roger."

Hailey studied the tire marks. Roger had done the same thing an hour earlier. What did the homicide inspector make of the fact that the car veered to the right side of the street before Dwight Stewart was run over?

Veered toward him rather than away.

Roger had worked more than a dozen hit-and-run homicides. There was definitely something strange about the tire marks. Normally, there was a heavy brake pattern behind where the body was found. In this case, though, there was heavy tread beyond Dwight's body. And then a second lighter set behind it.

"Can we tell which of these tread marks happened first?" Hal asked.

Roger stopped in the street. "I used a gelatin lifter on the tread marks. Once we have that in the lab, we will be able to create a cast and identify the layers of the tread in the order they occurred."

Hailey pointed to the reddish-orange powder on the tread. "This looks like fingerprint powder."

"It is. I had them use the electrostatic device, too," Roger said. "Otherwise, we don't get enough dimensionality to the photographs when they're taken in the dark."

"So, you willing to take a guess on how this tread happened?" Hal asked.

"I can't speak with one hundred percent certainty," Roger began.

Hailey and Hal waited for him to go on.

"It looks to me like the heavier tread happened first," Roger told them.

Hailey studied the tread again. "If the darker set happened first, then the driver didn't brake until after he'd run over the victim."

"Or she," Hal corrected.

"Or she," Hailey conceded.

Roger nodded. "It does look that way."

"So maybe she/he didn't see Stewart," Hal suggested.

Hailey squatted down at the spot where the tread started to darken. "But it's like the driver sped up before hitting him." She touched the asphalt right before the void in the tread that would have been the victim's body. "He hit the gas."

Hal got down, too.

"That's how I'm reading it as well," Roger said.

"Damn," Hal said.

"So, what do you make of this second set of marks?"

Hailey asked, pointing to the set of lighter tread marks that started past the body.

"It appears that he," Roger glanced at Hal, "—or she—backed up."

"He backed up over the body?" Hal asked.

Hailey stared down the street. "What about where the girl was hit?"

Roger shook his head. "The tread there swerves away from the body and there is one long, unbroken tread that suggests a single effort of hard braking."

"So, he braked for the girl, but sped up and ran over Dwight Stewart, then backed up to run over him again?" Hal repeated.

"That would explain why Schwartzman found three tracks across the victim's body," Hailey said. "The front tires went over twice—once forward and then back again—and then the rear tires when he left the scene."

"That should have been four," Hal interrupted. "Forward, back, forward, and rear."

"It's possible that the third set is overlaid on the second, so we didn't notice the difference," Roger suggested. "He would have backed up and then the same tread would have gone forward over the body again. We should be able to identify all four at the lab."

"That might explain it," Hailey agreed.

"But why?" Hal asked.

"Am I safe to use the pronoun 'he'?" Roger asked.

Hal chuckled. "Of course. Although let's be honest, this kind of driving makes the suspect seem like a woman." He winked at Hailey, who rolled her eyes.

"Go on, Roger," Hailey prodded, while Hal smiled.

"The existence of tread marks in front of the body means the car was going at a significant speed before it stopped. The hard braking is what created those marks." Roger leaned down and pointed to dark marks past the victim. Then, he pointed to the set in front of the body. "But if he had simply backed up over the body slowly, accidentally, it's unlikely that he would have left tread marks like this. These, again, imply hard braking."

"So he backed over the body intentionally?" Hailey asked.

"Obviously, I can't know that for certain, but that is one theory," Roger said. "That, or he didn't realize he was in reverse and was trying to speed away and ended up going backward."

"Which would mean maybe he got out of the car," Hailey said.

"I checked this area closely," Roger said. "No fresh shoe marks."

Hailey frowned.

"It's possible," Roger said. "It's possible his shoes were very clean, but it's unlikely that he would have been able to walk around the car and back without leaving some evidence."

"Which means, the best guess is that he ran over Stewart twice on purpose," Hal said.

Roger shrugged. "Like I said, it's a valid hypothesis."

"What about the girl?" Hal asked. "Any sign she was run over twice?"

"No," Roger said. "We see brake marks. Like the driver tried to stop." The scene where the young girl had been hit was also cordoned off, but it wouldn't be Hailey and Hal's case—she wasn't a homicide unless she died. As the first priority was to save the girl's life, the paramedics had little concern for preserving Roger's scene. His team would document it fully, but saying what had happened was complicated by the disruption of the paramedics and the ambulance.

Hal gazed in the general direction of the place where the girl was struck down. Perhaps wondering if the case would be his after all. Perhaps hoping it would not.

"Okay, Hal," Hailey said. "Let's find out who had a beef with Dwight Stewart."

"We also retrieved evidence of paint from the victim's pants," Roger said.

"What color?"

"White."

"What kind of paint?" Hailey asked. "If you were guessing," she added.

"It's consistent with the location where the car struck him," Roger confirmed.

"Will you rush the paint so we can try to find the perp's car?" Hailey asked.

"Will do."

"Thanks." Hailey spun in a slow circle, scanning the buildings that surrounded the victim. She was scanning for traffic or surveillance cameras in the vicinity. A good spot to run someone over. "I'll put a call in to Traffic and request any images they have from surrounding traffic cameras," Hailey said. "Maybe they caught him."

Hal pointed to a Chevron sign visible behind the low apartment complex. "Maybe the gas station camera caught something."

"Worth a try," Hailey agreed.

"I could use a cup of coffee anyway," Hal said. "Roger?"

"Not for me, thanks."

Hailey frowned at her partner like he was nuts. "Coffee?"

"Sounds good, right?" Hal said, bumping her shoulder with his.

"Are you crazy? After we talk to the gas station attendant, I'm going home to bed."

"Remember, it could be a woman," Hal said.

Hailey gave him a look and Hal laughed his deep, loud laugh that made it impossible not to smile. Roger watched as they started to walk toward the gas station. What an odd lot they all were, the people who worked these crimes.

"I got five bucks says it was a woman driver," Hal said as they walked down the road.

"What? That's just stupid. You might as well hand it over now."

Hal responded, but they were out of earshot by then.

How could Roger ever explain to Kathy that he had stood at the site of a gruesome hit-and-run in the middle of the night and laughed?

No. Some things about his job were not suitable for sharing in his home life.

Perhaps most things.

CHAPTER 9

TONY WAS MAKING dinner when Jamie came home the next evening. Exhausted, Jamie had spent the day trying to pin down the Bordens, trying to locate Delman, and trying to shift the workload of her other cases off her desk to focus on this one. Most of the efforts on all fronts had been unsuccessful. She'd returned home after 1:00 a.m. and missed seeing Z, then had left again early this morning. The only good news was that it meant there was no worrying about how she would keep the secret about his father. Keep it from Tony, too, for that matter. That was something she'd have to worry about tonight, though. He respected her need to keep aspects of her case from him, but this fell outside of that. They shared everything. This related to their son.

Everything seemed normal, except there was no music.

Recently, that was more common than not.

Tony always used to blare music when he was cooking. For a year and a half, it was the Black Crowes. Z liked them, too, so that made it easy for everyone but Jamie. Then, the lead singer of the band—Chris Robinson—went off on his own and his music replaced the blaring

Black Crowes. The music was slightly more acoustic, slightly less like someone screaming in her, and, therefore, slightly easier to tolerate.

Since announcing the move, though, Tony played music less often. When he did, it was Sam Cooke or Al Green. Maybe there was nothing to it. Maybe he'd finally gotten as sick of his selections as Jamie was. But she worried. There were other signs that Tony was uneasy about his move to Ohio. In the past month, he'd gone out alone after dinner twice. For a drive, he'd said. That was what he used to say when he was sneaking out for a drink. As far as she knew, he'd been sober almost five years—from within months of when Jamie officially became Z's foster parent. Tony had wanted shared guardianship, but their attorney warned that Tony's record might reduce their chances of a successful adoption.

He'd turned around then. He was accountable, went to meetings. He attended a few a week—or said he did—usually straight from work. Other than those first few months of his sobriety, Tony didn't share his feelings often. Jamie didn't either. In fact, most conversations about emotion revolved around Z. For whatever emotional dysfunction they recognized in themselves, they were determined to help Z work through his own issues.

But Jamie recognized that a move had ramifications far beyond what would happen with Z. There was no doubt that Z was an important part of the equation for Tony, but he certainly wasn't the only factor. For instance, never once had Tony brought up how the move, especially alone, would threaten his sobriety, but it would. He had to be thinking about it. As usual, in their awkward sibling-like relationship, Jamie watched closely, worried as little as she could, and waited for Tony to bring it up, which would likely never happen.

Jamie set her purse on the little bench by the door where the mail was stacked in piles. Jamie's, Tony's, anything for Z, and a household pile at the end. Computer bag still over one shoulder, Jamie picked up her pile and the house's and came into the kitchen, flipping through the stack. Nothing interesting. She checked her phone one last time for any new insights on the case.

Michael Delman's sister, Tanya, had called in sick to her job at Jack in the Box, which was odd because she wasn't at home either. Patrol went back to her house, but the only ones home were three children under six. Left alone. The patrol officers had called Social Services who were sending someone to pick up the kids. Jamie also received Charlotte Borden's credit card statement. She'd made the underwear purchase herself, five weeks prior to her attack.

Five years ago, Jamie would have stayed late, pored over the material again, and hunted down a new angle. There was a list of things she could pursue. First off, find out as much as she could about the Bordens and, second, look more closely at what Michael Delman had been up to lately. Plus, Tony had offered to pick Z up again; so, technically, she had no real home responsibilities tonight. With Tony's move coming, Jamie came home earlier. These evenings together were numbered and the closer it came to the move, the less willing she was to miss one.

When Z was younger, the three of them had made an effort to eat together most nights. Even with Jamie's crazy schedule, she tried to be home so they could act like a family. Everything she read about adopting a child in grade school—and she had read obsessively on the subject—supported the idea that a strong family unit was vital. As Z grew older, though, he was busier. More time was spent on school or activities and while they had standing movie nights most Fridays and family dinner on Sundays, many nights Z was with one or the other, instead of both.

The smell of Tony's cooking reminded her of the emptiness in her belly and also helped push away the frustrations from the day.

They'd lived together for five years—she, Tony, and Zephenaya. She'd expected it to be difficult to live with people. After all, she'd been living alone—aside from her dog, Barney—since her divorce from Tim. Almost two years. If she could call it living. Her post-divorce home had included precious little furniture.

Most of her belongings had been in boxes when Tony arrived in town and she agreed to be Z's foster mother. In fact, those boxes had been unpacked by the three of them in a mad rush the night before Social Services was due for an in-home visit to determine Jamie's suitability to be a foster mother. Somehow, she didn't think the boxes would make a great impression.

Earlier that same day, the three of them had gone to IKEA and purchased two new beds, dressers, and side tables for the extra bedrooms and a desk for Zephenaya. By the time they were done, it was a home. Having Tony there felt natural. After all, he was the man she'd lived with longer than any other, albeit like a sister. From the time her mother had died, Jamie had spent as much time in the Galens' home with Tony and his brother, Mick—or maybe slightly more—as in her own. Then, their mother died too, and the three kids had practically raised themselves while their fathers spent every third or fourth night at the fire station.

Tony had been married and subsequently divorced to a woman named Deborah whom Jamie had never met. Tony had never met Tim. The ten-year gap in their friendship meant they'd missed the relationships that might have made them seem like normal adults. Instead, when she looked at Tony, she saw the boy she'd always known.

"How was your day?" she asked.

"Fine," he answered, using a long slender knife to hollow out a red pepper. His tone suggested it hadn't been fine. Not the time to bring up Delman. It could wait until after dinner.

"Z," she called up the stairs.

"Not home yet," Tony said. He moved the knife with ease and confidence, nothing like those first months when his hands shook nonstop. She was proud of him. Though now that he was leaving for Ohio and wanted to take Z with him, she occasionally found herself resenting his presence as if it had been five years of frustration.

He didn't notice her staring.

"You were supposed to pick him up," she said.

He gave her a look. "He texted. Team was scrimmaging. He has a ride."

"With who?"

"He's fifteen, Jamie."

She set the mail on the kitchen counter. "He's a freshman in high school."

"High school," Tony repeated.

"High school? That's the time when we shut off the parental guidance?"

Tony julienned the red pepper, a dance between his fingers and the knife. It would have been impressive if he wasn't pissing her off so much. She'd have cut off a finger. "It's a ride home from baseball practice," Tony said.

Jamie crossed behind him to pour herself some sparkling water. The boys had given her a soda maker for her last birthday. She filled an empty bottle with tap water and screwed it into the machine. Standing behind Tony, she pressed the button, releasing carbon dioxide into the water until it made a loud, hissing screech.

"There's water made," Tony said.

She knew that. She was hoping the hissing would alleviate some built up frustration. No luck. She poured a short glass and watched the bubbles rise to the surface before she took a long drink. This was her evening vice. Before Zephenaya, Jamie had been a smoker. She was an alcoholic, but she'd given up alcohol after her divorce. Living alone, though, who would care if she smoked? The little voice in her head sometimes added, who would care if she died? Zephenaya changed all that.

Becoming his foster parent, then adopting him, meant she'd had to give up smoking. She had enough insecurities about parenting; she wasn't about to give anyone ammunition by smoking in the house where she was raising a child.

Closing in on forty meant she'd also had to give up caffeine after 10:00 a.m. if she wanted to sleep at all.

That left sparkling water. She refilled the glass and took another long gulp. It burned the back of her throat the way whiskey once had. Then the bubbles went up her nose and brought on the tickling sensation of a sneeze. When it passed, she crossed back around Tony and sat on one of the stools that perched at their makeshift breakfast bar and stole a pepper off the cutting board.

"You could have lost a finger," Tony said.

"I've got faith in your abilities."

Tony gave her a sideways grin. "Like I said, you could've lost a finger."

How did outsiders see them? Regular, single folks who had friends and dates. Though they hadn't talked about it, Tony had dated a few times in the past few years. Had the relationships ended as soon as Tony explained his living situation? She'd never asked, never let on that she knew about the dates.

Jamie hadn't dated since her divorce, so it was all the same to her. The truth was she liked Tony's company, and she trusted him. That he was moving to Ohio was a sucker punch, no matter how many times she told herself it wasn't about her. She would miss him. She wanted to ask if the new job was really worth it. A hundred times she'd tried to ask. What was wrong with her? Maybe he needed her to say that she wanted him to stay, that their life together—as odd and untraditional as it was—worked.

Tony looked up with the weight of her stare. "What?"

"I—" Her phone buzzed on the counter. Tony watched her, waiting, as Jamie lifted the phone to her ear. "Vail."

"Inspector Vail, this is Sondra Borden returning your call."

"Thank you for calling, Mrs. Borden. I wanted to follow up on the list of Charlotte's friends we talked about in the hospital yesterday."

"Yes."

"Also, I'd like to get contact information for any staff you employ at the house."

"Staff?" she repeated.

"Yes. For a background check," she lied. What she really wanted to do was locate the person who overheard Charlotte's argument about the art teacher.

Jamie waited for Sondra to say something else. "Would it be easier to e-mail them to me? Or I can take them down over the phone?"

The line was silent. Jamie pulled the phone from her ear to check that the call was still live.

"Mrs. Borden, the sooner we talk to Charlotte's friends, the better our chances that someone remembers something. I really need your help finding who did this to Charlotte." This wasn't the right time to ask about the underwear. "Perhaps I could come by tomorrow?"

"Let's meet at the house, then," Sondra agreed. "Say, 10:00?"

"10:00 will be fine."

Sondra rattled off an address that sounded expensive.

"One more question before you go," Jamie said.

"Mmmm," replied Sondra.

"Are you aware of any damage to your Mercedes?" Jamie asked.

"How do you mean?" she asked.

"I mean, are there any dents on the car? Has it been in any accidents or scrapes?"

"No. It's quite new," Sondra said. "Why? Has something happened to it?"

Jamie said nothing.

"It hardly matters," Sondra added. "I'll see you in the morning, Inspector. Good night."

When Sondra hung up, Jamie retrieved her laptop from her bag and turned it on. It was natural to ask about damage to the car. Sondra's reticence wasn't necessarily a sign she was hiding something. The thing that struck her as odd was that Sondra Borden should have been anxious to help Jamie. So, why was she reluctant to offer the names of Charlotte's friends? Was it possible Sondra knew who had assaulted her daughter? Or did she have evidence that it wasn't an assault at all, that her daughter had been involved in a relationship her parents didn't approve of?

Someone had pushed her down those stairs.

Curious, Jamie sat at the kitchen counter and read up on Sondra and Gavin Borden. Sondra was active in a number of San Francisco philanthropies, most notably the opera. Gavin was a partner at Bishop and Borden Law Firm. Bishop and Borden, Jamie read, was started by Sondra's grandfather, Reginald Bishop, the first African American attorney to open a law office in San Francisco.

Since then, a number of Bishops had joined the practice. Sondra had several cousins who headed a New York office and another in Atlanta. Sondra, in fact, was the first in Reginald Bishop's line who opted not to pursue law. Her degree was in art history.

Beyond that, there was precious little about them

other than images of fancy parties and ribbon cutting ceremonies. Charlotte and her sister, Katherine, were in a few of the pictures as well. Beside their parents, dressed in beautiful frocks, the girls smiled widely. They certainly seemed like the perfect family.

Tony shut off the burners and eyed the front door. Jamie didn't want to fight about Z tonight, so she pretended to be engrossed in the search she was doing of Michael Delman's known associates and their current whereabouts. No red flag waved from the files. Even Michael Delman's list of associates included little to go on. Delman's crimes were mostly solo ones—assault, robbery, B&E.

In his jail stints, he rarely shared a cell with someone for more than a few months; the ones he bunked with were similar, less serious offenders. If Delman were looking for help, his family was the most likely target. The thought made Jamie slightly uncomfortable. Zephenaya was not his family, she told herself. He was *her* family. Right now, a patrol car was stationed in front of the apartment building where Delman and his sister, Tanya, both lived. Tanya's kids were with Social Services, but one of them had to come home eventually. Jamie had no idea where they lived, had never seen where Z had lived before he'd taken refuge in her backyard.

"Your case was on the news," Tony said, pulling plates down from the cupboard.

"My case?"

"Well, I assume. You were at the hospital yesterday, and today they were reporting on that wealthy couple's daughter." He paused. "Borden?"

"It's mine." She watched his face, waiting for him to recognize the name. The press hadn't mentioned where the victim went to school. She imagined that fact was a relief to City Academy, and it was to her as well. The press didn't yet know that Michael Delman had dropped off the victim. That wouldn't be made public, not while the investigation was active, but it could easily be leaked. She did not look forward to having that discussion with Tony. What better argument for moving Z to Ohio than that his father had been involved in the attack of a girl at his school? Not just any girl. The wealthiest girl? The most popular girl? Jamie didn't know that yet, but it wasn't a stretch to imagine.

Tony set the plates across the counter while Jamie exited out of Michael Delman's record. She and Tony rarely spoke about her cases other than the occasional comment about what was on the news. Occasionally, Jamie ended up getting caught in the footage; Tony and Z liked to tease that she ought to try smiling on camera.

This case was relevant for Tony, too. If he hadn't taken the job in Ohio, if he hadn't been moving, she would have told him about Michael Delman. Tony was Z's father. He, too, would be worried about how Z would feel if he knew his biological father had attacked someone at his school. Not to mention how others would react. How long before they released Michael Delman's name?

It was a race.

Her stomach growled as Tony checked his phone. The smell of dinner filled the air, and her hunger was starting to make her a little ill. Tony was worried about Z. It was almost 9:00. Practice ended at 7:30. She watched Tony cross to the refrigerator and pull out a Diet Coke and pop it open, drain the first few drinks like a beer. Those things would kill him.

She wasn't ready to have a conversation about their son, so she remained nose-to-nose with the computer screen. She filled the time waiting for Z by running a background check on Brandon Shambliss. That guy was something more than the expensive suit and the hooked nose. Jeffrey Brandon Shambliss, born May 22, 1983. A juvie record that was sealed, then an assault charge in October 2005. It never went to court. Charges were dropped.

"Jamie," Tony said, sighing.

"What did he say about the scrimmage?"

"Nothing."

Zephenaya could be stubborn, but he was rarely late, and on the few occasions he was, he called. "Did you call him?"

Tony nodded. "A dozen times."

"Where do you think he is?"

Tony's expression was tight. "I don't know."

"He's not answering his phone?"

Tony shook his head.

"He was getting a ride with one of the guys from baseball? Would have to be Sam or Paul, right?"

"I don't have their numbers."

"I do." Jamie pulled out her phone and handed it to Tony.

Jamie started to close out of the file on Shambliss's assault charge when she saw the name of his attorney. R. Bishop, Jr. Bishop. She opened her browser and typed the name into the search engine. Ten thousand records. She added the words "attorney San Francisco." The first hit read "Reginald Bishop, Jr., Bishop and Borden Law Partners." She went back to the date of the charge. Shambliss had been twenty-two. Had he worked for the Bordens before he was charged with assault or if that somehow happened afterward? Another question for Sondra.

She closed her laptop and listened to Tony on the phone. "This is Tony Galen. I'm Zephenaya's father. Was he getting a ride home from baseball with you today? He's not home yet."

Tony stopped talking and Jamie caught pieces of the other end of the conversation. "Do you know who he rode with?" A frown set into Tony's mouth. It was like his father's—the deep crevice in his chin, hooded eyelids. "But he was at practice?"

Jamie got up and moved her laptop off the island where they would eat. Anything to keep from sitting and fretting.

"Thank you."

She halted.

"He didn't ride with Sam or Paul," Tony said.

"Why not?"

"Sam said they didn't see him."

Jamie's mouth went dry. "They didn't see him?"

"Well, that's where it got a little fuzzy. They saw him at practice, but not when they were leaving."

"Were they covering for him?"

"Shit," Tony said.

It wasn't like Z not to call. He wasn't always perfect, but he was usually responsible. Where could he be? Working in silence, Jamie spread out placemats and folded their everyday cloth napkins in their places. Her mind buzzed about Z, but she didn't dare talk out loud.

Tony was responsible for getting Z tonight. He had let someone else bring him home. That wasn't unusual. Z got rides regularly.

Her anger at Tony was caused by the fact that Z wasn't home. She crossed into the kitchen for water glasses as Tony plated the dishes. He set hers on her placemat and then his. Finally, he set Zephenaya's down, too. "He'll have to eat it cold."

There was tight pressure under her ribs. The mother pain. She'd never experienced something like it before Z came into her life. When she'd caught her ex-husband in bed with another woman, it was an explosive, searing pain that filled her lungs like smoke. In the divorce and the nights that followed, it waned into a wall of pressure in the pit of her stomach. This new pain, the ache of worry, was motherhood. It filled a very specific spot that felt like heartburn and shortness of breath. She resisted the temptation to press her fingers under her ribs. There was no alleviating the ache until she saw her son's face. Tony sat at the bar and Jamie took her spot on the counter. There were only two places at the bar, so this corner was her spot. Tony avoided cooking there, and it had become a joke that it was always cleared for Jamie's butt.

"You could sit here," Tony said, motioning to Zephenaya's spot.

Something cracked. "No." She lifted her plate up, then set it down again. She couldn't eat. He would be home. He'd always been home before. He was strong and smart. She thought of all the victims she'd seen. Was that what their mothers had said, too? "Jesus," she whispered and slid off the counter.

Tony's plate scraped across the countertop. "This is exactly why Ohio would be good for him," he said in a low voice.

Jamie spun back to face him. "Really? You're going to bring that up now? You were supposed to get him from school, and he isn't here yet."

"He said he had a ride," Tony responded.

"He's not going to Ohio, Tony. No way."

"You're making a decision based on emotion," he charged.

Jamie froze, raised her hands. "Versus what? I'm his mother, for God's sake."

"Then you should want what's best for him."

Jamie pointed to the ground. "This is what's best for him. I'm what's best for him." She jabbed her finger to her chest and for a millisecond, the mother pain vanished. Replaced by rage.

"Don't I count? I've been his father for as long as you've been his mother!" Tony shouted.

"Then stay and be his father. Just because you're moving doesn't mean we should all move. You made that decision without us."

"I can't give up this opportunity."

"Well, what then?" Jamie lifted her glass and drank down the fizzy water.

"Have you considered that there's crime in Ohio?"

Exactly. And as much danger for Z. Realizing what Tony was saying, Jamie stopped cold. She set the glass down and rubbed her palm across her pant leg. "You want me to move to Ohio?"

"Did you consider it?"

"No."

"You could."

"No," she whispered. "My job is here. My life is here."

"What life? Me? Zephenaya? You'll have that life anywhere."

"You want me to give up my life to go to Ohio to live with my childhood best friend?" she asked.

Tony shoved his stool away from the counter. The wooden feet screeched across the floor. "Jesus Christ, Jamie."

"Jesus Christ, what?"

"You're so rigid, Jamie."

"Rigid? What are you talking about?"

"You're rigid!" he shouted. "Stubborn, mulish, hard-headed, dense."

"I know what the word means, Tony. But why am I rigid?" She tried to focus on the idea that he wanted her in Ohio, that maybe he was trying to ask her to come with him. It was so frustrating—that he'd been thinking she would come. Hadn't she been thinking of asking him to stay? Why hadn't she done that? Because it wasn't her business. But how was it his business to ask her to uproot her life? "I'm rigid because I won't move to Ohio?" she asked softly.

"Not only that."

"What, then?" Jamie asked.

"Because everything is set in stone with you. Even us.

You're stuck in some idea you had of us when we were kids. That we're children. Like brother and sister."

The breath left her chest.

"It doesn't have to be like that, Jamie. We could be… more."

"More?" she whispered.

"Like a family," he said. "A real family."

She took a step back. "Us? Together?"

His expression stiffened. "Never mind."

"Wait. I'm sorry. I didn't mean it like that. It's just—"

"Forget it, Jamie. You've made yourself perfectly clear." He passed her on the way to his bedroom.

"Wait! Don't you walk away, Tony Galen," she called after him. "This conversation isn't done. You drop a bomb like that and then walk away? How am I supposed to treat you like an adult when you're acting like a fucking child?"

Tony was halfway across the room when the front door burst open.

Zephenaya dropped his backpack and threw his baseball bag down. His shoulders were hunched, his fists clenched. His baseball hat was pulled low, hiding his eyes.

"Not that you care," he said, "but I could hear you all the way down the damn street."

"Don't swear," Jamie barked out of habit.

"Where the hell have you been?" Tony demanded.

"What have you been doing for the last two hours?" Jamie chimed in. "And how did you get home?"

"What is this—bad cop, bad cop?"

"Watch the attitude, Z," Tony said, the warning clear in his voice. "And you better start talking. We know you didn't get a ride with your friends."

"Friends…?" Z's cap shifted.

Jamie spotted a shadow under the bill. She stepped forward and yanked the hat off his head. His left eye was bruised and swollen. Dried blood was smeared into his sideburns. It might have come from the cut on his cheekbone, but what struck her most was the hard glint in his eye that she'd never seen before. "Is that bruise from today?"

Z shrugged away from her.

"You got into a fight?" yelled Tony. "What the hell's gotten into you, Z? And shut the damn door!"

Z spun around and kicked the door shut. The side window exploded. Glass rained across the entry floor.

Jamie jumped, her heart pounding. Z tore past them, taking the stairs in twos. He slammed his bedroom door closed, sending stuttering tremors down the stairs.

Jamie and Tony stood in silence among Z's discarded bags and broken glass.

Tony's face was white. "What was that about?"

Jamie shook her head, her thoughts on what might have triggered that kind of rage in her son.

"He was in a fight," Tony hissed. "A fight."

Jamie's mind was still going. There was the blood in Sondra Borden's Mercedes. Zephenaya's blood type. But that was yesterday. That was not relevant. "That had to have happened today, right?" she asked.

Tony said nothing.

"You saw him last night," she pressed. "I'm sure you would've noticed that."

"Actually, I didn't really see him," Tony admitted.

Jamie took a silent swallow of air, but it was thin and insignificant, insufficient to fill her lungs.

"Z came in from practice, but I was working," Tony said. "When I went to check on him, he was asleep."

Both Jamie and Tony watched the stairs as though Z might emerge to explain his bizarre behavior. No answer came.

Tony used his foot to move the glass toward the wall. "I'll get someone out to repair the window."

"I'll get the dustpan and broom," she said. They moved gently, calmly, as though Z's outburst was not deeply disturbing.

CHAPTER 10

JAMIE GLANCED AT her son as she drove across the Golden Gate Bridge. Brooding, Z was more and more a teenager. In the passenger's seat, he had a single headphone in his left ear. His body was bent away from her, angled to the door. He would have been wearing both headphones if she'd allowed it. She did not.

Jamie didn't have a clear idea of what had happened last night. Z said it started during scrimmage. He and Paul were on opposite teams. Paul was stealing second and Z made a play, got to the bag first. When the coach called Paul out, he didn't move off the bag. "He started arguing with Coach," Z said. "So I gave him a little push and he swung at me."

"And that happened yesterday?" she asked again. The fifth time at least.

"How many times do I have to tell you? Yes. Yesterday at practice."

She had to push aside the sensation that he wasn't telling her everything. His explanation was believable enough. Paul seemed like enough of a punk, and it explained why Z hadn't gotten a ride home with Paul and Sam. It might explain why the boys would have lied to Tony. Z's coach had gotten him to the ferry. Z brought out the ticket and a bus transfer to show how he'd gotten from the ferry terminal in Sausalito to the house.

All of it fit, so why was it bothering her? Because it fit? Because her son had pulled the ferry and bus tickets out of his pocket almost as soon as he walked in the door? Like he'd known he'd need proof. Was it how little he'd said about the missing phone? Or was it the fact that his misadventure came on the day after Michael Delman's alleged assault?

They passed through the toll booth, her FasTrak beeping off another five-dollar toll. She took the Presidio exit and wound through the streets toward City Academy where, thanks to a number of scholarships, Z was a freshman. The fall had been an awkward transition. The majority of kids at City Academy were wealthy—extremely wealthy—and Zephenaya had experienced little of what money could buy.

While the families of his peers owned their own jets, Z had never been on an airplane or a vacation. Their idea of eating out was picking up burritos. The three of them had attended a single Broadway show with special tickets she'd bought through the department. It was around Z's eleventh birthday.

The show was the Lion King. Z had spent the entire show asking questions about how the animals worked. People on stilts, in costumes, it was all a complete puzzle to him. When he couldn't figure it out, he'd wanted to leave at intermission.

Many of his first experiences were more confusing

than enjoyable. When Tony first served pot pie with peas, Z refused it, saying he'd never had anything green before. Only his hunger finally broke him down. Though he never talked about it, Jamie imagined his situation at City Academy was tougher because of his size. While most of the freshman boys were short and scrawny, Zephenaya was the height of a man with a size twelve foot. He'd missed so much school before living with Jamie, the district held him back a year.

Getting him into fourth grade had been tough, and it had taken them a lot of evenings and weekends to get him caught up. Being a year older for his class would have been fine if he wasn't so tall. As it was, he was a freshman who could easily pass for a senior.

Baseball was the one place where Z could be himself. They were a few minutes away from school when she finally said, "I don't understand how you lost your phone."

"I told you, I lost track of it. It's not the same as being lost." He hunched lower in the seat and folded his arms.

"Did you have it after school?" she asked.

He knew this trick. She was always trying to pinpoint the details. The what, when, and especially who he was with when he got in trouble. Find all the suspects and work them against each other. A smart technique in investigative work. Not as effective with your own children, as she had learned when she'd called the father of one of Z's classmates in the fall. The man she called was the father of the boy Zephenaya had sworn had the cigarettes they smoked. Z looked Jamie straight in the face and swore it was Jimmy Woods.

It was bound to be an awkward conversation, but not

nearly as awkward as it ended up being. Jimmy Woods' father was a minister and head of the youth ministry in San Rafael, the same town where Jamie and Z lived. Robert Woods had never heard of Zephenaya. When he asked his son, Jimmy told him that Z was in his class but that the two boys had never spoken. They didn't share a single class.

On the night in question, in fact, Jimmy Woods was at his father's parish, leading the high school church group with thirty other kids. It was as ironclad an alibi as Jamie had ever heard.

"You have to find that phone."

"I didn't lose it."

Z had underestimated her last time. He'd thrown her the name of a kid she didn't know and expected her to swallow it. As a result, Z missed six weeks of his social life; while Jamie made a call to apologize to Father Woods, Zephenaya had to write a letter. When Father Woods called to invite Z to the youth ministry, Jamie made him go every Sunday of his punishment. But when the six weeks ended and Z went back to his regular routine, both Z and Jamie were a little more guarded and Jamie checked his story more often.

"If you didn't lose it, where it is?" she pressed.

"I'll get it back today."

Z shared less than he used to; Jamie had to push more often. She worried about pushing too hard, disrupting the balance that they'd created. He talked to her. He always had. Didn't that mean he would tell her if something was going on? How hard could she push without pushing him away completely? *A little further.*

"Z, it feels like there's something you're not telling me."

"What? What do you want me to say?"

She waited.

"It's like all of a sudden you're doubting everything I say. I told you I'd get the phone back and I will. Today. Why ain't that good enough?"

"Watch the attitude," she said softly.

"Or what? You'll send me to Ohio."

"Is that what's going on?" she asked. He was afraid of having to move to Ohio.

He crossed his arms. "Nothing's going on."

"Have you been thinking about that?"

Z shrugged.

"Do you want to talk about it?"

Z said nothing.

"Be good to hear your perspective."

"Want my perspective, it sucks," he said. A hair under six feet and one eighty, Z was the size of an adult.

Now, Jamie saw a ten-year-old boy.

"Sucks covers part of it," she agreed.

"It's like you guys are getting a divorce, but you're not married. It's all kinds of screwed up."

She took a moment to process that. It wasn't unlike how she felt. But that wasn't doing any of them any good. "It's not like a divorce, Z. We're family. Tony and I have known each other our whole lives. He's taking a new job, that's all."

"In Ohio." His voice cracked on the second "o." To a kid raised in San Francisco, Ohio was the middle of nowhere. The reality was that Tony would be able to afford a lot more there than she could here. There would be the same opportunities for schools and maybe something better. She imagined cornfields and boys playing ball in dirt fields. Who was she kidding? She was no different than Z; Ohio was the middle of nowhere to her, too. Worse, it was a million miles away.

"So?" Z asked as they pulled up to the roundabout in front of his school.

She started to reach over to straighten his tie, but he pulled away and fixed it himself. She purposefully held on to the gearshift to keep herself from reaching out to touch him. "So, what?"

"How will you decide?"

"Decide?"

Z cracked the door and swung his backpack on to his lap. "Yeah, Jamie. How will you and Tony decide who keeps me?"

Jamie opened her mouth, but Z didn't wait for an answer. He was out of the car, slamming the door, and walking away before she could stop him. Long legs and broad shoulders, hair trimmed short, Z was striking. Jamie wasn't the only one who thought so, either. As he crossed campus, girls gazed in his direction, giving him looks that they were too young to be giving.

She wasn't giving him up. Why hadn't she promised him that? Was some part of her afraid that it was a promise she wasn't sure she could keep?

*

Sondra Borden answered the door in a white pantsuit. Or, not quite white. Sondra would have a name for this color. Ivory, or alabaster. Or ecru. Sondra paused on the threshold of a room as large as Jamie's entire downstairs.

"Please." She put her hand out to invite them in. "We can talk in here. This room gets nice sun."

And sun it had. Jamie crossed toward one of three large couches upholstered in a light amber fabric that was probably silk, centered around a coffee table made of handblown glass. The four legs were swirled columns of oranges, golds, and hints of blue. It probably cost more than Jamie had made in her entire adult life. She gave it a wide berth. On the far side of the room, the Golden Gate Bridge was visible through the window. Beyond that were the spiky peaks of the Farallon Islands.

"Nice view," Vich said with his thick Boston accent.

"Thank you." Sondra perched on the edge of one couch. Her knees touched perfectly as did her feet. Her hands were folded in her lap until she rolled one out in front of her to display the porcelain teapot set on the table. "Can I offer either of you some tea?"

"Thank you, but no," Vich said.

"I'm fine, too," Jamie said.

Sondra replaced her hand in her lap and made no move to get more comfortable on her own couch. Jamie sat forward and pulled out her notebook. Vich gave her the small head dip that told her to take the lead.

"Has there been any change to Charlotte's condition?" Jamie asked.

Sondra stared at her hands, shook her head. Something like emotion crossed her face and was gone. "I made the list of her friends that you requested." Sondra motioned to an envelope on the corner of the table, and

Jamie reached for it gingerly. "The information on our staff is there, too. Aside from Tiffany Greene, we rely on a service. I've included their number as well as our account manager's contact information."

Jamie opened the thick, expensive envelope and slid out a card with Sondra's name—Sondra Bishop Borden—printed at the top. In small, neat print was a series of names and phone numbers. Four of them. One was Dr. Steckler's daughter. Not as many friends as Jamie had expected. Below the girls' names was "CPS Services." Beside the company name was Abigail Canterbury and a phone number. Sondra had called Abigail their account manager. It was an odd title for someone who handled cleaning ladies and gardeners.

Jamie slid the card back into the envelope and tucked it inside her notebook. "Can you tell me a little more about Charlotte? What are her interests? What does she like to do?"

"Oh, the same sort of things any sixteen-year-old likes to do."

"I'm afraid I don't have a sixteen-year-old, so I wouldn't know what they do." She didn't mention that she had a fifteen-year-old. "What does Charlotte do?"

"Talks to friends on the phone, texts, listens to music, hangs out, and goes to movies," Sondra said. "She's like any teenager. When she's here, she's usually working on her schoolwork. She carries her phone everywhere, always on Instagram and Twitter."

Vich raised an eyebrow at Jamie. Sounded like a normal teenager to her.

"What else?" Jamie asked.

"All that social media stuff, of course, and she spends time with her friends. Really nothing that is out of the ordinary. She gets good grades and works very hard at that. The academics are extremely rigorous at City."

"What about extracurricular activities?" Jamie asked. "I understand that Charlotte used to play lacrosse."

"She did. Freshman and sophomore years."

Jamie made a note. "Why did she quit?"

"Oh, I don't know. She said it was dull. The practices, the other girls, the coaches. I suspect she realized that she wasn't all that good at it. At this age, it's all about appearances."

Jamie pressed her lips together, thinking about this room, this house, Sondra Borden's life. What part of that was not about appearances? "So, she didn't quit lacrosse recently? She decided not to play last year?"

"I'm not sure she was decided at the end of last season. She went to the first couple of practices this year before deciding she had lost interest."

"When does the lacrosse season start?" Vich asked. "Where I'm from, we've got snow into April."

"I believe it's late February," Sondra answered.

Quit lacrosse recently, Jamie wrote in her notebook. "She took some music as well?"

"Yes. Piano and viola from Margaret VanEck. Margaret's talented, but also very demanding, and Charlotte didn't have the time to put in. The two sort of agreed to part ways. I hope she will go back to it. She has the fingers for the instruments—long, you know, and lean." Sondra pressed her lips together. Another wave of emotion perhaps.

"And she and Ms. VanEck parted ways when?"

"Oh, that was earlier this year. January, I think," Sondra said. Did Sondra recognize how much her daughter's life had changed over the past few months?

Or was it just occurring to her now?

"And art lessons?"

Sondra said nothing.

"She took art lessons as well, didn't she?"

"She did. She quit those as well. About a month ago," Sondra said. She stared into her lap.

"Sounds like Charlotte had been going through some changes recently," Jamie said.

Sondra looked up, eyes narrowed. "She's sixteen years old. That's what children do at this age."

"Did Charlotte say anything about new friends? You mentioned that she didn't have a boyfriend, but is there any chance she liked someone?"

Sondra sat up straighter. Her shoulders shifted back. "No. I don't think she liked anyone." Sondra's tone was clipped. Was she thinking about all that she didn't know about her daughter's life?

"I know this is difficult, but there is a strong possibility that she was assaulted by someone she knew. Is there someone who liked her? Someone she mentioned asking her out who she didn't return the feelings for?"

Sondra's shoulders dropped. "I've told you everything I know."

Right. Even Sondra's body language lied.

"What was the name of her art teacher?" Jamie asked.

Sondra's lips slid briefly into a flat line. It was the only sign that she didn't like the question.

"We need to speak to anyone who has been a part of Charlotte's life recently," Vich added.

"She hasn't seen him recently."

Jamie waited for the name.

"Heath Brody."

"Spelled B-R-O-D-Y?"

Sondra nodded.

Vich was on his phone. He was probably texting the department to get a handle on Brody.

"How about the people who work for you and Mr. Borden?" Jamie asked. "Are they around your daughters often?"

Sondra looked tired. "No. Not often. Tiffany Greene is around more because she's my assistant and she also helps with the girls when I'm at meetings."

"How about Brandon Shambliss?" Jamie continued.

"Brandon? No. He's not around much," Sondra said. "Occasionally he comes to the house, but he works with Gavin."

"Has Mr. Shambliss worked there a long time?"

"I believe he joined them out of school, yes."

"But what about before that? Did Gavin or your father know Brandon when he was younger?"

"You'd have to ask them," she said.

"Where were you yesterday afternoon?"

Sondra was surprised. "Me?"

"It's standard procedure to know the whereabouts of the family at the time of the incident," Vich interjected. "We're not accusing you of anything."

"I was at the office, working on the fundraising schedule."

"Which office is that?" Vich asked.

"The opera," she said.

"Were you there alone?"

"No. The executive director was there."

"And who is the executive director?"

Sondra's lips thinned again. "Helene Remy."

Vich made notes.

Sondra took a deep breath and stood. "You'll have to excuse me. I've got an 11:00 appointment that I need to prepare for."

Jamie remained seated. "I'm afraid I have one more thing that I need you to look at." She drew out the photograph of the lingerie that Charlotte had been wearing. They'd photographed it lying out on an evidence table. It looked like an autopsy table. Jamie passed it over. "Do you recognize that underwear, Mrs. Borden?"

She stared at it. Then she dropped onto the couch. "Charlotte was wearing this?"

"Is it yours?"

"No. It's not mine." She stared at the picture as she spoke. "Where would she have gotten it?"

"It shows up as an expense on her credit card statement," Jamie said.

"Charlotte bought this?" Sondra glanced at Jamie before returning her attention to the image, seeming simultaneously repulsed and entranced by what she saw.

"It appears that she did."

Passing the picture back, Sondra said nothing but smoothed her hands over her pants. A moment later, she rose and thanked them for coming by as though they had been guests for tea. She shook hands politely and headed for the door, more quickly than she'd been moving on the way into the room.

Which question had triggered the hurry?

Heath Brody, Brandon Shambliss, or the fact that her daughter had purchased the four hundred dollar lingerie that she'd worn when she was allegedly raped?

CHAPTER 11

AT THE LIGHT table, Roger worked beside Chase, measuring tire tread imprints from the photographs taken at the scene. Roger made careful notes, checked the measurements twice, made a little hash mark next to the ones that were correct. Went on to the next. His measurements didn't match Chase's. Before saying anything, he measured again. Same number as before.

"Check point fourteen," he told Chase who, despite multiple warnings, had a tendency to rush. Slightly flustered, Chase went back to re-measure.

Once the measurements were completed, they would be compared with the tread from Dwight Stewart's body to match the car and hopefully identify the make and model.

Roger appreciated the soothing momentum of the crime scene lab. Not the mad rush of a CSI episode—nothing moved that fast. The sense of things being uncovered one by one, over time, like moving through a haystack, one handful at a time. This was the slow process of narrowing in on the killer, the thief, the rapist. As with anything, there were times when this was not the case, when things halted. This morning was not like that. This morning, things were moving.

As he and Chase were finishing up, the lab door opened and Hal entered. He crossed to them in three long, clean strides. Roger enjoyed those kinds of things. He made a note to measure his own stride next time he went for the door. Hal scanned the images. "Any evidence of more than one car?"

"No," Roger answered. "All tires are the same make and model. I did notice something though."

"What's that?"

Roger sorted through the images to find the two he wanted. He spun them so they were upright for Hal then pulled them side by side for comparison. "One of the tires has significantly more tread than the other three."

"So it's newer?"

"Yes," Roger agreed.

"A replacement?"

"Maybe the spare," Roger suggested, using his pencil to point to the tread in the images. "The front right tire appears new, while the left rear shows signs of toe wear, more on the inside."

"What causes toe wear?" Hal asked.

"Could be underinflation," Roger said, "but, since it's more prevalent on one side, it may be an alignment issue. When we see it on the outside of the tire, it's sometimes a sign of the driver having too much speed when he or she takes corners." Roger was quiet for several seconds, considering another possibility. "Huh."

"What?" Hal asked.

"It occurred to me that if the tires were rotated, it's

possible that this tire with the toe wear was on the front of the car before they were rotated. Then, the wear would be a result of cornering, which is the most common cause of toe wear."

"So maybe the tires were rotated when the spare was put on."

"Maybe," Roger agreed.

"Those other tires are pretty worn. Wouldn't a tire store recommend new tires?"

"Most places would—more for the opportunity to upsell than for necessity, I'd think," Roger said. "But, if they fixed any alignment issue and put the toe wear on the inside, the tire could go longer." He shrugged. "Of course, I'm not a mechanic."

"Can you guess how long they've been driving on this new tire?" Hal asked.

Roger turned to Chase, who had been quiet. "That's probably more up your alley."

Chase lifted the image of the tire and put a magnifying glass to it. "Time depends on how far and how often they drive, as well as how hard they are on tires. There's maybe a thousand miles of wear. Maybe a little less." He handed the picture back to Hal and set the magnifying glass down before returning to his measurements.

"So the tires might have been rotated a week ago or a month ago."

"I thought you had all the answers," Hal joked.

Chase laughed like it was the funniest thing he'd heard all day.

The lab door opened and Hailey came in. It took her five strides to cross to Hal. "Here you are," she said.

All the men in the room—himself included—looked up as though Hailey might be talking to them. Of course she wasn't.

"Hey. I was studying these tire marks," Hal said. "How'd the interview with the victim's son go?"

Hailey wore a light gray pantsuit with a blue shirt. Where Roger's wife's full figure came from being tall and big-boned, Hailey was petite with an hourglass figure that men couldn't ignore. He was no different, although he'd like to think he'd grown subtler. Chase, on the other hand, was staring. Roger not so subtly stepped on Chase's foot. Chase winced and looked away. Thankfully, Hailey didn't—or pretended not to—notice.

"Dwight Stewart seems like a good candidate for stumbling out into the street and getting hit," she said. "But the idea that someone hit him intentionally doesn't ring true."

"How so?" Hal asked.

"There's nothing to suggest someone would want him dead."

"There's always something," Chase mumbled.

"What did the son have to say?" Hal asked.

"Warren—that's the son—" Hailey began. "Warren was well aware of his father's drinking. It's the usual story on that." Hailey rolled her hand like she was summarizing a long list. "Tried to quit dozens of times. Sometimes he'd go a week or maybe a month without a drink. Warren remembered one particular summer when he was eight, his dad was sober for the whole summer vacation. Said they played baseball every day. Everything was great, then bam. First day of school, Warren came home and his dad was on the couch with a bottle of malt liquor."

Roger had an uncle who'd been an alcoholic. "The addiction was always on his heels."

"Exactly," Hailey agreed. "Warren doesn't drink at all."

"So, the dad was a mean drunk?" Hal asked.

"Nope." Hailey settled onto a stool.

"Warren said his dad was about the nicest drunk you'd ever meet. Passed out, mostly. Could be a little cheeky with the women—Warren said that's what his dad called it, 'cheeky.' He had no debt, lived within his means on his Social Security checks. His son owned the house and paid the expenses. Dwight Stewart didn't drive. Got a DUI about six years ago and sold his car, stopped driving."

"And when he didn't come home two nights ago," Hal interjected. "Didn't the son think that was strange?"

"He said it happened sometimes," Hailey said. "Warren made sure his dad never went out with more than twenty bucks and knew where the hide-a-key was. He'd been rolled a couple of times, so Warren was pretty vigilant about what his dad took out with him. No house key or credit cards, that kind of thing. Warren would listen for him to come home, but every few months Dwight fell asleep somewhere else. He always showed up the next morning, so Warren stopped worrying about him." Hailey sighed.

"And no one had a beef?" Hal said.

"Nope. No enemies. Guy played poker with a bunch of geriatrics for nickels and pennies."

Hailey waved at the tires. "Anything interesting?"

"Nothing conclusive yet," Roger said.

"Any luck enhancing the surveillance video from the gas station?" she asked.

"I don't think so," Roger said, glancing over at David

Ting, who was hunched over his keyboard. "Ting, any luck with the video from the Chevron station?"

"Uh, not really," Ting admitted. He pivoted the monitor so they could see the image. "This is the best I could do."

In the center of the screen was a white shape. The image wasn't detailed enough to confirm that the shape was even a car. This was not going to help.

Hal walked toward Ting. "Isn't there some way to have the computer fill it in? Like a program that fills in the colors and shapes based on some statistical assumptions?"

Ting gave Hal a blank-faced look.

"A program that does what, Hal?" Roger asked.

"You know, they've got all these sophisticated computer programs that run crazy algorithms to fill in missing data and create full images from partial ones, that sort of thing."

Hailey waved a hand at him. "Ignore him. He watches way too much Science Channel."

"Going to have to side with Hailey on that one," Roger agreed. "We don't have anything like that, I'm afraid. If it exists, I'm guessing the price tag is too high for the public sector, except maybe the feds."

"Makes sense," Hal said. "Google probably bought it for fifty billion."

"Let me try something else," Ting said, ducking his head back down. His fingers moved across the keyboard so quickly they were hard to follow. The screen flashed black, then the image slowly reloaded.

As the first lines appeared, it was clear that the image was out of focus. It was better though. In this version, at least it was clear that it was a car.

Ting looked up at Roger as though begging.

"We can't do better than this, Hal."

Hal sighed and rubbed his bald head.

"We're lucky this camera got anything at all," Roger continued. "That equipment is meant to capture a license plate or a face at the pump, not something two hundred yards away at another intersection."

"I know," Hal conceded. "I was hoping we'd be able to pull something off that car. Without more detail, we're going to be searching for a white sedan in a city of a million people, and that's not including the suburbs."

"Okay, grumpy," Hailey said. "It's not perfect."

"Roger, do you have a request in to match automotive paint?" Sydney Blanchard asked from the doorway.

They all turned toward her voice.

"Actually, I do," Roger said. "It's from our hit-and-run last night." He checked his watch. "Did it come back already?"

"Not exactly," Sydney said, crossing the lab with a paper in one hand. "What time did that happen?"

"Seven thirty-seven is when we get the car on video, so we think the accident happened about then, give or take a couple of minutes," Hal answered. "Why?"

"There was paint transfer found on the driver's side mirror of a Mercedes that was involved in an assault case."

"The Borden girl," Roger said. He'd heard about that one.

"Right," Sydney confirmed.

"And?" Hal asked.

"The lab hasn't identified the make and model of the vehicle that hit the Mercedes yet, but I got confirmation that the paint from your hit-and-run is an exact match to the paint found on Sondra Borden's Mercedes."

Hailey crossed to Roger's computer. "Maybe Michael Delman's car is white."

"Hang on," Roger said, logging in to access California's DMV records. He typed in Delman's name and searched the results. "Nope. Delman drives a blue '90 Ford Focus."

Hailey pulled out her phone. "There has to be some connection. I'm texting Jamie."

"Delman might have had an accomplice," Sydney suggested.

"Roger, will you pull up Delman's record again?" Hal asked.

"I've got to get back," Sydney said, excusing herself as Michael Delman's record loaded onto the screen.

Roger scanned the rap sheet alongside Hailey and Hal. Assault. Burglary. Assault with a deadly weapon. B&E. Known accomplices: none.

Hal grunted. "Doesn't look like Delman is much of a team player."

"Right," Hailey agreed. "Maybe it wasn't Delman. Maybe the driver who hit and killed Dwight Stewart is the perp in the Borden assault. He assaulted her and was on the run when he hit Dwight Stewart and the girl."

"And Delman just happened upon a rich teenage girl and decided to put her in her own Mercedes, drive her to the hospital, and leave the car there?" Hal asked.

"Yeah," Hailey said. "Doesn't sound really feasible, does it?"

"At least we have a good theory about where Sondra's Mercedes was the night of Charlotte's assault," Roger said.

"I'll get a team back out there to look for evidence."

Hailey's phone buzzed in her hand. "Jamie," she answered. "I think we've found the location where Charlotte was attacked."

Something triggered in Roger's brain. An address that had come across his desk. He shifted several papers until he found it, then studied the two addresses side by side. He slid the paper to Hailey and pointed to the name and address. "Same place," he whispered.

"Shit," Hailey said then into the phone. "And Jamie?"

There was a muffled response.

"The place where we think Charlotte was attacked—it's also Michael Delman's home address."

CHAPTER 12

JAMIE RODE SHOTGUN while Vich drove the department car down 7th and turned left on 16th, then right onto 3rd toward the apartment building where Charlotte was attacked. The building where Michael Delman lived. She didn't want to think about Delman. She checked her e-mails for any further news about Charlotte's condition. If Charlotte woke up, if she could talk, all this would be over. They would have their answers. The thought was followed by an uncomfortable pain in her chest.

Z was keeping something from her.

What if it related to Charlotte? His school, his father, his blood type… how could she ignore that all these things led back to Z?

Vich found 23rd and followed it to Tennessee like he'd been driving these streets his whole life. He got along surprisingly well, Vich did, for someone new to San Francisco. Dogpatch had more than a few dead-end streets and the occasional road that looked like a throughway, only to take some bizarre turn. She didn't try to find her way anywhere without Google Maps talking in her ear.

Hal and Hailey met them at the curb. The crime

scene van's back doors were open, and two techs unloaded photography and lighting equipment onto the curb. There were also two patrol cars parked on the street, though Jamie didn't see any uniforms.

Hailey started down the street and Jamie fell in beside her. "Any sign of Delman?" Jamie asked.

"Nothing," said Hailey. "Patrol's knocking door to door again to ask if anyone has seen him." She motioned farther down the street. "You want to join Patrol?"

"Not unless they find him," Jamie said. Which door was his? "The only link we have to Charlotte Borden and this location is the white transfer paint on the driver's side mirror, right?" Jamie said.

"And the fact that Delman lives here," Hal added.

"But it is possible that there's no connection between Borden's attack and the hit-and-runs," Vich said.

"There is always that possibility," Hal agreed.

Jamie never liked coincidence. No police officer did. For her, it was almost superstitious. Coincidences did happen, but you would be hard-pressed to find a police officer who would argue it as a viable theory. For now, they had to go with the idea that the two incidents were connected.

Hailey motioned down the street. "Let's look at where the victims were hit."

They walked about twenty yards in silence. "Our first victim was found here. Dwight Stewart. Late fifties. Hit-and-run, carotid was shredded. He bled out internally."

Jamie studied the blood on the pavement. No rain in a few days, an unusual break.

"Stewart was a drinker," Hal added. "Lived nearby

with his son, who said he made the walk to the liquor store on 25th regularly. No sign of defense wounds, so it doesn't look like he knew the car was coming." Hailey and Hal explained how the driver had hit Stewart, halted to a stop, and reversed over him again.

Jamie squinted down at the pavement. "So, the driver wanted to be sure he was dead. Why else would he reverse?"

"That's what we think," Hailey agreed.

"Any possible connection between Stewart and the Bordens?" Jamie asked.

"No," Hailey said. "The son had never heard of the Bordens and his father really didn't leave the neighborhood, so chances are slim that their paths would have crossed."

"According to his son, Dwight was harmless," Hailey added. "A really mellow drunk. No enemies, people generally liked him. He didn't do much besides drink and play cards with his old buddies. The son is getting me a list of the friends so we can talk to them. Maybe they know something the son doesn't."

"It's possible the driver hit him because Stewart saw something," Vich said. "Or the driver thought he saw something."

"It's one theory."

Jamie glanced down the street. "Where was the other victim?"

Hailey started back down the street in the opposite direction. "Down here. A young girl, maybe eight or nine."

"How is she?" Jamie asked.

"Still critical."

"In this case, we see heavy tire marks before he hit her," Hal explained. "The driver swerved and hit the brakes hard."

Jamie looked up and down the street. There were easily a dozen cars parked within view. Across the street were several long warehouse buildings painted industrial gray, probably sometime in the '80s. Their windows were the frosted kind with what looked like chicken wire embedded in the glass. Several were crisscrossed with silver duct tape where the windows were cracked. "No one saw anything?"

Hal shook his head. "Not a damn thing."

"The girl was playing alone?" Vich asked.

"There were two other kids playing soccer in the vacant lot," Hal said, pointing farther down the block. "They heard her scream but that was all."

Jamie sighed. "They identify the car as white?"

"Not even that," Hal said.

"No security footage, either," Hailey said. "These warehouses have an alarm system, but the company isn't having it actively monitored. Company's called Party People. They bought these buildings back in the '70s, used them to store party rental equipment—like round tables and chairs. But this place is where they store the old stuff. Outdated. The company bought a warehouse in Alameda, but the owner died before the stuff was transferred, so they've been sitting on this place for a few years while the family irons out the estate."

Jamie scanned the curb. "So, based on the location

of the two victims, you're assuming the Mercedes was parked along the street."

"Right," Hailey confirmed. "The good news is that the crime scene team took images of the street last night. They also collected any evidence along this entire block."

"So, maybe they got something related to Charlotte," Jamie said.

"We'll get you a full list of the findings when Roger's group is through."

"Any ideas how to isolate the location of Charlotte's attack?" Hailey asked Jamie. "We found dust under Charlotte's nails," Jamie said. "The lab identified it as concrete."

"No paint?" Hal asked, looking across at the warehouses.

"No."

Jamie eyed the sections where the paint had peeled off the walls. "The concrete might've come from the warehouses, but Charlotte also had a contrecoup contusion on her skull. That's consistent with a big fall."

"Delman's apartment complex has two cement stairwells," Hailey said, pointing to the building behind them. "The main one is at the southwest corner of the building, and there's another one on the east side. We've got the crime scene team starting at the main stairs."

"Can the lab match another concrete sample to the one found under Charlotte's fingernails?" Hal asked.

"Not definitively," Jamie said. "Sydney told us that two samples—even from the same structure—can show relatively significant differences." She started toward the apartment building.

"So, even if we find the spot where the attack happened… " Hal started.

"We need something other than concrete to confirm the location," Hailey added.

"Right," Jamie confirmed. "Blood, and there should be a lot of it."

The two crime scene techs were surveying the front stairwell when the foursome approached. "Find anything of interest?" Vich asked.

One of the techs turned to them, pushing his glasses back up his nose with the back of his hand. "Not yet."

There was something on the concrete exterior. "See this honeycombing?"

"Honeycombing?" Hailey asked.

"The areas that are coarse and stony," Vich added.

"It's deterioration. Might have been caused by poor mixing when the concrete was made," Jamie said.

"Or insufficient fine material in the mixture or incorrect aggregate grading," Vich added.

"You do a lot of concrete work in Sex Crimes?" Hal teased.

"My dad was a builder for forty years," Vich said.

"Mine, too," Jamie said without detail. Every father-daughter bonding memory she had was of building something with her father. They had rebuilt part of the cement retaining wall in the basement and retiled the floor of their one small bathroom, built storage lockers for all the guys at the firehouse. Time with her father meant doing projects.

"The honeycombing?" Hailey prompted. "It's important?"

"I think Jamie meant the deterioration would be consistent with Charlotte being able to scratch into the concrete," Vich said.

"Right," Jamie agreed.

The other tech, an attractive black woman in her twenties, came back down the stairs.

"Any results from the luminol testing?" Jamie asked.

"Actually, yes." She turned the screen of her camera toward Hailey and Jamie. "You see the faint blue?"

The glare on the screen made it difficult to see much, so Jamie cupped her hands around the display. The cement in the image was speckled with blue.

Hailey studied it next. "Looks like it's all blue."

"Right," the tech agreed. "We've marked that area off."

An area maybe four feet by four feet was surrounded with crime scene tape. Much too large for the injuries Charlotte sustained. The splatter suggested something much more violent, like multiple gunshot wounds.

"I've never seen that much positive reaction from a luminol test," the tech added.

"What does it mean?" Hailey asked.

"It means that either the sunlight is messing with the camera and we're not getting an accurate read…"

"Or there's blood all over this place?" Jamie asked.

The tech nodded.

"Maybe there is," Hailey said.

"I'm going to get a tent to block the natural light," the tech said. "If we can make it darker, it will be easier to identify the most reactive areas. Luminol will pick up traces of blood that is years old, but the rain should have dissipated any older blood stains over time."

"You guys want to help me set up the tent?" the tech asked.

"Sure," Vich said.

"Hailey and I will check the east staircase," Jamie said.

"Delman's apartment is on that side, too," Hailey said.

"He's on the second floor. I'll show you when we get there."

Jamie fought to calm her nerves. Delman was not Z, she reminded herself.

The two women walked around the side of the building in silence. The other staircase was steel and tucked out of the sun. Jamie was cold before they started up the staircase. She peered at the cement wall.

"We should have brought the luminol," Hailey said. "It's plenty dark back here."

Jamie had no experience with luminol. Most of her victims could tell her where they'd been attacked. Finding the blood evidence was usually something that happened with homicides. The two women moved up the stairs slowly, scanning each step. The railing, the cement above the wall, the steel base. It took maybe nine minutes to reach the top. "Nothing."

"Me neither," Hailey confirmed, a minute later. She nodded to the next stairwell. "Keep going up?"

Together, the two inspectors searched the four levels of stairs for any sign of where Charlotte might have been attacked and found nothing.

"With that kind of injury, you'd expect some hair and blood evidence," Hailey said as they started back down.

"Unless someone cleaned it up."

"We'll get Naomi to check it with the luminol."

Naomi. That was the tech's name. Jamie had met her before. God, she was terrible with names.

"You want to see where Delman lives," Hailey said when they reached the second floor.

"Sure," Jamie said. "We sure he's not home?"

Hailey pointed to the street where a patrol car was parked. Unlike the patrol cars parked on Tennessee, this car had a full view of Delman's door. The officer in the driver's seat waved and Hailey waved back. "We've had a car parked there twenty-four seven. No sign of him yet."

Jamie started down the hall. "You sure the officers didn't miss him? People blink."

"Let's check." Hailey stopped at the third door.

Jamie stopped in front of the door. Red crime scene tape sealed the door. It hadn't been broken.

"It's not technically a crime scene," Hailey said. "Not yet, anyway, but…"

"We'll know if he's been back," Jamie finished.

"Exactly."

Jamie went back toward the stairwell. A small ray of natural light cut across the cement pillars. There was a graffiti tag that matched one behind the police department. Below it, inside the area highlighted by the light, was a thin orange line, bright against the dull concrete. Jamie halted.

Hailey came up behind her. "What?"

Jamie knelt down to examine the line. "This." She pointed to the orange and leaned in closer and sniffed.

"Orange paint?"

"Not paint," Jamie said. "Nail polish. Tangerine nail polish."

"Tangerine?"

"It's the color Charlotte was wearing."

"You know the name of the color?" Hailey asked.

"Not the nail polish, but the lingerie she was wearing. Matched her nails exactly." Jamie scanned the surface. "Look there." She pointed to several tiny spots of reddish-brown.

"I see it," Hailey confirmed. "Blood in a spray pattern."

Jamie pulled out her phone and dialed Vich.

"What've you got?" he answered a little breathless. She pictured him trying to put up an unwieldy tent.

"We're at the east stairs. I think we found the spot where Charlotte was attacked. Bring the techs to test for blood."

CHAPTER 13

IN ORDER TO make her meeting with Heath Brody, Jamie left without learning the results of the luminol testing. Was she crazy to assume the orange was nail polish?

It could have been a million things.

A hornet's nest buzzed in her mind. Questions about whether they were making too many connections, resting too much on one location. White paint wasn't uncommon. That Mercedes might have been hit anywhere. In the hospital parking lot or at City Academy, where Charlotte had parked it the day before her attack.

With all the buzzing, her mind also went to Z. His lost phone, his black eye. All the things he was suddenly keeping from her. Her inability to ask, to push him to open up. How would she do that? She lacked those skills. Just as her own father had lacked them. She thought of the concrete on Delman's building, of the times she'd spent with her father. His unending list of projects.

Were all those projects a way of not thinking too much about her own mother?

*

Heath Brody lived in a loft in a new trendy building by San Francisco's Yerba Buena Center. The sides of the buildings reminded Jamie of the game Jenga, which Z had loved and insisted they play almost daily for a full six months. The sides of the buildings had alternating protruding and inset cubes in a random design. The protrusions were lined with horizontal slats of clouded blue glass. The inset areas were large glass windows and decks that overflowed with plants. She'd never seen anything like it.

Vich was following up on Sondra's alibi and interviewing Charlotte's friends, while Jamie met the artist on her own. Jamie hadn't wanted to risk one of the friends recognizing her as Z's mother.

This area of town was expensive and nothing about the building suggested Brody could be a starving artist. Why teach, then? Usually that was what artists did before they made it. Were Brody's lessons a personal favor to the Bordens? Or did he have some other motivation for teaching a beautiful sixteen-year-old girl? Like maybe something in the color orange. Brody was as good a suspect as anyone. Certainly, he had access to Charlotte. A young woman falling for her older instructor—an artist, no less—was nothing new.

Jamie made her way to the front of the building and entered the foyer, which stretched half the length of a football field with ceilings easily twenty feet high. Aside from the blue glass doors and the bank of resident mailboxes, the whole thing was industrial gray concrete. A concrete bench ran along one wall, a concrete reception desk. Where it used to remind her of her father, concrete now reminded her of Charlotte Borden.

Maybe it always would.

Some of those connections never went away. Like the way that the smell of bleach would always remind her of a particularly violent rapist named Marchek, who had almost killed her in her own garage five years ago. Marchek stored his work boots in a shallow, rubber tub, its bottom filled with a half-inch of bleach. She assumed the bleach was an attempt to eradicate any evidence of where he'd been. Uncut by water, the bleach smell was pungent in his immaculate apartment. A small collection of hobby boats that he'd built sat on one shelf, the only decoration. Hobby boats, too, reminded her of Marchek.

Heath Brody had left a pass for her at the desk and Jamie took the elevator to his seventh-floor space. His was one of the work-live combination spaces. He answered the door in a pair of jeans and no shirt. A rag hung from his back pocket. His feet were bare.

"I'm Inspector Vail," Jamie said.

"Heath Brody," he responded, padding back into the apartment. His jeans hung low on his hips, showing off the cut muscles all the way from his shoulders to his waist. No question that Heath Brody was deliberately showing off his sculpted form.

"I'm finishing up a project," he said.

If Jamie had expected a sparse, starving artist residence, Heath Brody's apartment was anything but. The twenty-foot walls were covered in huge abstract canvases. A twelve-foot marble sculpture of a woman occupied one corner of the room. With her flowing gown, hair elaborately braided on her head, and the arms missing, the statue looked like it was straight from Italy.

Brody continued through the living room down a hall to another room. He slid a large, barnlike metal door open and they entered what must have been his workroom. He closed the door behind them, and Jamie surveyed the room. Three industrial grade fans hung from the ceiling and a complex venting system ran from one end of the room to the other, its own fans humming. Along one wall was a series of brilliant blue pieces that looked like some sort of marble. As Jamie got closer, she saw they were metal.

"Copper," Brody said. "It's oxidation. I use acids to bring out the colors."

"Is the art in front your work as well?"

"No. That's my personal collection. This is my work."

She studied the blues emerging from the metal surfaces. "Acid?"

"Acid," he confirmed. "I use different types for different lengths of time. That's how I create the color variation."

She motioned to his outfit. "You work with acid in no shirt and no shoes?"

"No. When I'm working with the acid, I wear clothes."

Jamie was tempted to touch the brilliant blue and green.

"It's coated. You can touch it."

She ran her fingers across the cool metal. "How much does a piece like that go for?"

"That one there is about fifty."

"Fifty," Jamie repeated.

"Fifty thousand."

"It's very beautiful."

"Thank you, Inspector."

"Is there somewhere we can sit and talk?"

Brody put his hand on the small of her back as he waved back toward the living room. She moved ahead of him so that his hand came off her back, then stepped aside in the living room. Without hesitating, Brody crossed the room and sank into a sleek, pea green couch with metal legs and arms. The coffee table looked exactly like the staples you fed into a stapler, all snapped together, only magnified a thousand times. She didn't want to imagine what something that ridiculous cost.

She pulled out her notebook.

Brody crossed one foot across his other leg and leaned back, stretching his arms up straight before settling them behind his head.

She didn't let her gaze drop to his chest. "I understand you know the Bordens."

"I do. Sondra bought one of my first pieces. She's connected me to a lot of my current clients."

"How long have you known them?"

"Ten years, plus or minus."

"And you taught Charlotte?"

"I did."

"The acid process?"

"No," he said quickly. "I don't think Sondra would like that."

Sondra.

"No, Lotti and I worked on more basics. Perspective, drawing." He rose from the couch and pulled a portfolio case out of a closet. "This is actually Lotti's stuff here."

He laid the case on the coffee table and unzipped it to display a large pencil sketch of Brody's marble sculpture—the woman with the long braid and flowing gown.

The artist had captured the sculpture extremely well. "Charlotte?"

"She has an eye for it," Brody said.

"Do you have other students?"

"Not really, no."

"Not really?"

"No. Lotti was the only one."

"And why did you teach her?" Jamie waved around the apartment. "Doesn't look like you needed the extra income."

He shrugged. "She asked. I said yes."

"Charlotte asked?" Jamie confirmed.

He hesitated. "Yes."

"She called you up and asked if you could give her art lessons?"

"Something like that."

Jamie wrote in her notebook: Sondra asked for lessons? Or Lotti? Why lie? When she glanced up again, she asked, "So, if Charlotte asked for lessons, why did she stop coming?"

Brody closed the portfolio and zipped it back up, setting it beside the couch. "I don't have any idea. You'd have to ask her."

Jamie waited for him to mention that Charlotte was in a coma. "You have heard what happened to her?"

"I did." No remorse. Not the slightest shift in body language. Either Heath Brody had nothing to do with what had happened to Charlotte or he was a full-fledged sociopath.

"When was the last time you taught Charlotte?"

Brody stretched his neck left and right. "January, I think, but Sondra would know better."

"What did you talk about during your lessons?"

Brody cocked an eyebrow. "Art."

"Really? Just art?"

"Well, she chattered about school and friends," he conceded. "I didn't really pay attention."

"She mention a boyfriend?"

He smiled like the idea was silly.

"Something amusing, Mr. Brody?"

"No. She never mentioned a boyfriend," he responded, drawing out the word "boy."

"A male friend?"

"No." The humor gone.

"You're close with the Borden family?"

"I'm not invited for Christmas, if that's what you're asking."

"You've been to their home, then?"

"Yes," he said. "Sondra's included me in a few functions to meet some of her friends. As I said, she's introduced me to quite a few of my clients."

"Do you have any idea who might want to attack Charlotte?"

Brody leaned forward, resting his elbows on his knees. His sculpted form created no strange rolls or bulges.

"A young, rich, beautiful woman. Seems like there would be a lot of suspects," Brody offered. Then, leaning back again, he added, "I can't imagine how you'd go about looking."

Jamie stared at Brody. He sat, unflinching. He was a liar. She could tell that much, but without a reason to request a search warrant, there was nothing more to be gained from Heath Brody.

She stood up from the couch and Brody led her to the door. A door off the hallway was ajar.

His bedroom.

She pretended to dig in her purse. "I'd like to leave you with a card," she said, palming through the bag as she stole glances into the room.

"In case you remember something useful," she added. Chin down as though searching in her purse, she scanned the room. A bed in the center of the room, dark covers strewn across it. A tall, dark bureau. No photographs. A wallet on the bureau, keys maybe. Assorted papers that might have been receipts. Her fingers found the hard case and she pulled it out. Removed a business card. Looked again.

On the far side of the bed hung a sketch. Done in heavy charcoal, it was a view of the Golden Gate Bridge with the land peninsula on either side. Unlike most pictures of the bridge, the bridge wasn't the focus in this one. Instead, the artist had balanced the bridge with the peninsulas on the Marin and San Francisco sides. "That's a lovely drawing," she told him, pushing the door open slightly. "The one beside the bed."

Brody crossed to the door to pull it closed.

Her foot was in the way. "Is it yours?"

Brody stared down at her foot.

She moved it slowly. "It's different from your others," she added. When he said nothing, she went on. "Can I ask who did it?"

"I can't recall, I'm afraid."

She took a last glance at the drawing. "So, it isn't yours, Mr. Brody?"

Brody closed the bedroom door and opened the front one. "Have a nice afternoon, Inspector."

"I'm sure we'll be talking again soon, Mr. Brody," Jamie said, walking away from the apartment.

*

Jamie hated parent-teacher conferences at Z's school. Even when the teachers had nothing but good news to report, there was always the sense that she and Z were both damn lucky to be there. Or the sideways glances at her slacks, inevitably wrinkled after the day, and once actually torn across the knee when she had gone to question a suspect and he'd taken off running. She'd caught the bastard but not before snagging her pant leg on the edge of a rusty swing when she chased him through a yard. Torn out a whole strip of the knee. There was no hiding that on the walk across City Academy's swanky campus. At least she kept an extra outfit in the trunk. Not that her extra outfit was anything worth mentioning.

The teachers at City Academy had nicer wardrobes than she did.

Brody was no boost to her mood either. The arrogant jerk. Then, getting a parking ticket on the street in front of Brody's apartment added insult to injury. She was parked in a twenty-minute loading area with her police credentials in full view on the dash. How did the parking enforcement officer miss that?

Even if she had been in the red, she'd like to meet the asshole who wrote her a ticket. Not that she'd have to pay it, but that wasn't the point. Maybe she'd send it over to Parking with a note.

She pulled into the lot at Z's school. Here she was again. Midterm review. Pre-term, mid-term, post-term, City Academy was all about communication.

Plenty of that was accomplished with the looks from the parents of paying students.

She parked the department car and opened the door, which emitted an ear-piercing creak from somewhere in the hinge. This was her car's latest issue. Thankfully, City Academy's parking lot was relatively quiet. Tony's Camry wasn't there. It would be tight for him to get to the school after teaching his last class.

She crossed through the lot toward the English building where Z's advisor was to meet them. A navy Lexus parked, occupying the center of two spots. Typical. As she came around behind it, the rear lights went on and the car began to back up. Jamie slapped the trunk. "Whoa."

The car hadn't actually moved, she realized, pulling her hand away and tucking her head down to walk past. From the corner of her eye, she saw the driver's side window go down. Expecting some snotty remark about denting the car with her hand, Jamie moved a little faster.

"Inspector," called a man's voice.

Jamie turned back. Windblown hair, big expensive sunglasses, a fancy watch on his wrist, she had zero idea who he was. With a tight smile, she kept walking.

He lifted his sunglasses onto his head. "Inspector, hold up. It's me, Travis Steckler."

She stopped. No recollection.

"Dr. Steckler, the friend of Sondra and Gavin Borden. From the hospital the other day."

"Oh, right. Hello, Doctor."

"Hang on a second," Travis said, and he quickly put his car in reverse, sped out, and pulled back in to occupy only one space.

Ten minutes until her meeting with Z's teacher. She would either have to wait in the anteroom or spend it talking to Dr. Charming. The anteroom seemed better, but she remained in place.

Moving quickly, Dr. Steckler locked the car and jogged to join her on the curb. He was dressed for work. A button-down shirt in some sort of fancy fabric that had a tiny pattern to it and a little sheen. A tie that matched the shirt perfectly. He propped his sunglasses up on his head and squinted in the sun as they started across the campus. "You here to interview some of Charlotte's teachers or friends?"

"No…"

"Good. Because the kids are actually off today. It's parent-teacher conference day."

Jamie said nothing.

"Ah, she doesn't comment. Can't leak any details of the case."

What did he want?

"Do you drink coffee?" he asked.

"Why? Are you going to tell me that my blood pressure is too high and I should quit?"

Looking startled, Steckler stopped walking. A moment later, he laughed out loud.

Jamie didn't know what to do, so she stopped, too. She frowned at him.

"No," he assured her. "I wouldn't say that."

"Then, yes. I do. Drink coffee, that is." Jamie started walking again, and Steckler quickly caught up.

"I want to take you out, Inspector."

"Well, then I'll remind you, Dr. Steckler, that you did almost take me out about two minutes ago—with your car."

"Call me Travis."

Jamie said nothing.

"I mean, I'd like to take you out for coffee... or dinner."

Jamie stopped walking.

Travis had pulled out his wallet and removed a business card. "Would you consider that? Like a date?"

Jamie glanced down at the card he handed her. It listed his office on Webster Street. It was close to Pacific Heights. "You want me to call the office and make an appointment?"

Travis grinned. Like she was hilarious. "That bottom number is my cell phone number. You can call or text, whichever."

With that, Travis touched her shoulder. "I'd love to hear from you. I'm afraid I've got to go. I have a meeting with my daughter's teacher." Then, leaving her there, he walked on.

After his hand was gone, the heat of his palm passed through her blouse. It wasn't him, she told herself. How long had it been since a man had touched her at all? Certainly, she and Tony had never been the hugging type, and the little cuddling she used to do with Zephenaya had completely stopped with the start of middle school.

She was reacting to the contact.

She thought again of Tony's comment. That they could be something more than friends. It wasn't true. They couldn't. She couldn't. He knew too much; she knew too much. Touching Tony would never have the spark she'd felt from a complete stranger. Did she expect to ever have that again? Her life was too complicated for dating. That didn't mean she would settle for something else either, like whatever Tony meant…

She folded Steckler's card in two and pocketed it to throw away later. As she walked across the campus, though, the notion played in her mind. A date with Dr. Travis Steckler. A date with a doctor. What would they talk about? He acted like she was charming.

She was as charming as a troll, especially with this case.

Truth be told, she was usually about this charming.

Was it some sort of joke? But why? To humiliate her? Surely, they were beyond that stage in their lives.

A date with Travis Steckler was completely impossible. She imagined being seen with him and trying to explain it to Captain Jules. *Sure, Captain. The suspect is my son's dad and I was on a date with the victim's close family friend.* Up ahead, Travis walked into the science building without so much as a backward glance.

The door closed behind him. She fought against disappointment. He hadn't looked back. Damn it. Who was she kidding? She was absolutely attracted to that man.

Tony called out to her. He jogged to catch up with her. "Hey, thanks for waiting," he said. "I didn't think you heard me calling."

She watched the door Steckler had gone through. "Sure. Of course."

The two walked toward the English complex.

"Should be good news, right?" Tony asked.

Jamie nodded. They hadn't gotten any reports on Zephenaya since the cigarette incident, so there was no reason to think the meeting would go badly. Tony tensed beside her.

What was it about this place that made every meeting like walking into a firing squad?

CHAPTER 14

THEY WERE GOING to try to pin Charlotte on him. He had no part of that shit. Innocent. Wouldn't make no difference to them. Not to the cops or the lawyers or the press. Hell, not even his family. No one would take his side over theirs. The public defender would tell him to plea. That's what they all did. No one wanted to take on the case of an innocent man. Not a poor one. Be rich like O.J. Simpson and leave your size thirteen bloody footprints all over and shit, no one could touch you. Be poor, though, and you'd better fly under the radar. Way, way under.

Which is exactly what he'd been doing. Biding his time, paying his dues. Saving. He'd thought this sort of shit was in his past. He was actually dumb enough to think that he could get out of here. That's what he got for listening to outsiders. For believing them. Especially her. Damn, how bad he wanted to believe her. Nothing was more addictive than hope and no drug was as painful to kick. That's what he felt. Like someone standing over him, kicking him in the head. How could he have been that stupid?

For years, he'd been careful not to let the hope get to him. Most of them were smarter than that. He'd been smarter than most. He didn't hope for anything. Not a new pair of sneaks or a ticket to the movies. None of that shit. He let the hope bead and run off like rain off a windowpane. No cracks. He held it all out. The attention, the way she looked at him like she really cared.

He'd effectively ignored it—seen it for the bullshit it was. He was like a mangy dog to them. Something you pitied, tried to scrub up and de-flea. But it only lasted as long as you were cute and pathetic. She didn't lose interest. She kept texting, kept calling.

He let her see the worst parts of him. He swore and cussed and didn't shave and got angry. But there was more, too. He told her the truth and, by doing that, he'd let her in.

Only four months and she'd splintered his strength, shattered the parts of him that protected against the idea that things might be different. As he huddled in the corner of the room, the fresh reality was excruciating. So much more painful than the time his father knifed him for "back talk," which, in his case, was confusion about what his father wanted, so thick was his father's whiskey slur. He was only six then. He hadn't known that hearing his dad sound like that meant it was time to hide and hide well.

Worse than watching the paramedics take his mother to the hospital because she nearly OD'd when his baby sister was eight weeks old, leaving him alone with her. This was worse than watching Justice Burrows get shot on the basketball court for no reason other than that some gangbanger was trying out a new clip. They were nine.

Finding her at the base of those stairs, he told himself it might be all right. She wasn't dead. Naive. The stupid dreams of a kid. They would find him. They would target him. There was no such thing as right and wrong. No matter what had happened that night, he was to blame. Born here, die here.

He'd managed to hold off that fate for a lot of years. He should be grateful that he wasn't already a lifer. So many of them were. It was where he'd been headed from birth. What happened in between was just a circular path back down into the gutter where they all ended up.

He pulled the carpet up in the corner and retrieved the bundle from under the busted floorboard. Crouched in the corner, he opened the soiled rag, smelling of gun oil and blood. A week ago, he'd thought about getting rid of the gun altogether. Starting fresh. Gone so far as to tell her that he was done with that. Made plans. No one here made plans. What a fucking fool he was. He clenched the gun and aimed it at the far wall. The desire to shoot, to fire off all the rounds was so intense. Then, he turned it up to the ceiling and brought it slowly toward his face, until he could see down the barrel. He lowered it to his mouth and opened, letting the barrel knock against his teeth. A sob caught in his chest and he pulled the barrel from his mouth. There was no room for self-pity. There was no suicide in the slums. That was for rich people, people who believed that life should turn out a certain way. Where he grew up, they knew it would never be fair. It was never about fair. Here, the game was survival.

He gripped the pistol in his hand, released the magazine, and checked the ammo. Snapped it back in place. No way he was going to Folsom without a fight.

CHAPTER 15

"IT'S BEEN GREAT seeing him on the baseball field. He's such a good player," added Mrs. Wilmington at the end of the conference. "I know he did track in the fall, but he clearly loves baseball."

"He really does," Tony agreed.

"Well, then, I'll see you both at the game tomorrow night."

"We'll be there," Tony assured her.

Jamie winced. The game tomorrow night. She'd already missed two.

She and Tony made their way outside. The weather had warmed up and the sun was bright above the blue-gray buildings. On the front of each building was the school crest and the department, set into stone like something out of ancient Rome.

Mathematics said the one they headed toward. Language Arts was where they'd met Z's teacher. It was an unreal place, City Academy. Not only the impressive stone buildings and the sculptures set regally around the campus, but the perfectly kept lawn, the rows of white lilies and daffodils that edged the landscape. Jamie had never seen an Ivy League school, but she imagined that this was what they looked like. She'd half expected the teachers to wear robes, but Mrs. Wilmington dressed in colored slacks and tops, ensembles Jamie would never have been brave enough to put together. At a weekend event in the fall, Mrs. Wilmington had worn a pair of bright green Chuck Taylors.

"An A," Tony said.

"What?" Jamie asked.

"He's got an actual A."

"In Spanish."

"He's really pulling it together. I'm proud of him." Tony nudged her when she didn't answer.

"What?"

"Aren't you proud of him?"

"I am. Definitely."

Tony put an arm around her and gave her a quick squeeze. "We've done some things right, you and me."

"We have." Jamie thought again about Tony's move to Ohio. She was afraid to bring up Ohio at all.

The baseball field came into view. City Academy had built a new complex three years before with money from a single donor. Not only the diamond itself, but also bleachers to hold several hundred fans and two boxes to hold up to thirty in case of inclement weather. It was a mini AT&T Park. All from a single guy. That had to have been a hefty price tag.

"You picking up Z?"

"He's supposed to be done at 4:30. Fifteen minutes."

"You want company?"

"No," she said. "Thanks, though. You want to go on home, I'll meet you there."

"I've a meeting at 7:00 tonight. I'm sure I put it on the calendar."

"Oh, right. I remember now," Jamie lied. She never remembered to check that damn calendar. "That's no problem. Maybe Z and I will go out for pizza or something."

Tony reached out as though to hug her. Jamie froze. Instead, he patted her shoulder. "I should be home by 9:30."

"Okay."

Tony hesitated.

"Bye," she said quickly and began walking toward the diamond. The shift in Tony was unsettling. She blew out her breath. Or maybe he, too, was nostalgic about leaving. They'd lived together five years. They were family and neither of them had anyone else. Their mothers had died when they were kids. Tony's brother, Mick, was killed in a factory fire. He had gone in after Tony when the ceiling collapsed, sacrificing himself for his baby brother. Their father died a week later.

Her own father passed seven years before. A middle of the night call that he'd suffered a massive heart attack. Tony had offered to go, but she'd flown to New York alone, sat in the hospital room with her dying father.

He woke only once while she sat beside him those four days. When his eyes opened, she was shocked by their hazy gray appearance. What she'd remembered was almost brilliant blue. In those minutes, her father squeezed her hand, lips lifting into a smile before he called her by her mother's name. He died the next morning.

Jamie entered the complex and took a seat on the end of one of the bleachers. She crossed her arms and watched Z, who was warming up to bat. He slid the metal donut onto the bat and swung it lightly through the air while another boy batted. Z was the only freshman on the team, but the boy on the plate looked to be at least a year younger than Z.

"Mrs. De—"

Jamie turned.

The coach jogged up the cement stairs to stand beside her. Bouncing on his toes, he snapped his fingers a couple of times then pointed to her. "Vail. Ms. Vail. I always forget that one."

"Yes," she responded as Z walked toward home plate.

"I'm Kevin Kushner," he said, pointing to the baseball field. "I'm Zephenaya's—"

"Coach," she finished for him.

"I left a message for you at your office earlier."

"I didn't get it," Jamie said.

Coach Kushner licked his lips, rocking on his toes. "Oh—"

"Sit down," she said.

The coach looked a bit startled before climbing over the row of seats to sit down beside her.

"What's going on, Coach?"

"Zephenaya was late for practice today."

Jamie focused on Kushner.

"Yesterday, he left early."

Again, she said nothing.

"There've been a few of those lately, which is unusual

for him. He's never missed any practice time before. He said it was a family emergency..." Kushner went silent.

Jamie eyed her son on the field. Z hadn't said anything about missing any part of practice. He was late coming home last night. If he'd left practice early, where did he go?

"Sometimes it helps if I understand the situation at home," Kushner continued. "That way I can be sensitive to what the player might be going through."

"I appreciate the concern," Jamie said. "I think everything's settled." She closed her lips, refusing to say another word. On the field, Z stood on first base, staring up at them.

"I wasn't sure if he'd gone over to General to see Charlotte."

A tightness in her chest. Z didn't know Charlotte. Did he?

"Some of the kids have been visiting her," Kushner added. "A few of the boys were out for that today."

"Z won't be missing any more practice." She pulled her badge from her pocket and slid a business card out from the pocket behind it. "My cell phone number's there. Call me anytime."

"Great. I'm glad to hear it. We've got him on the starting roster for tomorrow's game. Will you be able to come?"

"Definitely," she said. "I wouldn't miss it."

Kushner rose from his seat and started back toward the field as a ball was hit into the outfield. Without waiting for the play, Z ran toward second base. The left outfielder caught it on the fly as Z closed in on second.

He was slow to turn back. The ball got there first, and the baseman touched the base. He swung his hand through the air in frustration and hustled off the field. He didn't meet Jamie's gaze, but she didn't take her eyes off him.

She couldn't imagine that he would have gone to see Charlotte. Did they know each other? What else was Z hiding from her? She hoped to hell that no one else was considering Z's relationship with Charlotte. What was he doing today? And why would he have left practice early yesterday? And what sort of family emergency was he talking about? And what family? It couldn't be that.

Zephenaya hadn't seen his father in five years.

God, she hoped it wasn't that.

"Dr. Steckler, good to see you," the coach said as Travis Steckler walked into the bleachers.

The two men shook hands. Maybe Steckler was the anonymous donor who had built the stadium. She scanned the boys on the field for one who looked like the doctor. He'd mentioned a daughter.

"Inspector Vail," the doctor said, coming up the stairs. "You getting a feel for City Academy."

"Her son is Zephenaya," Coach Kushner said. "Our first varsity freshman."

Steckler glanced between Jamie and Z. "Aren't I a horse's ass?" he said. "How did I not put that together?"

"You mean because the family resemblance is so strong," Jamie said.

The coach laughed and walked away. Travis Steckler sat down beside her. "You're Zephenaya's mother."

"I am."

"So, you were here for the conferences?"

"Right again," she said.

The coach blew a whistle. "That's it. Bring it in," Kushner shouted, and the boys started off the field.

"Z! Come right out. We've got to go," Jamie yelled as he disappeared into the locker room.

"If it's anything like my house, that will be an hour," Steckler said.

"You have a son out there?"

"Just a daughter for me," Steckler said.

"I assume she doesn't play baseball."

"No. I come out to watch them while she's in choir. I played in school. Still love it," Steckler admitted. "Guess it's time to get going though."

Jamie started down the bleachers.

Travis Steckler followed. "Will I see you at tomorrow night's game?"

"I'm coming to watch Z, yes."

"Good. I'll save you a seat," he said, giving the back of her arm a gentle squeeze.

Before she could respond, Steckler vaulted over the bleacher stairs and bounded out of the stadium toward a group of girls walking across the grass. One, a small blonde, waved at Steckler. "How's the team looking?" she called out.

"Great."

She shook her head the way teenagers did at their parents. As the two came together, Steckler put his arm around his daughter. He leaned in and spoke to her. It was easy to see she adored him.

Z emerged from the locker room. Water dripped in a steady stream off his head. He was wearing his Adidas sports slippers with tall red and blue basketball socks. At least he'd been quick. "What were you and Coach talking about?"

"Family emergencies," she answered.

Z was silent as they walked toward the path.

"He said you were late to practice today."

"I was talking to Mr. Pike."

Jamie raised her eyebrow.

"My math teacher," he said.

"He also said you left early yesterday."

"Like ten minutes or something," Z said.

"Ten minutes early? Why?"

He wouldn't look at her, but instead focused on Steckler and his daughter talking to the other girls.

"Z," she said, trying to draw his attention back to her. "We're going to talk about this in the car. I am not putting up with lies."

He said nothing.

They walked along the path. There was no way to avoid Steckler's group without being rude.

Amanda turned to Z as they approached. "Hi, Z."

"Hey," he responded, staring at his feet.

What a charmer. Like mother, like son.

Moving as one unit, the group started toward the car. The wind had stilled and, beyond the chatter of the girls, traffic hummed from the road below the school. It was quiet. Somehow the trees around the school—pine, cypress, eucalyptus, and a few huge magnolias—created a barrier so the school felt more like a camp.

It was a nice break. Just then, a tinny pop and a long low hiss like a propane flame catching fire interrupted the silence. Jamie threw up her hands. “Stop.” A car peeled out of the parking lot, a flash of it visible through a cluster of trees as it passed. Jamie got a fleeting look. The light was fading but she thought it was dark and small, some sort of sedan.

“What is it?” Travis asked.

“Shh,” she whispered. The girls began talking.

“Quiet,” Travis repeated and they silenced.

Jamie moved two steps to the right, and saw the whirl of smoke, then several sparks.

“Everyone down!” She launched herself at Z, catching him off guard. Steckler huddled over the girls. They dropped to the ground moments before the deafening roar. A car was tossed ten or fifteen feet in the air. Something stung her forehead.

Debris showered down around them.

Jamie pulled her phone out and dialed 9-1-1 as smoke filled the air and made everything beyond it vanish.

“This is Jamie Vail,” she shouted, her own ears ringing. “I’m at City Academy. There’s been some kind of explosion. A bomb maybe.”

Steckler was on his hands and knees, checking the girls who were slowly sitting up in the grass. Two of them were crying. Jamie waited while Dispatch gave her an estimated wait time, but already, the sirens were audible in the distance.

“That was a bomb?” Steckler asked.

“I’m not positive.”

His eyes were wide.

“But maybe.”

Z blinked hard and stood up slowly. He crossed to the girls and offered them a hand. "I think it's over."

Jamie touched the tenderness in her ears.

Swiped her face.

Blood on her hand.

She wiped it on the grass. "You all stay here," she instructed and started for the parking lot as the sirens grew closer. She felt a presence behind her and expected Z. Instead, it was Travis Steckler.

"Dr. Steckler, you should stay back."

"I'm not letting you go out there alone," he said.

"I'm a police officer."

"An inspector, not the bomb squad."

She cast him a sideways glance, but he didn't stop moving. His shirt had come untucked, and there were grass stains on the knees of his slacks. His hair was disheveled and still he looked good.

Jamie reached the parking lot as the fire truck pulled in. Steckler halted beside her. "Christ."

A car was upside down in the center of the lot. Smoke poured out from the underside. "Your car."

Steckler pulled his hand through his hair. "Was that a bomb? On my car?"

Jamie stepped forward and flashed her badge at the fireman who came off the truck first. "It looked like it was a bomb, but it wasn't necessarily on the car. Might have been under it."

"Why my car?"

That she couldn't answer.

The fireman shouted back to his crew. There was a

flurry of activity as two men pulled the hose off its wheel, and another attached it to a hydrant.

Two firemen held the powerful blast on Travis Steckler's Lexus until the smoke had dissipated.

Travis started toward it, but Jamie grabbed his arm. "You can't."

He looked back at her, then to the car again.

"They'll want to make sure it's clear."

His mouth dropped open. "Like, another bomb?"

She nodded.

He reached for her forehead. Instinctively, she drew herself back. "You're bleeding," he said.

"I'm fine," she told him. "Go get Amanda. I'll get you guys a ride home."

"Inspector," one of the firemen called out to her. He pointed to something beyond her own car. From under the bumper, she spotted feet and legs. A man lay facedown not two feet from her car. The ambulance screeched to a halt five feet away, but Jamie couldn't wait. Pulling her shirtsleeves down over her hands to avoid contamination, she reached down to roll the man over. She was afraid of what she would find. When he fell onto his back, though, it took her breath away. There was so much Zephenaya in Michael Delman's face.

"Oh, shit."

Jamie rose and spun toward Z's voice.

He reached for her and she caught him as he leaned into her. Pressed himself against her like he had when he'd had bad dreams as a ten-year-old. "Oh, God. That's my dad, isn't it?"

Jamie tried to pull him away from the body, but he

didn't move. He stared at the dead man. Not willing to fight with him, Jamie held her grown son tight.

"Is he dead?"

"Yes," said the paramedic who crouched beside Delman, fingers pressed into his neck.

Z started to cry, heavy sobs that made holding him more difficult. "Oh, God. Why would someone kill him?" Z glanced around the school parking lot. "Why was he here?" In his face, she saw the frightened young boy he was five years ago.

"I don't know," she said.

He tucked his face against her shoulder, and she held him tight and rubbed his head. The mother pain was back, sharp in her chest. "I'm so sorry, baby. I'm so, so sorry."

"I don't understand. Why was he even here? Why did he keep coming?"

Her breathing halted. Z had seen his father recently. At this school where the children were protected from everything real on the outside, Z's worst nightmare had walked in. "Z, we have to talk about him. I need to know about him being here."

"Not now, okay? Please not now."

"Not now," she agreed. She put her arm around him and again tried to lead him away from Delman's body.

Z clung harder. "I don't want to leave you, Jamie. Please. Please don't make me leave."

"Never. I swear to you, Zephenaya. You never have to leave. I'm your mother. I will always be your mother."

There was a short break in the sobs as he exhaled in a hard, fast breath. She held him as tightly as she could, her son. She would not let go. Not ever.

CHAPTER 16

ANNABELLE SCHWARTZMAN ARRIVED at City Academy as Hailey Wyatt and Hal Harris were getting out of their department car. It was after 5:00, and Schwartzman was happy to be out of the morgue. The evening was cool, brisk, so unlike the South. Evenings in Seattle, where she'd gone to finish medical school, were like this. When it didn't rain. The cool air always made her breaths seem deeper, the air charged with an energy that made her feel both more alive and more on edge.

Hailey had gone ahead but Hal was by his car, facing her direction. She forced herself toward him.

"How's it going?" he asked. He had an easy smile that made him seem kind and gentle despite his giant size. Or that was how she felt now that she was accustomed to his size.

"Good, thanks. How about you?" They walked toward the scene.

She had been in the office for meetings today and was wearing heels a bit higher than usual, but Hal walked at a long, slow gait so that keeping up with him was easier than she'd expected.

"You from the South, Doctor?" he asked.

Schwartzman looked up, surprised.

"Hailey mentioned an accent, but I don't hear it."

"I was raised in Greenville, South Carolina," she said, hearing her own drawl as the name of her home city and state came across her tongue.

Hal laughed. "I heard it that time."

"I guess I haven't lost it entirely though I haven't lived in the South in a lot of years."

"Nothing wrong with a little drawl," he said. "I love listening to Merle Haggard. Wouldn't be the same if he didn't have that drawl."

"I suppose not," she said, careful to enunciate her words.

Jamie Vail sat in the back of the open ambulance. A man in slacks and a dress shirt was using butterfly sutures to close a small wound on her forehead.

"She could use stitches," Schwartzman said.

The man looked over. The front of his slacks was stained with grass at the knees and there was blood spattered on his shirt. "Oh, I told her," he said. "She's been fighting me since that bomb went off."

"I wasn't fighting," Jamie said.

"Then I'd hate to see you when you are fighting," the man said.

Jamie blushed.

"You okay there, Jamie?" Hal asked.

"I'm fine. I don't care about the cut. I need to check on Z."

"I'll check on him," Hal said.

"Would you? He's not hurt, but—"

"I'll check," Hal said.

Schwartzman hoped one day she'd be a part of the camaraderie the inspectors shared. How nice to be part of a team. How safe.

"I think Hailey's with him, too."

Jamie's gaze followed Hal as he left, avoiding eye contact with the doctor caring for her injuries. There was something between them, but it didn't feel like intimacy exactly. Maybe some past involvement?

"Can I do anything?" Schwartzman asked.

"You got a suture kit in your bag?" the doctor asked.

"I told you, no stitches," Jamie said.

"I'm afraid not."

The doctor gave Schwartzman a sideways glance.

"I'm a medical examiner," Schwartzman said. "We don't do a lot of sutures."

"Travis Steckler," he said. "I'm an ED doc at UCSF. I was here when the bomb went off. We got lucky. Somehow Jamie knew what was happening. Only one casualty." He let out his breath slowly, a technique she recognized for trying to keep his hands steady. "Could have been a lot more."

No one spoke. Jamie stared over the top of the doctor's head.

It wasn't a past intimacy that she saw but perhaps a potential one.

Schwartzman excused herself and went to find the body. Hailey and Hal stood with a teenager. Hal had his hand on the boy's shoulder. The boy held his hands over his eyes. As she passed, Hailey peeled away and caught up to her. "Bomb squad identified a single pipe bomb, placed under the Lexus."

A blue Lexus was being hoisted onto a flatbed tow truck.

"I haven't seen the body yet, but the paramedics think the blast killed him," Hailey said. "Once they confirmed he was dead, though, they didn't move him, so no one has done any real examination."

"Vail was already here on a case?" Schwartzman asked.

Hailey shook her head. "Jamie's son, Z, goes to school here."

Hal and the boy were still talking. "His name is Z? Like the letter?" Schwartzman asked.

"It's a nickname. His full name is Zephenaya. Jamie adopted him after his sister was killed. About five years ago."

Schwartzman stopped. "The bomb happened to go off while she was at the school?"

"I'm not a big believer in coincidences."

"Nor am I," Schwartzman agreed. "Do you have any suspects?"

"Nothing confirmed, but Jamie is working a case related to our hit-and-run."

Schwartzman had heard. "An automotive paint sample was matched to both cases."

"Yeah," Hailey said.

"I like to follow my cases through when I can," Schwartzman explained.

"Good. So, you're caught up." Hailey started walking again.

"Do we know who this victim is?" asked Schwartzman,

struggling to keep up with Hailey's pace. The inspector walked fast for someone her size, and Schwartzman was regretting her choice of shoes.

"Not yet. But whoever it was, it's really upset the boy," Hailey said. "He couldn't talk when I got to him. He's still not saying much."

They arrived at the body together. Face up, the man was younger than their last victim. In his thirties. Schwartzman studied his features and turned back to the boy with Hal. The resemblance was unmistakable.

"Jesus," Hailey said in a quiet breath.

Pulling on gloves, Schwartzman asked, "This is the boy's father?"

"Has to be," Hailey whispered, sounding as surprised as Schwartzman. The inspector didn't know about the relationship before.

Alan Wigby, a camera strap around his neck, flipped through the images on the LED screen. "Who?"

"Nothing," Hailey said quickly with a hard stare. "It's another case."

Realizing she'd said too much, Schwartzman hid the heat in her face by studying the victim's work shirt. There were several small burn marks in the fabric over his right shoulder and a series of abrasions along his neck, which implied he had been standing with his right side toward the bomb when it detonated.

"Do you have what you need, Alan?" Schwartzman asked.

Wigby glanced up as though surprised to hear his first name. "Yes."

"I'm going to move the body." Schwartzman nodded to the paramedics. "Let's get him on his side."

The two paramedics got down on their knees and rolled the victim onto his left side. "I'll work fast," she said. "You can see where the shrapnel burned into the fabric." Schwartzman pointed out burns on his shirt and two on the side of his jeans.

"Could one of those have killed him?"

Schwartzman studied the marks. "None of them seem deep or significant enough to be cause of death, but it's hard to tell. It's possible that the bomb triggered some secondary condition. Heart attack or a head contusion…" She reached up and palpated his skull for abrasions and found none.

"You can lay him back again."

The paramedics slowly lowered the victim onto his back. Schwartzman started to unbutton his shirt when she spotted another hole on the left side of his work shirt. She pressed her finger through the hole.

Schwartzman opened her medical bag. She pushed the clean, packaged Tyvek suit to the side and pulled out a pair of gardening shears. Taking hold of the flannel shirt, she cut a straight line up the side. Then, another straight line through a navy undershirt until she had exposed the victim's sternum.

She leaned down to take a closer look at an entry wound that had punctured the intercostal muscles. She fingered the area for evidence of the shrapnel under the skin. Then, she used her finger to press into the wound, feeling the break in the tissue between the fourth and fifth ribs.

Hal and Jamie joined them. Ignoring their presence, Schwartzman focused on the wound, trying to trace the path of the projectile. The silence buffeted around her like the warmth of a fire. Accustomed to finding her own focus, she fingered the entrance wound; the path was deep.

The projectile had likely severed the descending aorta, which would explain the rapid death. He would have bled out into his abdomen. She pulled her bloody gloves off and put on clean ones. She ran her gloved hands across his shoulders and chest, examining his head and neck. There was no visible blood. She was aware of Hal's bulk as he joined them, too. She was grateful that he didn't interrupt.

"I need to flip him over," Schwartzman told them.

Looking baffled, Hal knelt beside her. "Which way?"

"Onto his right side," she instructed. She counted to three and with only the slightest help from Schwartzman, Hal rolled the victim so that Schwartzman could examine his back.

"What did you find?" Jamie said, breaking the patient silence of the group.

Schwartzman spoke carefully. "I can't be sure without being at the lab."

"But—" Jamie prompted.

Hal lowered the body back down.

She pulled her gloves off, inside out, and laid them on the pavement. "The only evidence of an entrance wound is a single point on his left side. But the shrapnel from the bomb is all on his right side."

"So, what happened to his left side?" Jamie pressed.

"From what I can feel, the projectile cuts between his fourth and fifth ribs."

"So that's what killed him?" Hailey asked.

"From what I see, that would be my guess. Again, I can't be certain until—"

Jamie got down onto the pavement and studied the side of the victim's shirt. She examined his neck, shaking her head. "It's impossible."

Hal rose to his feet. "What's impossible, Jamie?"

"That explosion sent shrapnel flying two hundred feet," she said. "A piece of it cut me in the head and I was way out on the lawn."

"Okay," Hal said.

"Well, if it hit me way out there, how did Del—how did he get away with only a few scrapes? And if he did, then why the hell is he dead?"

In a soft voice, Hailey said, "You knew this was Zephenaya's biological dad when you saw him."

Jamie looked up.

Hal blew out his breath and rubbed his huge palm against his bald head.

Hailey gave Jamie's arm a reassuring squeeze. They were friends. Hailey was no nonsense. She was neither condoning nor condemning Jamie. She was reliable. Calm. Different from Jamie, but they seemed to be good for each other. Schwartzman had never had a friend like that.

Schwartzman rose slowly to her feet. The backs of her knees tingled from a lack of circulation and she bent them slightly to try to increase the blood flow back into her limbs. "The wound on his left side," she began.

All eyes turned to her.

"It wasn't shrapnel."

"You mean because there's only one entry point," Jamie said.

"Partly. If this had been shrapnel, it would be almost impossible to avoid other marks."

"But it's possible," Hailey interjected.

"Maybe, but not in this case."

No one spoke.

"The bomb's shrapnel hit him on the other side of his body. We can see the evidence of the burns on his clothes and the abrasions on his neck."

"It's possible he took one shot to his left side and then spun away, catching some debris on his right," Hal offered.

Schwartzman shook her head.

"What are you saying?" Jamie asked.

"The trajectory is too straight. The types of materials used in a pipe bomb are irregular in shape—nails and broken glass, that sort of thing. They enter the body and bounce all around." Schwartzman motioned to the victim. "This one projectile on the victim's left side entered and traveled straight through his muscles and between the two ribs."

Jamie's mouth dropped open. "You're saying he was—"

"Shot," Schwartzman said. "The autopsy will confirm it, but I believe the victim was killed by a single gunshot wound to the chest."

CHAPTER 17

JAMIE STARED DOWN at Michael Delman's lifeless body.

"We have to talk to Z." Hailey's voice sounded far away.

How many times had Jamie thought life would be easier if Michael Delman were dead? No worrying about tracking him. No concerns about how or if or when he might show up in their lives again. No more fretting about whether Z would one day want to reach out to him.

"Jamie?" Hal pressed. "You know that, right?"

"I have to be there."

"Of course you do. You know we can't interview a minor without a legal guardian present," Hailey said.

She wanted to take Z home. Get the hell out of this place.

Maybe Ohio would be good for all of them.

God, what if Tony was right? What if they should all start over in Ohio? When Tony found out…

"Tony can't hear anything about this," she said sharply.

"You're Z's guardian," Hailey said. "You have no obligation to inform anyone else." She paused a beat. "But Jamie, how will you keep it from him?"

She was right of course. "I have to be the one to tell him," Jamie said.

Travis Steckler walked toward them.

Jamie fingered the bandages on her forehead.

"Let me see those," he said. He wrapped his left hand behind her neck and used the other to raise her chin. She was staring right at his mouth. His lips were parted ever so slightly, and she could feel his breath on her face.

She pulled back. "I'm okay, really."

His left hand held her firmly by the neck. "Hang on a minute. You're not going anywhere yet."

From the corner of her eye, she saw Hailey, one eyebrow cocked. Jamie reached out a hand to swat her. It was too far.

"Don't wiggle or this will take longer," Steckler warned her.

Her skin was pulled, then pressed as he laid the sutures back across the bone of her brow. She winced at the pressure. "Probably a little bruising there, too," he said. "But it looks okay. If it opens up, though, I want you to call me." He gave her neck a little squeeze and let go.

She said nothing. Her face was on fire. It was not the time for this. She looked around for Z and found him standing with the three girls from City Academy. The two girls Jamie didn't know were huddled together, while Amanda Steckler stood beside Z. She wore his baseball sweatshirt, the sleeves pulled down over her hands. She and Z were talking softly, faces close. Amanda was a junior, like Charlotte. Were they talking about the bomb or was this something that had been going on before today?

Did Z know Charlotte, too?

"Z." She waved him over.

He squeezed Amanda's shoulder, like Steckler had squeezed her neck. Oh, hell.

"Your sweatshirt," she said, starting to pull it up over her midriff.

He waved it off. "I'll get it from you later."

"Thanks, Z."

"Sure." He was half smiling as he started toward Jamie, but his expression turned south when he saw her face. "What?"

"Hailey and Hal have a few questions they need to ask," she said. She tried to smile. Put him at ease.

"Okay."

Hailey and Hal stood with Schwartzman who was processing Delman's body. Jamie stopped Z from getting any closer.

"Hailey," she called.

Jamie motioned to Z, and Hailey reached out to tap Hal. The two of them walked over together. "The school has offered to let us use one of the math classrooms," Hailey said.

Jamie frowned.

"So we don't have to go to the station," Hal added.

Jamie wanted to talk now. Quickly. Then, she wanted the hell out.

"Room one twelve," Hal said. "You know where that is, Z?"

Z nodded.

"Lead the way," Jamie said.

Hailey and Hal followed Z across campus, Jamie behind them. Hailey took two steps for every one of Hal's and still they were synchronized. Or maybe it was the pounding in Jamie's head that made all this feel like some sort of weird dance.

Z's head hung as he walked off the path and cut behind the math building, leading them to the rear door. He held it open for the inspectors and Jamie. "It's down on the left," he told them.

The building was cold in the way that many of the old buildings in the Bay Area were for their poor insulation and thin single-pane glass.

Hailey and Hal sat at two of the students' desks and slid them to face another two. Hal tried to bend his knees, but he kept hitting the underside of the desk. So, he shifted his body to an angle and stretched his legs out in front of him.

Even Z seemed to have trouble making himself comfortable in the desk seat. Hailey and Jamie fit fine.

Hal pulled himself up in the chair and clasped his hands together on the desk. Just his two hands and a few inches of his forearm took up the entire desk. "You doing okay?" Hal asked.

"I'd like to go home, to be honest," Z told him.

"We only have a few questions," Hailey said.

"A few, sure," Z said.

Hal nodded to Hailey. Her lead. Same thing Vich always did. If she nodded back to him, it was his. Hailey didn't. "Did you know the victim, Mr. Delman?"

Jamie sat up straight. What kind of question was that?

Hailey gave her a stern expression, and Jamie sat on her hands to stay in her seat.

Z looked at Hailey like she was nuts. "The victim?" he

repeated like it was a crazy thing to call him. "Well, he was my dad, so you could say I knew him."

What was Hailey making of that connection? Z had answered it. It was a dumb question. Of course, he'd known his father.

What memories came to mind when he thought of his father?

There had been physical abuse and emotional, but mostly there had been abandonment. But the death upset him.

"But I don't know who killed him," Z continued. "It's not like we had a relationship or nothing."

Anything. A relationship or anything. That was true, too. The right answer. He knew Delman because Delman had fathered him. Not because they knew each other. They did not know each other. When Z came to her five years ago, his father had been in prison. Jamie took Z to see him once, early in the adoption, but Z had said he didn't want to go back. Jamie had never pushed. That fact was good news for Z. Unless he'd wanted a relationship with his father. Maybe they should have talked about Delman more.

Jamie wanted for this to be over.

"Did you see your dad regularly?"

"Shit, no," Z snapped.

"Language," Jamie warned him. The police were human. Humans made assumptions based on stereotypes. Kids who swore were presumed guiltier than those who didn't. Appearance, haircut, language, it all filtered in whether they wanted it to or not. Jamie knew that from her own experience.

Z leaned back into the chair and crossed his hands in

front of his body in a motion she had come to recognize as his "this is all bullshit" move. The tough guy exterior vanished. "What do you guys want from me?"

He sat forward, slumping on the desk. "I'm at baseball practice and a bomb goes off. Hits my mom right in the face—" He motioned to Jamie who felt the mother place squeeze. Had he ever called her his mom before?

"Then, I find out my dad—or my biol… whatever he is—he's dead. I don't know him any better than I know the two of you, but he was my…" Z stopped talking.

"That's fair," Hal said. "We gotta ask, man."

"So, you didn't see anything suspicious today?" Hailey asked.

Z shook his head. "No. We didn't have school today—parent conferences. I showed up at 2:00 for practice, been at the field the whole time. Can't see the parking lot from there 'cause of the bleachers. I didn't see nothing."

Anything.

"Then, Jamie came and we were walking across the grass and she screams at everybody to get down. Scared the shit out of me. Girls crying and everybody freaking."

"Z, it was scary, I know. But please don't use that language," Jamie said.

"It's okay," Hal said.

"No, it is not," Jamie responded. "I don't tolerate swearing. That's not your business," she warned Hal.

"Absolutely, right," Hal said. "Sorry, Jamie, Z. That ain't my business at all."

"Isn't," she said with closed teeth. "Isn't your business."

"That, too," Hal said.

Hailey stared at her. Jamie stared back. "I'm taking

him home now," she said, daring them to tell her she couldn't. "You have more questions, we'll answer them. But not tonight."

"One more thing," Hailey said.

Her entire body tensed.

"Did you see Mr. Delman today at all?"

Z's gaze traveled to the floor. "Nah. I didn't see him."

"You can talk to the girls. They were in the choir building," Jamie told them. "Maybe they saw something."

With that, she stood and waited for Z to do the same. Outside the building, she pulled a long, deep breath and hooked Z's elbow to pull him toward the car. Jamie passed Steckler and one of the uniformed officers on the way to the parking lot. Steckler said something to her as she passed, but she didn't stop to listen.

They were almost at the car when Z stopped short.

"I got to get my baseball bag," Z said. "It's on the lawn."

"Hurry up and go get it," she said. "I'll pull the car around and meet you by the walkway." As Z started for the lawn, Jamie jogged toward her car. Three steps in, she stopped. She didn't jog. Ever. Act normal, she told herself.

How many times had she watched a suspect and decided he was guilty by the way he held himself? She watched Z. His shoulders hunched over. Sad. Or maybe guilty. Was Hailey watching him, too?

She refused to turn back. Nothing screamed guilt louder than that.

And what could Z be guilty of? Did Hal or Hailey honestly consider that the child Jamie had been raising might have set up a pipe bomb? No. They hadn't implied anything like that. Was she simply projecting a piece of herself? The part that was actually scared Z was somehow involved.

"Impossible," she said out loud because hearing it out loud made it real. And it had to be real.

CHAPTER 18

WHILE Z COLLECTED his baseball bag, Jamie got in the car. Hailey and Hal were crouched next to the body, listening to Schwartzman.

Z knocked on the trunk, and Jamie jumped. She hadn't expected him to be so fast. She popped the trunk and watched him toss his baseball bag in the back.

As soon as the door was shut, she put the car in reverse. "You need to come clean with me," she said.

"I told them everything I know," Z said.

She stole a glance at him as she shifted into first gear. "You swear that you don't know anything about that bomb?"

"You think I made a bomb to kill my father? And set it off at my school?"

"Of course not," Jamie said, pushing the words off her tongue. And she didn't. He couldn't have. "I need you to come totally clean with me, Z. This isn't like getting caught smoking and lying about where you got the cigarettes."

"That again. Jeez, Jamie. How many times you gonna bring that up? I made a mistake. I did my time."

"I don't care about that," she said. "I care about this. I want to know what you know."

"I don't know nothing."

Anything. She felt the rise in her chest. Anger burned at the base of her throat. She sped from the parking lot. "Where have you been going when you're missing practice?"

"I told you. I was talking to—"

"Mr. Pike," she finished. "Right. About math. But Coach said there were a few times."

Z shrugged. "Nowhere really."

"But somewhere."

Z said nothing.

Jamie gripped the wheel harder. "Did you go see Charlotte in the hospital?"

Z remained silent.

"There will be a log at the hospital. They will know who went."

"I'm not on any log," he said.

"That's not an answer."

"No," he growled. "Okay. No."

Jamie checked over her shoulder to switch lanes. The tension in her neck was so tight, the motion was painful. "If there's something you know, Z, or something you've done, you need to tell me. You need to let me help you."

Z stared out the window. Said nothing.

"You hear me?"

He nodded without looking over.

"You've got everything to lose here," she whispered. "People are going to connect you with Michael Delman. He brought Charlotte to the hospital."

What was he thinking? Was he surprised? Afraid?

"You have to be one hundred percent aboveboard, Z. You have to tell me anything that might give someone the wrong idea."

A minute or maybe two passed in silence. She thought maybe he was gearing up to speak out, collecting his courage, but when he turned back, he said, "Can we stop for food?"

"That's your response to all this? You're hungry?"

"There's nothing to tell," Z said, staring out the window. "I'm starved."

"What do you want to eat?"

"Fish tacos at Bahia?"

A mother's primary obligation—feed and care for your child. "Call them and order so we don't have to wait."

Z took Jamie's phone out of the console and dialed. She didn't ask about his phone. She didn't ask anything else. She didn't know what to make of his silences, the absences from practice, the missing phone. She wanted to trust him. He was a good kid. He'd rarely gotten in trouble. But no matter how much she reassured herself, there was something he wasn't saying. She found herself remembering the slammed door. The broken glass. The anger.

Z was eating by the time they left Bahia and made their way through downtown San Rafael toward home.

"Let me break the news to Tony, okay?" Jamie said.

Z looked at her sideways, his mouth half full. "Which news? The bomb at my school? Or that my dad was killed?"

"He's going to be upset that we were there when it

went off and I don't want to break the news about your—" She halted.

"My father."

"Your biological father," she said. "I don't want to break that news yet."

"You're going to keep it from him?" He motioned at her face. "You've got all those bandages on your forehead. How do you think you'll keep him from finding out that my dad died at my school?"

Jamie went silent. His dad. Delman was Z's dad. She hated it. She'd worked so hard to keep Delman away from Z, to free her son of the history and baggage that came from him. The abuse, the losses one after another in that neighborhood.

"You thinking up some ideas about breaking the cable box or something?"

"Watch it, Z," she said calmly. "I'm going to tell him. I want to do it my own way. So, we're not going to blurt it out the moment we walk in the door."

Z picked up Jamie's phone to search for something on the web.

"Where's your phone?" She couldn't hold it back any longer.

"In my bag."

"So, you found it."

He made a grunt that might have been an affirmative.

Jamie looked at him, but he was staring out the window, phone raised to his face.

The smell of the food made Jamie a little nauseous. She couldn't imagine mustering an appetite. What she wanted was a drink. Amazing how certain things triggered the old desires, even after so many years. She'd go home and chug a liter of carbonated soda water instead.

The feeling would pass.

It always did.

Tony's car wasn't in the garage when she pulled in. That, thankfully, gave her a little time to unwind and decide how she would tell him. Z was right. She could hardly hide the news. On Tony's days to pick Z up, he always came home with gossip he collected from other parents. Mostly mothers.

Tony was the kind of person who women opened up to. Which meant hiding the news that there had been a bomb was not an option. The obstacles to hiding the news weren't the reason Jamie knew she'd tell him. Despite his move and the strain between them, Tony was her best friend. He was her oldest friend. He was her family. And, most important in all of this, he was Z's father.

As the garage door closed behind the car, Jamie unbuckled her seatbelt. "I need your phone."

Z wiped churro sugar off his face with the back of his hand. "What?"

"I need to see your phone, Z. I need to know who you've been in contact with."

"What the hell for?" Z snarled.

"Watch it," she warned. "Hand over your phone."

"Why do you need my phone? You're just like them. You think I killed him? You think I set that bomb?"

"No. I want to see your phone because that is exactly what the police will do, and I want to stay ahead of them."

"Them? You are them. Tell them I was with you."

Jamie shook her head slowly. "But you weren't with me. You were supposed to be at practice."

"I was at practice," he insisted. "Ask the coach. I didn't have anything to do with that bomb or killing him."

Jamie took hold of his arm. "You weren't at practice. At least not the entire time. And you weren't with me. It doesn't work that way, Z. This isn't like writing a note to get out of gym class."

When Z got out of the car, Jamie did too. She was faster. She went around the car, opened the trunk. Z's baseball bag was thrown in sideways. Jamie pulled it toward her and unzipped the top pocket.

Z grabbed the bag. "That's mine. Give it to me."

Jamie didn't let go. "I'm taking your phone, Z. I'll give it back."

Z let go of the bag. Jamie ran her hand through the pocket. No phone. She unzipped the second pocket.

"It's not in there," he said.

He was lying.

"I swear, Jamie."

"Where is it, then?" she asked.

"I lost it."

She pulled the bat out of the long pocket and tipped the bag on its end. The yellow donut he used for warm up fell into her hand but nothing else. "I don't believe you." She moved to the main pocket.

"I lost it two nights ago, the night I got in the fight with Paul."

"Why didn't you tell me then?"

"Because I was late. Because I knew you'd be angry. Because you guys were already yelling at each other."

He started to slide the bag away.

She grabbed hold of it. "How did you lose it? Where were you?"

"At the field."

Jamie stared at him. "I don't know why you're lying to me, Z. Coach Kushner told me you showed up late and left practice early."

Z said nothing.

"You go missing, then your biological dad is killed within fifty feet of you at your school. Do you understand how this looks? It looks like you were involved. Like you had something to do with it."

"It's not my fault. He started showing up at the bleachers. Always kind of out of sight."

Jamie gasped. "Delman started showing up?"

Z nodded.

"When?"

"A few weeks ago. To watch me play. He was careful not to stay long so no one really noticed him." Z leaned against the car.

"He showed up there to watch you play? Why didn't you tell me?"

"Not just to watch me play," Z said. "He worked there sometimes. Did some odd jobs for the school—maintenance and stuff. I'd see him around."

It was like she was hardly breathing. "Did he tell you that? That he was working there?"

Z's expression grew tight.

"So, you knew it was him?"

"I saw him," Z said. "I recognized him the second or third time he came to watch practice. I don't know. I went to round up a ball I'd hit out of the park in practice, and he came up to me. When he was walking up, kinda smiling, that was when I knew for sure."

"And you didn't tell me?" she said again.

"See? I knew how you'd react, Jamie. It's not that big a deal."

"Not a big deal?" she shouted, then worked to lower her voice. "That man is dead. He was killed at your school. Not only was he your biological father, but you knew him. People will have seen you talking."

Z pulled his bag toward him with an angry yank. "Why don't you trust me?"

"You want me to trust you? Be honest with me!" Her voice echoed through the garage, ringing in her own ears. "Tell me that you don't know Charlotte."

The color in Z's face darkened.

"Tell me that it isn't weird that your biological father was the one to bring her to the hospital after she was attacked. Is it a coincidence that he was killed at your school? And now I hear you've had a relationship with him." She was shouting. Her breathing strained. Her head throbbing.

"What was I supposed to do? Tell him to go to hell?" Z shouted back.

"Yes," she yelled. "He's bad news, Z. He's always been bad news."

"Jesus, Jamie. He's dead now. That good enough for you?" He swung the bag onto his shoulder and his mitt fell out, landing with a thud in the trunk as he ran into the house.

She picked up the mitt he had left behind. What

could she do to make him understand the risk? Understand how much was at stake? And he was lying. She couldn't help him if he lied to her.

The mitt smelled of glove oil, a scent that reminded her of being in the fire station after one of the men had died. When a firefighter fell, the men came to the station with their Sunday best. There, they dressed as a unit for the funeral. The bunk area would be pungent with the smell of shoe polish. It smelled of comfort. She lifted the mitt closer to her nose. There was a dark line in the leather; the section that covered the outside of his hand was stained. She shifted it in the light and studied the glove. Could glove oil darken the leather? Strange that it was only one part.

Once in the bright hallway of the house, she set her computer bag on the bench and placed Z's glove beside it, the stained side up.

The webbing of the trapeze was darkened too. But it was the knot at the base that caught her eye. Its X-like shape. She all but stopped breathing as she carried the mitt to the kitchen and laid it on a white paper towel. She reached for the silverware drawer and missed the knob twice, not taking her eyes off the mitt. She was wrong. She had to be wrong. With trembling fingers, she pulled a fork from the drawer and used a single tine to scrape inside the knot.

When she wiped the fork against the paper towel, it left a blackish residue. Dirt. Of course, it would be dirt. She was a little ill as she licked her own thumb and dragged it against the flakes on the paper towel. When she lifted her thumb, the smear was a dark red. Like blood.

She studied the edge of the mitt, remembering perfectly the smear of blood on the Mercedes. The pattern was similar, but it didn't mean they were the same. She'd have to compare them side by side. She needed access to that image. She could access it online but, with her login, there would be a digital record of her checking it. What she needed was to have someone send it to her without knowing they were sending it to her. Crossing the kitchen for her laptop, she dialed the lab. Let someone be there. Anyone but Sydney. Anyone but—

"SFPD Crime Lab. This is Sydney."

Damn. "Sydney, it's Jamie Vail."

"Hi, Jamie. How are you?"

"Good, thanks. Am I catching you on your way out?"

"Running a couple of searches, actually. Waiting for them to finish before I leave, another five or ten minutes."

"I'm having some issues with getting into the case database from home," Jamie lied. "I hate to ask, but is there any chance you can upload the images from the Borden's Mercedes into a Dropbox folder? I don't need full-size images or anything. I wanted to thumb through them tonight and see if anything pops out at me."

"They're already up there. I uploaded them for Hailey and Hal to work off, too."

Jamie wanted to be sick.

"Great minds must think alike."

"Yeah," Jamie said, praying that Hailey and Hal were not having the same thoughts she was. But why would they? Unless they'd found something that she didn't know about. Would they tell her? Z's mother?

"I'm sending you an e-mail with the access link to the folder. It should come across any second."

"Thanks a lot," Jamie said. The laptop was slow to boot—always slow when something was urgent. Tony would be home any minute. She could not be looking at this when he walked in the door.

The e-mail was waiting in her inbox. Jamie followed the link, opened the case file, and scanned the thumbnail images until she reached the close-ups of the side of the car. She clicked the files one at a time, careful not to download anything, until she found the first one that showed the impression. The area of car photographed was probably about eight or ten inches, which meant the impression was made by something almost that large. She zoomed in on the image so that the area that looked like it had been made by the knot was approximately the same size as the webbing knot on the mitt. She held the mitt beside the computer so that the stained webbing was next to the imprint on the car and slowly rolled the mitt against the image. A match. A perfect match. Not even a little doubt.

"Oh, Zephenaya," she whispered. "What have you done?"

Tony came in the front door.

CHAPTER 19

ROGER WAS RELIEVED that Sydney had gone out to the scene at City Academy today. After last night, his allergies were acting up, and he was happy to stay in the lab with his microscopes and fuming machine until he could get them settled down. Allergies were only one of the things complicated by having absolutely no hair anywhere on his body.

At the age of seven, he'd gotten a particularly bad flu. He remembered almost nothing about it himself. At least nothing outside the stories his parents told. At the time, they hadn't thought much of it.

Children—even only children—got the flu. What made this flu different was that shortly afterward, Roger began to lose his reddish-brown hair in clumps. A dozen or so of them. The resulting bald spots were about a quarter in size.

Over the following fifteen months, Roger lost all his hair. Not only from his head but also from his arms, legs, and everywhere in between. His condition, the most serious form of alopecia, resulting in total hair loss, was called alopecia areata universalis. Categorized with autoimmune diseases, alopecia is caused when the immune system mistakenly attacks the hair follicles.

Between the start of his significant hair loss and sometime around Roger's fifteenth birthday, his parents worked tirelessly for something that would grow his hair back. Roger's father had taken him to Paris for treatment, and his mother had retained the services of a Native American healer. Nothing worked. Not even temporarily. Roger became, and remained, stubbornly hairless. The fact that the hair follicles themselves were in perfect working order was of no consolation to his parents.

It should have been a teenager's hell. During the course of his early treatment, Roger had met others with alopecia and two with alopecia universalis. One girl, Heather, stood out in his memory. He was young then—maybe eight or nine—and his condition was relatively new. Heather was an early teen, perhaps fourteen, and had been affected with alopecia universalis since her tenth birthday. He and Heather had spent two weeks, side by side, in treatment. Heather talked a lot, and Roger listened.

For Heather, the hair loss came with extreme emotional turmoil. Her parents, particularly her mother, were very religious and early in Heather's hair loss, her mother had blamed the devil for the condition. Heather had been castigated for practicing paganism, while her mother demanded Heather reveal what activities she had engaged in that would have so angered the Lord.

Eventually, Heather said her mother had come to terms with the condition, but the anger and hate remained with Heather. Severely depressed, Heather was anorexic and had taken to self-mutilation. Roger remembered Heather sliding her skirt up her thigh to display the thousands of tiny lines she'd carved into her skin.

For Roger, on the other hand, his lack of hair became less and less an issue as he grew into his teenage years. Michael Jordan had shaved his head bald when Roger was thirteen, which gave hairlessness an edge closer to cool. Not that Roger was ever—with or without hair—going to be considered cool.

The biggest bother was the allergies. Sneezing in general was much more common because he lacked the nose hair that prevented pollen from traveling straight into his sinuses. And without eyelashes, he tended to get things in his eyes, so he carried both tissue and drops, causing people to treat him as though he were perpetually ill.

It was almost 7:00 when the crime scene van arrived with the evidence from City Academy. Roger had considered going home, but a bomb had gone off at the school Jamie Vail's son attended. Kathy and the girls were going to dinner and a movie with Kathy's mom after soccer practice, so he had the evening to himself. A Friday night in the lab didn't sound all that bad to him.

Naomi and Chase were first through the door. Carrying a box, Chase pushed the door open and held it for Naomi. "Ladies, first," he said, flirtatious as always. Chase had joined the crime lab almost two years ago; Naomi last fall. It was clear that Chase was smitten with Naomi, but Naomi was harder to read. While she seemed to enjoy Chase, she also deflected his attention enough to send off the message that she wasn't interested in more than a fun friendship. Which was good. Roger had been through the on-the-job romances with a few of his lab techs. Not one had ended well. Chase propped the lab door open and began bringing boxes in off a wheel cart in the hallway.

"Heard you had a bomb," Roger said.

"Wang's team confirmed it. A pipe bomb," Chase said, referring to Cindy Wang from the bomb squad. "We collected a lot of the shrapnel, but she's coming down for the bomb fragments. She wants to try to process it tonight for prints."

The women on the force felt a strong alliance to Jamie Vail. "That's fine," Roger said. "I'll be here."

"I can stay, too," Naomi offered.

"I can't authorize OT pay," Roger warned.

"That's okay," Naomi said.

"Sure," Chase added. "I was meeting some guys for drinks, but I can stick around."

"Well, then, let's see what we've got."

Naomi unloaded the first box, talking as she worked. "Jamie saw a car leaving the scene just before the bomb went off. A navy or black sedan. Two-door, she thinks. We didn't find any new tread marks in the lot, but there were tire marks in the grass at the corner of the lot. We think it might have been our guy, so we cast a mold in the mud there."

"Once it's dry, let's scan it and see if we get any matches in the database."

"Will do," she said.

Chase spread a thin layer of paper on one of the tables they used for larger projects and pulled out pieces of bomb and shrapnel.

Roger's cell phone rang. He recognized the coroner's office number. "Sampers."

"It's Schwartzman."

"Evening, Doctor. You working late, too?"

"I guess so. Didn't know you all were there. I thought I'd be leaving a message."

"We're all putting in a little extra time on this one."

"All right, then. I've got a clean slug I pulled out of the victim. I'll bring it over myself if you can stick around."

"I'll be here."

While Chase catalogued the elements of the bomb, Naomi scanned the tread into the system and compared it against the reference samples in the database.

At his computer, Roger went through the images from the scene to give himself a feel for the layout.

"Did you see the Lexus?" Chase asked.

Roger clicked through the images of the car lying upside down in the parking lot. "I'm seeing it now. Looks like it's totaled."

"It had to be," Chase agreed.

"Whose car was it?"

"One of the school parents," Chase said. "An MD, I think."

"Yeah," Naomi added. "UCSF. ER."

Chase watched her for several seconds after she stopped talking. Wondering how interested she was in the doctor, maybe. Roger was sometimes amused by his own gender.

They could be such a predictable bunch.

He glanced back at the image of the car. The Lexus

looked new. Maybe the doctor had been the target. "Did Wang mention if the bomb was attached to the car?"

"It wasn't. The origin of the explosion was at least a few inches away," Chase said. "They can tell by the burn pattern on the undercarriage."

"Well, I doubt he did that to his own car," Naomi commented.

Schwartzman arrived. By then, the three had settled back into work. The room was silent when she came in the door. In black dress slacks and a turtleneck sweater, she might have been dressed for a funeral. She always dressed that way. Maybe that was normal for a medical examiner. Maybe it was Shelby Tate's bright-colored scrubs that were odd attire for the job.

Schwartzman crossed the room, holding a plastic bag which she set on the edge of his desk. At the bottom was a small wad wrapped in paper.

Roger fingered the slug through the paper. "Great. Maybe we'll get lucky and find prints." Roger set the bullet up in the fuming chamber. Once the machine was powered on, he added four drops of super glue to the heating element and pressed "start."

"You joining us?" he asked Schwartzman, who remained at the desk.

"If it's all right, I'd like to see what you get from the bullet."

"Of course."

Roger was used to Hal and Hailey, or Jamie, the talkative ones. Even Vich had grown chatty in the months he'd been in the department. Schwartzman, though, remained quiet and still.

Roger was thankful when Cindy Wang showed up to break the silence. As always, she shoved the door open so hard it slammed against the far wall. "Sorry," she said, raising both hands. "The one in our unit always sticks."

Cindy joined Chase at the light table, and the two of them began to move around bomb fragments like some thousand-piece jigsaw puzzle. Naomi checked for matching tread in the database and joined them, too. Soon, the lure of the puzzle lured Schwartzman to the table.

When the cycle on the fuming chamber was done, a bell went off. Schwartzman at his side, Roger pulled the bullet from the chamber. She said nothing but Roger could sense her anticipation as he spun the bullet, studying for evidence of prints.

"Nothing," he said.

"Worth a try," she answered. She looked back to the group working on the bomb. She hesitated then said, "I'd better go."

"I'll run it through the ballistics database if you want to watch."

"I do," Schwartzman said.

Roger centered the slug under the scope and twisted it slowly with a long set of long needle-nose pliers until he located the striation marks. Then, he adjusted the marks until they lined up with the striations on the ruler and photographed the slug.

Normally, Kevin or Tess ran the ballistics comps. They were both gun fanatics—Tess's father had been a clay pigeon shooting champion in his twenties, and Roger was fairly certain that Kevin was, at least partially, a doomsday prepper. He lived clear out in Antioch, almost a two-hour commute. Every once in a while, Roger saw the magazines Kevin read on the commute. Titles like *Be Ready Magazine*, *OffGrid Prepping*, *Survivalist*, not to mention a particularly frightening-looking one called *The Preparedness Review*. Kevin was incredibly proficient with ballistics. Roger liked them both. They were only too happy to go fire test rounds on the weapons, which was fine with Roger. He could handle guns with confidence as long as they weren't loaded, but he was never at ease with them nor was he the least bit curious about them.

He'd have to do this one himself.

Tess was on vacation this week, and Kevin was out at a scene in the Tenderloin—a gang-related shooting. Roger tried to remember what they'd told him about how to best capture the striations. There was no harm in trying, anyway. They could always take new images on Monday.

Roger uploaded the image file into the database on his computer. Double-checking the parameters he'd set, he started the search.

"This might take a few minutes," he told Schwartzman. She shifted away a little when he spoke. He wasn't particularly great with new people, but Schwartzman was awkward. She seemed to be in a constant struggle between being close enough to watch and remaining as far from him as was possible.

Roger sat down at the computer and added his notes to the case file that Naomi had created. He included the steps he'd taken to document the striations. In case he'd done something wrong, the notes would make it easier for Tess and Kevin to figure out what. Schwartzman had migrated back to the bomb puzzle.

No more than three minutes passed before the program's icon flashed onto the screen. He clicked on it. A match. He had to have done something wrong. He'd never seen one happen that fast.

"Hey, boss," Naomi called over.

The program relaunched onto the desktop, and he stared at two bullets, side by side. On the left was his. He recognized the ruler beneath the image. The slug on the right was also set against a ruler, but the numbers were blue. His were red. Other than that, the pictures were identical. He double-clicked on the case file attached to the image on the right and scanned the name.

"Roger," Naomi said again.

"Yeah?"

"I got a reference on this tread," she told him. "Looks like it matches a case in San Jose last November."

Roger glanced up from his own screen. "Let me guess. Carmen Gutierrez?"

"Yeah," Naomi confirmed. "How did you know?"

"Because the bullet matches the same case."

Schwartzman returned to Roger's desk. "You found something?"

He nodded as Naomi joined them. "We have tire tread and a slug that match an old case."

"What case?" she asked.

Roger skimmed the case notes. "Gutierrez was the CFO of a company that designed geo-tracking units. Serious ones. Looks like most of their contracts were for the Department of Defense." Roger skimmed on. "Says Gutierrez was killed in an assassination-style attack in the parking garage of his San Francisco office building.

Dark sedan caught on the security camera. Single bullet wound to the head. 9MM. Striations are identical to the bullet that killed Michael Delman."

"What in the world does Michael Delman have in common with a company that makes geo-tracking units for the government?" Schwartzman asked.

"I have absolutely no idea."

CHAPTER 20

AS TONY ENTERED the house, Jamie stuffed Z's baseball mitt into a reusable Trader Joe's grocery bag and tucked it under the sink, hiding it behind the grout cleaners and scrub brushes that were used maybe once a year. Saliva filled her mouth, a sick churning in her stomach. Merely the act of putting the mitt in the bag, of hiding it. Hiding evidence. Evidence of her son's guilt.

She shut the cupboard door and swallowed down the feeling that she might vomit. Breathed slowly, deeply. Swallowed again. In under three minutes, she had jeopardized her entire career. Thrown away everything she'd worked for in the past fifteen years. The oath to protect and serve. Justice. She hadn't bent any rules for Tony and yet she was willing to throw it all away for Z. He was her child. She hadn't carried him inside her; she didn't give birth to him. She hadn't known him the first decade of his life. And yet, she would do anything to protect him.

She took a last look under the sink, praying that Tony didn't get into some cleaning fit. He wasn't a tidy person, but when something was really bothering him, he cleaned with the best of them. Not tonight. She would not let that happen tonight. When he was in bed, she would move it, find somewhere else to hide the evidence. *Oh, God.* She was hiding evidence. Her son knew Charlotte Borden. The same school. She'd assumed that because they were in different grades, they hadn't known each other. But Z had talked to Amanda Steckler. They knew each other. And that print on the Mercedes. It had to have come from Z's mitt. The knot was distinct; the stain matched the image of the car. There was blood on the mitt. Jamie saw her laptop screen open and moved quickly to exit out of the browser.

Her knees were ready to buckle as she balled up the towel in the sink and turned the water on high. She rinsed the paper towel until it was a shredded mess then tossed it into the trashcan as Tony entered the kitchen. Surely, if he saw her face, he would know that something was wrong. Instead, she pumped her hand full of soap and scrubbed and scrubbed.

"Hey," he said, sitting at the counter opposite the sink.

"Hey," she returned, shutting off the water. She pulled the dish towel off the oven handle and dried her hands. They were red. She'd been scrubbing harder than she realized.

"How was the afternoon?"

"Long."

"What happened?"

"A bomb."

"Jesus. Is that what happened to your head?"

She fingered the Band-Aid. "It's just a little cut."

"Where was the bomb?"

She hesitated. There was no way around this. *A bomb*

went off at Z's school, but everything is fine now. A bomb went off at Z's school and his father was shot. I found evidence that Z was at the scene where Charlotte Borden was attacked. Who is Charlotte Borden? Oh, she's the rich girl from his school. One of the rich girls. The richest girl. The one who's in a coma. And he knows her. His biological father brought her bleeding to the hospital and he's dead. I'm concealing evidence so next week I might not have any choice but to go with you to Ohio and work as a waitress.

"Jamie? What did you say?"

She jumped. Had she spoken aloud?

Z started down the stairs. For as long as she could remember, Z treated the stairs like they were bugs to be squashed. He always hit every stair with full power and speed. The house literally shook. Tony joked that they should be setting aside a special fund for stair repair. It drove her crazy.

Right now, the thundering was a gift.

Z's glance touched on Jamie and slid off like oil. "Hey, Tony."

"Hi, Z. Jamie was telling me about a bomb."

"Yeah." Z didn't miss a beat. "I was actually hoping you could help me with algebra. We started a unit on graphing parabolas and I'm lost."

"Sure. Sit on down."

Z sat in the chair next to Tony. Jamie wished she'd put his mitt in another room. She couldn't leave the room, knowing how close it was, but she didn't want to stay either. Instead, she puttered around the kitchen, pretending to be busy until it was clear that Tony and Z were focused on graphing whatever the hell they were called.

She made a bottle of soda water and chugged it until her stomach felt like it might explode. Then, taking a quick look to be certain the Trader Joe's bag hadn't somehow fallen into full view under the sink, Jamie left the kitchen. On the way upstairs, she grabbed her computer bag and set it in the hallway before entering Z's room.

She closed the door softly behind her and scanned the surfaces. Clothes were strewn everywhere—across the bed and chair, hung from the top of the closet door and the knobs of his dresser. In some places, the state of the room would be cause for alarm. With Z, this was normal. Not that Jamie was one to talk. Her room wasn't much better.

She found Z's backpack and checked it carefully—every pocket, opened each book and shook them to loosen any papers, then flipped through his notebooks. With every sound, she froze, holding her breath for a count of ten before continuing her search. She went through the drawers, checked under the mattress, inside the pillowcases, behind the dresser, ran her hand across the bottom of the desk for something that might be taped. Nothing.

Math normally took the better part of an hour. She was done in about fifteen minutes. She'd been a part of enough searches to have a pretty good idea where people hid things, but Z's room offered not a single clue. She hadn't unearthed so much as a cigarette or lighter, not a letter or a note, not a picture of him with someone… not that kids printed pictures anymore. Nothing suspicious and no sign of his phone. She needed that phone.

In her room, she left the door wide open and sat down with her laptop. Keeping one ear on what was going on downstairs, Jamie logged on to their cell phone provider and checked the history on Z's phone, then used the department's reverse phone directory to run some of the numbers she didn't recognize. A few names she recognized from school. Several were unlisted numbers. Those records would have to be accessed from the department. Travis Steckler was listed, probably Amanda's phone. Z had spoken on the phone with Amanda Steckler. What in the world was Z's relationship with Amanda Steckler?

She scanned the rest of the list of numbers, checked a few more of the names, ones that showed up more than three or four times. None that appeared too frequently or at odd hours. Probably other students. One could be Charlotte's number. Z wasn't much of a talker and none of the calls lasted longer than three or four minutes. Most were under forty-five seconds. The other calls were to a pizza place near school, Baja Burrito, and three separate numbers at the school. She was actually surprised how much Z used his phone, considering that he was always letting the battery run out or leaving it in his backpack or on his bedside table when she was trying to reach him.

None of the numbers came back to Michael Delman or Charlotte Borden. That might have been a relief except that she didn't have access to his text messages online. She had to request them. The message she got said it would take three to five days. That was a lifetime.

She tried to reassure herself that, as far as she could tell, Z hadn't dialed Michael Delman—at least not as of the end of last month when their billing cycle had ended. But somehow, in the last fourteen days, Z had found out his father and gotten wrapped up in the attack of Charlotte Borden. Not wrapped up. Maybe someone else had the mitt? Maybe Z had given it to his father? Or accidentally left it with him.

Maybe he'd been late to practice because he was getting the mitt back. But how? Had he left campus to meet his father? When would that have happened? Thursday, when he'd had the fight? Had he been telling the truth about that? Was it possible he'd been fighting with his father? She had so many questions and the person who could answer them was right downstairs, working on algebra like a normal fifteen-year-old kid. No, not normal. Better than normal. A sweet, respectful fifteen-year-old. A good kid. She could ask him. It might be that easy. Gathering her nerve, she stood from the bed. Blinked and saw her son in prison orange. Another statistic. Sank onto the bed again. How could she protect him?

On the dresser sat a framed picture of her, Tony and Z in front of the arrow sculpture at the base of the Bay Bridge. They weren't supposed to touch the sculpture or go near it for that matter. There were signs posted all around to stay off the natural grasses. There they were, though, standing right on that grass. The picture was taken some three or four years ago, when the three of them had taken the ferry into the city on a Saturday for the farmers' market, then walked all the way down to the IMAX theater to see the newest Spiderman movie before walking back for burgers at Red's. The day was focused on Z who had been dying to see the movie, but it had turned out to be one of those perfect days. Everyone getting along. Laughing. Even the movie wasn't awful.

On the way back to the ferry, giddy on soda, Red Vines, and french fries, Z sprinted up the side of the bow until he was almost at the top. As she thought back, he'd seemed little then, almost taller than her but not quite. Without hesitation, she ran up to join him while Tony watched from below and warned them not to fall. It was like that with Tony. He was fragile and didn't take the same risks Jamie would take, but he was the net. If she told him about the mitt, he would be her net now, too. Except for Ohio. Except that she worried the net he would offer was taking him away.

When she and Z were atop the arrow, side by side, she had been on top of the world. An older couple approached as she and Z finally made their way back down. Jamie was certain that they were about to get a lecture on respecting public property. Instead, the woman offered to take their picture.

The three of them stood half elated, half embarrassed in front of the arrow with the sun fading quickly to the west. The boys had framed it for Mother's Day, and Jamie kept it on her dresser, a memory of something a little daring but whimsical, fun.

How she would love to go back to that day.

When trespassing was their biggest concern.

Heavy feet trudged up the stairs. While Z thundered down the stairs like a charging bull, he climbed them more like a grazing elephant.

Z walked past.

She should have called out to him. Her mouth dropped open; she willed herself to say his name.

But she didn't, and she knew exactly why. She wasn't prepared to have this conversation or, more accurately, she wasn't prepared to hear the answers. She didn't want Z to lie to her. She would know if he lied, and she wasn't sure which would have felt worse. So, she let him pass. She went downstairs and sat at the counter with her laptop, staring at screens without the ability to focus until Tony disappeared down the hall to his room. She counted to ten after his door had closed and pulled the Trader Joe's bag out from under the sink, stuffed it into her computer bag, and carried it upstairs.

Safe behind her locked bedroom door, Jamie scrutinized the room. She wished there were some sort of crawl space or a hidden closet somewhere. The house was built in the '40s, so the rooms were small, the closets smaller. She had only one dresser with long, shallow drawers. Her closet wasn't lined with shoeboxes or big purses where she might hide something as bulky as a baseball mitt.

For the first time in a long time, Jamie wished fleetingly that she was a different kind of woman, one whose bedroom was stuffed with trunks and dressers, whose bed had a long frilly skirt, and whose closet was a sea of shoes stored in their boxes. At the back of her closet was a single cardboard book box. It had been there, undisturbed, since she brought it home.

The brown packing tape was yellowed; her father's print faded and bleeding from sun and moisture and age. As far as she knew, the box hadn't been opened after her mother's death. She had found it in her father's closet after his death. His handwriting looked like it had when she was a girl—blocky, confident cursive. The way he wrote before the tremors began and his cursive grew more tentative, more rounded, and long before he eventually started printing everything. In his youthful writing, he had written one single word, Catherine. Her mother's name.

At the time of his death, Jamie had gone through the apartment where he'd lived the last ten years of his life. He owned nothing of real value and very little of sentimental value. She kept the old Timex watch he'd worn his whole adult life and the few pictures she'd found, folded together with his birth certificate and hers. In the stack, too, was a single picture of a couple who had to have been his parents. The edges were frayed, the background silvering. She didn't recall having seen the picture before, but she saw her father in his father and perhaps a bit of herself in her grandmother.

The other photographs were familiar ones, most of them taken at the firehouse. They never had a camera in the house, so whatever pictures were taken at the weekly station dinners or the few holiday events each year were the only ones that existed of her as a kid.

This box had been in the closet of the small office he used as a den. While she had brought it home, she couldn't bring herself to open it. Only now did she cross to the closet, carrying the small pair of scissors she kept in her bedside drawer. Delicately, she flipped the box and cut through the brown tape, gummy after so many years. Beside her was the Trader Joe's bag. By the weight of the box and the way the contents shifted when she flipped it upside down, she knew the box wasn't full. She didn't need to look at the contents; she would simply put the bag inside.

Lifting the cardboard flaps at the bottom of the box revealed a pink book, maybe ten inches by thirteen. It fit snugly, side-to-side, end-to-end, and she struggled to wedge her fingers in far enough to pry it loose.

With the book loose, she couldn't help but look. She flipped it over in her lap. On the front was an etching of a little girl in a white nightgown, her feet bare. At the top it read, Baby Girl, and in the bottom right corner her name was etched in gold: Jamie Catherine Vail.

She held the book in her lap, terrified to open it. Her mother had died shortly after Jamie's second birthday. She had been sick almost a year before. Likely, the book would be empty, something her mother had planned to do but never had the chance. Jamie fingered the edge of the book and ran her palm over the smooth cover.

In the box were three bundles of letters and papers, another book, a small photo album, and a stack of carefully wrapped plates, surrounded by bubble wrap. Why had she never opened this box? She didn't remember her father ever showing her a photo album. Had he packed all of this up after her mother died? Had it all been hidden away for almost forty years?

With a deep breath, she opened the baby book to the first page and read her name in an unfamiliar script. She ran her fingers across her mother's handwriting, touched the impression the pen had made on the page. Studied the words: Born May 19, 1975. Six pounds, twelve ounces. Nineteen and a half inches long. Six pounds. That was tiny. Six pounds was about the weight of a police belt without the gun in it. It was the first time she recalled thinking of herself as a tiny human. Somehow, she never considered anything before the motherless three- or four-year-old of her earliest memories. The realization made her miss her father. She hadn't appreciated how difficult a job he had, taking care of her and living with the grief of losing his wife. Beside her was Z's mitt. What sort of things would she leave him? What sort of legacy would Z have? The mother pain squeezed in her chest.

Downstairs, the doorbell rang.

The mother pain was replaced by the hot rush of panic. Jamie made room for the Trader Joe's bag alongside the bundles in the box and laid the pink book back across the top of the pile. Her hands trembled as she folded the flaps in a circle so that the bottom wouldn't fall open.

"Jamie," Tony called up. "Vich is here."

Why would Vich be there? "Coming," she called out, hurrying to put away the box. It seemed lighter and more fragile. She set it down tenderly and slid it into the back corner, moving her laundry basket in front of it.

"Jamie!" Tony shouted again.

There was a stain on the front of her white blouse. Dark brownish.

It might have been a hundred things.

Blood was the first to come to mind.

But whose blood?

"Jamie. Are you upstairs?" Tony's voice called from the stairs. "Vich is at the door."

"I'm coming," she shouted, grabbing a sweater off the chair and yanking it down over her head before emerging from her bedroom.

CHAPTER 21

JAMIE WAS SURPRISED to find Vich in the entryway. "What's the matter? Has something happened to Charlotte?" As soon as the words came out, Jamie found herself studying Z on the stairs.

Her son was wide-eyed, worried. Her chest tightened. Did that mean something?

"No," Vich assured them. "No change with Charlotte."

"She's still in a coma?" Z asked.

"Yeah. What happened to your door?" Vich asked with concern. "You have a break in?"

"Wind blew it shut," Jamie said.

"Sorry to show up. I tried to call."

Jamie patted her pants pocket, which was empty, of course. She had no idea where her cell phone was. She'd had it in the car but so much had happened since then.

"I wanted to see how you were," Vich added. He looked up at Z. "Both of—"

"Vich," Jamie snapped, cutting him off. "I'll walk you to your car."

Tony hadn't moved. "Jamie?"

"I'll be right back. Z, go finish your homework."

Z lumbered back up the stairs. She hoped he would stay in his room. She hoped Tony would wait for her to come back. She needed to be the one to tell him. She should have already done it. *Damn it, Vich.* She opened the front door carefully, and Vich walked out into the dark.

"I am sorry for coming to your house," he said as they walked.

"Why did you?"

He stopped then and stared down the driveway before turning back to her.

She was edgy and angry. Back in the house, everything would be unraveling. Maybe not this instant but any time. Tony knew something was up. She waited for an answer and watched Vich's expression harden. He was angry, too, but why? What right did he have to show up at her house?

"I had news on the case," he said, through closed teeth.

"You didn't want to leave it on my voicemail?"

"You don't listen to your voicemail," Vich quipped.

She blew out her breath. "It's been a long day."

"Yeah, I heard," he said flatly. "That's why I came. Back where I'm from, when your partner's hurt, you show up." He started for the car. "So, I showed up. Sue me."

"Wait."

"I can update you on Monday."

It was like a block on her chest. Monday. That was almost three days away. "Vich."

He turned back, one eyebrow raised.

"Please. I'm sorry, but the shit's about to hit the fan

in there," she said, motioning to the house. "So, give me the damn news quickly."

"Matched the paint found in the automotive paint database. It's factory paint for a Buick Lucerne."

"What year?"

"Unfortunately, they used the same paint from 2005 to 2011."

Jamie exhaled. "So, we're looking for a white Buick Lucerne manufactured sometime between '05 and '11. That narrows it down to—what—a quarter million cars?" She wanted to sit down but hers wasn't the kind of yard to have a bench or a little bistro table, so she sat down at the end of the walkway. "Why don't these guys ever drive custom paint jobs?"

Vich walked back. "It's not that bad. Three hundred twelve thousand Buick Lucernes manufactured and sold in America in that time. Eight colors. That narrows it down to maybe fifty or sixty thousand."

"Sixty thousand?" she balked. "Like that helps. Did we run a DMV search for white Lucernes in the San Francisco Bay Area?"

"We did," Vich said, emphasizing the word "we." "Got twenty-four hundred eighty-seven hits."

Jamie said nothing.

"But none belonging to Michael Delman, the Bordens, or the second victim, Dwight Stewart." Vich paused a beat. "I assumed that was your next question."

"It was."

"Also, Sondra's alibi doesn't check out," Vich said.

"Really? She said she was at some opera meeting. They were working on a fundraiser."

Vich shook his head. "She wasn't there. I met the director, Helene Remy, and her assistant. Sondra had a meeting scheduled with them during that time, but she called ahead to cancel. She was supposed to call back to reschedule, but then there was the attack…"

Jamie needed to go back inside and talk to Tony. She started to push herself up when Vich reached a hand down. She accepted his hand and let him pull her up. "Why lie?"

"Don't know. Maybe we should go by and ask her."

Jamie brushed off the seat of her pants. "I can do it. I plan on going into the station tomorrow morning, getting caught up."

"What time? I'll meet you there."

"Tomorrow's Saturday, Vich."

"I don't take many weekends off, and I'm sure as hell not taking the weekend off on this one," he said firmly.

She nodded slowly.

"You can text me in the morning." He started to walk away. "Oh, I almost forgot the strangest bit."

"What's that?"

"The lab found an off-label tracking device on the Mercedes," he said.

"A tracking device on the car?"

"Yep. It was under the driver's side wheel well."

"Did they find any prints?"

"No."

"You think someone was watching them?" she asked.

"Maybe but not necessarily. Sydney thought it was possible that the Bordens or their people put it there for security. I guess that's something wealthy people do in case of a carjacking, especially if the daughter is driving the car. The lab's running a search on the serial number to see if they can determine where it came from."

Jamie took a step toward him. With everything that had happened at the school, she'd forgotten that Vich had actually been working the case all day. "Did you meet with Charlotte's friends?"

"All but one," Vich said. "Nothing to report from them. Nothing's come back on the Bordens or Bishops. No shady business deals, no disgruntled employees. It looks like they run a clean business."

Jamie considered making a lawyer joke but couldn't muster the energy. "And the kids at CA?"

"Clean. Teachers, the administration, her friends—everyone confirms that Charlotte was well liked."

"What about jealousy? Some sort of girl rivalry? No bitchy gossip about a secret boyfriend?" Jamie asked.

"Nothing."

"There has to be something."

"We'll brainstorm more tomorrow," Vich said. "Tonight, you'd better get back inside and give Tony the news about today."

Vich knew she hadn't told Tony, which meant Tony knew something was up. "Thanks, Vich."

He rounded his car and gave her a short, straight wave almost like a salute. "No problem, partner."

"Sorry if I was—"

"Enough said," he interrupted. He opened the car door and slid into the driver's seat before she could say anything else.

CHAPTER 22

IT HAD BEEN a relief to see Dwight Stewart's obit in the paper. The kind of relief that washed down your back like diving into cool water when it was hot. Done. The little girl didn't matter one way or another. Part of him hoped she'd make it, of course. He wasn't a monster, but she was irrelevant. She didn't know him from Adam. But Dwight Stewart. Old Man Stewart, that was a hell of a coincidence.

He was as drunk as always, but even falling down drunk he had an eye for trouble. How many times had Old Man Stewart called them out when they were kids? His eyes half closed from drink, his head tilted at an angle that looked almost unbearable on his neck, he'd raise the hand that wasn't clasping tightly to the neck of some bottle. "You—I know you…"

He'd shake his finger at them and they'd run away shrieking and making fun of him but scared shitless all the same.

What they feared wasn't Stewart himself, who was mostly too drunk to matter much. And not the kind of mean drunk that many of the men—his father included—turned into most Friday nights. The fear of Old Man Stewart was that he was tight with Herman Childers.

Back in the day, Childers ran the local gangs. Grown-up gangs, professionals. Not a bunch of kids running around, like they did today. Gangs that squeezed businesses into paying for protection, skimmed profits with threats. Gangs with guys who weighed as much as a small car and were all too happy to make good on the threats. Those gangs kept everyone under their thumb.

Old Man Stewart used to hand Childers the names of the punk kids who needed a little straightening out. Amos Barton got straightened out by Childers. He remembered Barton well. A big kid, Barton was as mean as he was dumb, which was very. Barton took what he wanted from anyone smaller than him, which was everyone. One day, Barton wandered into a convenience store just outside their neighborhood. Place was owned by an angry Chinese man who used to rant at them. Never understood a word the guy said. Well, whatever Barton was buying, he came up short on cash. When the owner didn't let Barton slide on the change, Barton took it anyway, leaving the owner with a black eye for the trouble. The place also happened to be where Stewart picked up his daily supply of malt liquor. When he heard what happened, he called Childers.

Next night, Barton was attacked a few blocks from home, thoroughly beat up and left for dead. As a result of the assault, Barton suffered a stroke that left the right side of his body limp and useless. He and Barton hung out some as kids, so he was pretty sure that Old Man Stewart would recognize him. No use risking that.

It felt like the world was smiling on him a little. After all, he didn't get the newspaper delivered, but he had wanted to see today's paper. Stewart had been on his mind. He'd wanted to search for the story, call the local hospitals, but he'd seen how these things went down. Anything he did on a computer—even a public one—they'd trace it to him somehow, so he had laid low and waited.

Then, that paper was lying on the table where he'd sat down, a nice neat stack to read while he ate fried eggs and hash browns, coffee with creamer—not milk—and sugar. The stress had been getting to him a little. He could tell by the food he was craving, but that wasn't evidence compelling enough to make a case. They could watch him and lean on him all they wanted. They were watching, he was sure of that. He knew the game and he played along. Did everything way out in the open. Made himself visible. People who were afraid hid. He would not let them see any fear.

He parked his car right in front of the diner. Set his phone on the table and ordered his breakfast. Ate exactly what he wanted. Dessert came in the form of an obituary. The paper was sitting on that table, waiting for him. He opened to the obits, skimmed them quickly. Didn't stop to read when he noticed Stewart's name. He was dead. What else was there to know? He certainly didn't care who Stewart left behind.

Now, Delman, too, had been taken care of, another piece of the mess that was tidied. That left one more connection between him and all this and he could leave it behind. Aside from Charlotte, of course. Time would tell on that one. Every day, it felt a little less urgent. The security around her would loosen. Access to her hospital room would be easier.

If nothing changed, one day he would walk in, sit by her bed like he belonged there. While he told her to have a long, restful trip to heaven—because girls like Charlotte had to go to heaven—he would insert the tip of a syringe into the IV tube and fill it with air.

CHAPTER 23

"THE BOMB WENT off at the school?" Tony asked again as they sat together in the kitchen. It was the third time he'd asked almost the identical question. She was ready for bed, exhausted, but neither of them would sleep until he'd had time to process what had happened. What it meant. Not that she knew.

This was the time to bring up the mitt, but she kept it to herself. It was the wrong decision; she knew that almost immediately. Tony was her partner. In everything related to Z, she had always been totally honest with him.

This was different. This wasn't something they could solve. She wished she didn't know about that mitt. She couldn't answer the questions Tony would inevitably ask if she told him the whole story. Questions about what it might mean. If Z had been the one… If he was capable of throwing Charlotte down the stairs and keeping it a secret. Or of watching her fall and keeping it a secret.

No, she was sticking with her decision. Until she understood how that blood had gotten on that mitt, how the impression had gotten on Sondra's Mercedes, how all of that could fit together in a way that left Z as the strong, morally centered boy they had raised. Until then, that mitt remained a secret. She had the desire to vomit again.

With every passing minute, she was acting more outside the law. There was no going back from hiding evidence. She was a mother first. A mother, and then a cop.

"What reason would someone have for planting a bomb at City Academy?"

She hesitated. "I don't know. I haven't heard anything from the lab or the—" She started to say "homicide" but caught herself. "And I haven't heard from Hailey either."

"Well, you know a lot more than I do, considering I don't know anything," he said, eyeing her. "There's something you're not saying." His face grew red when he was angry. Irish red as it was now. "So, why don't you tell me what you do know?"

"I don't know the motive behind the bombing, although it may have been to camouflage a murder."

"Murder? Someone was murdered at Z's school and this is the first I'm hearing about it?" He pushed his coffee cup away. He hadn't taken a single sip; small wisps of steam billowed into the air.

"Shh," she hissed.

"Someone planted a bomb at a high school to cover a murder? Damn, Jamie, I thought we had him at some prestigious school. Now it sounds like Columbine."

Before he could ask, she delivered the second piece of news. "The man who died—who was killed—was Michael Delman."

Tony's breath came out like air from a tire's broken valve—a fast, hard hiss.

"He's been visiting Z at school."

He stood, knocking the chair onto its back, and slapped the counter. "Jesus Christ, Jamie."

Before she could stop him, Tony sprinted up the stairs and marched into Z's room. Jamie entered as Tony was forcing Z out of bed. Z was half asleep as Tony inspected him head to foot.

"Are you hurt?"

"No," Z said.

Tony grabbed his son's face and ran his hand across it.

Z pulled away. "I'm fine. Jamie pushed me out of the way." He sank back onto his bed and let his head fall into his hands.

"Why didn't you tell us that your father had come to talk to you?"

Z didn't answer Tony either.

Tony, too, seemed distraught by the news that Z's father had come back in his life.

"I need sleep," Z said. He flopped onto his front, his feet hanging over the end, and yanked the covers over his head. He grunted something about the light, which Jamie shut off.

"I can't believe he's been seeing his dad," Tony said in the dark.

One more reason she couldn't tell him about the mitt. Tony would have insisted they confront Z, and Jamie was too terrified that he would lie. Or that they would prove he was involved. If they had proof, irrefutable proof, she would have to turn the mitt in. Did she have it in her to destroy evidence?

Even for Z, she didn't know if she could do that. If Tony knew the truth and they confronted Z, she might actually learn that Z was the one who pushed Charlotte. She couldn't stomach the idea. The part of her that knew it might be him warred with the part that prayed it wasn't. She refused to voice the possibility because to let those words out was to allow that doubt to overtake her hopes that somehow Z had nothing to do with any of it.

In the kitchen, Tony put his coffee mug in the microwave for something to do. She didn't tell him it was steaming. While it heated, Tony stared at the machine. When he finally looked up, he asked, "How did he take it?"

"What?"

"Delman's death."

Z's words were still in her head. *I don't ever want to leave you,* Z had said, clinging to her though he had thirty or forty pounds on her. Tony's eyes looked heavy as though his furrowed brow created weight that pulled them down. "He took it hard."

Tony retrieved his coffee, burning himself on the mug before using a dishtowel to set it by his place at the counter. He righted the stool and sat down. "Why would someone kill Delman at City Academy? What was he doing there?"

"I don't have any answers, Tony. All I've got are more questions."

"Should we be handling funeral arrangements?" Tony asked.

"No."

"He was Z's father, Jamie."

"Was," she said. "He gave up that right when he went to prison for the third time and abandoned him."

"At the very least, we should sit down together, the three of us, and talk about it," Tony said.

He was right, of course. Talking was exactly what they needed to do. She hated that Tony didn't know everything. Z was their child. He deserved to know and yet… all she kept thinking about was what might happen. Would Tony insist she enter the mitt into evidence? Or would he urge her to destroy it? Would he insist Ohio was their only option? Every possibility was terrifying. She didn't want him to condone that she'd hidden evidence, but she also wasn't prepared to turn it in. And she did not want to have to move to Ohio.

"Do we know how long they've been talking?" he asked, pulling her back from her own thoughts.

She shook her head.

"How about his cell phone records? Have you checked those?"

"I checked them earlier tonight. As of the end of the last billing cycle, there are no calls to a number listed to Delman or to any burner phone."

"When did the cycle end?"

"Fourteen days ago."

"So this all started in the last two weeks," Tony said. It wasn't a question, so Jamie didn't answer.

Sometime later, the brakes on the newspaper deliveryman's Corolla squeaked in the driveway. He always delivered the paper between midnight and 1:00, which meant it was late. Jamie went out in her bare feet to get the paper, opening it as she made her way back inside.

Sure enough, the story made the front page. MAN KILLED IN BOMBING AT PRESTIGIOUS HIGH

SCHOOL. Delman was named, so the notification had been made—to Delman's sister, Tanya, she assumed. She wasn't aware that Delman had other family. She would go on to read the article six or seven times. She and Tony read it through three or four times that night, sitting side by side at the kitchen counter.

There was no mention of her or Z or the other kids who were present. It wouldn't take the press long to link Michael Delman and Z. A few years back, Z had talked about changing his last name. To Galen or Vail, or some hyphenated version of the two. Jamie had never felt a close affinity for her name, which represented a ritzy ski town she would never visit. Tony had his own mixed emotions about his parents and heritage. Neither of them had offered any compelling case to Z for changing his name.

Now, it was stupidly obvious that he would have been better off with a new name. Especially living in the Bay Area, there was always a chance that Z's relation to Michael Delman, and Michael's long record, would sneak up on them. But Michael Delman was not front-page news. He was not a vicious killer or a sophisticated criminal mastermind. He was an average thief, a thug, a low-rent hustler, so how could she have imagined that his image would end up above the fold?

It was getting close to 2:00 a.m. "I have to go into the city to meet Vich early tomorrow. Z has to be at the school at 3:00 for practice before the game. I might make it back in time to take him…"

"I'll take him," Tony said.

"Are you going to the game?"

"Yes. Definitely. You?"

She nodded.

"Maybe we can go get something to eat afterward," Tony suggested. "I can't be out too late. I've got an early flight."

"Flight?"

Tony huffed. "I leave Sunday at 10:00 for Cincinnati. You're taking me to the airport, remember? I need to be there by 8:00."

Jamie hesitated a moment too long.

"It's been on the calendar for three months, Jamie. I can see it in bold print from here." He pointed to the family calendar that hung on a corkboard at the edge of the kitchen. In his print were the words "Ohio House Hunt Trip" across a whole line midmonth. There had been talk, at one time, of them all going. Talk from Tony, that is.

"It snuck up on me," she said. "I didn't realize it was this week."

"Should I cancel?"

"No." Slowly, calmly. Not emphatic, she knew exactly how Tony would react if she made it obvious that nothing appealed to her more than his absence. She didn't want to add to the hurt already there, but she would have taken an overnight at this point. Three whole nights to sort this all out was a gift from God. "We'll be okay, T."

He watched her. "If I don't see you in the morning, I'll meet you at the field?"

"Yes. I'll be there." She motioned up the stairs to where Z's door was closed. "Probably best to let him sleep in, after everything..."

Tony glanced up at the closed bedroom door but said nothing.

Her head was full of things she didn't want Tony to ask Z. Since the announcement about his new job, she'd been easing him out of their lives, while he was right there. Already she'd shut down so much of the input he had on raising Z. She watched him stare down at the cup of coffee, willing herself to make some offering.

When his chin lifted, though, his expression was changed. His eyes were narrow, darker. His shoulders rose and pulled back. "Z needs this move more than ever."

This move. As though moving to Ohio had ever been a possibility. Jamie folded the paper neatly and tucked it under her arms as she headed toward the stairs.

"I'll fight for this, Jamie."

She wasn't having this argument. He had no legal recourse. She was Z's mother, his guardian. Only her. Tony hadn't been on the papers. Yes, he was Z's father, and he was important to Z and to her. But he was only that because Jamie had let him.

"I'll petition the court for guardianship," Tony went on, gathering steam as his words came faster. He had the same snarling tone when he'd been drinking, but he was sober now. "I can offer him something in Ohio that you can't."

The words stung. She fought to calm herself. Her son was sleeping upstairs. Tony was hurt, worried, angry. This was how he handled it.

"I'm telling you," he went on. "I'll fight with everything I have."

She lost to the urge, swung around.

He wanted her attention and he had it. “A good school, new friends, away from his father’s murder. A stable home with a new start.”

Jamie took a deep breath. “Ohio would offer him a fresh start, Tony. I won’t argue with that.” She hoped he would drop it. *Not tonight. Let’s not do this tonight.*

“You don’t think I can win.”

She walked toward the stairs.

“You underestimate me. You always have.”

“No,” she said slowly. “I know the judicial system. With your record, there isn’t a judge out there who would rule you more stable than me.”

Tony said nothing. Jamie hated herself as she walked up the stairs and closed herself into the darkness of her bedroom.

CHAPTER 24

IT WAS MIDMORNING on Saturday, the morgue quiet, as Schwartzman ran the Stryker saw in a straight line diagonally from Michael Delman's right shoulder down through his sternum. Next, she did the same on his left.

Under the buzzing of the saw, her phone was ringing. She finished the cut through the breastplate and set the saw aside. Her mother's home number showed as a missed call. It was probably about time for her to check in. Schwartzman rarely called her mother. It wasn't as though she had news to share or stories to relay.

Her life was work, and her mother had no interest in her work.

It didn't seem as though her mother enjoyed their conversations any more than Schwartzman, although her mother did gain some satisfaction by sharing the latest society gossip from Greenville. Normally, her mother knew better than to call in the middle of a workday. Probably some bit of news she couldn't wait to share. Most of the time, Schwartzman didn't know the people her mother talked about.

Schwartzman lifted her red-handled pruning shears and cut through Delman's ribs so she could access his heart and lungs. The morgue had a pair of rib cutters, but the handles were solid steel rather than nylon coated. Plus, the morgue's pair was too large for her small hands and Schwartzman found them uncomfortable and awkward to use. She'd picked up her pair at Ace Hardware. They were perfect.

As she clipped through rib five on Delman's right side, her phone rang again. The call was her mother again, but this time from her cell phone.

It was unusual for her mother to call twice in a single day, but rarer for her to call from two different lines within a few minutes. It ran contrary to her Southern upbringing. Women should never be hysterical and calling twice in a row was a clear sign of hysteria.

As was leaving your husband for throwing you across the room and killing your unborn child.

At least, in her mother's mind.

Schwartzman managed to get through the remaining ribs before the phone rang again. The home line this time. What in the world was the bee in her mother's bonnet? Schwartzman set down the cutters, stripped off her gloves. The phone was still ringing when she stepped on the lever to open the trashcan and dropped the gloves in.

She raised the phone to her ear. "Schwartzman."

There was the faint sound of breathing. "Mama?"

"Ah, Bella," came the whispered response. There was no mistaking Spencer MacDonald's deep, Southern drawl.

Liquid heat pooled in her belly like food gone bad. She could hardly breathe. Shivers scampered across her shoulders and neck like cockroaches in sunlight. She shivered, spinning a full circle in the room. She was alone. Spencer MacDonald was not there; he was not in that room.

He was not even in the same state.

She was in the morgue. Alone. He was—she pulled the phone away from her ear and read the screen. Mama Home. He was in her mother's home.

"Bella?"

She considered hanging up. But this was her mother's home. She breathed in. "Where is my mother?"

"Bella," he said again, like a sigh.

She set the phone, facedown, on an empty autopsy table and walked away. She couldn't hang up. What if he'd done something to her mother. He had it in him, she knew he did. She fought off her repulsion. *There is no Bella here,* she told herself. *You are not Bella. You might have been her once, but you are not Bella. Bella is dead. Just like her daughter.*

He was calling that name again. His voice reverberated against the metal autopsy table, but she made no move for the phone. He could sit there on that line until she figured out what to do. But she would not speak to him again. He could not make her do that.

She would have to change her phone number again. That was nothing new. She had changed her number three times since she'd left Greenville seven years four months ago. She'd tried the restraining order route, but Spencer always found a way around that. Like calling from one of the local hospitals or the home of one of their old friends. Once, his voice had come across on a call from her credit card company. This was the first time he'd called from her mother's home. Her mother.

She lifted the phone. He was there.

"Bella, Bella, Bella," like cheering for some pathetic team.

Schwartzman drew a breath. "Let me speak to my mother."

"Oh, so you are there. Well, it's lucky you picked back up. You see, your mother can't talk right now. That's why I was calling."

"Explain," she demanded, struggling to ignore the physiological reactions she had to his voice. The accelerated breathing of hyperventilation, the constriction of peripheral blood vessels which made her cheeks flush, the increased muscle tension. The piloerection—or goose bumps—were explained by the contraction of the muscles that attached to each hair follicle.

Even with all of her knowledge, she was helpless to counteract these reactions in her own body.

"Your mama, she went to the hospital this morning with chest pain, Bella. How come you didn't know that and I—"

Schwartzman ended the call. She held the phone in her fist and forced deep breaths until her pulse no longer drummed in her ears. Her mother's physician was Dr. Hayes at St. Francis. That should be her first call. If she called an ambulance, they might have taken her to Memorial. The phone rang again. She sent the call to voicemail. Her finger barely trembled at all, her head triumphing over the fear.

She Googled Greenville Memorial and called the main

number. When the operator answered, Schwartzman told her she was looking for a patient who was admitted with chest pain. "Her name is Georgia Schwartzman."

"I'm sorry, ma'am. I don't have any patient with that name."

Schwartzman paused.

"Ma'am."

"Can you try under Montgomery? Georgia Montgomery."

"Sure thing."

It was well known that her mother had never loved the name Schwartzman but changing it—even after her father's death—would be out of character.

"No. No listing."

Schwartzman called Dr. Hayes's office next and asked where Hayes would have sent her. They said Memorial. "They don't have her listed. Do you have any record that she called in? This is her daughter, Dr. Annabelle Schwartzman. I'm calling from California."

"Bella?"

Schwartzman didn't answer. Dyspepsia fluttered its butterfly wings in her stomach. The muscle tension returned. It was like she was caught in some intricate ruse. It should have been impossible, but she had learned not to underestimate Spencer MacDonald.

"Is that Bella?" the woman said again. "It's Shelly Smith. It's been a long time, but I spent a lot of time with your dad when he was sick. Stayed at the house there at the end. Maybe you don't remember me?"

Schwartzman forced a long exhale. "Of course, Shelly. I'm sorry I'd forgotten." She strained to find a visual memory of someone named Shelly but came up empty. She wasn't certain if this was all part of some Spencer plan. "Have you heard from my mother today?"

"I have not, but let me check with the other nurses." Shelly placed Schwartzman on hold to check with Dr. Hayes's staff. She returned a minute later. "No. No calls to us today, and we haven't received notification from the hospitals either. They would contact Dr. Hayes as her primary care provider if she were brought in."

Unless she was unconscious and couldn't provide a name. Spencer knew where she was. Would Spencer ruin good graces with her mother to pull one over on her?

Or was this him pulling some stunt?

Part of his latest plan to get inside her head?

If so, how was he calling from her mother's house? Where was her mother?

She mumbled something that couldn't have been fully coherent and hung up. Though Shelly had assured her that her mother wasn't at any of the local hospitals, Schwartzman found the number for St. Francis and called them, too.

No Georgia Schwartzman there either.

The phone buzzed again in her hand. Four missed calls from her mother's home number. Four voicemails. She'd have to get another phone later today. Spencer wouldn't let up. He'd call day and night. She no longer kept a landline at home, so the cell phone was how her team got ahold of her. She'd keep a close watch on the phone numbers and hope he didn't find a way to route a call through the San Francisco Police Department. At least he was in Greenville.

Right now, anyway.

She wasn't sure she'd be able to ignore Spencer. If she couldn't figure out a way to get in contact with her mother, she'd be forced to call him.

Her mind was already working on the process of changing her number. She'd have to get the new number out to colleagues. She'd use the same excuse she always did with her first number change in a new city. Tell them she was switching to a local number from her current one with the Seattle area code.

She had known he'd find her eventually. In hindsight, this had been a relatively long hiatus. Almost six months had passed since the last time Spencer had sniffed her out. If he was back, it was unlikely that he'd give up after one contact. Every time she answered a phone—her work line, her mobile—she'd been waiting to hear that voice.

The morgue door slammed open against the inside wall. Schwartzman jumped.

Hal Harris halted in the doorway. He scanned the room. "You okay?"

She willed herself not to cry.

"Someone here?"

The phone buzzed in her hand again. Startled, she let it fall to the floor.

Hal crossed the room and picked it up. She made no move to reach for it. The phone looked tiny in his hand, and as he swiped his thumb across the screen, it covered the contact image of her mother entirely. "Inspector Harris," he answered.

Schwartzman backed away.

"She's right here." He lowered the phone, covering it with a huge hand. "It's your mother."

Schwartzman stared at the phone sandwiched between his palms. "Are you sure?"

Hal frowned. "I don't know your mom, so I'm not totally sure. But it's an older woman, and she said she was your mother. You want me to ask her some questions to be sure?"

Schwartzman reached for the phone and pressed the speaker button. "Hello?"

"Annabelle, are you all right?" Her mother's voice.

She scrambled to shut off the speaker and pressed the phone to her ear. "I'm fine. I was worried about you. I heard you were in the hospital?"

"What on earth would make you think that? I'm at home."

Schwartzman exhaled. The ruse hadn't been that he knew where her mother was and she didn't. The ruse was that her mother was fine. "Alone?" she asked.

Hal pointed to the door. She shook her head and put up one finger.

"I had some guests for lunch," she said. There was a little slur in her voice. Spencer was great at pouring drinks for guests. She couldn't count the times she'd watched him get guests smashed to squeeze some tidbit of information from them.

"We were out in the garden," her mother went on. "The gardenias and the ginger lilies are blooming, and the smell is glorious. Cornelia cooked up the most delicious grilled lamb chops with a lemon tarragon aioli and orange gremolata. We indulged in some wine." She laughed.

"Maybe a bit too much, but it isn't as though I've got to go to work. I'll have plenty of time to take a little rest before the auxiliary meeting this evening. We're planning for the annual fundraising ball at the club. You ought to consider coming home—"

"I'm at work," Schwartzman interrupted.

"Well, of course you are. You are usually at work, aren't you, Annabelle? I shall let you go on and get back to your important work."

"Well, and we don't want to keep your guests waiting," Schwartzman countered.

"Oh, no. They've all gone home. I only called because it appeared that you were trying to reach me—rather frantically, from the number of missed calls."

"Missed calls? I didn't dial—" How could Spencer have made it look as though she'd called her mother? Reprogrammed another number in as hers. Put in his own number as hers. He hadn't been particularly tech savvy when they were married. She refused to imagine he was better with technology. The idea was terrifying.

"Really, Annabelle. I don't know why you're so frantic."

Schwartzman closed her mouth. Frantic. Synonym for hysterical.

"I'll give you a call tonight," Schwartzman told her mother.

"I may not answer," her mother warned as though speaking to a young child. "It's the auxiliary meeting, remember? I wouldn't want you to start fretting again if you can't reach me."

"I'll be fine, Mama. Goodbye."

Her mother made a last tittering. Those were the

noises of a Southern woman, striving to come across light and carefree and also charmed by whomever she was speaking with.

Schwartzman hated those sounds.

She set the phone on the counter. There would be no arguing with her mother about Spencer. Her mother had Spencer MacDonald to lunch. Spencer had been bold to take her number from her mother's phone. He had assumed that Schwartzman wouldn't tell her mother about it.

He was correct. It wouldn't do any good.

Her mother was a staunch MacDonald supporter.

After coming to the hospital that night—after his brutal attack—her mother believed he was innocent. Her mother had listened as the doctor outlined her daughter's injuries. She had witnessed firsthand what Spencer MacDonald had done to her daughter. To his wife.

Her mother let him into her house after he had killed her first granddaughter. She invited him to lunch for God's sake. By inviting him to lunch, her mother had given him access to her phone number. And who knew what else.

How vulnerable was she to Spencer?

Did Spencer have her address?

Sweat broke out on her upper lip. Lightheaded, she moved toward her chair. Would changing her phone number be enough or would she have to move yet again?

"You okay?"

"I—"

"It's okay," he said. "You don't need to explain."

She opened her mouth to say something. Anything to deflect the attention.

"I may not be the person you want to talk to about—" He motioned to the phone, "—whatever that was. But I am always willing."

She didn't answer.

"And Hailey's good, too. You might not feel it, but you're one of us now. We protect our own." He gave her a smile.

"Hal—"

"Yes, ma'am?"

She wanted to say thank you. She didn't think anyone had ever reached out to her that way. Not what she expected from someone who looked like Hal. After Spencer, she should have known better than to judge a man by his appearance. But she couldn't bring herself to reach out for help. Instead, she asked, "Did you come down for something?"

"You know, I did," Hal said. "I was checking on Delman. We're working on how he got over to City Academy. His car wasn't there, and he wasn't scheduled to work yesterday. You run a tox panel yet?"

"I did." She crossed to the computer and signed in. She found the lab request and opened it to see if it had been completed. "Looks like it came in about a half-hour ago."

Hal stood at a distance. "Anything interesting?"

Schwartzman waved him over. "There is. Check this out."

Hal joined her as she pointed to the notation on the report. "The tox screen shows presence of a phenothiazine."

"What's a pheno-whatever?"

Schwartzman tried to make sense of it. "It's an anti-psychotic. Did Delman have a mental disorder?"

"Not that I know of," Hal said. "You're not talking about depression or something?"

"No. This class of drug would be for managing psychosis, like schizophrenia or bipolar disease."

"Can we tell how much he was taking?"

Schwartzman studied the numbers. The level was high, but there was no indication of prolonged use. "It doesn't look like he'd been on it for long, but I'd have to call the lab to ask if they can pinpoint it more exactly."

"Is it possible that Delman was drugged?"

"It's possible," she confirmed. "Phenothiazines are also sometimes used as tranquilizers if a patient is amped up on illicit drugs or suffering from a brief psychotic episode. It would have been administered at a hospital though."

"I'll send a request to the local hospitals to see if they treated someone with Delman's description." Hal's mind seemed to be turning. "What about the bullet wound?" he asked. "Is there a chance that Delman wasn't shot at the school?"

She hesitated. "It is possible. The shot wasn't a through and through, so the blood was contained in the abdominal cavity." She returned to the body. "But it isn't probable. Liver temp suggested he'd only been dead a short while when I arrived. But Roger has his clothes, so he should probably run a check for transfer. It's more likely that he was transferred to the school, unconscious, and shot there."

"But the drug would be powerful enough to render him unconscious."

"Absolutely," Schwartzman said.

"Okay," Hal said, rubbing his hands together. "I'll go talk to Roger."

"And I'll see if I can find any trace evidence on his skin or hair to give us a clue to how he was transported to the school," Schwartzman said.

"Keep me posted, then."

"Will do, Hal."

With that, Schwartzman gave Delman her complete focus. Her job was always her best shot at shutting out Spencer's most recent assault… at least until his next one.

CHAPTER 25

JAMIE HAD BEEN up most of the night. Every time her eyes closed, that mitt was there. The smeared blood on the window of Sondra's Mercedes. Once, she woke to a nightmare in which a ten-year-old Zephenaya stood over the body of Charlotte Borden. At 6:00 a.m., she gave up on sleep and got out of bed. She crossed the hall to her son's room and let herself in. Sat on his bed.

He didn't move.

"Z," she said.

His breathing deepened, then returned to normal. It was amazing how teenagers could sleep. Under different circumstances, she would have thought it amusing. She shook him harder. "Zephenaya."

"No," he said, flopping over.

"We have to talk, Z. This is serious."

He mumbled something she didn't hear.

"Z," she said louder.

Still no response.

Jamie rose and crossed his room, flipped on the light switch, bathing the room in bright light.

Z grunted. One arm emerged from the heap of sleeping teenager to draw the blankets over his head.

"Z, we have to talk." She shook him again.

Z groaned. "What time is it?"

The stairs creaked and Jamie froze. Listened. Someone was climbing the stairs. Damn it. She crossed the room and flipped off the light switch as the door cracked open.

Tony started at the sight of her. "You scared me."

"Sorry," she whispered.

"Everything okay?" Tony asked.

"I was telling him he needs to clean this room before practice."

Tony stared across the room, shaking his head. "He's dead to the world. He probably didn't hear a word you said."

Jamie stepped out of Z's room. "No, I'm sure he didn't."

"Don't worry," Tony said. "I'll get him out of bed in time to clean up."

*

Her head was throbbing, and she was wired on caffeine as she drove to work. She'd spent the morning at home reviewing the case file and her notes. At least, she reviewed the case file between the time she spent worrying about that damn mitt and about not getting to talk to Z.

What could she do? Take the mitt to the lab, fess up, and have Roger work on it? She couldn't do that. Not to Z.

It was only 9:00 a.m. and she was exhausted. She'd been up for three hours already. On a Saturday. It wasn't that she minded working the weekends. She didn't. In her pre-Z life, she worked most of them. She'd pull out the evidence and spread it out around the house. She'd leave case notes and tox screens and fingerprint cards and rap sheets across counters and the coffee table and couch.

As she moved from place to place, she'd read snippets of one thing or another until the case literally filled the air in the house.

Then something would click.

The pieces would fall into place, and she'd know the answer.

Living with a ten-year-old boy and a recovering alcoholic made the old process impossible. Certainly, any photographs had to be kept out of sight. She'd tried using her room instead, but early on, Z had spent many a night shuffling between his room and hers and she had gotten out of the habit. Maybe she'd lost her edge.

Too much thinking. Today, she wanted to immerse herself. She needed to. If she could find a way to get inside the case, maybe she'd find the piece that would pull it all together. If she knew Z was involved, she had to confront him.

As she pulled into the department parking lot, Vich was there. She steeled herself against the questions he would surely ask. Fortified, she emerged from her car, crossed to Vich's, and slid in beside him. Grunted.

"Good morning," he said. "Brought you coffee. Splash of milk, one sugar."

She stared at the cup in his hand until he pressed it toward her. "I don't deserve coffee."

"Sure you do."

"I'm a miserable person today, Vich."

"Okay."

She took the coffee.

"Thanks for the warning, anyway. Where to first?"

"Bordens," she said. "Any news on Charlotte?"

"Same," Vich said. "They released the little girl, though. The one from the hit-and-run."

Her pulse kicked up a notch. "Did she see—"

"She doesn't remember anything," Vich said. "Not the car, not getting hit, not playing right before."

Jamie blew out her breath. Damn it. "The Bordens know we're coming?"

"I left messages for Gavin and Sondra at the house and on their mobiles."

She took a sip of the coffee. "We ever get a response from the building manager on the request for information on Gavin's parking pass?"

Vich nodded. "Came in last night. Gavin had a late lunch meeting the day of the attack. We confirmed that he met two clients at Boulevard at 3:00. It's that fancy restaurant at the corner of Mission and Steuart..."

She knew the restaurant. In a thinly disguised attempt at bribery, the deputy chief of the department had given her a gift certificate a few years back.

"So, after lunch, Gavin arrived back in the building parking lot before 5:30 and didn't leave again until 8:07. That would have been about the time the call came in on Charlotte."

"So, he's got an alibi, but Sondra doesn't. You see Sondra Borden throwing her daughter down the stairs?"

"No," Vich said. "But I've been wrong before."

Arriving at the Bordens' house a second time was still a jaw-dropping experience. Built mostly of red brick, the house had three levels with four pop-out windows on the upper two levels, making it extravagant even in its silhouette. At the street was a heavy wrought iron gate that had been open on their first visit but was now closed.

As Vich rang the bell, Jamie spotted another thing she'd missed on the first visit. Two almost life-size lion statues sat inside the gate, facing one another across the wide brick walkway, as though ready to pounce on the uninvited guest.

The gate buzzed open, and Vich and Jamie made their way past the lions. Sondra Borden answered the door, dressed in a simple navy blue wrap dress with navy sandals. Her hair was pulled back into a low ponytail and, although her skin had the flawless texture of women in Botox advertisements, she wore no makeup. As with the other times Jamie had met her, she was elegant in the way that rich people were.

She led them into the same room where they'd sat before. Gavin Borden was at the window, his back to them. "Gavin," Sondra said softly. "The police are here."

Gavin turned without looking at his wife. He appeared to have lost weight in the days since Charlotte's attack. His face had a greenish tint around his eyes, as though he'd spent a week or two in a dungeon enduring some intense physical torture. In Jamie's experience, mental torture worked much faster than physical in breaking down the body.

Jamie caught Vich studying something on the floor. She saw a circular machine on wheels. A self-propelled vacuum cleaner. She couldn't remember what they were called.

Was it someone's idea as a hostess gift? Or something Mr. Borden bought for his wife?

"We won't take much of your time," she told the Bordens.

Sondra took the cue and perched on the edge of the couch while Gavin crossed the room to take a chair across the room from her. They made no eye contact at all. Vich was probably having the same thoughts.

Was there more to the cold shoulder Gavin was giving his wife than blaming her for letting Charlotte dress too provocatively?

"Mrs. Borden, I met with Ms. Remy yesterday from the opera. She said you canceled your appointment with her on Wednesday evening."

Gavin watched his wife.

"It's true, I did," Sondra confessed. "Our anniversary—Gavin's and mine—is the first week of May. Twenty years," she said with a glance in his direction that Jamie couldn't read. Sheepish or maybe coy. "I had the idea of putting together a sort of getaway night for us, so I went over to Union Square to look at the menus at a couple of restaurants and to try to find a dress. I didn't want to ruin the surprise," she said, shaking her head. "That seems so silly now."

If anything, Gavin looked slightly more tortured by the news.

"Did you see anyone there? Or have lunch with a friend?" Vich asked.

"No," Sondra said. "I didn't find a dress. I had one

on hold at Saks but then, at the last minute, I changed my mind and told them not to hold it."

Jamie made notes. "Do you remember the salesperson's name?"

"I'm afraid not," Sondra said.

"What did she look like?" Vich asked.

"Oh, my," Sondra said, shifting on the couch.

Jamie glanced at Vich. Sondra was lying.

"She was petite. Dark-haired," she added as though choosing traits out of a hat. "I don't remember much else."

Jamie hadn't ever been to Saks, but the description Sondra gave probably fit ninety percent of the Saks sales clerks.

"Would you mind if we looked at Charlotte's room?" Jamie asked, changing the subject.

Gavin sat up straighter. "Why?"

"Anything we can learn about your daughter will help us," Vich said.

Gavin and Sondra exchanged a glance. "I went through Charlotte's room after our last conversation. I didn't find anything," Sondra said.

Jamie and Vich waited.

"I don't understand why you'd need to see our daughter's bedroom," Gavin said. "She's the victim. Whoever did this is out there—" His voice cut off. He pressed the back of his hand to his mouth to muffle the sob that choked loose.

"It's okay, Gavin," Sondra said. "I'll show them." She rose from the couch. "It's down this way."

Jamie followed Sondra down a long hallway with rich wood floors and ceilings that were easily ten feet high. Paintings hung on the white walls. An oil portrait of a woman in a chair, a single flower, a watercolor of a country landscape with a barn, and something that was mixed media and abstract. She gave the paintings a wide berth and instead scanned the painted walls. The white walls were spotless. Her walls were white, too, but forever covered in fingerprints.

Sondra stopped at a dark wood door. It was oversized, the kind of door you expected to lead outside. Sondra pressed down a heavy-looking handle and opened the door. The walls and ceiling of Charlotte's room were painted a light purple. The bed was freshly made; nothing on the floor. On the walls were two poster-size pictures of Charlotte standing with people Jamie had seen in magazines.

"Is that Bono?" Vich asked, pointing to one that was taken when Charlotte was maybe eleven or twelve.

"Yes," Sondra said without explanation.

"Huh," Vich said and took a slow walk around the room.

Charlotte's makeup and bottles of perfume were lined neatly on a dressing table built into an alcove of the room. Lights lined the mirror but not like the big bulbs in the cheesy dressing rooms of movies. These were some sort of light panels. High-end, no doubt.

"I assume someone cleans the room?" Jamie asked.

Sondra nodded.

"Do they do that daily?"

"Yes. The staff tidies up after the girls go to school. They have a schedule where they clean certain things each day. I'd have to check my book to be certain. I believe they've dusted and done the floors since Wednesday."

Jamie opened the top drawer of the dresser. Sondra made a soft choking sound. Paired socks made neat rows. Beside them was cotton underwear, folded into little pastel cubes. Nothing similar to the outfit Charlotte had been wearing when she was attacked. Touching nothing, Jamie surveyed the contents and slid the drawer closed. She reached for the second drawer when Sondra stepped in front of her and pressed the drawer closed, avoiding contact with Jamie's hand. "I think Gavin's right. We shouldn't be in here."

"We understand that Charlotte had an argument about her art lessons."

"An argument? With whom?"

"That's what we were hoping you could tell us."

Sondra shook her head. "I have no idea. I don't know why she would have been arguing about that. She doesn't take lessons anymore."

"Perhaps the argument happened before she quit?" Vich suggested.

Jamie walked to the window. The entire Golden Gate Bridge was visible from Charlotte's window. Not only the bridge, but also the land peninsulas on either side. She'd seen this view before, or one almost exactly like it.

Sondra had said something, but Jamie wasn't listening. "Where is your bedroom, Mrs. Borden?" Jamie asked.

Sondra looked slightly stunned.

"I don't want to see it," Jamie assured her. "I'm just curious."

"It's down the hall," Sondra said, pointing.

"You have this same view?" Jamie asked.

"Almost."

The pieces fell together. "Thank you for your time."

"Of… of course," Sondra said, a little surprised when Jamie started for the door.

Vich followed. They didn't speak as they made their way back through the house and down the brick path to the car. Jamie slid into the passenger's seat and called the department. "Traffic, please," she said to the operator.

The phone buzzed twice. "Traffic. Roland here."

"Roland, Jamie Vail. I need you to pull all records for any recent parking or traffic violations for a Sondra or Gavin Borden." She recited their street address. "Citations on any vehicle."

Jamie put the call on speakerphone and set it in her lap, then lifted her coffee cup in a cheers motion toward Vich. "I've got a theory about why Sondra is lying about where she was."

"You going to share it?" Vich asked.

"As soon as I find out if I'm right." She drank from the lukewarm coffee. Even tepid, coffee tasted good. The one vice she hadn't given up completely.

They waited in silence until the clerk came back on the phone.

"Inspector Vail?"

"I'm here, Roland. What've you got?"

"I found four violations—one on a 2011 Jeep and three on the 2014 Mercedes."

"Can you give me the addresses?"

"One is on 301 Van Ness."

"That's close to the opera house," Vich said.

"And the others?" Jamie asked.

"Two are on Folsom—853 and 892. Same block. Wait. The third one is too. It's at 315 5th, which is around the corner from the Folsom locations."

Jamie smiled at Vich, who looked clueless. "What are the dates on the ones at the second address?" she asked.

"March 14th at 2:18 p.m., March 29th at 6:15 p.m., and the third is April 2nd at 4:58 p.m."

"Bingo," Jamie said. "Thanks, Roland."

Jamie ended the call. "So, Sondra is spending some afternoons at the city condo complex over on Folsom street."

"Who lives there?" Vich asked.

"Heath Brody."

CHAPTER 26

ROGER FOLLOWED HAL and Hailey into the darkened bar and smelled corporate beer. That's how he thought of this particular smell—thin, sour, acrid, the smells of beers made in huge plants. PBR or Old Milwaukee. Budweiser. Coors. To Roger, corporate beer smelled like the vat from whence it came and not unlike the urine that it would soon create. Not an opinion he shared all that openly. He knew it made him seem like a snob and although he had plenty of quirks—being completely hairless made you quirky whether or not you had quirks—Roger did not consider himself a snob.

He did not, however, partake in the average American's indiscriminate love of any and all beer. Not only was the taste bad, corporate beer conjured images of frat parties rife with atrocious behavior and thickly sticky floors. He was thirty-two on his first visit to a fraternity. He'd missed the party by about eight hours. Instead, he had come to collect evidence on the death of an eighteen-year-old freshman girl who had been repeatedly raped and who, it was later determined, asphyxiated on her own vomit. They never did determine if she was being raped at the time of her death, but there was compelling evidence that suggested it was unlikely that she was alone at the time she choked and died. One of her rapists might have simply moved her onto her side and saved her life.

It wasn't the fraternity rats that created Roger's dislike of the particular types of beer served inside their walls. Rather, for him, good beer had substance, like good coffee. A porter or stout might smell like chocolate, an IPA might be crisp with light citrus notes. His favorite was the oatmeal stout, made by Founders. Unless, of course, he could get his hands on a growler of the small batch ale by Sculpin from Ballast Point Brewing, but that was hard to come by. Sculpin normally sold out in San Diego within hours of being tapped and that was a bit far to travel for a beer.

As his eyes adjusted to the dim bar light, Roger scanned the room. The only natural light came from an eighteen-inch strip of window on the front of the building, maybe twenty feet long. The rest of the window had been painted black, although it was scratched enough that some sunlight leaked in through the tiny breaks in the paint. Hal and Hailey were there, so Roger crossed to where they stood at the bar.

Behind the bar was a man who appeared to have spent a lot of years in this room or one like it. Hal pulled a picture of Michael Delman from a folder and showed it to the bartender.

"You know this man?" Hal asked.

"Yeah. He comes in pretty regular."

Roger watched the bartender whose belly was precariously balanced on an old brown leather belt. The notches to the right of the buckle were each stretched and worn as though, one by one, they'd simply given in to his growing girth.

"When was the last time you saw him?" Hal asked the bartender.

Roger watched as the bartender mopped up a puddle of spilled beer with his wet rag, wrung it out in the sink, then proceeded to wipe off the bar with it. Maybe he had dunked it into a sink of clean water that Roger hadn't seen. Roger peered over the bar. Nope. The bartender worked the old beer into the bar. No wonder the place smelled so bad.

"Do you remember the last time you saw this man?" Hal repeated.

"Yesterday," bartender said. "Around lunch time."

"How long was he here for?"

"An hour, maybe a little less." He stopped mopping. "I don't really keep a timesheet."

It took nerve to backtalk someone Hal's size, especially someone with a badge.

Hal did not reply to the barb. "Anyone with him?"

The bartender shook his head. "Nah. He sat at the bar alone."

"He usually come alone?"

"Almost always. Sometimes there's a gal with him."

"Like a girlfriend?" Hailey asked.

"Nah. Think she's his sister."

"How about the rest of the bar?" Hailey asked. "Were there other people in the bar when he was here?"

The bartender filled the two sinks with water and added some sort of detergent to one. "Few of the regulars.

Carl and Steve at the back. They're in at lunchtime every day."

"They talk to Delman?"

"No. They're not big talkers. They sit in the back with their whiskeys and beer backers, eating stale pretzels. Stay for about forty-five minutes and leave again. They've got a standing tab. I bring back two whiskeys, two beers, and a bowl of pretzels. Most days, I don't even talk to them." He began dunking dirty glasses in the soapy sink then into the clean sink before lining them out on a thin rubber mat to dry. Roger imagined the bacteria that followed the glasses from one customer to the next.

How many sets of prints and DNA samples remained on them after the bartender's "cleaning" process? If he'd been considering ordering something to drink, he would have changed his mind now. There wasn't a chance they'd be able to isolate Delman's DNA in this cesspool. He didn't bother to open his evidence collection case.

The bartender looked up. "Delman did take a call. The phone rang a couple times before he finally answered."

"It rang a couple times," Hal repeated. "You mean like he didn't want to talk to the person calling?"

"I ain't a mind reader," the bartender said.

Hal leaned down over the bar. "Take an educated guess."

The bartender took a step backward. "It sounded more like he didn't know who was calling. Didn't recognize the number."

Hal kept his body leaned over the bar. At 6 feet 4 inches, two hundred fifty pounds, he was effective at encouraging folks to talk. What Roger liked was that Hal never threatened. He hardly ever raised his voice. Usually, merely shifting his body was enough to encourage people to talk. "You hear who he was talking to?" Hal asked.

"Nah. He only listened. Then, he pointed to the back door like he'd be right back."

They glanced at the back door. "He took the call outside?"

The bartender nodded.

"What's out there?"

"Feel free to look. It's a little square patio area. No tables or anything—" He waved his hand around. "We're not the patio service kind of place."

That was for sure.

"Beyond the patio is a gate that leads to the alley. The trashcans are out there and my truck, but nothing else."

"How long was he gone for?" Hailey asked.

"Not long. Four, maybe five, minutes."

"And when he came back?" Hal pressed. "He seem upset or angry?"

"Nah," the bartender said. "Maybe a little confused."

"Confused how?" Hailey pressed.

"I don't know, lady." He hitched his pants back up, but with his protruding gut, there was really nowhere for them to go.

"Watch the attitude, bub," Hal warned. "We're looking for a little assistance."

The man smoothed a palm across a bad comb-over. "He was here. He left. He came back. Had another beer and left. That's all I know."

"And there was no one else here at the same time he was?" Hailey repeated.

"I had a group of three German couples come in—or maybe they were Australian. Who knows?"

He must have meant Austrian.

"They were at a table in back, had a few beers and a round of lemon drops, if you can believe that." He swung the towel through the air. "Who would come in this place and order lemon drops?"

A light mist dusted Roger's face from the bartender's towel. He resisted the urge to wipe his face.

"Hey—" The bartender pointed to the bar. "The lemon drops remind me. There was one other girl."

"Girl?" Hailey repeated.

"Woman, whatever," the bartender responded defensively.

"How old?" Hailey continued.

"Legal. No question on that."

"But you didn't card her," Hal guessed.

The bartender stared at Hal. "She was easily twenty-seven."

"She was alone?" he asked.

"She came in with a book. Ordered a Belgian White. Like I've got that on tap. After some hemming and hawing, she settled for Coors."

"She a regular?"

"Never seen her before," he said.

"What did she look like?" Hailey asked.

"Decent looking. Pale. Don't remember much more." He started to shift on his feet. "Listen, I've got a lot to do before we open."

Roger scanned the area. There wasn't enough time in a month to do what had to be done in that place. This was a wasted trip. There was plenty to do back at the lab. He considered leaving, but he didn't want to interrupt Hailey and Hal. Instead, he settled in to wait and hoped they were close to done.

"We have a few more questions," Hal said, standing tall again.

The bartender sized up Hal. "Ask away."

"You think the woman was a tourist?"

"I doubt it," the bartender said. "She didn't carry a purse and no backpack. The tourists always have some sort of pack. Plus, she was wearing heels."

"So, she had no interaction with Delman at all?"

"None. In fact, she ordered her beer while Delman was outside."

Hailey motioned to the bar. "Right here?"

"Yes," the bartender confirmed. "Right there."

"Isn't this where Delman was sitting?"

"Yes, but he was outside, remember?" the bartender explained.

Hailey and Hal exchanged a look that Roger tried to read. The woman had ordered a drink when Delman was outside.

"Did Delman take his drink when he went outside?" Hailey asked.

"No. I don't allow people to take the glassware outside."

Of course.

"She put something in his drink," Hal said.

"What? I don't think—" He stopped cold.

"What?"

"She made me pour her another beer. Told me the

glass was dirty," the bartender said. "Asked for a glass off the shelf. Even offered to pay for both beers."

Hailey's phone buzzed. She pulled it from her pocket while Hal asked the bartender if he could find the glass Delman drank from.

Roger set his kit on a stool and opened it for a collection bag. If Delman had been drugged, there was a good chance that the drug had left some residue behind on the glass.

The bartender was pulling glasses out of the rinse and shaking his head. "They're all clean. Yesterday was slow, but it might have been any of these." He motioned to a dozen glasses. "And I did some last night, too, so it might be back on the shelf."

"We'll take them all," Hal said.

Hailey lowered her phone and leaned onto the bar. "What book was she reading?"

The bartender seemed shell-shocked. He was staring at the glasses that Hal had told him they were taking.

"The book," Hal repeated.

"Jesus, I don't know. It was a book. The cover was—"

"Was what?"

"Yellow, maybe. With red X's." He waved a hand. "One of those books I seen on posters for some new movie."

Hailey put the phone to her ear. "You hear that?" She asked the bartender, "Was it the Stone Temptress Series?"

"How the hell should I know what the—Stone whatever?"

Roger knew it well. Kathy and his older daughter were first in line at the bookstore to buy two copies of the newest book in the series the day it was released.

Two copies, because neither one was willing to wait until the other had finished it. He pulled out his phone and Googled the series. The image of the newest book filled his phone screen. He held it out to the bartender.

The bartender leaned back from the screen and squinted. "Yeah," he confirmed. "That's the one."

"Jamie? You get that?" Hailey asked.

"Great." Hailey ended the call. "Jamie said she thinks the woman sitting at the bar might have been Tiffany Greene."

"Who's Tiffany Greene?" Hal asked.

"I never heard of her," the bartender commented.

Hailey threw the man a look. The ability to communicate without words was something she and Hal had in common. He raised his hands and retreated to the far end of the bar.

"Tiffany Greene works for the Bordens."

"Figures Jamie Vail could get an ID from a book," Roger said.

"I hope it's the right one," Hailey added.

"Well, let's go find this Tiffany Greene, then," Hal said. "Roger, take these glasses to the lab and test them for residue of phenothiazines."

"I'll do one better. I'll set up the lab and do it right here."

Hailey patted him on the back. "Have fun."

Roger called the team. He didn't have nearly enough sterile sheets to cover the surfaces in this place. They'd have to bring him more. Lots more.

CHAPTER 27

WHEN JAMIE HUNG up, Vich was giving her a sideways look. "I missed all that. Why do you think it was Tiffany Greene at that bar?"

"It's a hunch," she said, but she was already second-guessing herself.

"Care to explain it?"

Jamie knew she might be totally off base. There were five million people between the ages of fifteen and thirty reading the newest Stone Temptress book. Vich drove by a billboard and Jamie saw the design.

The pendant she'd seen on Tiffany Greene at the hospital wasn't a flower.

It was the Temptress's stone.

Around it were Deception's flames, trying to break it open. "She was wearing a pendant at the hospital. It was from that series."

"The bartender recognized the pendant?"

"No," Jamie said. "He described the cover of the book she was reading. From what he said, it sounded like the third in the series, Temptation's Hand, that came out yesterday."

"That's a hell of a leap," Vich said. "I've never heard of the Stone whatever—"

"Temptress. Well, you don't have a teenager." Not that Z was reading the series. It was Jamie who had gotten totally sucked in by them, but Vich didn't need to know that. It was rare for Jamie to find the time to read. Between her caseload and Z, she stayed busier than she would like. On the occasional weekend day, though, without a pressing task, she'd download a book and usually finish it in a single sitting. For whatever reason, she was drawn to the young adult dystopia novels. Maybe it was because murder and suspense were too close to home, but the postapocalyptic worlds took her to another place. Not a happy one, of course. That would never work.

Home made her think of Z.

He hadn't called about his mitt. He'd have to realize it was gone before practice. Wouldn't he call her first, to ask if he'd left it in her car?

So far, nothing.

Just then, her phone buzzed. It wasn't Z. She slid her finger across the screen. "Hi, Hailey. What've you got?"

"Roger's still at the bar, so I sent him Tiffany Greene's photo from her driver's license, and he showed it to the bartender. Guess what?"

"It's her."

"Bingo. Nice work."

Jamie lowered her phone. "I was right," she told Vich.

"Damn," he said, shaking his head again.

"I wanted to let you know. Hal and I will reach out to Ms. Greene," Hailey said. "We'll keep you posted."

They drove about a block before Vich turned to her

at a red light. "What now?" he asked. "Do we follow up on Tiffany Greene?"

Jamie shook her head. "Hailey and Hal are doing it."

"Huh," Vich said. Jamie felt it, too. It was rare that they made a break and didn't get to follow up on it. There was the little zap of energy, the thrill of discovery about Tiffany Greene, a new lead to chase. But it wasn't theirs to follow.

"What about Brody?" he asked as the light changed.

Jamie considered Heath Brody. "Guy walks around like he's some sort of demigod. I don't see him giving us anything."

"Maybe we should pay him another visit, apply a little pressure. Find out what he knows."

"The guy throws acid on pieces of metal and sells them for fifty grand," Jamie said. "I think he's basically perfected the pretty-boy bullshit artist routine. I also doubt he'd do anything that might jeopardize the good thing he's got going with Sondra. She's connected him to a lot of clients."

"Maybe we need a little ammo first."

"What kind of ammo?" Jamie asked.

"Something to make him think his gigolo playboy artist gig might be up."

Jamie considered the idea. Her mind drifted then to Charlotte. "You mean like an inappropriate relationship with a minor."

"Don't imagine Brody's wealthy clients would take too kindly to the idea that he might be preying on teenage girls."

"We know Charlotte had a big fight with someone

about Heath Brody," Jamie said. "Maybe we can track down those housekeepers and find out who she'd been fighting with." She pulled out her notebook and scanned for the name. "Here it is. Abigail Canterbury." She dialed the number Sondra had given her. It went straight to voicemail for a company called Canterbury Personnel Services. She listened to the entire message, hoping for an in case of emergency cell phone number. Nothing. She ended the call without leaving a message. She hated voicemail. She dialed the department and requested they pull the cell phone number for Abigail Canterbury.

Jamie hung up, and the phone rang almost immediately. Too soon to be the department with a number. "Vail."

"Hi, Jamie. It's Sydney."

"Hi, Sydney."

"Heard about yesterday. Scary. Are you doing okay?"

"Yeah, fine. Thanks for asking." Jamie hoped to cut through all the condolences about the bomb. She didn't want to talk about it. "What's up? I didn't expect to hear from you on a Saturday."

"Actually, I'm at a Kindermusik class, but my son fell asleep, so I'm checking messages."

Jamie said nothing. She had no idea what Kindermusik was.

"I called Vich yesterday and told him we'd found an off-market tracking device on Sondra's Mercedes."

"Yeah. He mentioned it."

"We were able to track the purchase back to an online security company called SafeTrack. The purchase was made by a local company, R.I.P. Investigations.

Seems they've bought several of the devices in the past ninety days."

"R.I.P.?" Jamie repeated.

"I know, right? I did a search. Comes back to Ronald Ikerd Private Investigations," Sydney said.

"Can you text me his contact info?"

"I'll do it now."

"Thanks, Sydney."

"No problem."

"What's R.I.P.?" Vich asked.

"Someone was tracking the whereabouts of our Mercedes."

"Maybe Gavin knew about his wife's affair."

"It's possible, but it doesn't explain an attack on Charlotte. The guy finds out his wife was cheating on him, so he throws his daughter down the stairs?"

"What if Heath Brody found out that Charlotte was the one who spilled his secret?" Vich said.

Jamie nodded slowly. "And so he goes after her to keep her from ruining the good thing he's got going."

"Or… maybe she told her father," Vich added.

"Yes," said Jamie. "And maybe the argument the housekeeper heard was…" She stopped. It was like guessing in circles.

"How was Brody when you met him?" Vich asked.

"He certainly didn't seem like he'd been outed. But—" He'd showed no signs of remorse when she told him about Charlotte's condition. "He might also be a really good liar. Maybe Charlotte saw the sketch of the bridge and assumed Brody had painted it."

"The view from her mother's bedroom." He paused.

"Or—maybe Sondra saw it and assumed Brody had been in her daughter's bedroom."

"Either way," Jamie said, "we need to talk to Abigail Canterbury."

"And Brody," added Vich.

Jamie scanned her phone and saw a text from Sydney and another from a department number with Canterbury's cell phone number. Jamie hit the link and the phone dialed. She put the call on speakerphone when the greeting kicked in. "Hi, you've reached Abigail Canterbury. I can't get to my phone, so leave a message and I'll call you back."

With no other choice, Jamie left her name and number and disconnected.

"Same voice as on the company voicemail. Maybe Canterbury is one of those people who actually takes weekends off."

"A business owner, catering to wealthy clients? No way."

Z's game started in less than three hours. "I'll request her address and we can run by her house, then give a call to our private eye." She typed a reply to the department, requesting a current home address for Canterbury. Jamie looked up. "And somewhere in there, we could go by Brody's again."

"It's a plan."

Vich made a wide U-turn in the street and went off in the other direction. Jamie tried to press off her oncoming headache. Another hour had passed with no word from Z about his mitt. Practice was about to start. He had to know it was gone.

*

Jamie arrived at City Academy at 5:05. The day had been largely a wild goose chase. They'd gotten no response from the cleaning service. Ikerd's private investigation agency was closed for the weekend. No word from Hailey or Hal on Tiffany Greene. No luck finding Heath Brody, and no change in Charlotte.

As she came into the school lot, Jamie tried to push the work stuff away. Instead, she found herself scanning the asphalt and noted that the debris from the bomb was gone. Fresh paint lined the sides of the parking place where Steckler had been parked. Only a trace of the black burn marks from the bomb remained. What had changed was that four patrol cars were now parked in the lot. The sides of their cars were marked with the K9 logo. The bomb dogs were here.

The fans were loud enough to be heard from the parking lot. The police presence didn't seem to affect the enthusiasm. As usual, Jamie parked on the far side of the lot as another round of cheers erupted from the stadium.

City Academy didn't have a football team. If they had, Z would certainly have been recruited for the team. Jamie had read enough about the long-term effects of concussions in football players to know it was not a sport she wanted her son playing. Without a football team, baseball took center stage at City Academy; the games usually brought a large crowd. Tonight's game was against Marin Prep, City Academy's main sports rival, so the turnout would be even bigger. She'd have been happy to have some quiet time at home, especially as she had to get up at 7:00 to take Tony to the airport.

But she'd missed two games already. Despite everything else, she wanted Z to know she supported him. For her, supporting him meant all of the millions of things she did to protect him, to fight for him. Again, she thought about the mitt. The risks she'd taken on to protect him. What would she do if he was guilty? How could she possibly protect him then?

Unable to shake off the worry that had settled deep into her chest, Jamie entered the bleachers to see Z warming up in front of the dugout. Bottom of the inning. Zero-zero on the scoreboard so she hadn't missed much. Z swung the bat in a gentle rhythm. He seemed calm.

"Jamie!"

Tony waved from halfway up the bleachers. He always found a way to sit in the center. She had to crawl across all sorts of people to get to him. She shuffled awkwardly down the aisle to sit next to him. But Tony took her arm and gently pulled her past him. "Sit over here," Tony directed, patting the bench on the far side of him.

"What difference—"

Tony glanced at the woman seated beside him.

Jamie closed her mouth and moved past, settling onto the cold bench as Z walked toward the plate.

"Jamie, this is Brenda Newcomb. Brenda, this is Jamie."

Jamie shook Brenda's hand, returning the dead fish handshake with one equally limp.

"Now, how long have you two known each other?" Brenda asked Tony.

Jamie leaned forward, settling her elbows on her knees and resting her chin in her palms.

"Uh, since we were two or three," Tony said when Jamie didn't answer. They all went quiet as the first pitch was thrown.

Z didn't swing. Ball.

"Wow. That long. That was back in New York?"

Tony nodded.

Jamie risked looking rude and slid her fingers over her ears. Didn't Brenda New—whatever her name was—see that they were trying to watch their son?

Second pitch. Z hesitated then swung. Strike. Jamie held back the groan.

"So, your families were friends?" Brenda asked.

"Hang on a sec. This is Z at bat," Tony said.

"Oh, I'm so sorry."

Duh.

Brenda made like she was zippering her mouth closed.

Third pitch. Ball.

Fourth pitch. Z swung. The lovely crack of the ball and bat connecting. Line drive between second baseman and short. The ball was fielded by the center fielder, and Z rounded first with a single. Jamie sat up again.

"Sorry," Tony told his female friend. "Our fathers were best friends. They worked at the same fire station together for twenty-seven—"

"Twenty-nine," Jamie corrected.

"Right, twenty-nine years. Jamie's mom died when we were two. Mine when we were seven. After that, it was the three of us—Jamie, me, and my brother, Mick."

"Wow."

Tony smiled.

Jamie considered puking. But then she caught herself. What was wrong with Tony flirting? It wasn't like she wanted to be with him, and if Tony met someone, maybe he'd stay in the Bay Area. He could move out, and they could be like fifty percent of parents and simply split custody. Jamie gave Brenda what she hoped was an encouraging look, then turned back to see Z ease off first base to steal.

Brenda let out a little tittering laugh. "Talk about marrying your childhood sweetheart."

"No." The word was on the tip of her tongue, but Tony got it out first.

"No," she echoed.

"We're not married," he said.

"Or a couple," Jamie added. "Just friends." She gave Tony a friendly pat. "Family, really."

"Right."

"And you guys are raising Z together?" she said. "That has to be so hard."

"It's not the most traditional family," Jamie admitted.

"Z kind of came into our lives when I was staying with Jamie," Tony said.

Jamie watched as Brenda settled in a little closer. The attention was good for Tony. She didn't want to be with Tony. Not like that. Yet she felt oddly possessive. It was so awkward to watch. "I'll be back," she said.

Brenda gave a little wave. "Sure," Tony said.

Jamie started to climb the bleachers when a hand grabbed hers. She yanked it back. "What—"

Travis Steckler glanced up at her. "You're leaving while Z's on first?"

"No. I was just—"

"Sit here." He slid over. Jamie looked around.

"I—" There was no reason not to sit. Steckler had chosen a less crowded spot and maybe she wouldn't have to listen to Tony flirt.

"I couldn't help but overhear."

Jamie frowned.

"About you and Tony." He leaned in. "Brenda Newcomb has been asking questions about him for months."

"Oh, yeah?"

"There's quite a rumor mill among the divorced parents. New meat is always big news."

"Tony's new meat, huh?"

"Oh, you both are."

"Did you just call me meat?" she asked.

Steckler shook his head. "Not me. The rumor mill."

"And you're not part of the divorced parent rumor mill?"

Steckler's smile faltered. "Nope. Widows and widowers aren't invited. Too sad."

Jamie cringed. "I'm sorry."

"Don't be. It's been almost ten years."

"Still hard."

"Yes," Steckler agreed. "Like losing your mom, right? And that was probably before you could remember."

"It was."

He motioned to Tony. "You two had an interesting youth. Tony made you guys sound like boxcar children."

"Boxcar children?"

"You don't remember those books? The kids who lived in the boxcar? It was great. Only you and Tony and—his brother was it?"

She nodded.

"You guys had a firehouse instead of..."

"A boxcar," Jamie said.

"Right..."

The crowd around them cheered, and Jamie turned to the game as Z slid into home. Oh, God. She'd been flirting and she'd missed her son's run.

"He's playing great. You missed the top of the inning. He made a great play at second."

"Second?" Z normally played left field.

"Yeah. Paul Shay lost his mitt, so the coach benched him for misplacing it. Put Z in at second."

Something hot rolled up her spine and settled at the base of her neck. "Paul lost his mitt?"

"He pitched a fit about it, too. Directed most of his fire at Z, in fact. Was really out of line."

Two words echoed above all the rest.

Paul's mitt.

CHAPTER 28

HE STARED DOWN at the ground. A rectangular shape, piled high with rich, dark soil, surrounded by grass. It looked more like an expensive garden plot than someone's death. His permanent resting place—no, final. Final resting place. Resting. Like he was taking a short nap. The bullshit they tried to sell. Dead. He was dead. Autopsy said he was drugged, then shot.

Shot at least made sense. They knew all about getting shot. That happened in the neighborhood. Probably most days, but drugged? He didn't buy that Michael was doing drugs. He wasn't into that. He knew who was using. Could see it in their eyes. There had been plenty of heroin around. People he knew had died from heroin. Even that was changing. Kids these days were starting with meth.

A twelve-year-old girl—Jamal and Shawna's girl—had died using meth. Some nasty stuff, meth, but it was a known entity where he came from. Known entities—even the ones that killed you—were safe. They were familiar. Known entities were the things that happened in his shitty neighborhood.

But Michael was drugged by some fancy drug with

a long name. He made them spell it out for him so he could Google it. Some sort of tranquilizer. Didn't they know that they could have given him a few beers and he'd have tranquilized his own self?

Michael was drugged with something that came from Charlotte's world, not his. Her people had killed him. Or at least, they had drugged him. He'd been the one to convince Michael to help him get her to the hospital. He told Michael he'd owe him one, pick up the next six-pack or run some errand. A six-pack of Old Milwaukee or PBR was what Michael's life had been worth in the end.

Michael's death meant they were after him, too. Had to be. And what about her? Would they come after her? If she lived—God, he hoped she lived—what would they do to her? Or was she safe because of who she was? Were any of them safe?

You were a product of your environment, but they weren't that different, Charlotte's people and his. They were playing gangs up there, same as down here. The rule was still an eye for an eye.

What would she think of that?

She pretended to have disdain for people like her, but when push came to shove, didn't they all protect their own kind?

How soon till they came after him?

CHAPTER 29

SCHWARTZMAN UNCORKED A bottle of her father's Evan Williams bourbon. At the time of his death, eleven bottles remained. Schwartzman was drinking the second to last bottle. For more than four years after leaving South Carolina, Schwartzman didn't drink at all. She had never been a heavy drinker, but some nights the bourbon went down a little too easily.

One bottle remained after this one. One last bottle of a lifetime of them. This had been her father's celebration drink. The familiar label was present in her memories of holiday parties, birthdays, her father's work functions, celebrations of cases won, and the toasts her parents made to one another at anniversaries. Her father often raised his crystal lowball, the ice ringing against the glass, to her for report cards and merit scholarships, whatever milestones parents celebrated.

There was always a bottle in his den and, more than once, her father had said Evan Williams was practically part of the family. As a child, she'd taken that literally. Once, she'd asked her mother how they were related to Evan Williams. To which her mother had responded, "By now, clear through your father's liver." Her mother could be witty.

Schwartzman herself took her first sip of Evan Williams after her acceptance to Duke Medical School. It wasn't what most young people tried their first taste of alcohol, and she hadn't loved it at first.

She'd sipped it politely, while her father read her like a book. "You'll grow into it," he said. "Then, you won't want anything else."

Unlike most college kids, Schwartzman had consumed little alcohol in her undergraduate years at University of North Carolina. She graduated high school at seventeen and college at twenty. By twenty-three, she was through three years of med school at Duke.

By the time she drank alcohol again, her father had died. She had left Spencer. She might not have thought about Evan Williams again were it not for her mother. When Schwartzman had packed up her Jeep to move out to Washington, her mother loaded the case of bourbon into the back of her car. She hadn't touched it since his death. "The sight of the label is devastating. I couldn't possibly bear the taste," her mother had told her.

In those first months in Seattle, back in medical school, a bottle of the bourbon sat perched on Schwartzman's dresser as a beacon of her father. Pushing her to make it through another day, to stay awake, to study, to not fail. It was only after her first finals that she cracked the bottle and then only for the smell.

It was sometime during her internship that she actually poured it. The occasion had seemed special at the time, although she'd forgotten what it was. These days, she sipped it rather freely. Not every night, but perhaps a third of them, creeping toward half recently. Never more than two fingers, always with three ice cubes, never more than two in a night.

The supply would soon be gone.

She had kept the first empty bottle. It remained on her dresser and, when she bent over and uncorked it, she smelled her father inside. His smell was a mix of the bourbon and his cologne, his soap, and the smells of ink and paper. Those other scents had fallen away until her memory of his smell was no longer distinguished in her mind from the smell of the bourbon.

She dreaded the day the bourbon ran out. It wasn't a matter of the bourbon itself. The distillery was in business. She could source the bottles locally if she chose. It was silly, but the case he had bought held more than the bourbon he had loved. Those bottles held some essence of him. A living piece. Once they were gone, he would be gone, too. He resided in other places, but for her, the bourbon had been the only thing of her father that she'd taken from her mother's home.

While her mother was living, the other items Schwartzman would one day keep to remind herself of her father remained in her mother's house.

The dearest one to her was his 1928 first edition Napoleon Hill law book, signed by Hill, which lived in a glass case in her father's den.

For as long as Schwartzman could remember, her father was rereading Hill's *The Law of Success*. Her father would turn a page of the book where it would remain open, in its locked, glass case, for several days or a week.

Long enough to give him—and also her, or the staff, or her mother, or whoever else was interested—a chance to read the page. Then, he would don a pair of white cotton gloves, open the case, and turn the page, closing it up again for another five days or a week. Schwartzman rarely saw him perform the changing of the page, but when she had, it was like watching a ceremony.

Schwartzman had read the last page dozens of times. She never had the heart to turn it.

She had come upon a Napoleon Hill quote when she first arrived in Seattle. His name was only familiar to her because of the book in her father's study, so she'd been surprised to read the inspirational words. At the same time, the message seemed to have been sent directly from her father, delivered to her that day in the shape of a poster on the wall of a bookstore. It read, "Opportunity often comes disguised in the form of misfortune, or temporary defeat."

Now, Schwartzman set the glass down and pulled herself from her reverie. The thoughts felt foolish floating in her head. She was a medical examiner. Dead men did not send messages via other dead men through posters in bookstores. The borders of life and death were well known to her. Yet, she always found herself imbuing the Evan Williams bourbon with something of her father that her rational mind knew couldn't possibly exist.

Enough for tonight, she told herself, pulling David McCullough's *Truman* into her lap and settling back into the settee. Tomorrow, she would cross the Golden Gate to hike the Dipsea Trail that ran from Mill Valley to Stinson Beach. In her months in San Francisco, the Dipsea had become a sanctuary, though she didn't get there as often as she would have liked.

The trail was almost ten miles. It might take her three hours, or she could spend seven. She had been known to stop among the redwoods or under the arching laurel with a book, and she often spent several hours on the beach when she arrived.

Even in the rain, or when the fog was so dense it was difficult to see beyond her own feet, the trail brought immense relief, something that she struggled to find in her regular life. She was due. She would have liked to go today, but between finishing Delman's autopsy and arranging for a new phone, the time had gotten away from her.

The front bell rang in the entryway. She saw the clock on the far wall, 8:00 p.m. She couldn't imagine who would have been calling up, but perhaps it was a package. Normally, the doorman called her phone. She sat up, remembering. Her phone number had changed. Another person she needed to update.

She retrieved the front desk number from her old phone and dialed down.

"Nob Hill Manor," the evening clerk answered.

"Martin, it's Dr. Schwartzman."

"Good evening, Dr. Schwartzman. How can I help you?"

Schwartzman settled back onto the settee. "I forgot to let you know that I have a new phone number. I got it today."

"Oh, certainly, Dr. Schwartzman. Go ahead and give it to me. I'll update your record right away."

Schwartzman recited the new number, already memorized.

"Is there anything else?"

"I heard my front bell ring. Were you trying to reach me?"

"Your front bell?"

Schwartzman sat upright. "Yes. It rang in my unit."

"Recently?" Martin asked.

"Just before I called you."

"I've been at the desk the whole time. You haven't had any visitors."

"You're certain?" she asked.

"Absolutely."

"Can you hang on the phone a moment, Martin?"

"Of course, ma'am."

Schwartzman carried the phone to the front door. It trembled in her hand. Her legs were shaky from the rush of adrenaline. Her heart sprinted in her chest.

"Dr. Schwartzman, would you like me to send someone up? I believe Caleb is still here. Or Francis, if you prefer."

"No, Martin. If you don't mind holding on, I want to check outside the door."

"Of course."

Schwartzman rose on her tiptoes to look out the peephole, which had been installed for someone at least six feet tall. The hallway was empty. She had heard the bell, she was certain. There was one bell outside the apartment door, but she'd never had anyone use it. Normally, the bell rang from downstairs. Anyone coming into the building would have had to pass Martin to get access to the intercom keypad.

She pressed the metal knob at the end of the chain into the slide and slipped the chain across before unbolting the door. She peered through the narrow opening. There was nothing.

"Dr. Schwartzman?"

"One more second, Martin." She closed the door again and pressed her forehead to the wood. She would have to open it. She would have to unlatch the chain. "Martin," she said out loud.

"I'm here, Doctor."

"I'm opening the door. If I don't come back on the line—"

She didn't finish the sentence.

Martin said something indiscernible.

Schwartzman was already going. She unlatched the door, pulled it open, and stuck her head out into the hallway. The left was clear, but against the wall to the right of her door—just out of view from the peephole—was a huge bouquet of flowers.

They ranged from the palest to the most brilliant shades of yellow.

Yellow.

Spencer.

Schwartzman ducked back into her apartment and slammed the door. She spun the bolt and latched the chain. Shaking uncontrollably, she slid her back down the door until she was seated in a ball on the floor.

"Dr. Schwartzman? Are you all right?"

She was crying. "Send someone up immediately.

Caleb. Send Caleb and tell him to remove the bouquet in the hallway but not to dispose of it. Martin, remove it from the hall but do not discard it, do you understand?"

"Yes. Of course, Doctor. A bouquet—of flowers?"

"Yes. Flowers," she confirmed. "And have Caleb wear gloves."

"Gloves?" he repeated.

"Or use a towel to carry it. Tell him not to touch it with his hands. I'm calling the police. Martin, do you understand?"

"Yes. Remove it, don't touch it, don't throw it away."

Schwartzman got unsteadily to her feet. She didn't have Jamie Vail's number in her new phone. She hurried back across the apartment and lifted her old phone to check her contacts.

On the front screen was an iMessage from an unknown number. *So nice to hear your voice yesterday, Bella.*

CHAPTER 30

CITY ACADEMY BEAT Marin Prep in an extra inning. It was a good game. Each team spent part of the game in the lead and the two were tied at three separate points. By the time it ended, it was after eight. Jamie was exhausted. Something about watching Z play baseball wound her nerves into a mess of frazzled yarn. Every time the ball came near him at second base or—later, after Paul was off the bench—at center field, she held her breath, tensing all the muscles in her body as though she might send him the right energy to make the catch or the play. It was worse when he was up to bat.

And she was calm compared to a lot of the parents.

Now, the exhaustion of all her worries pressed into her shoulders like lead hands, holding her down. She stood from the bench and arched her lower back, which was tight and sore. A talk with Z was her primary goal. The mitt was Paul's. That was the biggest piece.

There were questions Z had to answer. She needed to know what he knew. He was evading answers. They'd missed the window for a family dinner, which was a relief. Traffic would have died down leaving the city, so she could be home by 9:00. That would give them an hour to talk before bed. She had to be up by 6:45 so that would give her nine hours. Nine hours of sleep…

She blinked, and Z bounded up the stadium seats. "The team's going out. Can I go?" he asked, breathless. "I'll get a ride home, I promise. Be in before midnight. Please." He clasped his hands together for emphasis.

Travis Steckler chuckled.

"I don't think—" Jamie started.

"Absolutely," Tony said, giving Z a high-five and a man hug with lots of back patting. "You should celebrate with your friends."

Neither Tony nor Z looked at her for input. Tony pulled forty dollars out of his wallet and handed it over. "Before midnight," Tony said.

"Absolutely. I'll be home before midnight."

"You don't have a phone," she called to him as he was jogging back down the bleachers.

Z raised a hand at her. It was one part wave and one part something she couldn't read. Was he agreeing that he would answer his phone? That he'd found it? Was he telling her to stop bothering him? Or was he reminding her that he couldn't answer it because it was lost?

"We got his phone back today," Tony said over one shoulder.

"You did? How?"

"It was at a friend's house."

"What friend?" she asked.

"Jacob, I think was his name. I didn't meet him. Z ran into the Westfield Mall to get it."

"The mall?" Jamie asked.

"Yeah. Guess he works there."

Brenda touched Tony's arm and he turned to talk to her.

Z had never mentioned a Jacob. She found her son back in the crowd of boys. She recognized Paul and Sam because they lived in the north bay. She knew them because they often drove Z home. But she didn't know the others. Sure, they were familiar, but she didn't know their names. Was Jacob on the baseball team?

Jamie recalled watching Z with Amanda Steckler and the other girls yesterday. Z had never mentioned Amanda Steckler. Or Charlotte. Or any girl. But he had talked to Amanda on the phone, talked to others Jamie didn't know. Maybe he had talked to Charlotte.

The request for names on the unlisted phone numbers Z had called wasn't back yet. Some embezzlement case was in front of her request and it was two thousand phone numbers or something. Jamie might have called in and gotten her small request bumped up, but not without calling attention to it. She wasn't prepared to do that.

That was just Z's phone calls. Who knew how many people he texted. Jamie was waiting for the phone company to get back to her on that. And she had no good way of seeing where else he was communicating. Not without getting his password to Instagram and Snapchat and whatever else he was doing. She saw all his public posts, but those apps all had private message boards.

He's a teenager. A teenager who has settled into his new school. The first semester of his freshman year, he'd come home after school or practice every night. Now, he occasionally had sleepovers and went to the movies with other kids. Tony usually picked him up because his schedule was so much more predictable. And normal. Tony probably knew more about what Z was doing than she did. She was his mother, but Z needed a father, too. What on earth would she do without Tony?

She touched Tony's back. The smile on his face stiffened slightly. "The parents are going to a local place for a burger or whatever…"

Tony was making plans to go to a bar.

"Do you want to come?" he asked, and she saw in his expression how badly he wanted to go.

"No," she told him. "I've got some things to follow up on, but you should go. Have fun. Maybe you can coordinate with Z and make sure he has a ride home."

He squeezed her shoulder. "Yes. I absolutely will." He started to leave but turned back. "You're okay with taking me to the airport in the morning?"

"Of course. I'll be up and ready at 7:00."

"Great. Thanks, Jamie." Tony returned to Brenda and the two started down the bleachers. Soon, Travis Steckler, who had wandered away to greet some other parents, headed back her direction. "You joining the celebration?" he asked.

"Not me," she said.

"You've had a long week."

She thought again about that mitt. Down on the field, Z was in a huddle of boys, swatting each other in the way that boys did with their friends. Paul Shay was there, the whole mitt thing forgotten. She had so many questions about that damn mitt. She would submit it as evidence. For all the lab knew, she had only just discovered it. She'd have to create a story. She could say it had ended up with Z's things. That Z and Paul often carpooled together, and it had probably been left behind. That was reasonable. It made sense. But she wanted to talk to Z.

There he was. Down on the field, laughing and smiling. His father hadn't been a significant part of his life. Hadn't been any part of his life in the past five years. But Michael Delman was his father and he had been killed yesterday. Right now, Z was distracted. He wasn't thinking about his dead father or where he came from, what he'd been through. He wasn't thinking about how his life would change if Tony left—when Tony left. He wasn't thinking about any of the things that might have driven his surge of violence the other night.

They'd let it go.

Everyone except Jamie seemed to be enjoying a break from reality.

Jamie glanced around the stands. How many of them were thinking about the bomb that had gone off yesterday? Maybe a few, but even the police officers with their German Shepherds looked relaxed.

A hand pressed on her shoulder.

"You okay?" Steckler asked.

She nodded.

"Not very convincing."

"Like you said, it's been a long week," she admitted. "I'm heading home."

"Me, too." He started down the bleachers. "Come on. I'll walk you to your car."

"I—"

"Not that you need a chaperone," he added quickly.

She gave him a smile.

"I'm heading that way, too," he said. "In fact, I'm the one getting a chaperone, after all. A decorated police inspector, you've already saved me once."

"Stop," she said.

He raised one hand. "Done."

They walked quietly through the parents, many of whom greeted Steckler. A few told them they'd see him at Presidio's, the pizza place where they were all headed. None said more than hello to Jamie. And why should they? She'd never made an effort to speak to any of them. This part of Z's life had felt foreign. It also felt temporary. Of course, she had hoped that he would have four years at City Academy, but they always reminded her that there was no guarantee. That they might not be able to continue his scholarship. That it depended on grades. On behavior. On school politics and the board and… on and on. But she might have looked at it differently.

Steckler made no commitment either way. He, too, seemed tired. "Why aren't you going tonight?"

"I'm not much for crowds," he answered. She was taken aback by his honesty. They walked a few more steps, and he added, "And it has been a long week."

They matched their stride, and the tension in her back and neck unwound a bit.

"How is Z doing?" Before Jamie could answer, he added, "About his father, I mean. His biological father."

Normally, all her hackles would have stood on end. Instead, she considered how to respond. How was Z doing? How could she answer that when the truth was that she had no idea?

"When Mary died, Amanda was only seven. We'd been separated for a short time before that. Amanda lived with me. She had little interaction with her mother that last year."

"I'm sorry," Jamie said softly. She'd expected cancer or some awful car accident. In her mind, they'd been this perfect family until something tragic pulled them apart.

"She was an addict, Mary was."

"That's very difficult," Jamie said.

"Amanda rebounded from it fairly well," he said. "I mean, of course, she was upset. How could she not be? But she always seemed more distraught about the idea of losing a mother than about losing her mother specifically."

"I can't tell what Z feels about it," Jamie offered, surprising herself. She didn't think she'd ever spoken about Z to anyone other than Tony and the required conversations with his social worker and therapist after the adoption. "He was so upset when he saw his—father. But he hasn't talked about it. Not that we've been together much since yesterday afternoon."

"It's hard to have a parent who fails on the basics of parenting," Steckler said softly. "And it's not entirely easy to be the parent who has to pick up after that. Mary left a bit of a mess after her death…"

Jamie waited for him to continue and when he didn't, she said, "It's got to be tough to do it alone, too."

"Right," he agreed. "I'm sure it's been good that you two have each other."

"I didn't mean that," she said.

"Oh, no. It's the truth, isn't it?"

"He's moving," she said. "He got a teaching job in Ohio."

Steckler stopped. "Really? He's leaving?"

"He hoped we'd come with him."

He stared at her. "But you're not, are you?"

"This is home for us," Jamie said. "I couldn't leave."

"But he thinks that getting away would be good for Z," Steckler said, as though he could read it on her face.

"Especially now."

"Right."

The case details had been kept under wraps, but Delman's death meant all bets were off. Tomorrow's paper would certainly include Delman's involvement with Charlotte Borden's assault. That he had delivered her to the hospital would make him look guilty. Even if he wasn't. She had a hard time imagining he wasn't. The press would have full access to create a giant exposé of his life. If they didn't already…

She was guilty of exactly what she expected from the other parents. She was already judging Delman the way others would judge him. Worse, she had transferred that blame onto Z. She blamed the son for the sins of his father. Otherwise, why wouldn't she have confronted him? She was no better than the others.

"Having a criminal for a parent doesn't make you a criminal," Steckler said.

She felt stunned and ashamed that he might have read her mind. "You think everyone agrees with you?"

"I know they don't," he said. "But they're not raising Zephenaya. Or Amanda."

They arrived at Jamie's car. She glanced around the

parking lot. He couldn't be driving the blue Lexus. "Which one is yours?"

"I bought that one, there." He pointed to a black sedan. It was a BMW or a Lexus. She couldn't tell the difference. Expensive. Nice. "Kind of boring," he added.

"I really liked the color of the Lexus," she said.

"The blue. Me, too."

She unlocked her car and he pulled the driver's side open for her. "Good night, Jamie."

She slid into the seat. "Good night, Travis." The word filled her mouth.

He shut her door and walked away. As she started her engine and pulled her seatbelt across her chest, she watched him in the rearview mirror. He was surprising. She was grateful.

CHAPTER 31

JAMIE'S IPHONE SCREEN announced that the call was coming from the new contact number Schwartzman had sent, but she was startled to hear the medical examiner's voice. Jamie's thoughts circled like a lasso around her head. Schwartzman would call if they'd found another body, but Jamie should have heard about another attack directly. Something about Delman that related to Z? But Z was innocent. He had to be.

But what about that damn mitt?

"What's going on?" Jamie asked into the phone as she swung her feet onto the floor to ground herself for the news.

"I'm sorry to call so late. On the weekend." Schwartzman's voice was slow, but there was a breathless quality that Jamie hadn't heard before.

"It's fine," Jamie assured her, glancing at the clock. It was 12:33 a.m. She must have been asleep, and yet it didn't seem like the phone had awakened her. "I didn't get a text," Jamie said. "Is there another victim?"

"No." Schwartzman exhaled. "Yes. You could call it that. It's me."

"Where are you?"

"I'm home. I'm safe."

Jamie eased back down onto the bed. "What happened?"

"It might have waited until morning, but…"

"It's okay. Tell me what happened," Jamie said.

Schwartzman exhaled. "I received a gift."

"Of?"

"Yellow flowers."

Schwartzman was from the south. Early to mid-thirties meant she was old enough to have been married. And from the phone call, Jamie guessed she'd married badly. "An ex?"

"Yes."

"Is he in town?"

"I don't think so, but he's found my address, which isn't good."

"How long since you've seen him?"

"Seven years four months." She stopped, but Jamie suspected Schwartzman could have told her how many days had passed if she'd asked.

"Any idea how he found your address?" Jamie asked.

"Some idea."

When she didn't expand on the comment, Jamie said, "How can I help?"

Schwartzman took a breath. Jamie could tell it wasn't easy for her to ask. "I have requested the security footage from my building, but it's not as easy as getting them to send me the file in an e-mail. I was hoping maybe the crime lab would look at it."

"Of course. We'll have Roger do it."

"Thank you."

"What else?"

"I want the lab to run prints on the flowers—the vase and packaging. If that's possible," Schwartzman added.

"I imagine you're hoping to keep your name off the case file?"

Her exhale was audible. "Yes."

"We can do that. I'm not in the city now, so I'd like to call Vich to come over." Jamie sensed Schwartzman's hesitation. "He's good, Schwartzman. And trustworthy. I wouldn't put him anywhere near my victims if he wasn't."

"Okay," Schwartzman said. "That's fine."

"In the meantime, do you have somewhere else to stay?"

"I'll be fine."

"You have an alarm?" Jamie asked.

"I have several precautions, and the building is secure. I've let the management company know about the break-in."

"Someone broke in to deliver the flowers?" Jamie asked.

"Yes. Well, I assume," she said. "There is no record of a flower delivery person being let into the building."

"Isn't it possible that they buzzed an apartment and someone let them in?"

"Every visitor to the building has to come by the front desk. You either have a keycard and pass through the gate or you sign in the guest log and are announced. Then, you're issued a temporary keycard. Security is twenty-four seven."

A high security building. On Schwartzman's salary

that was a big expense, which meant it was a high priority. Maybe the ex was more dangerous than Schwartzman was letting on. "There have to be other ways in and out. The garage, for instance?"

"Yes, but again, there's a guard station there, too. You need a keycard to access the garage and then again to access the door from the garage to the elevator bank."

"So even if someone snuck through with a car…," Jamie began.

"They couldn't get out of the garage and into the building," Schwartzman said.

"It sounds secure."

"I'd thought so," Schwartzman said.

"So, it's safe to assume that every time a keycard is used, it is logged?" Jamie asked.

"I think so, yes."

"Text me your address and the contact information for the management company. Maybe I can get access to that log," Jamie said.

"They won't give it you," Schwartzman said. "Not without a warrant."

"Oh, I don't know," Jamie told her. "I'll bet it costs a lot to live in that building. That security is probably a big part of how they can command those prices. People might not react that well if they knew it was so easy to get in without being detected."

"Thank you, Jamie."

"No problem, Schwartzman. Really. You want to give me your ex's name? I can see what he's been up to?"

Schwartzman hesitated. "Not yet."

"Okay," Jamie said. These days, people had all sorts

of access to when someone checked up on them, even if that someone was the police. It was sometimes best to wait to dig into a suspect's record. "You let me know if you change your mind."

"I will."

"We'll catch up Monday, if not before."

"Enjoy the weekend," Schwartzman said.

Jamie didn't respond. She wasn't going to enjoy the weekend and neither would Schwartzman. The fact that Schwartzman had chosen to call Jamie was telling enough. She'd been close enough to these cases to know that whoever Schwartzman was avoiding had already done enough to prevent her from resting this weekend. "Call if you need me."

Jamie hung up and called Vich. Her feet were on the cool wood, and she pressed her toes into the solid floor. Vich answered on the third ring, wide-awake. She explained Schwartzman's request and gave him her number. He promised he'd get over there and take care of it.

"Keep me posted," she told him as she hung up.

Jamie set her phone on her bedside table and walked out of her bedroom. She had left the downstairs hall light on, but it was off now. The boys would have turned it off.

She listened at Z's door. With her palm against the wood, the door swung open, and she saw his unmade, empty bed.

"Z?"

She checked his room and then the bathroom, and then made her way down the stairs. No sign of him in the kitchen or the living room.

"Z?" she called out in a whispered shout.

No response.

She made her way down the hall to Tony's room. "Tony?" She heard him moving in the bed. "Tony," she said again.

The bedroom door swung open, and he stood in boxer shorts and a white T-shirt. His hair was on end and his eyes were barely open. "What? What is it?"

"Z isn't in his room."

Tony exhaled, leaning against the door jam. "He's at Sam's. They all went up there after the pizza place."

"Sam's?"

He nodded, stifling a yawn.

"I thought he was coming home."

Tony studied her face. "What's going on?"

"I thought we'd talked about him coming home."

"We did," Tony said. "And then I was out with the group and about five of the boys from the team were sleeping at Sam's. Sam's parents, Kate and Tom, were there, and they assured me that Z was welcome and that they would be home. So, I let him go."

Jamie crossed her arms.

"Are you okay?"

An uncomfortable knot formed in her throat. "Fine," she said. "It startled me when he wasn't in his room." She started back down the hall.

"Jamie—"

"Yeah?"

"You can talk to me," Tony said, running his palm over his nest of hair.

"What? I know."

"I mean really talk," he added softly.

Jamie fought off the onslaught that followed. The tightness in her chest, the dense weight behind her eyes where the tears were building up.

Tony stepped into the hall. Not closing the space between them but minimizing it, leaving that gap that always existed between them. The safe space. "I know this has been hard."

He was referring to his move to Ohio. But it wasn't only about Ohio. "This" to her was their living together. Raising Z. Losing their mothers. Growing up with their fathers and so many things that had happened in between.

Their relationship was built on these things—these trials.

Maybe that was what it was like to have siblings. It wasn't as though they'd chosen each other.

They were thrown together.

He cared for her, and she would have done anything for him. To help him.

But despite all the love and respect they might have for each other, there was always the burden of those difficult experiences at the base of their relationship.

"I felt like I needed to step up," he whispered. "As a man, as a father, and be a provider."

"I never asked for that."

"No," he said. "You didn't. You've always taken care of me. Hell, you mostly took care of Mick, too, and he was three years older. When I came out five years ago, I didn't plan on—" He let out a dry laugh. "Well, I didn't plan anything, but I definitely didn't plan on moving in. Living in your house. Then, becoming a father to your son."

"I don't really think of it as my house, T. It's our house. And Z—he thinks of you as his father. And so do I." She drew an unsteady breath. "I wished you'd talked to me first. About Ohio and all of it...," she said.

"We haven't been talking much, have we?"

"We *are* a family, Tony," she said. "Not the traditional kind where the mother and father share a bed," she added softly.

"I know."

She exhaled. "But we will still be a family if you're in Ohio. We'll need to save more for plane tickets."

"Speaking of which, it's an early morning," Tony said.

"Right. You need to get some sleep."

"We both do." He started back toward his bedroom.

"Hey, T."

He looked back.

"Z will miss you," she said.

"I'll miss him, too."

"But he won't be the only one." There was so much more to say, but it was a start.

Tony retreated into his room and closed the door, and Jamie made her way back upstairs to her bedroom. She crawled under the covers and tucked them in along her sides.

What would their lives be like with Tony so far away? She'd never imagined it before and now she couldn't.

CHAPTER 32

SCHWARTZMAN WOKE MIDMORNING on Sunday. Bright daylight streamed in along the edges of the dark shades. She didn't remember her dreams, but she felt as though she'd barely slept at all. Thankfully, it was Sunday and nothing was expected of her today.

She would not leave the apartment.

She had intended to go to the Dipsea trail, stop for some groceries, but facing the real world was too much to take on today. She would order from her favorite Indian restaurant, Curry, and have it delivered. Enough for lunch and dinner.

What she needed to do today was pull herself together so that she could walk into work tomorrow. That meant sifting through the emotions that were churning on the surface. From experience, she knew that they would not be dragged back down. Not without being felt and heard first.

The first thing was to let the memories come.

Lying in her bed, Schwartzman was flooded with images of their first date, to the country club. Eight weeks after her father's death, Spencer MacDonald had called to invite her to dinner at the country club. His low drawl, his manner of speech so unassuming, the call made Schwartzman feel like he was a young colleague of her father's. Safe.

"It sure would make me happy if you'd join me for dinner, Bella." No one had called her Bella. It had seemed so loving, so intimate, even before they knew each other. How easily she'd been lured in. How desperate to get out of that house, filled with the emptiness her father had left behind, the gap between her and her mother impossible to fill.

Her father had been their bridge.

Now there was nothing to connect them.

Spencer MacDonald stepped in as though to build a new one. How gracious he was that first evening. Arriving to the front door in seersucker pants and a navy blazer, he brought her mother flowers. A bright bouquet of yellow flowers. Not something so large as to be gauche. Just the right touch of respect and something to brighten her day.

Her mother, of course, was thrilled. Spencer offered his arm to walk her to the car, opened her door, let her sit, and waited for her to gather her skirts before closing the door for her.

At the club, their table was in a prime corner, looking out at the room and, beyond it, the golf course. They were the center of a constant swarm of visitors. Spencer addressed each and every one by name. Polite but brief, he asked after their mothers and children. Then told visitors that he was there on a very special date, using her name. Bella.

"You haven't met Bella Schwartzman?" he would ask with surprise in his voice when they said they hadn't had the pleasure. And all of them said that. Her parents belonged to the country club, a concession to her mother. But her father never went and so she avoided it as well.

That night, she felt like some sort of celebrity. The way he reached out to touch her hand, she was the centerpiece of the entire room.

The envy of the women who passed their table was obvious. Spencer MacDonald was sought after. Wealthy, gorgeous, powerful. He was Greenville's prize bachelor. Already thirty, he was wise to the world. And he had chosen her—barely twenty-three and finishing her third year of medical school. Her life had been studies.

Naïve and much younger than her peers, she was a child.

She'd had few friends and no experience with men.

At the time, she did not consider any other option. There was no chance that those girls knew more about Spencer MacDonald than she. No chance that what she'd interpreted as envy was actually pity.

That night, when Spencer suggested a nightcap, she'd accepted. There had been champagne and wine at the club, but the real buzz came from him. Back in his home, he poured a second nightcap only minutes before he pinned her down and raped her on the expensive Persian rug in his den. The sex (her first) was painful and rough. She had struggled against him for its duration.

But as soon as he had finished, he cupped her face for a kiss as though the act had been loving and consensual. Then, he led her, bleeding and crying, to the bathroom and ran her a bath. He insisted she soak, lit a candle, brought her ice water and Advil which she did not take.

Afterward, he delivered her home, clean as new.

The last thing he said was that he would call her the next day.

Which he did not.

Nor did he call the next day after that. Or the one that followed. Not for an entire week, while her mother asked for every detail of the evening, trying to discern where her daughter might have gone wrong and lost the interest of Spencer MacDonald.

She told her mother nothing about the sexual encounter. When pressed, Schwartzman recounted some of the details of the evening. The club, of course. The names of a few of the people she'd seen there. The glass of champagne. The Cajun shrimp risotto. The lemon crème brûlée. After that, the story became purely a work of fiction. They'd driven down to the water, she'd told her mother. Walked in the moonlight.

There had been almost no moon that night.

Not that her mother cared.

Fiction was fine by her.

Each day, her mother scratched for some new detail, commented again on how strange it was that, after such a lovely evening, Spencer MacDonald hadn't called. Before leaving Schwartzman to suffer, her mother would offer some backhanded encouragement. "I'm sure he's busy with other things," she would say. "We can only hope he'll call. Keep your fingers crossed."

Which was not at all what Schwartzman wanted. Her plan was to write him off completely. She'd read plenty of cases in her studies about women losing their virginity by rape. More in the south than in the north or west. More in broken homes, more in impoverished areas.

It wasn't her fault.

All the books said that.

It was never the victim's fault. She was the victim. It wasn't her fault. She had repeated that mantra over and over.

Sometimes out loud.

The steady stream of her mother's feedback fed her own insecurity about what had happened, what she'd lost to him. Lost to him. That first night it was what he had stolen, robbed from her. But the brain was an amazing organ. Much more powerful in its subconscious than in anything she had trained it to do.

Over the course of one week, Spencer MacDonald was silently transformed from a monster into a modern prince. Without a single word from him. Of course, he had wanted to have sex with her on the first night. He wasn't about to waste his time courting someone blindly. He was a highly prized bachelor. If they weren't compatible, he would want to know immediately. And hadn't he bathed her afterward? Hadn't he let her know that it was okay, that she was safe?

The lovemaking—that was how she came to think of it after only a single week. The lovemaking had been painful, but that was to be expected with her first time. Like a bandage. Just rip it off. Surely, he would be gentler the next time. Now that he knew they were compatible. But they were, weren't they? Hadn't he seemed pleased afterward? She had certainly felt it when they'd kissed, hadn't she? Yes. She was sure she had. The rest, well, she couldn't have been expected to enjoy that, could she?

By the time ten days had passed, Schwartzman was convinced Spencer MacDonald was the man of her dreams.

When he called on the eleventh day, his voice was enough to make her cry with joy.

CHAPTER 33

JAMIE HAD ONLY seen Z for all of thirty minutes since the ball game. He'd arrived home while she was at General Hospital Sunday, doing rape kits on three women who were attacked Saturday night across the city. Three who were attacked and had reported it. She'd finally gotten home at almost midnight on Sunday, and Z was sound asleep. His phone was on his bedside table. She'd taken it into the bathroom and read the two text messages displayed on the front screen.

The first was from Amanda at 10:29 p.m. Amanda Steckler. *Nice game.*

The second came in at 11:09 from Jake. *Wat up?*

Sitting on the edge of the bathtub, Jamie had swiped the screen to access his messages. The words "Enter Passcode" had appeared at the top of the screen. Below were four dashes and the numbers 0-9. She tried his birth month and date. The screen flashed, returning her to the passcode screen. What else would he use as a passcode? His birth year? No. Their street address. No. Her birthday. Jamie crept back into Z's room, replacing the phone on his table and went to bed.

She had changed her alarm on Sunday morning to take Tony to the airport, then forgot to reset it, so when her alarm did go off on Monday morning, she was a full forty-five minutes behind schedule. Thankfully, Z had been able to catch a ride to school with Paul. But it had left them no opportunity to talk.

Worse, with Tony gone, her whole day was going to be cut short. She went to the lab first. The mitt was in a proper paper evidence bag, she'd turned it into the same tech who had been at Delman's apartment building that day. Nadia or something. God, she was terrible with names.

The tech slid the evidence slip in front of her and Jamie stared at all the things she needed to log. Where it was found. When it was found. Day and time. Jamie stared at the form. She didn't want to lie. She couldn't be entirely honest.

"Everything okay?" Roger asked.

"I've got a piece of evidence that may be related to Charlotte's attack."

Roger waited.

"It's a baseball mitt."

"Okay," Roger said.

"It isn't Z's mitt," she said, happy to be able to say that with total confidence. "But it does belong to one of his friends."

Roger looked at the form. "And you're not sure exactly when or where it was recovered." It was less a question than a statement.

"Something like that," she said.

"You know the name of the kid who it belongs to?"

Jamie nodded.

"Put his name there and record the date and time of collection as now. We'll see what we can find."

Jamie froze, conscious of how she reacted to this request. The desire to bask in the relief, or let tears fall, was almost overwhelming.

Roger took it for something else. He put his hand on her shoulder. "It'll be okay."

As she left the lab, her sense of relief waned quickly. Just because the mitt wasn't Z's didn't mean he wasn't involved. She'd done what she had to do.

No matter what Roger found out, she would stand by her son. She hated the idea that she had to wait to learn whether the blood on the mitt was Charlotte's and if there was anything to link it to Z. After all, the mitt had been in his baseball bag.

Only she knew that.

She had to keep her head down and work until Roger called.

The bad news rolled in. Jamie and Vich made Brody's loft their first stop of the day. No Brody. And his cell phone went straight to voicemail, so no way to track him by GPS either. The front desk manager told Vich and Jamie that Brody was out of town for the weekend, attending an art festival in Telluride. But the manager also thought he was due back last night.

On top of an AWOL Brody, the DMV database search they'd been running for white Buick Lucernes in San Francisco had some sort of program failure, so they had to start it again. The office told Jamie they'd hope to have something by Thursday. Three days away, Thursday was forever.

Jamie had identified one of the unlisted numbers on Z's phone as belonging to Gavin Borden, so Z was communicating with Charlotte. Two short calls, each under two minutes. She'd also learned that over the ten days prior to Charlotte's attack, Z was in touch with someone on a burner phone and a phone number that traced back to Michael Delman. The calls were all initiated from Michael Delman to Z and most were under a minute long.

One had lasted for almost fifteen minutes.

Long enough to make a plan to get Charlotte to come to Delman's house?

Of course, but that didn't make sense. What about the lingerie? Was she dressing up for Z? The calls between Z and the burner phone had gone both ways, including the day of the attack. Some as long as twenty minutes.

She tried to imagine that beautiful sixteen-year-old dressing up in that lingerie for her son. Couldn't. The image of her son in her mind was of a young boy. An undersized ten- and eleven-year-old. How could he have become a man that would make a woman want to wear underwear like she'd seen on Charlotte?

Z was suddenly two different people, and she didn't know either of them.

Tonight would be the night that she and Z talked. She had the phone records. It wasn't his mitt. Fine. But it was his phone. He'd made those calls. He'd spoken to Charlotte. He knew her. He knew something. Tony was gone, so there were no excuses. It was all closing in. She pictured the garbage pit from *Star Wars*.

Her life was only missing the monster lurking beneath to come up and grab her ankle and pull her down.

Or maybe the monster was there, too.

Jamie was at her desk, gathering case files and waiting for Vich who had run down to the lab on something related to Schwartzman's unwanted floral arrangement. The department was empty. It had been a rough weekend. The Saturday night rapes, plus a handful of other assault cases, and every inspector was juggling a new case as well as at least a dozen open ones. She and Vich had been split up on a few of the cases to handle the load.

This morning, they were meeting the private investigator who was linked to the tracking device. After that, Vich would head to talk to one of his victims and Jamie would figure out where to go on her own cases. The department door opened as she was dropping her notes into her computer bag.

"Jamie."

Hal stood in the doorway.

"No one here but me," she said.

Hal didn't move.

She barely glanced at him as she said, "What's up?"

As he moved toward her, she sensed something was wrong. She knew it as she focused on packing up her things. He held a folded paper in both hands, running his fingertips along the creases nervously.

"What is that?" she asked.

"It's a subpoena."

Jamie shrugged. "Okay. You want Vich and me to deliver it?"

The door swung open again and Hailey thundered in. "Hal, it's almost done."

Hailey froze as Jamie looked up.

"What's almost done?" Jamie asked.

"The subpoena, it's for DNA."

Jamie pressed her lips closed and took the sheet from Hal's fingers. A subpoena for DNA.

"Hal," Hailey said again.

"Jamie, we all want the same thing," Hal said. "This is the best way to clear him."

As though working on their own, her fingers reached up to unfold the document. But then she stopped. No. She would not read this. She did not need to read it. She already knew exactly what it was.

"Clear him of what?" Jamie could hardly believe the words had come out. She didn't want to know the answer.

"She doesn't know about the blood, Hal," Hailey said. "I told you that I was coming to talk to her."

"I can do this," Hal said.

"Stop it!" Jamie shouted. Her hand trembled as she shoved the paper down into her bag and pulled it closed.

The department door opened and the admin, Marcia, poked her head in. "You okay in here, Inspector?"

"Thanks, Marcia," Jamie said.

"We're fine, thanks," Hal said.

Marcia gave Hailey and Hal her evil eye, an expression that was at odds with the kind-old-lady look of her old-style big hair and full skirts. "Inspector?" Marcia asked.

"It's okay, Marcia," Jamie said. "Thanks."

Hailey took Hal's arm. "Can you let us talk?"

"I'm sorry if this is hard for you, Jamie," Hal said.

Jamie yanked the paper out of her bag. Saw Zephenaya's name. Jabbed her finger at the air in front of Hal. "Why should it be hard for me, Hal? You come in here, asking for a DNA sample from my son? Without explaining yourself? What do you know about hard? You have a son who attends a fancy prep school on the charity of a bunch of rich people? Then, that kid's deadbeat dad is linked to a rich girl's assault and, a few days later, he's murdered at the school where your son goes?" The rage simmered across her shoulders and back. "You don't know shit about that." Jamie turned to Hailey. "But you do. You know something about having a child you want to protect, don't you, Hailey?"

Hailey held Jamie's gaze, but Jamie could tell it wasn't easy. Hailey was proud, and she had worked hard to put her past behind her. It was low to bring it up again, but Jamie was desperate. Every tool, every weapon was drawn, and she would fight.

"The blood where Charlotte was attacked isn't Delman's," Hailey said. She took a step toward Jamie.

Jamie tensed. She knew what it meant.

The blood wasn't Delman's.

"It's not a match," Hailey clarified. "But the two are related."

"They have markers in common," Hal added.

Markers in common. Jamie set her palm on her desk, fighting off the desire to sink down onto the ground. Related. That didn't mean it was Z. Delman had a sister, Tanya. Maybe Tanya had a fight with Charlotte. Jamie leaned against the desk. Damn DNA.

"We need to be able to rule Z out," Hailey said. "He doesn't need to know that we're collecting DNA."

Jamie seized on another opportunity to fire at them. "You want me to lie to him? To my son?" She considered the evidence she'd concealed, the lies she'd told to Roger in the lab and to Tony and to Hailey and Hal, for that matter. All of it made her sick.

"I want you to know we're on your side," Hailey said slowly, motioning between her and Hal. "Both of us."

Hal said nothing.

"Leave," Jamie said.

Neither moved.

"Get the hell out of here!" she shouted again.

The department door burst open again, but it was Vich, not Marcia, who came through the door. He crossed to Jamie.

Jamie took her time folding the subpoena back up and putting it in her bag.

"We've got the last of Charlotte's friends in Interview One," Vich said. "And I pushed our meeting with Ronald Ikerd back to 10:30."

Jamie turned her back on Hailey and Hal. The air in the room shifted as they left.

Vich put his hand on her shoulder. "I heard about it in the lab. Tell me what you want me to do."

"Let's go do this interview. What's the girl's name?"

Vich glanced at his notebook. "Claire Delger."

"I'll meet you there in five."

*

Jamie took the five minutes to pace the bathroom. The bathroom was empty. She considered going in the handicapped stall but locked the main door instead. She needed the whole space to think it through. They wanted Z's DNA. Of course they did. She had known it would come to this eventually.

What were the laws about subpoenaing a minor's DNA? Surely the judge who signed it knew he was a minor. Worth a check.

She imagined a judge would sign it. After all, Z was a kid who would have DNA similar to Michael Delman's and Michael Delman had no other children. They had found DNA with familiar markers to Delman's. Familiar markers. That didn't necessarily mean his child. She tried to think of all the people who might have familiar markers. How close a relationship did that have to be? Schwartzman would probably know.

Michael had one sister Jamie knew about, Tanya. She had come to several of the adoption hearings when Michael Delman was in prison. She was an obese woman, her upper arms tattooed with the names of her husbands and boyfriends. There had been two or three on each arm.

What Jamie remembered most was how cold it had been those days—bitter outside and the heat in the old courthouse wimpy and ineffective against the chill. But there was Tanya in her sleeveless shirts, her brightly scripted boyfriends and husbands on either side. Delman didn't have a large family. The court always looked to family first in a case like Z's. His older sister, Shawna, had been his guardian before her death, but now there was no one else besides Tanya.

At the time, Tanya was recently divorced and on probation for her second drug charge—possession of methamphetamine with intent to sell. She had a handful of young children of her own and they, too, would become wards of the state if Tanya couldn't straighten herself out. Which is how Jamie had been awarded Z. Did they issue a subpoena for Tanya's blood, too?

*

Jamie arrived in the interview room angry. She was angry that this whole thing wasn't over. That she suspected Z was involved with Charlotte, that he'd been with her that night. That she didn't know what happened that night. That Z wasn't being honest. Irrationally, she was angry with Hailey and Hal and with everyone at City Academy for making her feel like Z was being judged and, mostly, angry at herself for not knowing how to deal with it. But as she settled down across from the young friend of Charlotte's, sitting politely at the table with her hands in her lap, it was impossible to stay angry. This was just another kid. She didn't control that she'd been born with money any more than Z controlled that he'd been born without it.

In her job, Jamie had interviewed her share of teenagers—boys and girls. As a group, they hadn't changed all that much in her seventeen years on the force. Fewer of them smelled like smoke, which was nice, and there was an increased predilection for piercings that were no longer limited to the ears. They had more tattoos than they used to.

But like the one sitting across from her, most

teenagers exuded discomfort in their own skin like a cloying floral scent and, like Z, they alternated radically between being apologetic and furious. They were also consistently bad liars.

Even the good ones were unsure and unpracticed in their craft and gave themselves away. Claire Delger was neither good nor practiced, so it only took about five minutes to suss out two important facts: first, she—along with her friends—knew that Charlotte had a boyfriend who didn't go to City Academy and, second, she had neither met him nor knew his name. Claire thought Charlotte's mystery man might have been older or much older. Other than that, she knew precious little.

"Assuming he wasn't a student at CA, when would Charlotte have met him?" Jamie asked.

"A couple people thought maybe it was the school service day we did about two months ago," Claire said. "We went to serve lunch and dinner at a homeless shelter."

"Do you remember Charlotte meeting anyone there?"

"No," Claire said. "Not at all, and we stood together the whole time. I was on green beans and she did potatoes. Mostly, we talked to the people who came through the line. They were so grateful to have us there." Claire stared at her lap, and Jamie thought of a term she'd heard recently about kids who grew up with a lot of money. The article had referred to these kids as suffering from "affluenza." Jamie assumed that was true of most of the kids at Z's school, but she had to admit, this one was pretty levelheaded.

"Can you think of anything else that might help us find out who Charlotte's boyfriend was?" Vich asked.

Claire checked over her shoulder as though to see if anyone was there, then began to play with the bottom of the ponytail that hung over her shoulder. Using both hands, she twirled the locks around her fingers.

"Claire?" Vich pressed.

"Lotti wouldn't talk about him. She said she had to keep him a secret because her parents would go batshit." Pink flushed across Claire's cheeks. "That was what she said."

"But she never said why they'd go batshit?" Jamie asked.

"But there was something..." Claire said.

They waited.

"She mentioned quitting her art lessons—she took from a guy—"

"Heath Brody," Jamie supplied.

"She said something happened, and she couldn't take lessons from him anymore."

"And that made you think he might be the boyfriend?" Jamie asked.

"I don't know. Maybe... There was something about how she talked about him. Like she was embarrassed."

"But you didn't ask her if it was Heath Brody?"

"No," Claire said. "We all wanted to know who he was; she seemed so into him."

"I thought girls shared their secrets," Jamie said. "Why didn't anyone push Charlotte to tell you who he was?"

"You know how it is. We're a close group. It's impossible to keep things a secret once more than one person knows. And our parents all know each other, so if her parents found out and pressured our parents, who pressured us, it would be bad," she explained. "I didn't want to be the person who knew if she didn't want people talking about it." She opened her mouth to say something else but stopped.

"What is it?" Jamie asked.

"It's nothing important."

"Please tell us," Vich urged.

"It's not about Charlotte," Claire said. "It's more about secrets."

"Okay…"

She shook her head, embarrassed. "There's this series we all watch—like on Netflix. It's called *Pretty Little Liars.*"

"Pretty Little Liars," Jamie repeated. "Okay."

"The theme song goes something like, 'If I show you then I know you won't tell what I said 'cause two can keep a secret if one of them is dead.' Charlotte knew that once someone knew who he was, there was no keeping it quiet."

Unless one of them was dead. God. That was one more thing that had changed about teenagers—the shows and books they watched and read were so much darker than they'd been when she was a kid.

Claire stared down at her hands.

"Did you know that Charlotte had a secret?"

She looked up, startled. "You mean, her boyfriend?"

"No," Jamie said. "Another secret."

Light-eyed and skinned, Claire's red face gave away the answer.

"What do you think she was hiding?"

"I don't know," Claire said. "She never told me. I swear."

"But if you were to guess," Jamie pressed.

"I can't guess."

"You have to," Jamie snapped. "She's in a coma. You have to help us so we can find out who did that to her."

Claire blinked her wide blue eyes but, to Jamie's surprise, she didn't cry. Instead, her resolve shifted. The redness in her cheeks faded and she raised her hands onto the table. "I think something happened with the art teacher."

"Heath Brody."

"He did something to her," she went on. "Lotti wouldn't say what it was, but I could tell she was uncomfortable. She felt ashamed. He made her feel really awful about something." Claire raised her chin as though angry.

"You think he assaulted her?" Vich asked.

"I don't know. She wouldn't say what happened. I told her she should talk to someone. The school counselor is too intense—she's like a Catholic nun or something—so no one would go to her. I pushed Charlotte to talk to her parents. Her dad's an attorney, so he could definitely do something."

"What happened then?"

"She totally freaked out when I mentioned talking to her parents. It was like she was sure they'd blame her. Especially her mother," Claire added. "That guy was, like, her mother's favorite artist ever."

Vich thanked Claire for her help and led her out to meet her mother. When he left, Jamie wrote HEATH BRODY in her notebook and underlined it twice. She pulled out her cell phone and called Patrol, requesting that they please send a car back out to Heath Brody's residence.

Everything circled back to Brody. She was relieved.

Brody was the key to all of this.

The DNA sample would clear Z.

Why, then, were there still so many unanswered questions?

CHAPTER 34

ROGER HAD LIFTED one hundred and thirteen partial prints from forty-three "clean" bar glasses. Most of those were probably the bartender's, but there was no way to be sure until they were run. He had also lifted ninety-some prints off the bar itself, plus seventeen off the front door handle, and another five off the door that led to the bar's small back patio and the alley. In addition, he collected eleven cigarette butts and four cans from the patio and alley. The process had taken almost five hours. His team had joined Sydney's to work a nasty office building fire scene, so Roger had worked alone. Just him and the funky smell of cheap beer. It was better than what he smelled at most of his crime scenes.

He spent much of that time cataloguing where each glass, fingerprint, and other evidence was found. Cataloguing was one of Roger's favorite parts. Before he married Kathy, he had a specific way of keeping the food in his pantry and the refrigerator. Not only meat in the meat drawer, but turkey on the right, salami on the left, pastrami perpendicular at the front of the drawer because it was his favorite. Mustard between the mayo and ketchup, pickles on the far side of the ketchup, and so on. Early in their marriage, Kathy had made an effort to keep things in his special order, but then they had Kimmy and all bets were off. Which was fine by Roger. He had plenty of places to exercise his OCD proclivities.

Like mapping out the location of the glasses on the bar shelf. If they were fortunate enough to match a fingerprint, they'd need to be able to prove to a jury that it was reasonable to believe that the glass might have been used by the suspect on the day in question based on the timing of visitors and washing. Often, it was the tracking of the evidence and not the work they did on the evidence itself that took most of their time.

The weekend techs had prepared the prints onto slides, and this morning, Naomi was scanning the images to run through the database. All in all, it was easily a seven- or eight-hour process. For evidence work, that wasn't bad, especially if they got a hit.

Roger was focused on the baseball mitt Jamie Vail had brought in.

According to Jamie, it wasn't Z's mitt.

He believed her. He hoped that whatever he found on it left no doubt about who had attacked Charlotte.

Roger prided himself on letting the evidence tell the story. He wished the rest of his team was as discreet. Already this morning, Chase had been talking about the fact that Hailey and Hal subpoenaed a DNA sample from Zephenaya. Vich had been in the lab when Chase was talking, and it had taken all the restraint Roger had not to call Chase out in front of everyone.

Instead, Roger waited until Vich had left and pulled

Chase aside to give him a special assignment. Chase was on his way to the scene of a potential stalker case where he would spend the remainder of the day, alone, combing the outside of the apartment building, its garage, and the dumpsters for signs of a break-in or evidence of how someone smuggled a huge bouquet of flowers into the building. Normally, Roger wouldn't have sacrificed the manpower to something like dumpster-diving, especially in a case where they had no punishable crime. Unless they could prove that the deliveryman broke in first before leaving the flowers in the hall.

What jury would send a guy to jail for confessing his love with a huge bouquet of flowers?

For whatever reason, Vich was taking this particular case personally, and Chase needed some time to realign his priorities. The convergence of the two was a perfect opportunity.

Roger had told Chase to come back fifteen minutes before the end of his shift or when he found something. And not a minute before.

Earlier in his career, Roger had done his share of grunge evidence collection. His own mentor, a strangely angular man named Keith Hobart, had taught him some valuable lessons by making Roger spend time in some less than ideal conditions. Dumpsters or people's trash or—the worst—combing through a getaway car after four burglars had died in a wreck. The inside—where he was supposed to locate evidence that would identify the crew's henchman—was a mess of blood and tissue. He'd spent almost five hours searching for a single hair or print. In the end, they'd had to tie the leader to the crime without any physical evidence. Thankfully, the police's forensic accountants had been more successful than Roger.

Roger turned to his work. Using an ethyl alcohol solution to moisten the stains on the mitt, Roger confirmed that what had stained the mitt was blood. He knew it was. Enough years on the job and he could taste the coppery scent of blood from a hundred yards, but he never assumed. Using sterile swabs, he took eight separate blood samples from the mitt. He ran the first four for blood type, the other four would go for DNA testing. Within minutes he confirmed that all four samples matched Charlotte's blood type.

Next, he would have to cut apart the mitt to test it for other DNA. He wasn't a ball player himself, but he could tell the mitt was well worn. That took a lot of energy. It was a shame to cut it apart. Roger set the thought aside and, opening a medical pack with a clean scalpel, he began to saw it apart at the stitching. He'd only made the first four-inch incision when an incoming e-mail made a dinging sound on his laptop.

He pulled off his gloves and went to his desk. He normally didn't let himself stop a task for e-mail, but something about pulling apart that mitt was extremely unappealing. Most of the evidence that came across the lab was adult-oriented. Guns or clothing or fingerprints. They were usually connected to an adult, to adult crimes. Even when evidence was clothing from a child, he could somehow distance the material from the child. The mitt was harder. Knowing it might belong to Jamie's son was awful.

The message in his inbox was from City View

Condominiums. The building where the flowers had been delivered. It included a zipped file. Roger watched the file run through the department's antivirus software. The attached e-mail was a list of video files that covered the four hours before and one hour after the package was delivered. Five hours wasn't much. The guy could have snuck in the building much sooner than that, but certainly this was a start.

Each of the eleven files was footage taken from a different security camera view. The front, rear, and garage level of the building, as well as the camera on the floor where the package was delivered.

The process would take a few minutes, but Roger waited, using the time to clean out his inbox which had accumulated forty new messages since he'd checked it last night.

The lab phone rang. "Crime Lab. Roger here."

"Roger, it's Chase."

Roger frowned. "You found something already?"

"I think so," Chase said, a little breathless.

"Where are you?"

"I'm standing in the building's dumpster."

Roger suppressed a smile.

"I found a black gym bag. It's empty other than a few leaves and two petals."

"What color?"

"Yellow," he said. "Two different kinds of flowers, and there is a little orangish-red residue that looks like that stuff inside those big flowers."

"Lilies," Roger said. "It's pollen that comes off the stamen."

"What?" Chase yelled over the noise of a truck. "Ah, shit. The garbage guys are here. Should I tell them to come back?"

"No," Roger said. He didn't have an actual crime scene so there was no real way to hold off the garbage collectors. "Check around where the bag was found, then come back in."

"Okay," Chase shouted. He'd actually gotten in the dumpster. Roger had assumed he'd half-ass the job and was pleasantly surprised.

On his desktop were the eleven files. Curious, Roger double-clicked on the last video file, the one that covered the hallway floor where the flowers had been left. He set it to play. The video captured the hallway from the elevator doors to the stairwell at the end of the corridor. There were three doors on either side of the hall. He watched nothing happen for a minute or so, then held down the fast-forward button.

For more than two hours of film time, nothing happened. Then, the elevator doors opened. Roger slowed the film to watch a man in his late thirties or early forties walk off the elevator and disappear into one of the apartments. Maybe forty minutes later, a woman exited the elevator and entered the same unit. The two emerged a short time later, together, and passed an older woman with a small dog on a leash who entered a different apartment.

A short while later, another woman came off the elevator. Her body language gave her away. She was their victim. It was in the way she looked over her shoulder as she stepped off the elevator, though there was nothing but wall there. The dipped slope of her shoulders. The forced rise of her chin as she fought some internal battle. She was afraid.

He recognized her. Stopping at her door, Annabelle Schwartzman glanced up at the camera, then let herself into her apartment. The time stamp on the video read 7:19 p.m. on Saturday night. Less than a half-hour later, the elevator door slid open again. A figure dressed completely in black walked slowly down the hallway. The bouquet of yellow flowers was held slightly above eye level, blocking any view of his—or her—face. In a black hoodie and black baseball cap, not a single part of the face was visible. Hands were covered in thick leather gloves, like the kind that were fleece lined for snow.

This time, the elevator door didn't close. It remained open while the figure walked slowly down the hall and set the flowers by Schwartzman's door.

A hand reached out and rang her bell and then, head down, the figure returned to the elevator, pushed a button, and the doors slid closed again.

Roger rewound the film and watched it again. Not a sliver of face. He rewound the film a third time, all the way to Schwartzman and studied how high her head hit on the door. Roger watched the deliveryman. He wasn't that much taller than Schwartzman. A little broader, a little larger. Schwartzman was tall so Roger put this guy at about five feet ten and maybe one hundred sixty pounds. Could be a woman. He let the video play on.

Nothing happened for about fifteen minutes of film. Then, Schwartzman's door opened. First, only several inches and then, fifteen seconds later, all the way. When she spotted the yellow flowers, she pressed her hand to her chest. She scanned the hallway quickly and pulled herself back into the apartment. Roger pressed the fast-forward option in slow bursts, studying the screen for motion.

The elevator opened again. A man walked down the hall. He was too big to be the deliveryman. Over six feet, close to two hundred pounds. He gave the flowers a long look, then let himself into the apartment past Schwartzman's. Next, a man in a uniform arrived at Schwartzman's door. He knocked, knocked again, and Schwartzman stepped out, pointed to the flowers, motioned to his hands, and returned into the apartment. She wanted him to take the flowers. Wear gloves.

Another gentleman appeared at her door in a suit along with a second man in a uniform. More building staff, Roger assumed. Schwartzman stepped into the hall to talk to them before retreating into her home again. Just before the film ended, Roger watched Vich arrive. Schwartzman hesitated slightly, then opened the apartment door to let him pass.

Roger saved the videos onto the lab's shared hard drive and crossed to David Ting's desk. "You got time to work on something else?"

Ting glanced up. "Sure. I'm trying to repair the jpg file we pulled off that phone."

One of Saturday night's rape victims. If they could repair the file, they might have an image of the young woman's attacker. Roger couldn't pull Ting off that, even for Schwartzman. "You almost done?"

Ting nodded. "Another ten minutes or so before I can run the repair program. Might take the program a while though."

"That's okay," Roger said. "I want you to look at something else while it's running."

"What've you got?"

"I need to try to ID a guy from some video that came in."

"Sure. I'll let you know as soon as I'm done."

The mitt lay beside the scalpel and gloves he'd set aside.

Instead of returning to his work, he dialed Chase's cell phone. "You close?"

"Coming down the stairs now."

"Good." Roger hung up the phone and waited for Chase. He'd work on the bag first, then force himself to get back to that damn mitt.

CHAPTER 35

RONALD IKERD PRIVATE Investigations was not what Jamie expected. The office was in a small, sunny, '40s style bungalow home in Cow Hollow, an area mostly filled with young urban professionals of a much higher ilk than the seedy PI office she'd expected. The stucco front was beige, the front door and windowsills black. The paint job was immaculate and recent. The small yard was rimmed with a manicured hedge; along the front of the house was a line of droopy, pink peonies about to bloom.

Jamie rang the bell. She and Vich were greeted by a woman who introduced herself as Mrs. Ikerd. "Please, come in. They are waiting for you in the den."

The entrance was old hardwood, across the floors and also up the walls in a rich wood paneling, capped with an attractive chair railing. The ceiling, too, was an inlaid wood design that appeared original, or at least restored to original. While the downstairs had the feel of an office, Jamie glanced up the stairs and was certain that this was also where the Ikerds lived.

"You said 'they' are waiting for us?" Vich asked.

Mrs. Ikerd offered no explanation as she led them

down a short hallway. Along the walls were images of the city that dated back to the early 20th century. Mrs. Ikerd paused at a smoky glass window and gave three quick raps.

"Come in, please," a man's voice said.

She pushed the door open and stepped inside, moving aside for Jamie and Vich.

"Please join us," said a gentleman seated behind a large mahogany desk. His mustache was waxed and curled at the ends, like a character from the old westerns her father sometimes left on TV while he was making dinner or cleaning up. While the man's hair was salt and pepper, the mustache was solidly brunette, making it the center of focus of his whole head. The room smelled so faintly of cigar smoke, it might have been bathed in it a decade or so ago. There were no ashtrays visible, and the windows were spotless with no evidence of recent smoke.

As Jamie stepped into the room, she looked at the second man. Easily late sixties, he was trim and tall, dressed in a light gray three-piece suit. A chain ran from the center button of his vest to his pocket where Jamie imagined he carried an old gold pocket watch.

Beneath a pair of small round spectacles, the high arch of his brow and the almond-shaped eyes were familiar. Unlike his daughter's though, his eyes were gray and smoky with cataracts. Sitting in the room with the private investigator was Reginald Bishop, Sondra's father.

"Mr. Bishop," Jamie said. "I'm Inspector Jamie Vail." She stepped forward to shake his hand. "And this is my partner—"

Bishop nodded. "Alexander Kovalevich." He made no move to shake. "I hope I pronounced that correctly."

"You did," Vich told him before raising an eyebrow at Jamie.

"Please join us, Inspectors," Ikerd said, motioning to the empty seats before addressing his wife. "Marjorie, would you please bring us some tea?"

"Of course, Ronald. I've got some black for you if you'd like it, Reginald."

"You're a dear, Marjorie," Bishop told her.

Marjorie excused herself, closing the door behind her, while Vich and Jamie sat in the two empty chairs across from Ikerd's desk. Jamie removed her notebook and flipped it open to the first free page. "I assume by your presence that you were the one who placed a tracking device on your daughter's car."

Saying nothing, Bishop drew the gold watch from his pocket by the chain and studied the face as though it would take him some minutes to ascertain the time.

"Mr. Bishop," Jamie pressed.

"We have invited you here so that we might address your concerns," Ikerd said. The mustache bobbed as his upper lip moved. "We shall do that as long as it can be done without disrupting my client's efforts to protect his family."

The protection of his family was illegal, Jamie thought, but didn't say. Instead, she exchanged a quick look with Vich. She would have liked to have asked him if he, too, felt as though they'd stepped into some 1950s noir film. Instead, she ignored Ikerd's warning and pressed on. "When did you put the tracking device on the Mercedes?" she asked.

"The device was installed when the car was purchased," Ikerd said.

"So, Sondra knew that the car was being tracked?" Jamie asked the question to Ikerd, but kept a watch on Bishop. No reaction from him as he focused on his watch.

"Mr. Bishop purchased the car," Ikerd said, which offered no actual answer.

"So, Sondra didn't know that her car was being tracked?" Jamie asked again, waiting for clarification.

"What are you really after, Inspector?" Ikerd asked. "You want to know why Mr. Bishop tracks the expensive cars he purchases, or who attacked Charlotte?"

"We believe one may lead to the other."

"That's hogwash," Bishop said, drawing out the words as he slid the gold watch back into the small pocket of his vest. Moving slowly, he pressed his hands into his knees and leaned forward so that the buttons of his vest strained against the bulk of his chest. "I'd like to make a request that we kindly cut the crap. Please?"

"Happy to," Jamie said. "You first, Mr. Bishop."

Bishop raised an eyebrow like he found her slightly amusing.

"Inspector, you requested an audience with me, and I have granted that," Ikerd said, and there was a small sense of relief when he reached up and stretched out one end of his mustache into a long thin strip which reached almost to the edge of his jaw. "Neither Mr. Bishop nor I are under any obligation to speak to you, and we certainly will not tolerate your insults."

Jamie couldn't think of what she'd said that would have insulted either of them. She opened her mouth when Vich cut in.

"Mr. Ikerd, Mr. Bishop," he began, and Jamie forced herself to sit back in her chair. Her instinct was to tear them to shreds, but Ikerd was right. She had nothing to hold them on, no ammunition to load that could pressure them to answer any of her questions. In fact, she was surprised—suspiciously so—that Bishop was here at all. What incentive did he possibly have to talk to them? Unless he knew something about Charlotte's attack that he wanted them to know... or make sure they didn't find out.

"I assume we are all here for the same purpose," Vich continued. "The tracking device is of little interest to the police unless it is somehow involved in the how or why of Charlotte's brutal attack." Vich folded his hands into his lap. Jamie saw that he was infinitely more suited to this old boys' game than she. "From our perspective, we can only assume the device is related because it is both unusual and not yet accounted for by the Borden household."

Jamie watched the silent exchange between Ikerd and Bishop. Damn, Vich was good.

"I agree, Inspector Kovalevich," Bishop said.

"Please," Vich said. "Call me Alex."

"Alex," Bishop agreed. "Let me explain the origin of the tracking device."

Ikerd cleared his throat, but Bishop waved him off.

"Ronald worries for me," Bishop explained. "But I am confident that I can answer this question and assuage any of your concerns about my family's involvement in my granddaughter's attack."

Ikerd made another cough-like noise, but Bishop was silent.

"What I will tell you is not police business. It is merely family laundry as they say," Bishop began. "But I am confident that by knowing it, you can set aside this piece of trivia and get back to finding my granddaughter's attacker."

Neither Vich nor Jamie moved. She was terrified that Mrs. Ikerd would enter with tea and interrupt Bishop's confession. Despite Ikerd's warning, it felt like a ruse to throw them off Bishop's real motivation for tracking Sondra's activities.

If that was the case, Bishop was selling it hook, line, and sinker.

"Sondra is a bright woman," Bishop said. "Like her mother that way, God rest her soul. Sondra is an only child, and I blame myself for some of my daughter's shortcomings. Her mother wanted more children, siblings for Sondra, but it never worked out. The result was that Sondra got more of her way than was good for a child. And, of course, children of her generation were offered more freedom to choose their own path. So, one must account for the times as well."

Jamie resisted the temptation to turn to Vich to see if he had any idea what the hell Bishop was talking about.

"Sondra found quite a passion for art," he continued, enunciating the word as though it were a synonym for dirt. "Artists, the lifestyle…" He removed the small horn-rimmed spectacles from his nose, then, drawing a white linen handkerchief from one pocket, scrubbed them clean. Was this guy for real? "After her mother's death, I let the behavior go, attributing it to some form of grief and acting out. Perhaps for too long…" He replaced the glasses on his face and tucked the handkerchief back into his pocket. "Eventually, she was introduced to Gavin and she settled down."

"Heath Brody was not the first?" Jamie said.

Bishop was quick to look at her, surprised that she knew.

"Yes," he said after a short pause. "Brody."

"How long have they been together?" Vich asked.

"One and a half?" He considered Ikerd. "Has it been two years?"

Ronald Ikerd pressed his lips into a thin, straight line that suggested he didn't think any of this was a good idea.

Bishop clicked his tongue. "That's actually relatively long for Sondra. She must be slowing down in her old age." He chuckled thinly to himself.

So, Heath Brody wasn't Sondra's first lover.

"So, you know about your daughter's… dalliances."

Both men nodded their approval at Vich's choice of words.

"But you didn't try to stop her?" Vich asked.

Bishop shook his head. For the first time, he seemed grim. "There was no stopping Sondra when she had her mind set on something. I hired Ronald to make certain that Sondra's—" He waved a hand at Vich. "—dalliances didn't bite the whole family in the… Well, you know what I mean to say."

Jamie sat back up in her chair. "If you know about Sondra's affairs, surely Gavin knows, too."

"No. Mr. Borden is not aware of his wife's proclivities." Ikerd made it sound like a perversion.

"How can you be sure?"

Ikerd glanced at Bishop. The two shared some wordless conversation before Bishop said, "In the way Ronald keeps track of Sondra, he does the same of Gavin. By my request, of course."

"So, you track Mr. Borden's car."

"We do," Ikerd said.

"That's not enough to prove Gavin's whereabouts. If he suspected you were tracking him, he could've followed his wife a million different ways..." Jamie stopped.

"I am a professional, Inspector," Ikerd said.

"With all due respect, gentlemen, in this investigation, you're not the professionals," Vich said. His tone was clear, even.

Bishop waved his hand toward Vich. Ikerd took this as permission to speak. "We also track Mr. Borden via his phone and—"

"So—" Bishop interrupted. "We are confident that he's not aware of my daughter's indiscretions."

"We can confirm that Sondra was with Heath Brody at the time of Charlotte's attack," the investigator said. "I know you don't consider Sondra a suspect, but I also understand it is police policy to confirm all alibis. I would be more than happy to provide an affidavit of Mrs. Borden's alibi should you need one."

"You?"

Ikerd twisted his mustache. "I was the one who

contacted Mrs. Borden at Mr. Brody's home when I got word that Charlotte had been brought to the hospital."

Sondra had been in her lover's arms when her daughter was being attacked.

"I don't believe that will be necessary," Vich said. "Confirming Mrs. Borden's alibi, I mean."

"No," Jamie agreed. She couldn't imagine a situation where Sondra had thrown her daughter down the stairs. Either Borden for that matter.

"Sondra's affairs, while unfortunate...," Bishop began carefully, "...do not seem relevant to my granddaughter's attack."

When neither Vich nor Jamie disagreed, Bishop went on. "It would be best for the family—certainly during this trying time—if Gavin were not to find out about the relationship my daughter had with the artist."

"I wasn't under the impression that it was over," Jamie said.

"Oh, it is," Bishop said. "I can assure you of that."

"If you were tracking Sondra and Gavin," Jamie began. "How about—"

"I'm afraid not," Bishop said before she could finish. "To me, Charlotte is still a sweet, young child. I can't picture her a day past nine." He sighed. "I suppose that makes me an old man. I ought to have been tracking her, too."

"Who else were you tracking?"

Mr. Bishop said nothing.

"I can confirm the location of Mr. Borden at that same time, if that is useful," Ikerd said carefully. "Would you like to see?"

"Sure," Vich said.

Ikerd sat up and began to peck away at an ancient-looking computer. "Reggie and I have been through this carefully."

"I can assure you Gavin was in his office the entire afternoon," Bishop echoed.

Ikerd continued to peck before hitting a button with a particularly loud jab. "Here we go." He waved to the monitor. "It doesn't do any of that fancy swiveling, I'm afraid, so you'll have to come around."

Jamie and Vich circled behind Ikerd's desk. On the computer screen was a map overlaid with a red blur. Ikerd clicked on the red and the image zoomed in so that the red line crisscrossed the screen. Only one rectangle remained white.

"The red line is a device on Gavin's phone."

Vich pointed to the void area. "What is that?"

"Gavin's desk."

Jamie stared at the web-like lines of Gavin's movements. It appeared that there were two separate red lines, moving exactly side by side. "Are there two devices?"

"Just the way the program works," Ikerd said.

"It appears that he only covers this one space. What are we looking at?" Vich asked.

"I've zoomed it in so that we're only seeing his individual office." He pointed to the sidebar which showed the date and the time range between 17:27 and 19:52.

"You're saying Gavin didn't leave his office from 5:30 to almost 8:00, three and a half hours, on the day his daughter was attacked?" Jamie asked.

"Right," Ikerd confirmed. "I started the time stamp

after he returned from a business lunch, before the conference call started." He clicked on the time clock and expanded the range by ten minutes on either side. When he hit enter, the screen zoomed out and the red line extended to two additional locations, one within the office which might have been the bathroom and the other Jamie assumed was his parking place in the lot.

"Is it possible that he left his phone on his desk and left the office?" Vich asked.

"I get a signal every ninety seconds," Ikerd explained. "Any four consecutive periods without movement show as yellow." Ikerd expanded the time range by an hour on the front end; a yellow blur appeared, probably when Gavin had been sitting at a lunch table.

"So, you're saying he's in his office, pacing around, for almost three hours?"

"We had a partner call," Bishop said. "We have offices in Chicago and New York as well as the San Francisco office. In addition, we're opening one in Atlanta. Gavin, myself, and my nephew, Henry, were on a call with our attorneys, our chief accountant, and two people from the Atlanta office."

"That entire time?"

"Yes," Bishop confirmed. "The call began at 5:30 and ended when we got the news on Charlotte."

"Was the call recorded?" Jamie asked.

Bishop frowned. "It was, but only so that we can have a transcript made for our records."

Jamie rubbed her face, then looked back up at the screen. "But wouldn't he be on speakerphone or something? It's like he's actually carrying the phone around the office. Who does that for three hours?"

"Gavin does."

"It's true," Ikerd said. "Mr. Borden uses a headset that plugs into the phone. So, the phone is in his shirt pocket while he talks but the phone is on him."

So, the Bordens didn't throw Charlotte down the stairs. She'd probably known that already. But Heath Brody had been her best bet. She wasn't sure what she expected. Once they'd ruled out Brody, this whole meeting had been a waste of time. They didn't have a single lead. Her thoughts went to Z. Did he know something that could help them? She pushed the thought away and worked to pull Vich from his questions about how the tracking system worked.

"This thing is amazing. If I had a daughter, I'd probably track her, too," Vich said.

Ikerd agreed and clicked on a few more buttons. The time narrowed to fifteen minutes and a dozen red lines crossed the screen. "The police could use something like this," Vich said. "Track all the criminals in the city."

"I'll bet," Ikerd said.

Jamie turned to Bishop. "You knew what your daughter was up to. But why would you track Gavin, unless you thought he was guilty of something?"

Bishop said nothing.

Vich snapped a photo of the screen. "I'm serious. This would actually be great for our undercover guys."

"Mr. Bishop?" Jamie pressed.

"In my experience, Inspector," Bishop began, "everyone is guilty until proven innocent."

"So, who else do you track?"

Bishop gave her a wry smile.

Vich looked up from the computer.

"Mr. Bishop, we all know it's illegal to track someone without their knowledge," she said.

"But we're more interested in finding out who hurt Charlotte," Vich added. "Is it possible that you are tracking someone else who might know something?"

Bishop might be able to confirm that Tiffany Greene was at that bar with Michael Delman the day he died, but getting that information meant tipping her hand. She wasn't willing to do that.

"Just my children, I'm afraid," Bishop said.

Ikerd rose from his desk. "If there is anything else," he said, "please feel free to contact me directly."

The door opened.

"Ah, thank you, Marjorie," Ikerd said to his wife in the doorway.

"I'll be happy to show you out," Mrs. Ikerd said with a polite smile.

Vich and Jamie followed her down the hall. As Jamie stepped into the bright sunshine, she realized that Mrs. Ikerd never brought the tea. Jamie checked her watch. They had been in Ikerd's office for exactly fifteen minutes.

Tea wasn't tea. Tea was code for Marjorie to come to the door after fifteen minutes. Jamie had to give them credit for cleverness.

Did any of Ikerd's visitors ask about the tea?

CHAPTER 36

"YOU KNOW HE'S probably tracking that entire office," Vich said on the drive back to the station.

Jamie was fighting off a strange sense that she was missing something obvious, something right in front of her. Every step forward on the case dragged her a step back from finding out who was responsible for Charlotte's attack. Worse, it was like they'd been running down the wrong path entirely.

"Did you see anything on Ikerd's computer?" Jamie asked.

"No," Vich said. "He only had Gavin's tracking up on the screen. I checked the sidebars, but nothing showed. I'm sure he's got others being tracked, but I couldn't tell who." He handed Jamie his phone. "I did get a picture of it. Thought I'd forward it to Roger."

Jamie studied the red web. "Not sure what Roger can do without the actual software program."

"We could try to get a warrant." Vich shook his head as he finished the sentence. "Never mind."

"There has to be something we're missing."

"The attack, you mean?"

Jamie nodded.

"Maybe it was random," Vich said. "We've been entirely focused on a few people, but maybe Charlotte was pulled down the stairs by some drugged-up addict. Michael Delman happened upon her and brought her to the hospital. Or maybe Delman knew the person who did it and decided to do something right for a change."

Jamie wanted badly to believe that Michael Delman had been acting in good faith. "More likely, it was Delman himself."

"Maybc it was."

"Then, who killed Michael Delman?" she asked.

"That's where we ought to be looking at Bishop and the Bordens," Vich said. "You should tell Hailey about that tracking deal. They could check where the Bordens were when Delman was shot."

Hailey. Jamie did not want to think about Hailey Wyatt. She had until 3:00 to respond to the subpoena for Z's DNA. The smartest course would be to bring Z into the station after baseball practice. Get it over with.

"Sorry," Vich said.

"Not your fault."

"There's no way Z's involved," Vich said, and Jamie told herself that there wasn't the slightest doubt in his statement.

The question of Z's involvement rested in the air. As it would until she could scare him into talking to her. Or until some piece of evidence either condemned or exonerated him.

She'd read how teenagers were dangerous to themselves and sometimes to others. Their brains aren't fully developed until they're twenty-five. Inhibitions are lowered. Less control over themselves and their reactions.

Like Z slamming the door? Was that a moment of emotional overload?

Teenagers also lie more easily—even when presented with the risks and the possible repercussions.

Even then, they fail to really understand the consequences of their actions.

Hailey and Hal were right. Obtaining Z's DNA was necessary. It might not prove whether he was there, but it would certainly help answer the question of whether or not he'd had a hand in the actual assault. A question she had refused to face head-on because she'd been so sure she could get him to tell her. To confess to whatever it was he was hiding. But she couldn't.

On the sidewalk, an old woman wheeled a shopping cart, her back a strange hump that reached higher than her head. A professional woman in a dress and heels moved quickly around the old woman without so much as a glance. As though the older woman was a lesser creature, a nonhuman. How poorly humans treated each other. Not protecting those who needed protecting and instead working tirelessly to shield those who could not be harmed.

She considered the defense attorneys she'd come into contact with in her years on the force. Plenty of them had gotten their clients off. Even guilty ones. The thought was followed by a sharp pang in the mother place.

"Something will break," Vich said.

Jamie was thankful when he pulled the department car into the parking space beside hers and she could get out. She'd gotten used to working with Vich, but right now some alone time would be good. Plus, they had to split up; there were too many cases for them to focus on Charlotte alone.

With the pressure from the mayor's office, Captain Jules had instructed them to shift their focus to some of the new cases. Jamie wished she could do that. No matter how she tried, Jamie wasn't able to get her mind off Charlotte. Because taking her mind off Charlotte meant taking her mind off Z, and any mother knew that was impossible.

Once alone, Jamie called Abigail Canterbury. Again. This was the third message she'd left so far. Jamie checked in on two of her victims—one at the young woman's apartment and one who was staying at her mother's home—and made some follow-up calls to set up interviews with two witnesses.

At a little past 2:00, she drove to Canterbury's home address. The building was along a block of converted warehouses, south of Market Street. The woman who answered the door was petite, dressed in a black skirt and white button-down shirt. She wore simple black flats and her hair pulled back. She didn't look a day over twenty-six.

"I'm looking for Abigail Canterbury."

"I'm Abigail."

Jamie hesitated. She'd assumed the woman was Canterbury's help. "I'm Inspector Vail."

Canterbury said nothing.

"I have been trying to reach you to discuss a cleaning

person who was at the residence of Gavin and Sondra Borden," Jamie explained.

Still nothing.

Jamie checked the street address above the doorway. "You are Abigail Canterbury?"

Finally, Canterbury said, "I'm sorry. My father had a stroke." She touched the place on her wrist where a watch might sit. "I haven't checked my messages..."

Jamie was taken aback. "I apologize for bothering you, but I'm trying to locate a woman who did some cleaning at the Bordens' house recently."

"I've had a few people there," Abigail said. "Mrs. Borden hasn't found anyone she particularly likes, so we've been sending new staff every week or so."

"This woman has a turtle tattoo right here." Jamie touched behind her own ear.

"Bianca."

Bianca. A name. "Do you have a number for Bianca?"

"Sure." Canterbury waved to Jamie to follow her as she walked into the apartment. Beyond a short entryway, the unit opened up. High ceilings, an open steel staircase that led to an upper loft; it looked like something out of Architectural Digest. Between this place, the Bordens', and Heath Brody's place, Jamie was beginning to feel self-conscious about her little split-level house with the original knobby carpet. She was obviously in the wrong business. This place screamed trust fund baby. That, Jamie decided, was the business to be in.

Abigail Canterbury turned from her desk and handed Jamie a piece of paper with a phone number.

Jamie handed it back. "Will you call? You might have better luck getting her to tell you what she overheard."

Abigail hesitated only a fraction of a second before nodding. "Yes. Of course." Abigail lifted a cordless phone off her desk and dialed the number. "What should I ask her?"

"We believe she overheard a girl named Charlotte arguing with someone about art lessons. I need to know who that person was."

Abigail repeated the message.

"She's helping me out," Jamie confirmed. "She's not in any trouble."

After ten or fifteen seconds, Abigail put her palm over the receiver again. "She didn't know his name. She says he is tall, with dark hair—not Hispanic. With a prominent nose."

Bianca said something else and Abigail said, "She thinks his name is Brian."

"Brandon?" Jamie asked.

"She's not sure," Abigail said.

Shambliss seemed like the kind of guy whose Facebook profile picture would be of himself. "Can we send a picture of him to her phone? So, she can confirm it's the right person?"

"Yes," Abigail confirmed. "Send her a picture. She'll call us right back."

On Facebook, Jamie found four hits on the name Brandon Shambliss. Only one in California. She zoomed in on his page. Bingo. She enlarged his face and took a screen shot of the image. He looked better on Facebook than he did in person. No surprise there. She texted the image to Bianca's number.

She'd start a full check on Shambliss but not until she was certain.

A minute passed. Finally, after what felt like an hour, Canterbury's phone rang. "Yes, Bianca says that's the man who fought with Charlotte about the art lessons."

Jamie folded Bianca's number and tucked it into her back pocket. "Tell her thank you," Jamie said, starting for the door. "And you, too." She put her hand on the door. "I hope your father gets better."

Jamie let herself out, closing the door firmly behind her. What a stupid thing to say. Did people get better from strokes?

She dialed the lab.

"Crime Lab. Roger."

"It's Jamie."

"Hi. I'm glad you called." Jamie's stomach lurched. Had he already processed the mitt?

"I've got Ting working on the video surveillance footage from the flower delivery. And we—"

She didn't want to think about Z. "Roger," she interrupted. "Sorry. I need a rush on a full background and financial check on Brandon Shambliss. I don't know any of the forensic accounting guys, but—"

"It's in process."

"What? What's in process?"

"I started a full background check on Brandon Shambliss about thirty minutes ago."

Jamie glanced at the clock. "How did you know?"

"We matched his prints to a cigarette found behind

the bar where Michael Delman was drugged before his murder."

"Is there a warrant out?"

"Hal is working on one now. I called him about ten minutes ago. Actually, you were next on my list."

Jamie held her breath. Not the mitt, please not the mitt.

"I found something in the initial run on Brandon Shambliss," he said.

"You did? What?"

"In November 2005, Shambliss moved into an apartment building on Fell Street. Apartment 312."

"And that means something?"

"It jogged something in my memory. Kathy used to live near that building. It was kind of a dump."

Jamie had no idea where he was going with this. "Roger?"

"Right," he said quickly. "Well, guess who lived in apartment 315 at the same time?"

"No idea."

"Heath Brody," Roger said. "They lived down the hall from each other for almost two years."

Jamie opened her notebook and started writing. "When was Shambliss charged with assault?"

"October 2005. So, he moved in right after the assault. Brody had been living there about seven months. They moved out about four months apart. Shambliss first, then Brody."

"Roger, you're brilliant."

She was afraid what the homicide inspector might tell her, but Jamie needed to talk to Hailey Wyatt.

CHAPTER 37

HE LISTENED AT the door to Brandon Shambliss's apartment. Eyes down, he noticed his shoes were in need of a polish.

It was Monday, and Shambliss's Monday schedule included coming straight home. Mondays were pretty well set in stone—most of his nights were. An odd thing about Shambliss. He came across as someone who was used to accommodating himself to whomever he deemed the most powerful person. But he didn't often adjust his evening schedules.

Sunday night would have been preferable, but that was the Shambliss family night. Every Sunday afternoon, Brandon Shambliss went back to the East Bay to see his mother, stepfather, sisters, and their kids. He talked about barbecues and lawn games like croquet or cornhole. Cornhole—that was actually the name of a game. This was some big family gathering he raved about. Not married, no family of his own, but Shambliss went home to his mother on Sundays and pretended like it was something to be proud of.

Maybe he was bitter about the joy Shambliss found

in that pseudo family. After all, he certainly didn't have the big happy family scene. Never had. He had promised himself he'd never be as miserable as he was as a kid. But here he was. More miserable. And maybe Brandon Shambliss was happy with a shitty fake family. That made him want to hurt Brandon Shambliss. Had made him feel that way from day one, really. Now, he got to actualize the dream. And he could blame Shambliss. Things would have been fine if he hadn't involved Tiffany Greene. Why she had fallen for Shambliss was a mystery. She would do anything for him. But that wouldn't last. It never did. Before long, Tiffany would recognize the situation and she would give up Shambliss to the police. If Tiffany gave up Shambliss, he had zero doubt that Shambliss would give him up. No. Shambliss should have kept Tiffany out of it. Why should he suffer for Shambliss's stupidity?

Sure that Shambliss wasn't home, he let himself into the apartment with the key he'd stolen and looked around. The place was pathetic. Filled with uninspired furniture. The kind of stuff that was all made out of North Carolina, places like Ethan Allen. It belonged in some beach house rental. All light woods and cheap finishes. The walls were white, of course, and mostly bare. A poster of an Ansel Adams photograph hung over a pastel striped couch. Shambliss had never had any taste, but the apartment was worse than he'd expected. He could have afforded to have someone make it look presentable, at least. What the hell did Shambliss spend his money on? Clearly, it wasn't his place. Or his appearance. And the little black sports car was at least five or six years old. Nothing special about it.

As he moved through the apartment, he tried to

imagine what Shambliss would do first upon arriving home. Most people stopped in the kitchen. Mail was piled on the counter, so it seemed like a safe bet. The element of surprise would be essential. Not that he couldn't overpower Shambliss. That wouldn't be an issue. Shambliss was maybe five-ten, but scrawny with a thin man's gut developed from years of playing croquet and cornhole instead of doing real exercise.

He surveyed the bedroom, too. Bed unmade. Of course. Dress shirts and slacks were piled onto a single chair, like some animal might be living in there. The smell of the place. Body odor and socks. God, it was awful.

Out of habit, he checked for his watch again. Remembered he didn't have it and checked the time on his phone. Shambliss would be home any minute. As he smoothed his gloves across his hands, he searched for a good hiding place. Clothes spewed out of the closet like vomit, leaving no good spot for hiding. Best to hide in the little pantry off the kitchen. He made his way back down the hall and pulled the length of cable from his pocket. Unlike the bedroom closet, the pantry was practically empty. Some tomato soup, an empty box from a twelve-pack of diet root beer. Pathetic.

He stepped into the pantry and closed the door until it was ajar. He wrapped the cable around each hand, leaving a length of maybe ten inches between them. And he waited.

He was cool under pressure. He had to give himself credit for that. He'd been in some pickles in his life, but this one was the worst of it. Still, he'd managed to find a way out. Clever. Smart. A key scratched in the lock and he felt a little start. Maybe best not to get ahead of himself yet.

The door opened and the apartment was filled with Shambliss's nasal voice.

"I already told him," he whined.

Christ, he wasn't alone. He backed quickly to the rear of the pantry, looking around as though a door might magically appear. He hadn't considered a second person.

"He says you didn't," came the response.

"That's horse shit," Shambliss said as he came into view, a phone held awkwardly between his shoulder and his ear. In one hand, he had the same worn leather brief-case he'd had forever; in the other, a thin plastic bag. A pair of chopsticks poked through the bottom of the sack, but he knew from the smell that it was Chinese. Shambliss loved his moo shu pork.

"You want to call him?" echoed a voice from the phone.

His chest deflated as the pressure released. There was no one with Shambliss. For whatever reason, the idiot had the phone on speaker.

"No," Shambliss barked in the tone he took with people he judged were beneath him, which was most everyone. "You tell him I said so. And don't call back until it's taken care of."

What was Shambliss talking about? He didn't recognize the voice on the phone. Then, there was no time to wonder. Shambliss entered the kitchen and walked straight for the pantry. What could he possibly want from here? His own heart thundered in his neck. Shambliss's face was visible through the open door. Shambliss seemed to glance up. He stopped breathing, certain that he'd been seen. But there was no reaction from Shambliss.

Shambliss hadn't noticed him in the dark pantry. He was still safe. Shambliss set the bag of food down, dropped his briefcase on the floor, and removed the phone from between his chin and his neck, setting it on the counter. It was almost time. He tightened the cable, got ready to spring.

Go now!

A moment passed in hesitation, then he took a small step as Shambliss walked away.

Damn. Shambliss was no longer in the kitchen. Other than his blood rushing across his ears, the room was silent. He waited, adrenaline coursing like hot water down his spine. He didn't hear the front door. Shambliss must have gone to the bedroom or the bathroom. He hadn't thought about waiting in the bathroom. That might have been smarter. Now, he was stuck.

He shifted to look out the cracked door and spotted Shambliss's phone. Considered grabbing it as a shadow crossed the kitchen. He jumped back as a hand reached for the phone. He shifted his angle and watched Shambliss slide the phone into the front pocket of his shirt. Then, he opened the plastic bag and pulled out the carton of Chinese.

He'd be going for a fork. Shambliss had never mastered the art of chopsticks, something Shambliss found bothersome. He'd seen chopsticks around his old apartment the times he'd visited. On the table by the couch or on the counter, like maybe Shambliss practiced when no one was watching. That would be something Shambliss would do. A drawer slid open. He pulled the door ever so slightly, saw the narrow expanse of Shambliss's back. Pulled the door farther.

The hinge creaked.

Shambliss turned.

With a quick breath, he pounced.

"What the—" Shambliss lifted a hand to shield himself as he encircled Shambliss's neck with the cable. Not quick enough. Shambliss was facing him, making it difficult to pull the cable taut. Shambliss's face went red. He ducked back as Shambliss reached out to claw at his face. Shambliss was half facing him, making it easy for Shambliss to take swipes at him. He loosened his grip. Shambliss choked and sputtered. "What the fuck—"

He didn't let Shambliss finish. He used his knee in Shambliss's back to push him away, then came behind him and crossed the cable over itself on the back of his neck.

Shambliss was trying to say something, and it felt unnatural not to stop and listen. He was starting to feel short of breath himself. Meant to protect his arms from any clawing, the jacket he wore was too heavy for inside. He was a little light-headed. Sweat poured down his face. Into his eyes. He blinked hard as Shambliss clawed at his arms and then swung around to try to reach his face. He responded by pulling the cable down with a hard yank so that Shambliss fell off balance. His arms spun like a pinwheel before he fell hard.

The landing knocked his wind out, and he clutched his chest. The cable was underneath Shambliss, the position of his hands holding up the man's head. Which left him looking directly down at Shambliss's face. He pulled harder. Blinked away the sweat. Gave the cable a hard pull.

It wasn't working. Shambliss was still breathing. He doubled the cable back across Shambliss's neck and pulled tighter. He stared into Shambliss's brown eyes, bulging slightly, and down that hooked beak. The cable tore into the skin of his neck, blood seeping from the wound.

Shambliss flopped his legs to one side, trying to roll himself over. His hands clawed into the thick fabric of the jacket, occasionally bucking his hips and trying to reach his attacker's face. Die already. Shambliss reeled back and tried again, unable to get his hips over with the tension on his neck. While Shambliss struggled, he pulled and yanked, twisting the cable to make it tighter, finally shifting to Shambliss's side and using his foot to press against his chest and increase the tension. Shambliss's face grew steadily redder before taking on a purplish shade and finally something more like blue. His hands were focused on the cable at his neck. It was bizarre to watch the man claw with such ferocity into his own neck. A fingernail snapped off and bounced across the linoleum floor.

Finally, Brandon Shambliss's body went slack. He didn't release the tension at his neck until he was sure Shambliss was dead. A dark stain spread across the front of Shambliss's slacks. Followed by the ripe smell of feces. He scrambled up off the floor and away from the body, burying his nose in the crook of his elbow.

He gagged. Breathed slowly through his mouth. He had to get the hell out of there. He needed the cable first. He returned to the body and reached down for the cable. The cable had cut deep into Shambliss's skin. He tried to pull it straight out, but the skin gripped the cable. He tried wiggling it from one end and finally pulled the cable straight through the wound. The last bit broke free and sent a chunk of tissue into the air. He recoiled; his stomach heaved. He pressed his lips together. He would not be sick. He swallowed slowly. Counted to ten. When he had control, he retrieved the cable and wound it around his gloved hand. He placed it in a trash bag he found in the kitchen.

The last task was to check for any footprints he might have left. He used the back of his glove to swipe at the area of Shambliss's shirt where he'd placed his foot for purchase, though he didn't see any footprint there. Then, he studied the floor. It was clean enough. As he bent down to get a better look, Shambliss's phone rang from inside his shirt pocket, giving him a start. Once again, he was half-tempted to take the phone off the dead man and see who was calling. This is where people make mistakes, he told himself. Instead, he waited until the phone had finished ringing and slowly backed out of the kitchen and down the hallway until he was at the front door. He checked the peephole before stepping outside where he locked the door with the stolen key, dropped it and the gloves into the trash bag with the cable, and walked toward the rental car.

He concentrated on walking slowly, not hurried. Like a man on regular business. Just visiting a friend. When he reached the car, he ducked in, put the bag on the floor beneath his feet. He would keep an eye out for a dumpster once he'd gotten a few miles away.

He started the car, felt a rush of relief when the engine

turned over. And why wouldn't it? He was thrilled to hear the low purr. Checked all his mirrors twice before pulling onto the street and taking a right at the first corner.

All in all, not a bad job for an amateur. And that was the last of the mess to be cleaned up.

Unless Charlotte came out of that coma… But he wasn't thinking about that now.

CHAPTER 38

JAMIE SENT Z a text message to tell him that she'd pick him up from baseball practice early. Practices were going until 8:30 these days, but that was too late if they were going back to the lab to take care of his DNA sample. And they were. They were doing that, and they were coming clean about Charlotte. She would tell him that she'd had the mitt and he would tell her where the blood came from and why it had made a print on the side of that Mercedes. The thought filled her with dread.

As soon as she hit send, a message displayed on the screen from Hailey. *Brandon Shambliss is dead. Home. Patrol found him.* The next message was his address. Followed by one more. *On my way. Meet you there?* Shambliss was dead.

In the meeting with Bishop and Ikerd, she had asked point-blank if they were tracking anyone else. Of course they'd said no. But she was almost certain that was a lie. If they were tracking employees, Shambliss was an obvious choice. Had she and Vich planted the idea that one of their employees might be involved and, as a result, gotten Shambliss killed?

Jamie texted back. *How long?*

A line of bubbles showed on the screen as Hailey typed her response. Jamie resisted the urge to call.

Two hours.

So, it might have been Bishop. She imagined his three-piece suit, his gold pocket watch and tried to picture him a killer. It was a hard fit. He wasn't the type to get his hands dirty. Didn't mean he wasn't involved.

Jamie called Vich to share the news. He was finishing up some profiling on another case. "I'll check out the Shambliss scene and be in touch," she told him. He was quiet on the phone. Maybe tired. Or maybe it was the case coming between them. That would be on her. After tonight, she'd be able to come clean. With him. With Hailey and Hal. With Tony. First, Z had to come clean with her.

By the time she arrived on the scene, Shambliss's small apartment was crowded with police. Sydney Blanchard stood in the living room with three techs. The room might have belonged to anyone. No magazines, no pictures. A poster on one wall and the kind of bland furniture reminiscent of corporate housing. There was a single glass, half full of something like soda and some catalogues on the coffee table. A sweatshirt hung over the back of the couch, tennis shoes on the floor.

Sydney gave Jamie a short wave and pointed. "Body's in the kitchen." She passed two patrol officers in a narrow hall and entered the kitchen where Hailey and Hal were watching Schwartzman, crouched by the body. Shambliss had soiled himself, so the room smelled like an overflowed bathroom. The cop shows made it seem like that sort of thing happened often, but thankfully that wasn't the case. Hal pulled out a little green bottle and sprayed it into his mouth.

"We've been living on this stuff," Hal said, offering it to Hailey. She took a couple hits, too, then passed it toward Jamie.

"No, thanks," she said. She smelled the Listerine over the other smells, and she knew it would help, but she didn't use mouthwash. Anything with alcohol was a no-no for a recovering alcoholic. Not a drink in eight years, but she'd be a recovering alcoholic forever.

"We know what happened?" she asked.

"He was strangled by some type of wire or cable," Schwartzman said.

"They just finished with the photographs of the body," Hailey explained. "Schwartzman thinks she sees some sort of particulate in the wound. She's trying to get some samples so we can get them to the lab."

"They break-in?"

"Nope. Looks like someone had a key," Hal said.

Bishop came to mind again. Not hard to get if you work with someone. House keys would be in his jacket pocket or in a briefcase while he was at work.

Schwartzman pulled a length of packing tape off a roll and laid it against the wound on Shambliss's neck. With gloved hands, she gently pressed the adhesive to the skin then pulled it free and laid it down onto a clear plastic sheet. That she lifted into the air above her head and stared up at the length of tape.

She pointed to several specks. "There is evidence of

some plastic residue in the wound." She motioned to his hands. "It's under his nails, too."

"What do you think it is?" Hailey asked.

"The wound appears to have been caused by some sort of thin cable."

"No signs of any cable in the apartment," Hal said.

"So, not a crime of opportunity," Jamie said.

"No. Killer came prepared."

"We have a BOLO on Heath Brody," Hal said, referring to a police notice to "be on the lookout" for a suspect. "He's not at his apartment, but we'll pick him up when he gets home."

"So, one of them throws Charlotte down the flight of stairs because she was going to out Brody to her dad?" Jamie said. "I might buy that, but then Shambliss comes to Brody's rescue? Why would he do that? I hardly get the feeling he was an especially nice guy." She shared Roger's discovery that the two men had lived down the hall from each other. "It's hard to picture them being close friends," she added.

"I agree," Hailey said.

"Maybe Shambliss wasn't helping," Hal suggested. "Maybe Shambliss figured out it was Brody and was threatening to give him up," Hal suggested.

Her phone vibrated in her hand.

A text from Z. *Can't leave early. I've got a scrimmage tonight. Done by 8.*

"But Shambliss was the one at the bar where Michael Delman was drugged," Hailey countered. "Why drug Delman if you're going to out Brody?"

"Maybe so you've got the corner on the information.

Maybe Shambliss meant to set Brody up for the Delman murder, too."

Jamie told them about Bishop's tracking devices.

"Sounds like we need to talk to Mr. Bishop," Hal said.

"I'd suggest talking to Ikerd and Bishop separately," Jamie offered. "Maybe you can put some pressure on them that way."

"We'll check out Shambliss's car and phone for tracking devices, but without something to link Bishop to the scene, we've got no probable cause," Hailey said.

"We did link Shambliss to Carmen Gutierrez," Hal said.

"Gutierrez?" Jamie repeated.

"Gutierrez was the CFO of a company that designed geo-tracking units for government use. We matched the slug in Delman to a slug in the database—the one that killed Gutierrez," Hal explained.

"And they're connected how?" Jamie asked.

"Gutierrez was the one who pressed charges against Shambliss as a minor," Hailey answered.

"And we never looked at Shambliss for Gutierrez's death?"

Hal shook his head. "Not even on the radar."

Jamie sighed. "And where's Tiffany Greene?"

"We haven't been able to reach her," Hailey said. "We spoke to her roommate. She was in Yosemite with two of her girlfriends this weekend. They're due back tonight."

Jamie sighed.

Schwartzman stood up. "I think I've got everything I need for now. I'll do the cut first thing in the morning."

Jamie checked the time. It wasn't yet 6:00 and she

couldn't pick Z up until 8:00. She considered going to the school and pulling him. He'd be angry, but so what? He was in some serious shit.

"Nothing to do but go have dinner," Hailey said.

"You hungry?" Hal asked.

"A little, but tonight's the Rookie dinner at Tommy's."

"Rookie Club is tonight?" Jamie asked.

"Yes, ma'am," Hailey said.

"What's Rookie Club?" Schwartzman asked.

"Ah, hell," Hal said. "You guys go on. I'll finish here."

Jamie couldn't remember the last time she'd gone to a dinner. No. She could remember. It was around the time she adopted Z. She did not want to go tonight. She wanted to pick up Z, get his DNA, go home, and sort everything out. "I—" But then, she couldn't think of anything to say. She didn't have an excuse. She wasn't pulling Z from the scrimmage. She couldn't go home. The investigation was at a standstill until Shambliss was processed, Brody was brought in, or they got in touch with Tiffany Greene. Nothing could be resolved right now. Plus, she had to admit she was hungry. "Okay," she conceded.

"Come on, Schwartzman," Hailey said. "We'll introduce you to the Rookie Club tradition."

Schwartzman seemed a little reluctant, but Jamie gave her arm a soft squeeze.

"It's a good thing," Jamie promised. "It's gotten me through some tough times."

"Me, too," Hailey added.

Schwartzman gave a nod, and the three of them walked out of the apartment, leaving Hal with a dead body and the terrible stench.

CHAPTER 39

THEY WERE THE first to arrive at Tommy's. Rookie Club dinners normally began closer to 7:00. The three of them sat at the same table in the back. The restaurant was quieter than normal. Maybe it was because they were early. Maybe it was because it was Monday. Or perhaps it was her state of mind. At her last Rookie Club dinner, she'd been working to catch a serial rapist who was attacking women on the force.

When the waitress arrived, Hailey ordered a Coors in a bottle.

"Seltzer with lemon for me," Jamie said.

"Me, too," Schwartzman said.

They agreed on an order of nachos to share. As soon as the waitress left, Jamie addressed Schwartzman. "You doing okay?"

"Better," Schwartzman said, turning to Hailey. "I got a bouquet of flowers yesterday from my ex-husband."

Hailey looked at her. "You don't have to explain."

"I left him after he threw me into a dresser," Schwartzman said, her voice carefully modulated. "I lost my baby."

"I'm sorry," Hailey said.

Jamie touched her hand.

Schwartzman hitched her chin a little higher. "Every once in a while, he finds out where I am and calls."

What triggered him to get in touch with her? "Have you gotten flowers before?"

Schwartzman shook her head.

"Gifts of any kind?" Hailey asked.

"He's escalating," Schwartzman said.

"Any idea why?" Hailey asked.

"No. It's been more than seven years. And as far as I know, he's still in South Carolina."

"Do you know if he's involved with anyone?" Jamie asked. A recent breakup might explain the renewed attention to his ex. Or some sort of anniversary.

"My mother gives me the occasional updates," Schwartzman said. "Despite my request that she not talk about him," she added. She looked up at Jamie. "Vich told me that Roger's tech found a black duffel in the dumpster behind my apartment building. Roger thinks maybe that's how he got the flowers inside."

"You think it was your ex? Inside the building?" Jamie asked.

"I don't, but I'm not sure. Roger's working on the video footage, too."

"Does the date mean anything?" Hailey asked as the waitress brought their nachos. "An anniversary?"

"No. We were married in July." Schwartzman reached for a nacho. "Let's talk about something else, please," she said before taking a bite.

Jamie knew exactly where she was coming from. Hailey did, too. They didn't have to be asked twice.

Shifting off the subject, the three talked about other ongoing cases. Schwartzman and Hailey were working a recent stabbing. Schwartzman was able to do a cast of the wound, and they were thinking it would match a knife found in the suspect's possession. Eating nachos and talking about stab wounds was par for the course at these dinners.

Before long, several others joined them. Mei Ling arrived with Ryaan Berry. Linda James. Cameron Cruz. Cindy Wang from the bomb squad. Soon the table was loud and raucous and, instead of talking about cases, they were sharing gossip about the department. Which of the attractive men were married, which weren't. Interoffice romances, which were discouraged but happened all the time, often to married officers.

Mei mentioned to the group that Ryaan was dating Hal and that things were hot and heavy. Ryaan bumped Mei, who seemed at home in the group. The others teased Ryaan about Hal. Jamie was happy for them. The banter bounced around the table. Finally, Cindy looked at her. "How about you, Jamie? Is there a man in your life?"

"Just my son," Jamie said.

Cindy was one of those women who always had a boyfriend though she never appeared to take them too seriously. Highly motivated in her job, she didn't act interested in the idea of settling down. Perhaps if your job was dealing with explosives, settling down wasn't really in your nature. "Come on, Jamie," Cindy pushed. "There has to be someone ringing that bell."

A wave of laughter erupted, and Jamie found herself thinking about Travis Steckler. She deflected the questioning by asking Cindy for an update on her own life, which spurred a long conversation about another officer in the drug unit whom Jamie didn't know.

More food arrived, drinks. Another round of seltzer water for her and for Schwartzman. She watched Hailey get up from the table to take a call. Cameron Cruz pulled out her phone to share pictures of her son. Then, Hailey was back. Jamie noticed her expression and stood from the table. "What is it?"

"We got Brody," she said. "I've got to go back in."

"I'll meet you there," Jamie said. "I've got to get Z at practice."

Hailey came around the table to talk to her. "Hal also told me that they pulled Shambliss's financials. There's a recent charge at a place called Fresh Start Auto Body in Alameda. Almost a thousand dollars."

"A white Buick."

"Think so. But we don't know who it belongs to. I'll keep you updated." Hailey left a few bills on the table and walked out.

Jamie pulled a twenty from her wallet and put it on top of Hailey's. She touched Schwartzman's shoulder. "You okay if I go?"

"Absolutely. Thanks, Jamie."

Jamie said goodbye to the group and started for the door. Behind her, the conversation shifted to the annual policemen's ball. Something Jamie had never attended. She was sorry to miss the story, whatever it was. Theirs was a unique group. To make an ongoing dinner work for them, it had to be. Some wouldn't come, sometimes for years. But when they showed up again, they were welcomed as though they'd never been gone. New additions were included without any weird female antics, and when someone got up in the middle of dinner to take a call or to leave on a case that was perfectly fine, too. Jamie had few girlfriends growing up.

It was nice to have women friends.

Without all the female drama.

The Rookie Club fit her perfectly.

CHAPTER 40

A GROUP WAS huddled in the school parking lot as Jamie drove in. Staring back toward the school, they appeared to be waiting for something. It was the baseball team. They stared into her headlights like terrified deer. Something was wrong. She parked where she was and shut off the engine, got out.

Coach Kushner ran to her. "He's got a gun." He grabbed her arm. "There's a kid with a gun. He's got a gun."

The mother pain seared her chest. A gun.

Instinctively, she grabbed his arm. "Where is Z?"

"Another boy showed up—maybe ten minutes ago. Came onto the field. He was looking for Z."

"Who?"

He shook his head.

"They're on the field?" she asked.

Coach nodded. "They were."

She started toward the baseball complex.

Zephenaya. She had to fight the desperate need to run to him. She forced herself to stop. Listen. Understand. "This is a boy from school?"

"No," Kushner said. "None of the other boys know him either."

She knotted a fist and pressed it against the hollow ache. "A random boy showed up looking for Z?"

"It was someone Z knows. His brother maybe?"

"He doesn't have a brother," Jamie said.

"I don't know who he is," Kushner confessed. "But he's angry."

"A gun," Jamie whispered. All the effort to bring Z here, to this impenetrable learning institution, and he was facing a boy with a gun.

"I tried to get Z out of there, but I had to clear the other kids," Kushner said.

Jamie pulled her phone from her pocket and dialed. "Are there any other kids on campus? Beside the boys here?" she asked the coach.

He licked his lips, thinking. "Choir is practicing for this weekend's concert."

Dispatch answered. "This is Jamie Vail. I've got a two-two-one at City Academy. Requesting any available units in the area for four-oh-six. Repeat requesting officer assistance for an armed suspect at City Academy High School." It hurt to breathe.

She ended the call and took hold of the coach's shirt-sleeve. "Get over to that choir building. Take the back way. Stay totally clear of the diamond. Tell the choir group to lock down. I don't want anyone out on the campus grounds until the police arrive." She waved to the baseball boys. "And I want these kids out of here. Tell them to load into the cars of those who can drive and head out. Pick a safe meeting spot off campus. You got it?"

"Yes. Get the boys off campus and warn the choir group."

She dialed Vich.

He answered on the first ring. "Jamie."

"Vich, I'm at City Academy. There's a kid with a gun. Z—" She choked. "He's got Z."

"I'm on my way."

"I called Dispatch, but get Hailey and Hal, okay?"

"I'm doing it now."

She ended the call and popped her trunk, pulled out her Kevlar vest, got it over her head, and yanked the straps across her sides. She ran toward the baseball diamond, gun in her hand, with everything she had.

She hadn't made it more than a hundred feet when there was a gunshot. She stumbled, tripping over her feet. "Zephenaya!" she screamed, catching herself from falling, and sprinted across the uneven grass.

Breathless, she reached the cement entryway to the diamond and pushed herself faster. Her panting reverberated off the walls as she paused in the tunnel to shove her gun down the back of her pants so the suspect wouldn't see it, then ran ahead. *He has to be okay. Please let him be okay.* The lights on the field were blinding. She stopped at the edge of the tunnel and stared out. She'd be a sitting duck if she stepped into the lights. She covered her eyes in the glare, blinked. *Come on, eyes. Adjust.* "Z," she shouted.

She listened.

"Z!" she shouted again, a shrill of desperation.

"Jamie," he called back.

She focused on his voice. She had to go to him. She thought about the shooter. Hitting a target at more than fifty feet was difficult, even for a good shot. Cameron Cruz could do it. Would they call in Special Ops?

They were at least fifty feet away. Hopefully, she could reason with him before she got too close. If he managed to shoot her, she hoped it would be in the vest.

She stepped into the light.

"Stay the hell back," the boy shouted.

She stopped cold, raised her hands. Squinted at the figures on the field. The voice was familiar. Not Zephenaya's voice but similar. His brother. Could Z have a brother? His mother was dead before his fifth birthday. His older sister, Shawna, had been his caregiver before her death. Could there have been a brother she didn't know about? From a different father, maybe? Or Michael Delman had a baby with another woman? The blood showed familiar markers that matched Delman's.

She took another step forward.

"I swear to God, lady. Don't take one more step or I'm gonna waste you."

She halted. Hands raised. "Z, are you hurt?" She squinted at the two figures in center field.

So far away.

She could shoot at the boy, but she couldn't be sure she'd hit him. He held a gun pointed at Z who sat on the ground, feet in front of him. If he wanted Z dead, there was nothing she could do.

Z's upper body was bent over to his knees, his left hand gripping the opposite shoulder. "Z, where are you hit? How bad is it?"

Z rocked forward and back. "It hurts like hell, Jamie."

"Is it your shoulder, Z?"

"Yes." The answer came through gritted teeth.

"On the arm or closer to your chest?"

"It all hurts."

"You have to let me see him," she said, taking another step forward. "You want to shoot someone, you can shoot me."

"Jamie, no!" Z shouted. "Leave her alone, Jacob. She didn't do shit to you."

The boy, Jacob, looked between them, unsure what to do. His features were similar to Z's. His hair was longer. He wore a black DC baseball cap and long basketball shorts. A hoodie, where one hand was tucked. The other held a gun. She considered whether there was something else in his pocket. Shoes with no laces would make it hard to run away. She wished he'd run but knew he wouldn't. Kids like this didn't run. He would hold his ground. She studied his gun. Might have been a Springfield. Some of those held nineteen rounds. Illegal in California, but that didn't stop them from showing up.

She took a step forward, then another. Jacob was watching Z.

"Jacob," she said softly.

"Stay away," Jacob shouted, waving his gun at her. "This is between me and him."

"I have to be sure he's okay," she said. "You don't want him to die. I know you don't. He's your family, right?"

"Damn it, Z," Jacob shouted. "Why you gotta be so mouthy?"

"He didn't tell me," Jamie said. "But you two look alike, you know?"

"No, we don't," Jacob said. "My cousin looks like one

of them." He waved his gun in a circle. "Uniform with his name on it and shit. Here he is at this fancy school, in his fancy baseball uniform. Like some rich kid and shit."

His cousin. Their similarities were undeniable. Looking into the other boy's face was like staring at an angry, scared Zephenaya.

"You do. You have the same eyes," she said, although she wasn't sure if that was what was so similar. "Your voices, too. Michael Delman was your uncle."

The boy stared at his cousin. "Shit."

"Z had your mitt? I found it in his bat bag."

"Wasn't mine," Jacob said. "Belonged to one of those rich white kids. I took it."

Z rolled onto his side. "But you gave it back, Jake. That counts for something."

"Yeah. I gave it back all covered in blood. Christ." Jacob wiped his face.

Jamie inched forward.

Z moaned. "It really hurts, Jake."

"You ain't gonna die," Jacob shouted. "That bullet barely hit your sorry ass. I been shot through the gut and I didn't die."

"I'm going to check him," she said. "We need to get him to a hospital."

He turned his gun on her. "No. He ain't going nowhere and you ain't getting one step closer."

"Jacob, man. It hurts."

"You don't know shit about pain, Z. Where you been the last five years? I been living in that shit hole. I been shot. I been beat to shit. My mom kicked me outta the house like four, five times. I spent four weeks on the street, man, when your dad wouldn't take me in neither. Said I was a punk. I almost shot some poor fool just to get me a warm bed." He lifted his face to the sky. "And you? You been at this fucking school, gone all white and shit."

"Jacob, I can help you," she said, easing closer. "If you let me."

Jacob narrowed his gaze at her. "What are you going to do, lady? Adopt me too?"

"If that's the best thing," she said.

"What the fuck? You walk into the poor neighborhoods, adopting up the sorriest looking kids?"

"No," she said carefully. "Not normally. Z ended up coming to me, but I'm glad he did. I'm glad I can help him. He's very important to me. I'd like to help you, too."

"Jacob, she's not lying," Z said.

Distract and move in, that was her plan. "Can you tell me what you saw? When Charlotte fell?"

"Fall my ass. Someone threw her down those stairs," Jacob said.

"Did you see anyone?"

"No. I didn't see shit. I'm walking in front of her. It's dark. I hear something and look back and wham, I'm slammed in the head. I went down. Woke up and Charlotte was at the bottom of the stairs. Not moving." He choked on a sob. "Fuck, I was so scared. I ran and got Mike."

"Your uncle." She moved two steps closer.

"He wanted to call the police, but I couldn't," he said. "I got two strikes and, as a juvie, one more and I'd go away for good. And not to some kiddie place neither."

Jamie spoke around the tightness in her throat. “Michael Delman wanted to call the police.”

“Now, he’s dead.” Jacob looked around, his back and arms tensing.

“Let me help you,” Jamie said softly.

“She can help, Jake,” Z said.

But Jacob was wound up now. He scratched at his neck, leaving bright red lines where his nails scratched into his skin. “Bullshit,” he screamed. The gun quaked in his hand. “I didn’t do nothing. You hear me. Nothing. Only thing I did was fall for her. I let her get in my head, man. But I didn’t come after her. She tracked me down.” He waved his gun at Z. “She came to Z for my digits.”

“Jacob,” Jamie said. “This doesn’t have to end this way. We know you didn’t hurt Charlotte Borden.”

“How the hell you know that? Far as the police care, I threw her down them stairs. Ain’t no evidence says I didn’t. You’d all love to send me away for that shit. Three strikes, I be gone for a decade.”

“I know she loves you,” Jamie said. “Charlotte loves you, Jacob.”

“Listen to her,” Z said. “She’s not shitting you. Charlotte’s crazy ’bout you, man. She told me herself.”

Z lied. He knew Charlotte well. Well enough to have that conversation. If he had told her the truth… She stopped herself, focused on Jacob.

Lips pressed together, he said nothing. Tears streaked his face. He used his free hand to wipe down his face. “Why the hell she pick me, man?”

“Because you’re a good person, Jacob,” Jamie said.

"She knew that. Just like Z knows it. He's been protecting you."

Sirens blared in the distance.

"The police coming." Jacob glanced at Z. "Where I go now?"

"Nowhere," Jamie said. "You stay and I'll help you work this out." She took the final steps to crouch by Z. She touched his shoulder. He grimaced.

"You," Jacob shouted.

Jamie looked up.

He waved at her. "Uncle Mike got hisself killed on this thing. No way I'm going down like that." He pointed his gun at her and waved it to get her to move. "You going to help me get outta here."

"I'll help you."

"No, bitch," he shouted. "Not your way. My way. Put your hands up and come here, or I'll shoot him. I swear I'll do it."

Jamie reached behind her back.

Jacob took a step forward and aimed at her, his gun maybe six inches from her face. "Let me see that other hand."

She pulled the gun out and held it upside down by the stock. "I'm removing my service weapon so no one gets hurt."

"Un-fucking-believable. You got a gun." His own weapon stiffened in his hand. Aimed directly at her head.

Jamie exhaled and tossed the weapon across the grass. "I don't want anyone to get hurt, Jacob."

"Bullshit, lady." He spat as he spoke. "You as full of shit as the rest of them. You can't never trust a cop." He aimed his gun toward the ground and pulled the trigger. The low boom of the gun. Then, a searing pain in her shin. Jamie dropped.

"Jamie," Z screamed, struggling to sit up.

"I'm okay," she said quickly. A quick breath. "Z, lie back down."

"What the fuck, Jacob?" Z screamed at his cousin.

"Shut the fuck up, rich boy!" Jacob shouted. His teeth were bared. "Just SHUT. THE. FUCK. UP."

"Z, do it," she said, shaking. "Lie down. Be quiet."

Jamie drew in a couple of tentative breaths, then tried to pull one to the bottom of her lungs. Her leg had a pulse of its own. She reached for it, rolled her pant leg slowly.

Jacob held his gun aimed at her head. "Now, you get me out of here or I'll do it again. This time I'll shoot higher."

"It's okay," she told him. Her voice was breathy. She glanced down at the wound. Touched her skin. "I'll get you out of here."

She fingered the center of the wound. Not a through and through. Not deep enough to be a bullet hole. Had to be a piece of shrapnel. Ricochet maybe.

"Let's go lady. Hurry it up."

"She can't get up," Z screamed at him. "You shot her."

"One more word out of you and I'll put a bullet in your motherfucking brain." He shoved his gun down in Z's face. "You hear me?"

"It's okay. I'm getting up," she said. She used her hands to push herself up onto her good leg.

Z quieted.

Standing, she locked her right knee and put a little

weight on her left foot to test it. Roaring pain. Her knee threatened to buckle. She reached down, clasping both hands across her knee. Vomit rose in her throat. She swallowed it down. Took a deep breath. Stood up.

The sirens wailed closer.

Jacob waved her over with his free hand. She watched his movements; the front pocket of his hoodie appeared empty.

"Hurry up," he said.

She moved toward him. "Okay. Let's get out of here."

The sirens blared one last time then silenced. The police had arrived. Jacob would know it was only a matter of a minute or two before they were surrounded. "We need a way out of this place. Now. You better make that happen, cop lady."

Jamie thought about the choir group. "Sure. There's a back entrance. Leads right into the Presidio."

Jacob shoved his gun into her neck. She stumbled forward, weight on her bad leg, and cried out.

"Jamie!" Z cried out, reaching for her. "Don't hurt her," he shouted. He was fighting back tears.

"It's okay," she whispered. But it wasn't. She had no way out. She scanned the grass behind him. Her gun was too far. Only one thing to do. She took a step toward the far side of the baseball diamond and hoped someone would be out there, waiting for her.

CHAPTER 41

JAMIE MOVED STEADILY forward in the dark. As much as she could with a gun pressed to the base of her skull and a bullet in her leg. Behind her, Jacob's breathing was rapid and raspy, like someone suffering from an asthma attack. They exited the baseball diamond on the first base side and were suddenly shrouded in darkness.

She stumbled once on the uneven grass and caught herself with all her weight on her injured side. She cried out, tears flooding her eyes. Jacob stopped, too, and for a moment, he didn't push her. She wiped her face with her sleeve and started moving again, all her energy focused on finding level footing.

She had lied to Jacob. She'd never been to this side of the campus before. She had no idea where it would lead them. But they were moving away from the others and that was good. To their right was the main campus. Lights were on in the math building and in the one beyond where the choir had been practicing. To their left was a standard wire fence, maybe six feet high. Its cheap utilitarian nature was at odds with the school's penchant for expensive aesthetics, which made her think it was the neighbor's fence. Beyond it was an expanse of woods. It smelled of the cypress, eucalyptus, and pine trees planted by the army men who lived there a hundred years ago.

The fence seemed to continue indefinitely. Its presence would make it difficult for the police to come around and overtake Jacob from the forest side. Nothing to do but keep walking. Jacob's breathing grew raspier, louder. The pain in her leg more acute. More crippling. It became harder to put weight on it.

As she struggled to keep moving, she prayed that the paramedics had reached Z. "Jacob, I'm not going to make it much farther."

"You have to." The desperation was audible in his voice. "I have to get out of here, okay?" He came around to her left side and wrapped his arm around her. "Lean on me."

She put her left arm over his shoulder and let him carry some of her weight. He moved gently, almost tenderly. He'd shot her and now he was holding on to her. Tears streamed down her face as they made their way. She tried to think of some way to change his mind. To make him drop the gun and come in peacefully. He might go to jail, but at least he wouldn't get shot. "Jacob—" she started when Vich appeared in front of them.

His gun leveled at Jacob. Jacob pressed his gun into Jamie's skull and pulled her in front of him again.

"Jacob, this is my partner, Vich," she said. "Vich, this is Jacob. He's Z's cousin."

Vich didn't take his eyes off Jacob.

"I want to help him, Vich. He's a kid."

She started to cry. What the hell was wrong with

her? Was it that she could feel Z's presence in the scared, confused boy behind her? That the stroke of luck that brought her son to her was all that had saved him from this same fate? Could anyone really argue that anger was in a child's nature? Was there really some crime gene? Or did we simply have too many people who had no way out?

"Let her go, son."

"Fuck you," Jacob replied.

"One of you is going to tumble down this hill and get hurt."

Jamie looked at him. The finger of his left hand pointed to the ground. Then, she saw three fingers.

He stared straight at Jacob. "You understand me?"

"Screw you," Jacob snapped back.

Jamie understood.

From the trees came the rustling sounds of others getting into position. There were cops all around them. Jacob tightened his grip.

"Hold your fire," Vich shouted out.

Jacob looked around frantically, yanking her off balance to glance behind them. "I'll shoot her. I swear, I will."

"You don't have to do this," Jamie whispered.

"I got nothing," Jacob said back. His voice cracked with desperation.

Jacob shuffled to the side, pulling Jamie along with him.

Vich merely pivoted to track them with his weapon. There was no way out. All Jacob could do was move a little one way or another. He was surrounded. Holding Jamie at gunpoint wouldn't prevent a sniper from taking off his head. If she could get away, maybe she could save his life.

"Jacob, if you let go, you won't get hurt."

Jacob said nothing.

Vich flashed three fingers on his leg. He was giving her a count. She tensed. She was afraid to leave him. They would shoot.

"Let them take you in," she urged. "I'll talk to the DA. We'll work something out."

"You can't help me," he said. "I shot a cop."

Vich pressed the three fingers into his leg again.

Jamie shook her head.

Vich nodded.

"I can talk to them, Jacob."

Jacob didn't respond.

Vich wiggled one of the three fingers. "No one shoots without my go ahead," he shouted again.

Then, one finger vanished. Two. She had to go. Jamie stooped slightly to make herself as small as possible under Jacob's hands. Vich flashed one finger. Jamie took a breath and exploded upward, driving the gun's barrel toward the sky, then dropping like a stone to the ground. Clasping her hands over her face, she rolled. Something hit her shin and she cried out but kept rolling.

A single gunshot.

Jacob screamed.

Jamie stopped herself, scrambling to her feet. Cursing the pain in her leg. Crying outwardly. She was too far down the hill to see Jacob. "Jacob!"

Vich raised a hand in the air. "Clear."

"What did you do?" she screamed, struggling back up the hill on two hands and one leg. "He's a kid. He's Z's cousin."

Vich walked to meet her, pulling her up and half carrying her up the last part of the hill.

Two officers stood over Jacob. One had retrieved Jacob's weapon and released the magazine, removed the bullet from the chamber. The sight of the 9mm bullet was dizzying. Would he have shot her in the head?

She pushed the other officer aside. "Let me see him."

Looking more like a kid, Jacob was curled on the ground, crying.

She stooped over, afraid to put her injured leg down on the uneven ground. "Jacob? Are you okay?"

He shook his head.

She touched his back and shoulders, put her hands on his head.

He tried to push her away, but she knocked his hand away. No blood. She couldn't find any blood. "Where is he hit?"

"He's not," one officer said.

"I shot the gun out of his hand," Vich said.

Department policy. Never shoot to maim. If you have to shoot, shoot to kill. "You broke department policy," Jamie said, ignoring the voice in her head reminding her of her own recent policy breaches. Big ones.

"No," Vich said carefully. "I missed."

Jamie stepped back as the officers pulled Jacob to his feet. They cuffed him and led him away. He said nothing, nor did she. Just watched them go. She could think of nothing to tell him and she wouldn't make any promises. Not now, anyway.

She turned to Vich, gripping his arm as her vision swam. "I've got to get to Z."

"He's on his way to UCSF."

Dizzy and nauseous, she tried to balance.

"We need to get you there, too," Vich said, putting his arm around her back. She wrapped her arm across his shoulders, using him as a crutch. They made it back onto the campus grass before they met the paramedics pushing a gurney. In its wake was Travis Steckler. "Get her up on the gurney," he instructed the paramedics. He took her hand. "I came to get Amanda and heard what happened."

Jamie let them lift her. Her head hit the hard surface, and she was freezing.

Steckler was talking gibberish about pulse and blood pressure.

"Z," she whispered.

Steckler didn't answer.

She grabbed his hand. "Please. Z."

He leaned over her and pushed her hair out of her face. "He's fine. I saw him first. The bullet only grazed him. Took out a tiny chunk of skin from his bicep but no muscle tissue."

Z was okay. A chunk of skin. No muscle.

"He's not nearly as tough as you are."

The gurney bumped across the campus. Jamie focused on her breathing and the smooth skin of Travis Steckler's hand on hers.

CHAPTER 42

ROGER WAS STUDYING the evidence from a hit-and-run case that was going to trial. As the prosecutor's key witness, Roger would be called to testify. It meant he had to go back through every piece of evidence and know where it was found, how it was interpreted, and how it supported the DA's case that the family of four had been killed by negligence on the part of the defendant. He was due to meet with the DA and two of her assistants in the morning. He should have been prepping himself on the case for weeks, not half an afternoon.

He stood from his desk to stretch and saw the image Vich had sent him. Red lines crisscrossed the page. Charlotte's grandfather was tracking his daughter and her husband. Now that tracking devices were cheap, it probably happened more often. Drones flying through the air taking pictures. Tracking devices. GPS in cell phones. George Orwell's *1984* might have been a few decades off, but he had gotten a lot of it right.

The image was an overview of Gavin's movements during a two and a half-hour conference call. The images showed two lines across the screen. Roger couldn't be certain, but he'd suggested that there were likely two devices. Or one device with two antennae.

Now, he reached his hands behind his back to stretch out his shoulders. Chase was pacing in front of the fingerprinting chamber.

"That doesn't make it go faster," he commented, returning to his chair.

"Helps me though," Chase said.

"If you think so." Personally, pacing made him uncomfortable. It made him think of someone waiting to hear if a loved one was dead. A hospital waiting room. That was where people paced. He stared down at the image again. Then, back up at Chase, pacing across the room.

It was totally wrong.

He dialed Jamie. When she didn't answer, he left a message with his cell phone number. Then, he looked at the clock. It was after 8:00, and he wasn't halfway through the evidence on the hit-and-run case. He would be there all night.

CHAPTER 43

ON A GURNEY in the emergency department, Jamie watched Travis Steckler work on her leg. From her position, she couldn't see the wound, which was fine since it looked like a little bomb had detonated there. No bullet though and that was a good thing. In fact, Jacob hadn't technically shot her. He'd shot the ground where the bullet struck a piece of granite from the baseball diamond. Acting as its own little bullet, the granite embedded in her skin. A few stitches and she'd be good as new. Steckler was there to pick up Amanda from choir and insisted she and Z be brought to UCSF.

Jamie refused to be treated until Z was stitched up.

"Can it wait?" Vich asked. "She's bleeding a lot."

"It can wait," Steckler said. "If I was worried, I'd hold her down and put her under myself." He said this with a big smile.

Vich seemed to think it was funny, too.

She lay on her gurney and watched Steckler sew up Z's arm.

"You sure she's okay?" Z said to Steckler more than once.

"Your mom's fine," Steckler said. "She insisted we stitch you up first."

"Are you the only doctor?" Z asked.

"Just the best," Steckler said with a wink.

She wasn't letting Z out of her sight for a month, but she hadn't told him that yet.

"Nothing you need to do. Stitches will disintegrate on their own," Steckler told him.

"How long will it hurt?" Z asked with a grimace as he moved his arm.

"You'll be sore for a couple weeks. After that, the pain should be gone and there's no reason you can't go back to playing ball."

"Really? Two weeks?" Z complained.

Jamie interrupted before the two of them could start plotting ways to get him back on the field. "We'll see how it goes."

As Steckler finished her sutures and bandaged her leg, Vich arrived back with her phone, which one of the officers had found in the woods.

"Looks like Charlotte is coming out of her coma," Vich said.

"They called me about an hour ago. She started bucking the ventilator."

Jamie sat up, still dizzy. "Bucking what?"

"They removed the breathing tube."

"Is she awake?" Jamie asked Vich.

"In and out," Vich said. "Not ready to talk to us yet."

"We've got security on her?"

"Three patrol officers on her floor. Only family allowed in. Her parents are with her now."

Jamie winced as Steckler put pressure on her wound. She lifted her phone over her head and saw a missed call from Roger.

She hit the call back button on the off chance he was at the lab. She hated voicemail.

"Roger here," he said.

"What are you doing there at 10:00 at night?"

"Waiting for you to call," he said.

"What?"

"No. Studying for a trial. Did you get my message?"

"No."

"You should really listen to your voicemails."

"I'll put it on my New Year's resolutions," she said.

"It's April."

"Right. Next year's resolutions."

Roger chuckled.

"What's going on?" she asked.

"I've been staring at this picture that Vich sent. The tracking one."

She put the phone on speaker. "Vich is with me. What about the image of the tracking?"

"Have you seen Gavin pace?" Roger asked.

Jamie glanced at Vich. She thought about the first time she'd met him, in the hospital room. Then at his house. "Not really." She glanced at Steckler.

"Me, neither," Vich added. "Why?"

"What's weird about this tracking is that he paces all across the room," Roger said. "You look at the picture, it's really a multilayer star pattern. Like random pacing but almost mathematically perfect randomness because he touches almost every place in the room. In fact, if the tracker captured his location more than once a minute, I think we'd be looking at a solid red blob."

Jamie turned to Vich. "Do you have that image on your phone?"

Vich scrolled through the images.

"Hang on, Roger."

Finally, Vich handed her his phone. The red crossed the entire room. "You're absolutely right." She sat up, pulling her leg free from Steckler's hands.

"Hey, I've got to get it bandaged."

"The only void we see is his desk," Roger said.

"Roomba," Jamie shouted.

"What-a?" Roger asked.

Jamie pushed herself off the gurney. "Roger, you're brilliant."

"I'm not done yet," Steckler said.

Vich stared at her. "What?"

The bandage came loose and started to fall off her leg. She was already moving. "What room is Charlotte in?"

"Six nineteen," Steckler said. "But you have to wait. You're going to pull those stitches out."

Jamie didn't stop. "Vich, call 9-1-1. Get those patrol officers into that room. Gavin's in there with Charlotte."

The two men followed her out of the emergency department and down the hall.

"What's a Roomba?" Vich asked.

"It's a robotic vacuum cleaner," Steckler said. "It bumps all around the room at random."

Vich caught up to her. He lifted his phone to his ear but tucked the mouthpiece under his chin. "You think he attached his phone to a Roomba and went out and threw his daughter down a flight of stairs?"

"Yes. Only he thought it was Sondra. Remember how angry he was at her? He acted like it was inappropriate to let Charlotte wear her clothes." Jamie jabbed the elevator button again. Nothing. "I think he was really angry because he actually mistook Charlotte for Sondra." She saw the door to the stairs. Blood was running down her leg. "Damn it."

"Which means Gavin knew about the tracking," Roger said, still on the line.

Jamie started up the stairs. "Yes."

Behind her, Vich was speaking to Dispatch. "Alert the patrol officers on the Borden assignment that they need to remain inside the room until we arrive. No one should be left alone with Charlotte under any circumstances."

Jamie huffed up the first level and rounded the stairs to the next.

CHAPTER 44

SWEATING, IN PAIN, Jamie hobbled onto the sixth floor with Vich on her tail and scanned the walls for room numbers, signs. A nurse walked past. "Six nineteen," Jamie demanded. "Where's six nineteen?"

The nurse pointed down a hallway and moved on quickly.

At Charlotte's room, Jamie pushed through the door without hesitation. Inside, two patrol officers stood as sentries on either side of the door. Sondra sat at her daughter's bedside. Opposite her—on the far side of the bed—was Gavin.

"What is going on?" Sondra demanded.

Jamie and Vich moved into the center of the room.

"These officers insist on being here," Sondra continued. "Not outside but in this room. We are waiting for our daughter to wake up. Can't we have some privacy?"

Jamie shook her head, wiping her brow with the back of her hand. Sondra glanced at her pant leg, which was crusted with blood. "You found the boy who did this?"

"We found the boy Charlotte was dating behind your

back," Jamie said slowly. "And we know how Charlotte went down those stairs. But they are two separate things."

"What do you mean?" Sondra said.

Jamie studied Gavin. "Would you like to explain it to your wife, Mr. Borden?"

Gavin shifted slightly but held his ground. "I have no idea what you're talking about."

"Mrs. Borden, I noticed the Roomba at your house." She spoke to Sondra but held her gaze on Gavin.

The nodule at the base of Gavin's throat gave away his silent intake of breath. She had him already.

Sondra frowned.

"The vacuum cleaner that moves across the room," Jamie continued.

"Yes," she agreed. "Gavin bought that. But what does it have to do with Charlotte?"

"Does your husband have a Roomba at his office?"

"I'm not going to stand by and listen to this," Gavin said, rounding the hospital bed.

The patrol officers took hold of Gavin.

"Please check his pockets," Jamie said.

The officers frisked him. One of them stopped on his pocket and drew out a large syringe, still in its packaging.

"That's mine."

"What's in it?"

"Nothing," Gavin said proudly. "It's an empty syringe."

Vich nodded to the IV beside Charlotte's bed. "Injecting air into an IV is a pretty good way to kill someone. Excruciating way to die though."

Though Gavin's jaw dropped, his eyes narrowed.

Instead of shock and outrage, what Jamie saw was pure anger.

"What are they saying, Gavin?" Sondra crossed to her husband. "Why do you have that syringe?"

When he didn't answer, she shoved him. He stumbled back. "What have you done?" she screamed.

"Me?" he charged, spit flying through the air. Only the police officers' hold kept him from launching himself at his wife. "You did this. All these years, Sondra. One after another. Why the hell did you marry me if what you wanted was to be with one of them?"

Sondra gasped.

"Yeah," he said. "I've known about them. Peter the sculptor. Andre. Those were before Charlotte. Did you know I had a DNA test done when Charlotte was four months old?" He let the question sit. Sondra grew smaller. "I had to have my infant daughter tested because I didn't know if she was mine." The words cut through the room like a scythe.

Jamie wished she could be anywhere else.

Sondra held her hand to the base of her throat. Her long delicate fingers, her thin regal neck, were suddenly so fragile. She struggled to maintain her composure. "You were following me? All this time?"

"I didn't need to follow you, Sondra. Your father was doing it for me. He's been tracking us for years. All I had to do was get the username and password and log in to your father's tracking. Guess how hard that was? Your birthday is his password."

"But why hurt Charlotte? If you were so angry with me, why would you—" Sondra halted. Pressing both hands to her mouth she began to sob. "You thought she was me."

She pressed trembling fingers to her lips. "That's why you were so angry," she went on. "She had borrowed my clothes that day. I let her drive the Mercedes. You weren't mad because of the clothes or the car, but because you thought it was me. You went there to throw me down the stairs."

"No," Gavin said without conviction. "It wasn't like that," he said. "I was so angry. How many times had I logged in to that stupid system to see that you'd been with someone? Heath Brody and Jack Coleman before that. And the others." He sank into the chair. "So many others. Sometimes I followed you. I thought things with Brody were ending." He set his head in his hands. "It was such a relief when they ended. But then your car went to that new place. I thought you were starting something up again. So soon after Brody. I couldn't bear it, Sondra. Not another one."

"So, you left your phone on the vacuum in your office," Jamie interjected. "How do you manage to be on the conference call if your phone was in your office? Was it a burner phone?"

"I had the call forwarded to a disposable phone," Gavin admitted.

"Bishop made it sound like he had been tracking you another way, too," Vich said. "Not just your phone."

"My watch," Gavin said. "My car."

"So, you left your watch on the vacuum, too," Jamie said. "And you borrowed Tiffany Greene's car."

Gavin gave the slightest shrug.

"Mom?" Charlotte whispered from the bed.

"Oh, sweetheart." Sondra ran to her. "Oh, baby. Thank God, baby."

Gavin didn't approach the bed. Tears streamed down his face, his arms at his sides. Defeated.

"Dad?" Charlotte whispered.

Jamie watched Charlotte look at her father. She didn't seem afraid. Had she seen him attack her?

Gavin rounded the bed to her side. His expression held such relief. Had he really intended to hurt her?

"What happened?" Charlotte whispered.

"She doesn't remember?" Vich whispered to Jamie.

"Head injury. Who knows?"

"Would be a blessing," Vich said.

Jamie nodded.

"You'll be okay," her mother whispered. "Everything's going to be okay now."

Charlotte looked much younger awake than she had in the coma. There was no alarm in her features. Just confusion. Exhaustion. Nothing to suggest she had any memory of her father throwing her down the stairs. The three whispered for a minute or two before Charlotte's eyes drifted closed again.

Clutching their daughter's hands, Sondra turned to her husband. "You weren't really going to hurt her, were you?"

Tears streamed down his face. "No. Of course not. I couldn't. I was so afraid. I was so, so afraid." He reached out to take his wife's hand, but Sondra pulled away. Angry. Cold. All the times she had met Sondra, Jamie felt that they were different creatures.

But right then, it was like she could feel the exact emotions that were coursing through Sondra.

"What now?" Sondra asked.

"Mr. Borden will need to come with us," Jamie said. The pain in her leg making it difficult to remain standing.

Gavin reached for his wife again. "It was an accident, Sondra."

Sondra said nothing.

"Please read Mr. Borden his rights and take him into custody," Jamie directed the officers.

"How could you think I'd hurt her?" he charged at his wife.

The officers stepped forward and led Gavin away from the hospital bed. "Mr. Borden, you have the right to remain silent…"

"This is your fault!" he screamed at his wife.

The officer continued the Miranda warning.

Charlotte began crying and Sondra leaned down over to whisper to her.

"You have the right to an attorney…"

"You made me do it, Sondra. You broke me. All those years—" As they passed Sondra, Gavin launched himself toward her. "Sondra!"

The officers grabbed him back, pushed him through the door. "Do you understand these rights as I've explained them to you?" the officer repeated again.

Gavin silenced. His head dropped. "I understand."

After they'd taken Gavin away, Jamie left Charlotte in the arms of her mother. There was more to discuss. They hadn't charged Gavin Borden with the death of Brandon Shambliss or for his part in the death of Michael Delman.

She didn't ask Sondra if she had been prescribed phenothiazine for postpartum depression. Jamie suspected that they would be able to tie the medication used to drug Michael Delman back to Gavin Borden as well. There was time for that later, when Charlotte was well, when the girl didn't have to hear every detail.

Jamie hobbled back into the hallway where Steckler stood, watching Gavin go by. The two men said nothing to each other. Then, Steckler was by her side, helping her into a wheelchair.

"I'm going to patch her up again, and then she has to stay off this leg for at least a few hours," Steckler told Vich. "I swear, I'll strap her down myself if I have to."

She listened as Steckler and Vich talked about her as though from a dream. The ding of the elevator, the odd flighty sensation in her stomach as they rode back down. Then, she surrendered. To the pain and exhaustion, and she let herself fall deep into sleep.

EPILOGUE

Ten days later

Z'S PACE SLOWED as they walked through the jail halls. Jamie was in no rush either and, with her crutches, she was slow anyway. She couldn't compare her own emotions to what Z was feeling, but seeing this boy who looked so much like Z, whose life was only a single degree separated from her son's, was excruciating. What would she have done differently if she'd known about Jacob when she adopted Z? That, although Z had no living siblings, he had a cousin who had been left behind when Z was adopted. She might have saved Z, but, in the process, she had unknowingly contributed to Jacob's failure. Could she have done something differently? Would she have?

The prosecuting attorney, Colin Burch, was standing outside the door of the interview room. At least six-three, he smiled easily for a man who spent his life with a front row seat to the grimmest side of humanity. "Hi, Jamie."

"Colin. I appreciate you letting us talk to him."

"Don't take too long, okay?" Colin nodded to Z as they entered the room.

Jacob looked younger than he had three days before. The orange jumpsuit he wore was big around his shoulders. His hands were cuffed through a lead loop on the surface of the table in front of him. A can of Coke rested between his palms, the outside of it dented as though it were empty and had been there awhile.

Z pulled out a chair and sat across from his cousin. Jamie watched the two boys. Nine months older than Z, Jacob would be tried as an adult, though he was so clearly just a boy.

The resemblance was striking. She had found out that Michael Delman and his sister Tanya were twins. Jacob and Z might easily have passed for brothers.

"You doing okay?" Z asked.

Jacob shrugged.

"I'm sorry," Z said. "That I left you. I should have come back for you."

Jacob shook his head. "You was a kid."

"But I knew what it was like down there."

Jacob raised his hands, the handcuff chains clanking against the steel loop. "Guess this was always where I was headed."

Neither boy said anything.

"We'll be here," Jamie told him.

Jacob's eyes were hooded, less angry but distrustful.

"During the trial and after," she continued. "Whatever happens."

"It's true," Z said.

"You're Z's family, Jacob," she told him. "That means you're mine, too." For better or worse.

Jacob began to cry. Jamie crossed on her crutches and

put her hand on his shoulder as he dropped his head and sobbed. "I'll see you soon."

Leaving the two boys, Jamie entered the hall and drew a deep breath. Colin was waiting. Vich was there, too. She turned back to the interview room door. Z needed her, but he also needed to begin the process of closure with Jacob. That was not something she could do for him. More and more, he would have to maneuver through his life without her constant involvement. That might be harder for her than for him. Jamie made her way toward Colin and Vich.

Vich put a hand on her shoulder and squeezed. "How you holding up?"

She said nothing and knew Vich understood. She was grateful for him. One of these days she'd have to let him know. Finally, she said, "He's so much like Z."

"Yes, and no," Vich reminded her.

"Okay, but he's a kid. They say that the brain isn't fully developed to make good choices until we're twenty-five. And yet, we try them as adults as young as fourteen or fifteen."

"Some of them need to be treated as adults, Jamie," Colin said.

"I don't think this kid's one of those, Colin." He said nothing, so she went on. "I know this case is going to get a lot of press, but most of that is because of Gavin Borden. What Jacob did was run. Gavin Borden killed Stewart and Shambliss. Borden threw his own daughter down the stairs and hit that girl with his car, left her in the road… Don't make Jacob pay for that."

Vich cleared his throat as Z walked toward them. Jamie leaned into her crutches. "Bye."

"It was good to see you, Jamie," Colin told her. "I heard what you said about the boy."

"Thank you, Colin," she said.

She caught up to Z, who had stopped in the hall.

Vich joined them and the three walked out of the jail. Z shaded his eyes against the bright sunlight. "Damn, it's dark in that place."

Neither Vich nor Jamie said anything. Probably they were used to the dark.

"I'll let you know if there's any news," Vich told her.

The ride home began in silence. This last week they had talked so much. One on one, and with Z, and with a counselor, too. She had been sure Tony would be angry at her for keeping her suspicions from him, but he hadn't judged. She kept waiting for it to come up. For the anger to come. So far, Tony was mostly distraught for what Z and Jamie had gone through. Or, perhaps he was thinking of how it would be to leave them in a few weeks.

Despite all the talk, there was so much to say, so much unanswered. Tony and Jamie had done most of the talking at first. They were both trying to let Z initiate conversations, giving him the opportunity to talk when he was ready. Tony had been gone the night before for training in Sacramento. He had surely spent the drive time thinking, so there would be more to talk about tonight.

Plus, today was Z's first day back at school. So far, he hadn't said much. It wasn't awful, but she gathered it hadn't been easy either.

Z reached over and opened his backpack, pulling something out.

"Homework?" she asked.

"Not much." Z pulled out an envelope. "They gave me the decision on next year's scholarship."

Jamie could tell from his face it was bad news.

"They didn't renew it."

He stared out the window. "Says I showed... questionable decision-making, inconsistent with the high moral standards at City Academy..." That he could repeat it verbatim meant he'd read it multiple times.

"What do you think that means?"

"I withheld information that could have assisted in a police investigation. Maybe I could have saved some of those people."

Staring out the window, Z traced his finger along the edge of the door handle. When he first lived with her, he would sit at the kitchen counter up on his knees because the stool wasn't tall enough and trace the faint swirl of the porcelain. Lost in thought, he might spend an hour that way. These days, he almost always had a phone or some other device in front of him.

"Maybe," Jamie said.

Z waited for her to continue.

"Jacob's family. You protect family." She waited a beat. "I'm guilty of it, too, Z. When I thought you were involved, I—" She stopped.

"You lied."

She studied him. "I wasn't totally honest."

He continued tracing along the door. "Because I'm family."

"Because I'm your mom, Z," she said.

He stopped tracing. "You're not mad?"

"Oh, I'm mad as hell," she said. "But I'm not mad because you protected Jacob. I'm mad because you didn't trust me enough to tell me."

Z started to talk but Jamie raised a palm to stop him. "Some of that's on me. Tony and I haven't been the most united front lately. His move has been tough, and we haven't done a great job talking it out."

"And Jacob's a kid," Z said. "That's what you told that lawyer."

"He's a kid who will probably be tried as an adult, Z."

Z exhaled a long breath.

"There's no going back from what he did," she continued. "And in some ways, there's no going back from what you did either. At least, no easy way. You put yourself in danger—not only physical danger—which you did also, but the danger of being implicated in Jacob's crimes. We're lucky they're not going after you as an accessory."

"He didn't hurt Charlotte!" Z argued.

"But he didn't come to the police either. He had a responsibility to Charlotte to tell the police what happened. We might have homed in on Gavin Borden a lot sooner." She thought about her own actions. She was as guilty as Jacob. Worse because she was the officer sworn to duty. If she could go back, she tried to imagine doing something different, not yielding to the mother over the police officer. No. She would fail again. She reached out and touched Z's leg. A grown-up's leg on the boy she still saw as a child. The push and pull of letting your children grow up. "From now on, Z, there are no secrets."

"Okay."

"I don't just mean this stuff," she went on. "I mean all of it. I can't help you if I don't know what's going on."

"I'll tell you," he said. "I wish I'd told you about this. It was awful, keeping the secret."

"I know the feeling," she said.

"It made me sick to think about it sometimes," he went on. "All the things you and Tony didn't know."

She remembered all the times she'd been sick to her stomach from hiding the truth. "You'll know better next time," she told him. "And so will I."

A Budget moving van was parked in the driveway when they arrived. The sight of it took her breath away. A moving van. Tony was really moving. Her exhaustion felt heavier as she pushed her door open and got out on one foot. Z brought her crutches around and waited as she hobbled into the house.

The smell of barbecue filled the kitchen. Tony was at the stovetop, sautéing onions.

"I thought you weren't getting home until midnight or something," Jamie said.

He shut off the stovetop and crossed to them without speaking. He gave Jamie a long hug and then Z.

"We saw the truck," Jamie said. "So, you found a place and you're moving already?"

"Come sit down," Tony said.

Jamie crutched her way into the kitchen and sat up on one of the stools.

Tony set her crutches on the floor by the door and crossed behind the bar where he filled three glasses with sparkling water. He set one in front of Z and one in front of Jamie then lifted his own. "I want to propose a toast."

"A toast?" Z asked.

"Really, Tony? This isn't maybe the best—"

"I got an apartment," he said.

"That's great," Jamie said flatly.

"Yeah, Tony," Z agreed.

"It's on C Street."

"Is C Street good?" Z asked.

"Yeah, Tony, it's not like we know Cincinnati," Jamie agreed.

"That's okay," Tony said, clinking his glass against hers. "It isn't in Cincinnati."

"What do you mean?" Z asked.

Tony smiled. "It's in San Rafael. A little over a mile from here."

Jamie didn't move. "What about the job?"

"I kind of decided that I like the one I have," Tony said. "And I really like where it is."

Z heaved a sigh. "Really? You're not moving?"

Jamie's tears flooded down her face. "You're staying? You're not moving?"

Tony came around the counter, and Z slid off the stool to hug him. "I couldn't leave my family," he said. "But I thought it was time I got my own place. It has two bedrooms, Z, so you'll have to come decorate yours."

The two men embraced. Really embraced. Z was teary, and Jamie was crying outright, up on her stool, her crutches out of reach. "You guys."

The two of them turned to her, sitting on her stool, waving her arms. "She's stuck," Z said, laughing.

"She's like a turtle on her back," Tony said.

"That is not nice," Jamie told them.

"Should we help her out?" Tony asked.

"Probably," Z said with a wide grin.

"Poor Jamie."

"Get over here," she said.

The two men moved to her, and she held one under each arm. Her guys. Her family. Her bizarre, untraditional family. Her perfect family. "Thank you, Tony."

"It's no—"

"Tony," she interrupted. "Thank you. Thank you for staying."

"That's what family's for."

And it was. This was her family. But it was growing, too. Vich was like family. And Jacob. She would take in Jacob, too. Whatever that meant. He was her family, too, and you didn't let go of family. Ever.

AUTHOR'S NOTE

The first person I would like to thank is you—the reader. Thank you for reading this book and for following the Rookie Club stories. While we're at it, thank you for every book you've ever read. It is the greatest gift you can give an author like me. Without you, there would be no books, and what a terrible world that would be.

If you have enjoyed this book, please consider taking a moment to leave a review on Amazon or elsewhere. Reviews and recommendations are vital to authors. Every good review and every recommendation for one of my books helps me stay hunkered and warm in my basement, doing what I love best—writing dark, chilling stories.

To claim your free short story, to learn more about the Rookie Club or my writing, please visit me at www.daniellegirard.com.

Now, please turn the page for a preview of Exhume.

Excerpt from

Dr. Schwartzman Series

PREVIEW: EXHUME

CHAPTER 1

San Francisco, California

DR. ANNABELLE SCHWARTZMAN threaded her half-circle number-five suture needle, the kind normally used in orthopedic surgery. Pinching together the edges of the Y-incision she'd made an hour earlier, she began the process of closing the victim's chest.

The chest and torso had been badly burned, and the fire left the skin fragile. Since there wasn't going to be an open casket, the standard protocol was to use staples to close the incision. Schwartzman preferred sutures. Staples were effective but seemed too industrial. The sutures were slower, and she enjoyed these last minutes with the victim, the time to fully process the death before contacting the investigator.

Both the intensity and the reward of the medical examiner's job were in being the final voice for a victim. Schwartzman was the last person to have access to the body, the one who decided if death was from natural causes or at the hand of another. It was intense and quiet work, the hours spent studying each piece in a puzzle that needed to be worked out.

In medical school, many of her peers chose specialties in order to interact with patients—gynecology for the joys of birth, or pediatrics for the children.

But those jobs came with sadness, too. Fetuses didn't always make it to full term. Children developed diseases and died.

As an ME, Schwartzman interacted with patients in the most intimate way—limitless in the depths she could go to diagnose a death. For many, forensic pathology would seem like an impossible choice. For her, it was the only one. People chose medicine for the heroics—to cure disease, save lives. In forensic pathology, there were no heroics. Just unanswered questions.

The overhead light shut off. She waved her arm in the air to trigger the motion sensor. After 7:00 p.m., the lights automatically turned off after ten minutes. The halogen in the corner crackled angrily as it flickered on and off before settling into a solid glow. The hallways were dark, the room silent.

Some of the department's other medical examiners worked with loud music, but Schwartzman appreciated the silence. One reason she enjoyed being in the morgue at odd hours.

She had been heading home from a dinner with some women from the police force when the morgue called to her, left her energized, ready for work.

She didn't go to the morgue because there was

work—the work was always there. What she loved about the morgue was the space. The smell of the grapefruit lotion she used after she'd washed up and before she donned gloves, the vinegar scent of the clean instruments and table.

She always smelled these before the body.

The girls' night out with her coworkers on the force had given her a chance to talk to Homicide Inspector Hailey Wyatt, to get to know her away from the crime scenes they had worked together. Schwartzman had surprised herself by opening up about Spencer.

How long since she had done that?

Melanie in the last year of medical school—six and a half years ago—that was the last time she'd allowed herself to get close to someone.

Her phone buzzed. A text from Hailey. *Glad u came tonight. See u tmrrw.*

Schwartzman smiled. She had felt a growing closeness. They might become friends.

Spencer kept her isolated, certainly while they were married but even after she'd escaped. He had planted the notion that he was always close—confiding in someone was offering a key that might be used against her.

Dinner hadn't felt that way at all. It was a relief to get her truth out there—a man she hadn't seen in more than seven years was stalking her. He'd made her believe her mother was in the hospital. Had managed to elude building security at her apartment and deliver a bouquet of yellow flowers. A color Spencer loved and she despised.

But he was a fool to think he could get to her.

She was with the police department. That bouquet

of flowers was being processed by Roger Sampers—the head of the Crime Scene Unit himself. In only six months, San Francisco had started to feel like home. Here, for the first time, she had her own space. She was in charge of her own work, which gave her the opportunity to give it the focus it deserved and to excel at something she loved.

Because she was good; she was appreciated. She had the support of her peers. She had… friends. A ridiculous thought for a thirty-six-year-old woman, but there it was. She liked it here.

Seattle had always been temporary. The first city away from Spencer, a place to regroup, finish her training. Seattle was perfect for that period of her life.

She was a doctor now, ready to begin her career, put down roots. She had spent long enough looking over one shoulder. She was determined to stay in San Francisco, even more so after the evening with those women.

She made her final notes and signed off on the work. Her phone buzzed in her pocket as she was sliding the body back into the drawer. She snapped off her gloves and pulled the phone from her lab coat. *Hal.*

"You're psychic," she said in lieu of hello.

"Oh yeah?" Homicide Investigator Hal Harris said. In the six months they had worked together, she and Hal had created a comfortable banter that made cases with him her favorites.

"How's that?"

"I just finished our burn victim."

"And?" Hal asked.

"Autopsy showed massive bilateral pulmonary thromboembolism with pulmonary infarction."

Hal groaned. "English, Schwartzman."

"Natural causes," she said. "He died of massive blood clots in his lungs."

"Guy dies of natural causes, then drops a cigarette in bed and torches his own house." Hal had a knack for pointing out the ironies of their job, but they were always relieved when the autopsy revealed a death was due to natural causes.

"Yep. You want me to call Hailey?"

"No. I'll tell her," Hal said. "You ready for another one?"

"Sure," Schwartzman said. She was always game for another case. Lost in a case at the morgue, home alone with a book or occasionally an old black-and-white movie—usually one her father had loved—those were her best moments.

The distractions were all the more important now that Spencer had found her again. The phone calls, the creepy bouquet of yellow flowers that had appeared outside her apartment door. Worse was the fact that no one in the heavily secured building could explain how the deliveryman gained access to her floor. Seven years and five months since she'd left, and he would not give up.

"I'll text the address and send over a picture from Dispatch," Hal said. "I'm about five minutes out."

"I'll try to leave here in the next ten."

"Great," Hal said. "See you then."

She was ready to end the call when he said, "Hey, Schwartzman?"

"Yeah?"

"Nice work on that last one."

She smiled. Hal was good at praising his peers—herself, the crime scene techs, the patrol officers. It was another of his endearing qualities. "Thanks, Hal."

She ended the call and removed her lab coat, hanging it in her narrow locker. After exchanging the orange Crocs she wore in the lab for her street shoes, she packed up her case for the scene. Her phone buzzed with the address Hal had sent. She double-clicked on the attached image. Waited as it loaded.

The image came into focus.

A woman. About Schwartzman's age. Wavy, brunette hair. Laid out on her bed. Shivers rippled across Schwartzman's skin like aftershocks. Someone had already put a sheet over her legs and stomach, as though she'd been found nude, but a thin stripe of her clothing was visible above her waist. Other than the pale color of her skin, she might have been sleeping.

In her hands was a small bouquet of yellow flowers.

CHAPTER 2

San Francisco, California

SCHWARTZMAN STUDIED THE flashing lights of the patrol car parked on the curb. Between the rotating bursts of blue, her vision was stained the color of blooming daffodils. She couldn't shake the image of the flowers she'd found outside her door. No call from the front desk to tell her she had a delivery. The sole alert had been the sound of the bell right outside her door. Through the peephole, she'd seen an empty hallway. Then she'd opened the door and found the huge bouquet beside the door. Pale- and bright-yellow roses, calla lilies, freesia, mums.

She clenched her fists, fought off the fear.

On the street, the lights painted shadows across the front of the stucco building and washed the undersides of leaves on the small oak trees that lined the boulevard, giving everything the appearance of being underwater.

Neighbors stood along the sidewalk, jackets closed over pajamas or sweats to ward off the chill in the San Francisco night air. They huddled in small groups, arms crossed, watching. Waiting for answers. This was not the kind of neighborhood where people were murdered. They looked cold and frightened. Schwartzman felt the same.

She would not give in to it. She didn't know that Spencer was behind this death. Rule one of forensic pathology: never expect an outcome. Something she appreciated about the job. Shortcuts didn't work.

She emerged from the car and popped the trunk to remove a hard-sided black case. Focused, she crossed the sidewalk to the building, showed her credentials at the door, and stepped over the threshold.

Ken Macy was the patrol officer at the door. "Evening, Doc."

Schwartzman smiled at the friendly face. "Evening, Ken. I didn't expect to see you on tonight." She removed her short black boots and slid into the pair of navy Crocs she used for indoor scenes.

"Traded a shift for Hardy. He got tickets to the Warriors tonight, taking the family."

"Lucky him," she said, enjoying the moment of banter.

"I know, right?"

Schwartzman stretched blue booties over the Crocs. "Any new restaurants to add to my list?"

"Did you try that Lebanese place I recommended?" he asked.

"Mazzat," she confirmed. "Yes. I did. Last week. I meant to e-mail you. I had the kafta. It was amazing."

Ken smiled. "That's one of my favorites, too. That and the bamia."

Ken had a seemingly endless list of the best spots for ethnic takeout in the city. "I'm ready for a new one."

"Absolutely," he said. "I'll have something for you when you come back out."

"Perfect. I'm sure I'll be starving." One of the things she'd noticed about her new life in San Francisco was how her appetite had grown. Seattle had amazing restaurants, but her time there had been intense and focused. Stressed by Spencer and by school, she'd rarely eaten out, and the food she did pick up had been for sustenance rather than enjoyment.

Now, living in a new city, out from under some of that weight, her appetite was rejuvenated. It wasn't unusual for her to have a second dinner after a late crime scene. She picked up her bag and turned her attention to the building, shifting into work mode. She glanced into the foyer, unsure where she was headed.

"Oh right," Ken said, shaking his head. "Sorry. Take the elevator on up to four. It's real clean. No blood at all."

"Thanks, Ken," Schwartzman said, carrying her case into the foyer.

The building was probably built in the 1940s. Narrow entry, large marble tiles in the pinkish salmon that was popular then. She passed a woman in pajamas and stepped into the empty elevator just as the doors were closing. The elevator bumped and shook slightly as it rose. Schwartzman was grateful for the lift anyway. She was not a fan of stairs, especially not with the case.

The interior of the victim's apartment had been recently remodeled. Wide-plank hardwood floors throughout. Walls finished in a concrete-like texture that she recognized as American Clay. Sage green. Two large oils hung on the biggest walls. Both rustic scenes, one of a river and a mill, the other an old barn. A tasteful chenille couch with silk floral throw pillows.

Despite the decor, dark undertones were palpable. The room was too bright. Too perfect. Pictures framed on the table, set at perfect angles to one another. Nothing out of place.

Someone used to controlling things.

Or making it look that way.

Her first thought was domestic murder. People assumed domestic murders were committed by alcoholics and druggies, but a perfect home was as clear a sign of dysfunction as a slovenly one.

Under all the illusion of perfection, something ugly was often at play.

In Spencer's house, everything had its place. Down to the white porcelain cup where the toothbrush lived when it wasn't being used. The way the towels were folded in the towel rings, the direction in which the toilet paper unrolled. Her towels were never folded now. Not in more than seven years. She wondered which way the roll in her bathroom faced. She hadn't noticed. Progress.

Hailey Wyatt was on the far side of the living room with one of the crime scene analysts, working intently. Like herself, Hailey still wore the clothes she'd had on at dinner. Not wanting to interrupt, Schwartzman passed the kitchen. A single wineglass with an inch of red wine sat on the counter next to a dark-wood cutting board with an inlaid bamboo center. A thin knife lay across its edge, the blade jutting off the side as though, at any moment, it might fall. Crumbs. Dinner perhaps. Wine and cheese with bread. Schwartzman's favorite meal.

Three doors opened off a short hallway. The rooms were tidy and feminine, similar in style to the living room. No sign of a second inhabitant. She paused at the office door. Nothing out of place there either. A desk with an open book. A yellow bookmark lay between the two pages. No computer, no papers. Tidy. Too tidy. She moved on.

The body would be in the next room.

The dead did not spook her. Skin slippage, blistering, the blackness of putrefaction—those were all natural parts of death. Even the smell had lost its sharp edges and grown manageable. Especially when the body was discovered early, as it had been here.

The room smelled faintly of a candle that had been lit. Something earthy with a slight spice. Perhaps sandalwood.

Homicide Inspector Hal Harris stood by the bed, staring down at the victim as Schwartzman entered the room. Detectives in San Francisco were still referred to as inspectors, though she had yet to find someone who knew exactly why.

Even in the large room, he took up a sizable chunk of real estate. An imposing figure at six four and somewhere north of 220, Hal had flawless dark skin that made his hazel eyes look green, especially in bright light. His expression stern, he gave off the impression of being someone not to mess with. Behind the facade, Hal was both easygoing and extremely kind.

She was particularly glad that he and Hailey had caught this case. She had seen them solve a couple of tough cases since her arrival in San Francisco. A combination of smarts and determination. Those flowers unnerved her, and she felt calmer knowing that they were here.

He didn't bombard her when she walked into the scene. As usual, he didn't say a word.

It was a grand bedroom, particularly for an apartment in a city whose square feet sold for a multiple of hundreds of dollars each. As she did in every case, Schwartzman studied the space before the body. Often the surroundings gave context to the body. What she saw here was more of the same. A single, generic painting on the wall of a meadow, tall wheat bent in the wind.

There were several photographs in small frames on the coffee table in the living room, but none in the bedroom. Nothing personal at all.

The body was arranged on the neatly made-up bed. The sheet that had covered her in the image from Dispatch had been removed. She was not nude. The victim wore a lightly patterned yellow dress.

Schwartzman was reminded of the matching outfits from Lilly Pulitzer that Spencer so loved. Christmas, Easter, even the Fourth of July were occasions marked with a new dress for her and a matching button-down for him. Like they were children dressed by a wealthy housewife.

There wasn't a spot of yellow in her closet. In her house.

The victim's yellow dress had been fanned out and smoothed across the duvet. Gold flats. Tory Burch. Schwartzman could see the familiar emblem on the soles.

And the yellow flowers.

They were not the same as in the bouquet she had received from Spencer. That had been formal, almost a wedding-style bouquet, while these were more like wildflowers, long greens with tiny blossoms, the bunch held together by a piece of white string like cooking twine. Altogether different. Two different bouquets of yellow flowers. A coincidence.

Everything did not tie to Spencer.

He only wanted her to think that.

She set her bag on the ground and opened it up for a fresh Tyvek suit, reining in her thoughts.

The victim had been found in her bedroom. Affluent, white, early to midthirties. In a secured building.

Schwartzman stepped into the suit and raised the plastic-like fabric up over her dark slacks. It was warm in the apartment. With the suit at her waist, she unbuttoned her gray cashmere sweater, removed it, and placed it in her scene kit beside the box of gloves before pulling the suit up over her tank top. She hated the feeling of the fabric on her arms, but the room was too hot. Sweating under the Tyvek was distracting. She needed to be comfortable enough to give the scene her full attention.

She checked that her kit was open, made a mental note of her thermometer and the notebook where she would record her initial findings.

"What do we know?" she asked, snapping on her gloves as she crossed to the victim.

"The sister called it in," Hal said. "Came for a visit from Southern California and found her like this."

Schwartzman pressed her fingers into the skin. Lividity was apparent on the right side of her arm. "She's been moved."

"I agree. It's too clean to be the original crime scene."

Schwartzman examined the skin for early signs of bruising, checked the eyes for petechiae and found none. She fingered the victim's rib cage, then her neck. "Not strangled. No obvious trauma. I'll have to get her to the morgue to find cause of death."

"I figured," Hal said. "What about drugs?"

With a penlight, Schwartzman checked the victim's nose and mouth. The passages were clear. She leaned in to smell the victim's mouth. A little halitosis but no hint of drugs. "It's possible. But I wouldn't guess overdose. I don't see any residue in the nose and mouth." She pulled off one of her gloves. "There's a wineglass in the kitchen."

"I've asked Roger's team to collect it." Head of the Crime Scene Unit, Roger Sampers was extremely thorough. Somehow Hal managed to have Roger at most of his scenes, a testament to how much people respected the inspector. Roger was meticulous, comfortable with his own intelligence. Humor came easily to him, and, while he was often self-deprecating, he was careful not to make jokes at the expense of others.

"Good." Her skin was hot and her hands cold and clammy. Coming down with something maybe. "What do we know about her?"

"Victoria Stein. Lived alone. The sister wasn't aware of a current boyfriend. According to the sister, Stein divorced a couple of years ago. Moved to San Francisco and bought this place."

Schwartzman replaced the gloves with fresh ones and raised the victim's top, pointed to the lividity. "Appears she died on her side. Makes the overdose possibility less likely. OD tends to result in death by aspiration."

"Could she aspirate if she was on her side?"

"They can," she said. "But it's not common." She examined the victim's scalp for signs of contusion. "You said she's not from California?"

"From somewhere down south."

"Oh yeah? You know where?" The skull was normal. No trauma to indicate cause of death there either.

He checked his notebook. "Here it is… Spartanburg. The victim's sister said it's close to—"

"Greenville," Schwartzman finished for him. One town over from her own hometown.

"You know it?" Hal asked, surprised.

The victim's earlobes were pierced, but she was not wearing earrings. No jewelry visible on the dresser. "The sister mention if there was any jewelry missing?"

"No. Stein didn't wear any, I guess."

A bit unusual. In her experience, most women wore jewelry. The more affluent the woman, the nicer the jewelry. There were exceptions, of course. She herself was one. Schwartzman had gone so long without earrings, her holes had closed up.

Spencer didn't like earrings. Lobes were to be bare.

One of his rules. Something always reminded her of him. Maybe one day it wouldn't. She hoped.

Schwartzman raised the victim's hands, studying the palms for defensive wounds.

"You seeing anything?"

"Not yet," she admitted. "Victim's nails are pretty short, so it's possible we wouldn't see breakage with defensive wounds." She studied the underside of the nails. "But I don't see any tissue underneath." She flipped the hand back over and studied the fingers for the telltale indentation or sun mark that would indicate a ring. None.

No earrings, no ring. Could be skin allergies.

She shifted the neckline of the victim's dress and found a thin gold chain. She pulled it free of the dress to see the pendant. A gold cross. On the right side was a small hole, about the size of a pinhead. Like the kind jewelers used to let light through to gems. After laying the cross in her gloved palm, Schwartzman used her free hand to flip it over.

Embedded in the gold of the right cross beam was a Star of David.

"Oh, God." She dropped the pendant, pedaled away from the body. Snapped the gloves off and let them fall to the floor.

"What is it?" Hal said, crossing to her.

His hands gripped her shoulders. The pressure was reassuring, settling the waves of panic that made it hard to stand. It couldn't be a coincidence.

"Schwartzman," he said firmly. "Talk to me. Are you okay?"

She leaned into his hands, shook her head slowly.

"What happened?" Hailey Wyatt appeared in the doorway.

Just hours earlier they had been talking about Spencer. She had opened up to Hailey and the others about Spencer. She'd told Hailey about being trapped in that marriage. And now... Schwartzman hugged herself to fight the shaking.

"My God, you look like you've seen a ghost, Schwartzman," Hailey said. "Are you okay?"

If only Spencer were a ghost. But he was all too real. The victim's dress was yellow. She wore no jewelry. These were just coincidences.

"Shit. Did you know her?"

"No. It's not her—" She pressed her palm to her chest. Hers was there. She felt suddenly exposed. As though by speaking of Spencer at dinner, she had conjured him into being right here. She had allowed herself to open up about him, and here he was.

"Why would you think she'd know the victim?" Hal asked.

"I don't know, but they look alike," Hailey said. "The wavy hair, the shape of the face, the nose. It must have freaked her out."

They did look alike. God, how had he managed to find a woman who looked like her? She wasn't imagining it. The lack of jewelry, the dress, the flowers. It was all him.

"No," Hal said. "She didn't freak out until she saw the necklace."

Schwartzman remained against the wall. Her bare hands pressed to the skin on her neck. It was icy cold and also slick, like a body coming out of the morgue refrigeration unit after being washed down.

"It's a cross with the Star of David on it," Hailey said. "And a little gemstone in the star."

Would they think she was crazy when she showed them? She had spent months building up their trust. It took so little to break it.

What choice did she have? She couldn't hide the pendant from them.

Schwartzman forced herself to lower her hands. "It's a Christian cross with a Star of David on it," she said, struggling to get the words out. "The Star of David is placed exactly where the heart would be if the cross were a woman. A tiny diamond in the center of the star."

Schwartzman fingered the chain on her neck, located the pendant under her tank. To celebrate their first wedding anniversary, her father had designed a pendant for her mother.

The room tipped, and Schwartzman closed her eyes.

A pendant identical to the one on the dead woman.

ABOUT THE AUTHOR

Danielle Girard is the bestselling author of *Chasing Darkness*, The Rookie Club series, and the Dr. Schwartzman Series—*Exhume*, *Excise*, E*xpose*, and *Expire,* featuring San Francisco medical examiner Dr. Annabelle Schwartzman. Danielle's books have won the Barry Award and the RT Reviewers' Choice Award, and two of her titles have been optioned for movies.

A graduate of Cornell University, Danielle received her MFA at Queens University in Charlotte, North Carolina. She, her husband, and their two children split their time between San Francisco and the Northern Rockies. Visit her at www.daniellegirard.com.